A SHARD
OF HISTORY

- - - - - - - - - - - - -

MOMENT OF TRUTH

J.Y. LILLY

Produced by:

FriesenPress
Suite 300 – 852 Fort Street
Victoria, BC, Canada V8W 1H8

www.friesenpress.com

Distributed to the trade by The Ingram Book Company

"Prophecies, predictions and life itself all have the same common thread; no one knows for sure what will happen until the end. Fate leads you to your destiny but the choice to take up the challenge is still unknown until that very moment of facing your inner truth. Remember, fate does not care what you do, but your heart always does."

- Wizard Ke-Hern.

Chapter 1

"Where could she be?" Ke-Hern asked as he checked the forest on the other side of the valley. He was usually a patient Wizard, but Eirian's tardiness was winning the battle of his nerves. He chanted a few words under his breath and the old stand of massive fir trees began to groan and sway, passing on his message of urgency. Her insolence bothered him but his worry for her ate at him, agitating him all the more. Gripping his torn cloak, he shook off the chill from the wind and headed back to his campfire.

He tossed another log on the glowing embers then went to check on his two new wards, Leif and Jelen. He wasn't happy that he had used magic to get the adolescent boys to wander away from Solveig, but he felt he had no choice. It had taken much faith, hardship and even a little insanity to connect the signs but Ke-Hern felt sure this time.

Standing in front of the arching branches of a Hemlock tree, Ke-Hern gently waved his ebony hands and the drooping branches magically parted. Both of the lads were asleep on the ground. "Unstoppable young mavericks," he muttered with some pride. They had been brave and had taken to this adventure with ease, except when it came time to eat. Ke-Hern could still hear Leif's loud and strong complaints. Ke-Hern shook his head. It was hard to believe that Broan, of all Warlords, would be neglectful about teaching these young men how to live off the land. Huffing, he gave an almost imperceptible flick of his hand and the boughs of the Hemlock closed.

Ke-Hern returned to the fire and sat down. He studied his hands and the power they wielded. There were only three known types of magic powers in this land. The Alzmer Power of the Ancients was now only a quiet whisper in the scheme of things. The Venler power was controlled by two Off-World beings, Queen DaNann and Sobus.

The third was Natu; its power came from the land itself. Few Mortals sensed it and even fewer controlled it. "But with direction from the Queen one could actually do much with it…" Ke-Hern chuckled as he concentrated and another log floated over and dropped onto the fire. It was easy to move matter around once you understood the make-up of form. It was one of the first lessons that Queen DaNann had taught both him and Lija, some seventy full seasons ago.

"*It's so simple,*" the Off-World Queen said. "*The fundamental nature of all things is that they are all created from the same energy, which for some reason concentrates temporarily into a form. Once you learn how to shift this energy you can use it to your will.*"

Ke-Hern shook his head. "There is more to this fundamental nature of things… a hidden…" His intense devotion to his surreptitious knowing was almost obsessive but he had his reasons. "Still too many secrets, too many lies," he whispered to himself. He got up and wandered to the top of the hill again. A sharp breeze kicked up making his old eyes water. "I'll not be tempted to waste my magic on shifting your direction wind. Go find someone else to torment." He waved his hand in the direction to the east. "Be useful and go find her."

He paused for a moment and calmed his nerves then looked out towards the distant southern islands and Queen DaNann's prison. He spoke to the Queen in his mind, an old trick she had taught him long ago. "There is no sign of Sobus, although there has been much talk of a Wizard being around here and there are definitely signs of magic being used."

"*Well, the only other Wizard is Lija and I can't see Sobus letting him come this far south on his own. No, this just doesn't sit right with me. Sobus has got to be involved somehow.*" Queen DaNann stated firmly.

"So this could be it?"

"*NO!*" Queen DaNann replied heatedly, "*I'm still not convinced. Sobus has always played us like puppets, getting us to waste our resources while you chase your dream.*" She paused in thought for a moment. "*I even wonder if it is at all possible that Faeries and Mortals can come together. There is much distance between them, a chasm of ignorance, fear and hatred.*"

"I think you may be wrong this time," Ke-Hern whispered."Just listen to me…"

"*Listen to you!*" she retorted. "*The last time I listened to you and gave the Faeries the ability to briefly shape-shift back to their Mortal selves, it didn't help one bit. I should never have listened to you.*"

"As much as it has further divided the Mortals and Faeries, it has saved many Faeries from going into the cursed void. So it did help…in a way." Ke-Hern sighed deeply. "Life is neither accommodating nor is it entirely capricious."

"That's why I need you to keep your eyes and ears open. You are my only link to the world outside my prison and there is much evil that Sobus can still do even though he has been exiled beyond Duronyk." She paused, "I know. Rest for now," Ke-Hern said lightly. He was very worried about the Queen and the pending war. He saw it for what it was even if…"Too many secrets," he repeated to himself, "Too many lies".

As of late, thousands of images from the past seem to enjoy plastering themselves over his present time. It was a daunting task to keep the present in the foreground so he could keep hope alive for the future. It was as if the past knew the secret, knew that the story had not ended some twenty seasons ago. It was as if the past had a life of its own and it had begun to rumble awake from its long silence.

Time and weather had dulled Hargrave's good humor and now more than ever neither was on his side. A peculiarly vigorous gust of wind pushed his long hair across his face. He grunted and swiped it back just as a squall of rain began. He tried to ignore the drops as they began slapping against him. Hargrave couldn't believe that he, a seasoned warrior from the Fortress Solveig, had been so invested in finding the two lost boys that he had missed the warning signs. Something was definitely hunting him. *"But what?"* he wondered.

He wiped the rain off his face with the sleeve of his leather tunic. Slowly he peered out once again. He narrowed his hazel eyes, peering deeper into the woods. The frown on his face deepened quickly. If his hunch was right then the reality of his predicament was staggering. Hargrave waited, trying hard to listen beyond the raindrops. The extreme quiet unnerved him. Impelled by a sense of urgency, he stepped out from behind a boulder and quickly started up a slope.

Kibria, a beastly Ny-dick male creature, sniffed the air with his flat snout. He had been on a mission when he happened upon this slight diversion and he couldn't pass it up. He stretched his head upward from his thick neck, which protruded from his massive chest, and took in all he could see in the dim light of the night. Violently, Kibria shook the dripping snot from his nostrils and sniffed the air again. "*Fear,*" he thought to himself and smiled. "*These useless, sub-Mortals are so easy to kill. It doesn't matter if they're Manliken or Elfian, they're as stupid as rocks.*"

"Damn!" spat Eirian. Her mystical wings twitched with growing irritation as she hovered above a branch just behind the Ny-dick. Eirian had followed the Manliken and the Ny-dick for most of the afternoon, careful to keep out of sight. She wasn't going to get involved unless she absolutely had to. Messing with Mortals or Ny-dick never proved to be good for any Faery.

Hargrave heard the sound of a bird taking flight, which meant his enemy, was getting closer. Holding his breath, he artfully inched his way to his right and looked out from the side of the tree. There it was, a Ny-dick, close enough that Hargrave could see the black coldness of its stare. Gripping the handle of his sword, he pulled himself in tightly - calming his mind and his fear - focusing on what he needed to do. *"I know death always lingers in the shadows, ready to slip in at will... but not today."*

Kibria's wicked toothy grin quickly turned rapacious with the anticipation of bloodletting. He sneered as the Mortal stirred and gave itself away. A low sound that began deep in his belly swiftly rose and turned into a sick laugh. *"Like I said, stupid as a rock."*

Suddenly Hargrave spotted the sparkle of wings in the dim light just beyond the Ny-dick, and cursed his bad luck. It was hard to believe that a Faery, something as small as the palm of his hand, could cause such disquiet in a man his size, but it did. It infuriated him to think that this vindictive shape-shifting being, that was once Mortal like him, had come to join in on his slaughter.

Wondering what his next meal was looking at, Kibria glanced back. When a flash of light caught his eye, he growled and hissed. Narrowing his eyes he turned towards the flicker. "Ah... Faery... It's about time you showed yourself."

Eirian calmly began her metamorphosis from the petite whimsical form of winged Faery to that of a normal Elftan. Gone was the sparkling energy; in its place was the tediously normal grouping of flesh and bone. Now in Mortal form, she stood on the other side of the Ny-dick, slyly keeping just out of its reach. "Shall we begin?" Eirian said in a sweet voice as she began to hum an unusual tune.

Hargrave could see the Faery gently stepping, stopping and turning, sure-footed as a cat, leading the Ny-dick in the opposite direction as she sang to him. He couldn't decide if the Faery had just saved him by drawing the Ny-dick's attention from him or if the Faery had not noticed him and was simply joining the Ny-dick for reasons of its own. In truth, right then and there, it didn't matter. He took the diversion with gratitude, and without hesitation he backed away into the dense forest.

"More bad news for Broan, I fear." Hargrave scowled as he made good his escape. "It looks like the Ny-dick have moved into the fringes of the region and the Faeries are back at making trouble, or worse, have formed an alliance."

Leif's eyes shot open. He sat up and peeked through the protection of the Hemlock branches and watched Ke-Hern at the fire. Daylight was still a little ways off, but the glow from the fire made it easy to peer about. He didn't know what had awoken him, only that a quick energy ran through his body as if to herald something wonderful. He nudged Jelen from his sleep and whispered, "Can you feel it?"

Jelen slowly sat up and rubbed his eyes. "I'm not half Elftan, remember."

"Well I feel something," Leif retorted. "Come. You'll see that I'm right once again."

Jelen crawled up next to Leif. "The last time I listened to you we got lost in the woods." He took in a deep breath and was filled with dread. "My father...NO, my mother will have both our hides for running off!"

Leif kept his eyes on the still figure of Ke-Hern. "Not before my mother - or worse - Broan gets his hands on us."

"Don't remind me! My backside already hurts just thinking of it."

"Look! Look!" Leif exclaimed, pointing to where Ke-Hern sat.

Jelen looked up in surprise. A sparkling image, like from a cluster of stunning diamonds, twinkled and floated in front of Ke-Hern. It was no more than six inches in height and came complete with gossamer wings. "Fa..Fa..Faery!" Jelen stuttered, barely able to get the word out.

Leif nudged him hard this time. "I told you so."

They both turned and looked at each other. With sly little boy smiles of mischief, they both nodded to each other and slowly began to creep out from under the Hemlock tree.

"You better change form Eirian or you'll scare the two young lads," Ke-Hern said as he quickly looked their way.

"I hate the way he always knows what we're doing," Jelen whispered to Leif as they stood up.

Leif just shrugged as he studied Eirian in Mortal Elftan form. He marveled at all the colors that played upon her clothes. Her tunic was of Aventurine, a dark green of jade, her tights and boots were of Chrysocolla, a beautiful blue–green that shifted as she moved. He could just pick out the edge of her Calcite colored undershirt, a translucent color of green and honey. "She's beautiful," he breathed.

"How do you know it's a she?" Jelen whispered incredulously. Many had told him that Faeries were neither male nor female but both in one. They were not like Mortals at all.

Leif just stared back at him and then raised one eyebrow. "How do you think?"

"You mean you can see her breasts?" Jelen spoke a little too loudly as he leaned slightly forward to take a better look.

"Come here you two. I want to introduce you to a friend."

Leif and Jelen shuffled forward until they were next to Ke-Hern and standing face-to-face with a real live Faery, the very creature that most talked about and that many feared. No one was going to believe them.

"This is Eirian and she is going to take you back home to Solveig," Ke-Hern said smiling.

"I'm WHAT?" Eirian choked, in disbeLeif. She stared in shock at the young boys. "I cannot go into Solveig! YOU of all people know what would happen!"

"You have to. I can't take them - not with Ny-dick in the area searching for fresh meat. Only you can get them back to safety."

"Now I know you're crazy."

"I'm not crazy. You have to trust me. Broan will be happy that you brought back his nephew and companion."

"Not the Broan I know of."

"Broan has integrity and honor. It took character to rally against his uncle about the building of Solveig."

"He's a tyrant. He's a bully. No! He's an idiot!"

"He is the future, Eirian, just as you are."

Ke-Hern turned and scooted the boys back under the Hemlock tree. "Back to sleep both of you, Eirian and I need to talk." He whispered a short spell and soon heard the even breathing of deep sleep. "That will keep them out of trouble for a short while."

Eirian watched Ke-Hern do his simple magic. He was a quiet man, tall and lean. His broad hands and ebony colored skin attested to his royal lineage while his face, a road map of sleepless nights and too many worries, told of a difficult life.

Eirian squared her shoulders as Ke-Hern approached her. The glow of the fire could not hide the invasion of gray in his hair. Although it was still mostly black, she could no longer ignore that the sides now gave way to the approaching signs of aging. "You have more gray than last time."

"I may be older than most Mortals thanks to Queen DaNann, but she did not give me immortality."

"No," Eirian hissed through her teeth, "the witch gave that curse to us, the Mortals of Duronyk that she so graciously changed into Faeries over twenty seasons ago. And just because her daughter Haidee ran off and married our Governor Cian!" Eirian fumed. Ke-Hern stood silently allowing her to vent.

She continued with a vengeance "As always with that Queen of yours, her so-called gifts bring a host of problems with them. Who would have thought that someone could so easily twist a thing like immortality into something so vile? SHE created the void for us to live-out her gift of perpetual life. How cruel and brutal that place of total isolation and helplessness is. I know because I feel the depth of pain clearly experienced by those held there." She glared at him as anger continued to possess her. "How would you like to be trapped in a place of darkness? You see nothing, you hear nothing, but yet you are aware of everything back here...a punishment that lasts forever."

"Not forever! You know there is one thing that will break the spell which holds the Faeries." Ke-Hern paused briefly, looked deep into Eirian's eyes, and then finally said, "...and its time has finally come."

Eirian glared at him for a moment. "I'll ignore that for now. What I don't comprehend is why you defend her. You've seen firsthand what has become of us because of her."

"Don't be so hard on Queen DaNann. There's much you don't know."

"And what is that?"

Ke-Hern paused briefly and wisely changed the subject. "I've never doubted that the Duronykians were tougher than any horror visited upon them. Sometimes things happen for reasons not yet understood." Ke-Hern took hold of Eirian's arm and walked with her to the top of the hill. "Our lives are made up of more than one dimension. It's time for you to take up your destiny."

She tensed at his words. "What makes you think I haven't already?"

Ke-Hern took in a deep breath; he had hoped that she wasn't going to behave like an angry child being forced to do something she didn't want to. "Flying around the land is not the only thing you were born for," he spoke in a harsh tone.

"I do more than just fly around. The land's energy needs constant balancing," she snapped back at him. "Manliken's plundering has laid waste to both land and animal. How long before it is unsuitable for even the bugs and the maggots?"

"Don't be so callous and don't think Faeries are so much better than anyone else. We all take what we need from the world around us," replied Ke-Hern.

"Some take more wisely than others." Eirian huffed. "You yourself taught me that the elements of the land only reflect the soul of the people who live off it. You have silly dreams of uncorrupted people living in harmony, in touch with the land and the living."

"Faeries live here too." Ke-Hern took hold of her hands. "Besides, it's a good dream and one that you play a very important part in: a part you cannot continue to avoid. A dark evil from beyond Duronyk is seeping south, reaching its hand to grab all it can. This is not news to you. And you know neither one voice nor one being will prevail over this evil. Unity is the only way."

Eirian pulled her hands away, turned, and looked at the peaks of the mountains that guarded Solveig's back. "But you want me to go into the lion's den."

"It will take the courage of a visionary." Ke-Hern said encouragingly.

"Or of a fool!" she scoffed.

Ke-Hern turned her around and looked down at her. She had always shied away from greatness. She would most likely protest, kicking and screaming the whole way. *"Poor Broan,"* he thought to himself as he rolled his eyes. "Take the boys back to Solveig. Talk with Broan. You need to begin." He watched her eyes for any hint of a break-through.

"Why start at Solveig?" she asked miserably. "Why Broan?"

"While others will argue, even try and ignore this war, he will fight long and hard. He will do whatever it takes and stay the course."

She gave him a scowl. "All I've seen of Broan so far is that he is nothing but a tyrant. He demands, he yells, and he expects everyone to do his bidding and to never sway from his decree. Why would I ever want to get involved with him?"

"He is a Warlord. He commands attention but he also has the ability to inspire others to grasp for the unattainable. I would think that you, of all people, would want that on your side." He chuckled, "interesting to see that you've been spying on him."

Eirian's eyes flashed with anger.

If looks could maim, Ke-Hern thought he would have spent the next week on his back. "Eirian only you can do this. You must do this despite all that the others have done by turning their backs on Faeries...."

"DURONYKIANS," she corrected him sternly. "The OTHER regions ALL turned their backs on us even before that so called Queen diminished us into Faeries. We belong to the northern region called Duronyk. We still do even if we can never go back there. Call us by our true name or not at all!" she demanded indignantly.

"Sorry. Duronykians," he restated. He paused and looked down at her. "Eirian please listen to me. You need to make this decision from trust and your deep love of this land. Don't make this decision from the bitter taste of revenge or the blackness of anger." He half-smiled at her. "I do agree your most rancorous dispute will be to convince Broan that the Faeries of Duronyk have a role in this coming war."

She groaned. "I'd rather fight a Ny-dick."

"Well you may just get that wish." Ke-Hern pointed to the ridge above a coulee in the distance. "The Ny-dick are coming and there's no more time to waste. They've caught our scent and will be on us soon."

He grabbed her hand and pulled her along quickly towards the sleeping boys. With a sharp clap of his hands, Ke-Hern barked, "Leif, Jelen, wake up. It's time to go back to Solveig." He bent down and picked up a sling that he'd made for just this moment. "Here Eirian, put this over one shoulder."

Eirian complied with a puzzled look. "You really think I can get the boys safely back to Solveig?"

"I'm counting on it." He could feel the enemy approaching. Their heavy weight made the ground shudder and the air cry with the twisted spell of silence.

She adjusted the sling to fit more comfortably and then looked at the two young lads. "Together they weigh more than I do. I don't know…" she said shaking her head, "Even as an ox, I doubt I'll be able to hold any form the whole way to the fortress."

"I know. That's why you'll need to travel as a Faery."

She quickly turned and looked at him. "Faery! That's impossible!"

"Not with a little magic," Ke-Hern said with a twinkle in his eye. He hurriedly motioned the boys to come and stand in front of him. "I'm going to make you both smaller so Eirian can carry you on her back. Once she changes back to being a Faery, you'll all fly back to Solveig and to safety. I promise you won't feel a thing." He studied them for a moment for any signs of panic but saw none. He smiled. "Once Eirian breaks from her Faery form you'll return to your normal size. Are you ready?"

Both boys nodded, excitedly. Ke-Hern conjured his magic and then scooped up the boys and placed them into the sling.

"Talk to Broan. Tell him I will make it there as soon as I can. Begin what you know needs to be done."

"And if this isn't...?"

"GO!" Ke-Hern pushed her on. "GO! The Ny-dick are almost here."

Eirian took flight and immediately plunged down the far side of the hill, plowing through the leaves of trees. Entering the deep narrow canyon, Eirian struggled to adjust to the burden on her back. She had no choice but stick close to the rocky wall, keeping to the pre-dawn shadows.

"Will it take long?" Leif asked

"Just hang on!" She tossed a quick glance over her shoulder at them. They were in their glory, dark hair blowing in the wind, huge radiant smiles on their faces and eyes that sparkled with the 'awe' of flying. She softened her tone of voice. "At this low level it will take as long as it would a horse to run it."

As soon as Eirian flew out of the shadows, an axe blade nearly cut her six-inch body in half. Dipping under the blade, she flew around the Ny-dick and onto the back of its head. Gently gripping its hair she hung on as it began to swing its head looking for her. Muffled screams from Leif and Jelen alerted Eirian to the second Ny-dick approaching from behind. She waited until the last second and then shot off, avoiding the drop of the axe that now embedded itself in the skull of the first Ny-dick.

Skirting the jutting rocks, she flew upward as fast as she could, hoping she have the strength to reach the top of the canyon and freedom.

"Watch out!" yelled the boys and Eirian forced herself to drop back and avoid a thrown knife that was aimed to kill. Unable to reach the top now left her no other choice.

"Grab on!" She could feel the tightening grip of their fingers as she closed her wings once again and plunged towards the ground.

Skimming the floor of the canyon she darted around and over rocks, shrubs and boulders as she rushed towards an Ancient monolith on the edge of a clump of trees. Reaching it, Eirian latched onto its worn etching of the old forgotten language and scampered up. Pausing in a deep weatherworn indentation, she looked below her. "Nothing, not good," she muttered under her breath, "...an unseen Ny-dick is more dangerous than one you can see."

A sudden jolt almost threw her from her perch. The Ny-dick stood at the base of the monolith, its large arms wrapped around it. With loud angry grunts and groans, he began pushing and pulling the monolith from side to side, trying to dislodge it from its formal resting place.

Eirian wished she could simply use the voice spell; it worked so nicely on the Ny-dick she ran across earlier. But the only way she could use her spell was in Mortal form and that would return the boys to their normal size as well, putting them in grave danger.

Calming her nerves and senses, Eirian drew from within herself an idea. She smiled and pulled a single hair free from under her skull-cap. Knotting her hair into a mysterious shape, she laid it across the open palm of her hand, blew on it, and set it into motion. It glistened in the fading moonlight, slowly moving on a light current of wind.

The Ny-dick saw it and a terrifying roar rent the air. In a flash, it was off after the sparkling illusion. This gave Eirian the chance she needed. She made a huge leap onto a nearby tree branch. She ran from one tree to another moving with silent speed, away from the Ny-dick, away from trouble.

As Eirian neared the edge of the stand of trees, she paused and scanned the area. There were only two ways to reach Solveig and both had clear advantages and very clear risks. There wasn't sufficient time to battle the pros and cons of each way. So standing stoutly in the midst of the leaves, Eirian scanned the area around her once again and then simply… took flight.

The Dark Lord, Sobus gloated fiendishly as he stood on the balcony of his castle. It was far to the north beyond Queen DaNann's land but not far enough for him to lose control over Lija. He enjoyed the ability to be in residence of another being's body and mind. He smiled wickedly. *"A little concentration, a little twist of the hand and I can get the Wizard Lija to do anything I want."* Sobus focused on Lija and then spoke directly into the Wizard's head. "You know what to do, now get on with it."

Sobus smiled as he watched through Lija's eyes. Ten of his Ny-dick had just surfaced on top of the ridge not far from Ke-Hern and a Faery. From this distance, Sobus could only make out a general form of the Faery and from what he could tell; she was a wisp of a woman, hardly what he would have expected Ke-Hern to pick to teach Wizardry to. He studied her for a moment. "Kill Ke-Hern and bring me the Faery," he hissed. "Let's see how much he's taught her."

"But if the Ny-dick kill him, it will bring much attention from the Queen. Are you sure you want that?" Lija questioned out loud. "Not everything is in place yet."

Sobus raised his hand and focused his thoughts and energy into it. A mist formed quickly around Lija's head. Sobus squeezed his fist tight and the mist pressed in on Lija. "Do not question me. You may have once been the adviser to that thing you all call a Queen, but you will never be one to me!"

Lija's screams lessened and he fell to the ground, panting for breath. After all this time in Sobus' control he should have known better. He rubbed his head and rose to his knees waiting for Sobus' permission to stand up.

"Ke-Hern's a bumbling fool. Kill him. I'll handle DaNann when she comes."

Lija stood up, nodded his head, and then gave the orders to the captain of the Ny-dick.

All of Eirian's reasons for picking this route were erased the moment she started crossing the last of the rivers. She had just started over the rushing water when she peered up and saw them — three Shadow Dwellers in the form of ravens!

Her choice of routes now held the worst hideous possibility - death in the claws of the Shadow Dwellers, the dark Faeries. She felt her stomach convulse. Was this to be her true fate?

"NO!" yelled Eirian to herself. "Not this time." And with that she pushed and willed herself to fly faster and harder than ever before. She smiled when she spotted a rodent's hole at the top of the nearing embankment. As soon as she was close enough she dove into it.

Using her fingers as her eyes, she ran them along the inside of the hollowed out passage, moving deeper into the blackness that surrounded them. She wasn't sure which way to go as she ran through the maze of passageways, she only hoped one would lead outside and not to the den of whatever animal made this it's lair.

Eirian noticed a dim light to her right and rushed through roots that hung in ethereal forms - motionless and twisted. She paused near the new exit disappointed that they were back at the river's edge.

Leif and Jelen both screeched with fear at the sight of larger than life ants running down one of the roots. Shaking with fear and anticipation, Leif reached out and picked up a rough stone, ready to throw it.

"DROP IT NOW!" Eirian hissed as she glanced over her shoulder. "They'll leave us alone if we leave them alone. Now be still and quiet!"

Leif's eyes narrowed. Not wanting to let go of his only weapon, he quickly tucked it into his belt and motioned to Jelen to grab a stone as well.

Jelen leaned over and reached towards a stone that caught his eye. He paused briefly to look at this unusual stone. A brief glimmer of light sparkled along its dull gray surface. He picked it up and found that it tingled in his hand. Leif elbowed him hard and Jelen swiftly tucked it away into the pocket on his shirt. He patted it twice wanting to make sure it would remain there.

Eirian craved to use the power that was buried deep inside her but Ke-Hern had warned her too often about the price she would pay. She inched back from the opening, if seen the Shadow Dwellers could simply shift back to their natural shapes of half-beast, half-Mortal, and claw at the ground until her and the boys were found.

Feeling she had no choice she whispered. "I'm going to try and make a run for it but if all does not go well, I will have to turn back to Elftan form. If this happens, it will cause you to return to your real size. Take to the water and make your way to Solveig. The Shadow Dwellers are after me, not you, and I believe they'll leave you alone." She hunched down and gazed ruefully out of the burrow. She caught a glimpse of only two of the Shadow Dwellers as they landed nearby. She cursed, "*If DeSpon is hiding, we're in big trouble!*"

Her skin quivered with nervous anticipation. She would have to time it just right. Her wings trembled and began to glow like a tidal wave retreating and advancing, keeping time with the energy building within her. She took a deep breath. "Here we go."

Eirian surged forward; it was now or never. She slipped out of the hole, up the embankment and quickly dove under a bunch of half-rotting leaves. Hastily she moved away from the river noise and towards the stillness of the predawn. Finally she burst free of the ground covering and fled unheedingly up a tree and into the broad leaves that were there. She waited for any sign of danger. When there was none, she bravely poked her head out. A hushed silence overtook everything and everything was motionless – her fear rose quickly. Slowly she started to slip back into the foliage when suddenly, banshee shrieks pierced the dawn.

"HERE THEY COME!" Leif's voice shook with panic as he pointed.

Two Shadow Dwellers exploded towards them into the leaves of the tree, missing them by mere inches. Eirian tucked her wings in tight and dove down along the tree trunk and towards the deep thicket. Suddenly, a large raven whistled past her on its way upward. It swiftly nipped in and out of the branches getting in the way of the other Shadow Dwellers. Scared and startled, Eirian quickly shot away. She didn't question what had just happened; all she could do was hold on to that one little thought in the midst of all the chaos, "get to Solveig."

Chapter 2

"Unfortunately guilt lingers well past its due date."

- Warlord Broan

Broan couldn't sleep. Even though the search parties had covered wide, vast areas, they still had nothing to show for it. Frustrated, he ran his hands roughly through his short black hair and got up.

"It's been too long," he said to himself. "The old forest is chock-full of dangers." Broan rolled his neck to loosen some of the muscle tension and then rubbed the cold spring dampness from his strong arms - arms that had been created by years of wielding heavy weapons in hard training and even harder battles. The rubbing didn't help; the cold clung to him like the heavy feelings that clung to his heart. "It's as if the boys have been plucked from this world. Neither a leaf upturned nor a stick broken." He had to wonder, "Faery?"

Broan shook off his exhaustion and began to dress. He proceeded to pull his white linen shirt over his head. He thrust his large arm into one sleeve and then the other only to hear it rip. He cursed and continued to dress. He wasn't about to let a simple piece of clothing control the day. After sliding a knife out from under his pillow into his boot he left his room. He carried on through the gate of the inner wall, across the outer bailey, and up the stairs to one of the watchtowers.

The sun had not yet risen over the high mountains, yet the night's blackness was fading into shadows exposing his part of the world. It didn't comfort him. Times like this brought out all his fears. He was driven to the extreme to protect his family and friends and he would go to any lengths to avoid a painful ending, like the one that had taken his younger sister and mother, many seasons ago. Their deaths were still unsettling. The wound would not heal.

Laeg quickly walked out of the barracks and onto the training field. The sun had yet begun to burn off the low laying morning fog as he made his way to Broan. Long muscular legs flowed with an unusual grace as his boots kicked up small wisps of mist. He had tied his long blond hair back with a strip of leather. He preferred to bind the sides back with braids behind his Elftan ears but he hadn't taken the time that morning. He had woken with a fresh idea playing in his mind; his determined gaze and firm bearing said it all. As he passed under an informal archway, Laeg turned and headed towards the one place he knew Broan would be - up on the parapet - just like he had every other time he was under stress.

"You didn't sleep very long," Laeg said as he came up next to Broan.

"Long enough," Broan replied. His ice blue eyes still focused on their surroundings.

"Trying to will them back?" A half smile graced Laeg's face.

"IF only it was that easy."

"Hargrave's back. No sign of the boys but he said he needed to talk to you."

"Later," Broan turned and looked at his second in command. "How's BroMac doing?"

"Just about as good as you, I'd say, which is amazing seeing that it's his…" A sudden flash caught Laeg's attention. Something reflected the sun's rays as it moved through the air. He stared at it and was surprised to see that it was heading straight for Solveig. He quickly pulled Broan inside the tower. Startled, Broan was about to say something when Laeg put his finger to his lips. Laeg slowly removed the knife from his belt.

The sun had just broken free of the mountain's shadow and caught Eirian in the eye. She faltered for a moment. The flight had been harder than she expected and she was so exhausted that she had to fight to keep afloat. She rushed passed the Ancient stone statues near the Blue River of the West. It wasn't long before she flew over the last fortification, hooked up with an upward draft and sailed to the top of the outer wall.

When she turned into her Duronykian form on the top of the outer wall, the extra weight of the boys behind her made her stumble and rush towards the door of the tower.

Laeg's knife hit the inside doorframe at the same time as he growled "Faery!"

Dodging the knife, Eirian quickly backed away from the tower with Leif and Jelen tucked safely behind her. "Stop! I have children!" she yelled as she quickly scanned the area around her. This wasn't going to be an easy escape. "I have the boys you lost. Ke-Hern sent me to deliver them to you."

"It's us!" screamed Leif and Jelen.

They were greeted with silence.

"I only want to hand the boys over and talk with Lord Broan," she called out.

Still silence.

"Fine. If you care not, I'll just take them back or perhaps I'll make my life a whole lot easier and just dump them over the wall!"

"How do we know this isn't just one of your tricks?" Broan asked.

"It's no trick Uncle Broan. It really is me and Jelen."

"Send the boys through the door and then be on your way," he demanded.

"Ke-Hern told me to hand them over only to Lord Broan. I have a message to give him."

Silence once again. She did not like this one bit.

Broan raised his hand to still the guard and Laeg. "I AM Lord Broan. I'm coming out." He said as he leaned over to Laeg and whispered, "Give me your Faery Binding Cord." Taking it, he used a slip-knot to fasten it loosely around his right wrist. Then he tucked the cord under his tunic sleeve as he stepped through the door.

There in that early morning of late spring, destiny won out and Eirian came face to face with Broan the Warlord of Solveig. He was tall, broad and very much in command.

Broan assessed the Faery just as quickly. Other than a strange skullcap, she was dressed much like other Faeries in boots, leggings, tunic, and shirt. She stood still - looking quite striking and profoundly confident - still guarding Leif and Jelen with her hand. She suddenly forced them further behind her, which surprised him.

"It's okay. You can let them go." He turned his hands over exposing his palms. "No weapons." That was all the two young boys needed to hear, as they quickly broke free and ran to him.

Eirian still eyed him cautiously. "Now if you want I'll tell you what Ke-Hern…"

"Not here." He cut her off, "Let's go into the Keep. It's more comfortable and much more private." Broan smiled at her as he pushed the boys into the tower and into Laeg's protection. "So, what is your name?"

"Eirian. But here is just fi…"

"Well Eirian I'm very grateful to you for getting the boys back to us in one piece. I apologize for the knife but we've not had any good come from any encounter with Faeries." He rushed on as he extended his hand and offered it in welcome.

"And neither have we upon meeting any Mortals." Eirian felt uneasy by his gesture, but maybe Ke-Hern was right and this little misunderstanding was going to be the most vexing problem she would have to face. Slowly, cautiously she put her right hand in his to complete the shake.

Broan gripped her hand so hard she could feel pain right through to her bones. With one smooth motion, he slipped the cord off his wrist, onto hers and pulled it tight.

Eirian pulled back as soon as he let go and tried to remove the offending rope but couldn't. Eyes wild with defiance, she glared at him. He had just committed an offence that was virtually impossible to forgive. She struggled through a series of fight and flight urges. Refusing to give up, she swung around nearer to the wall and tried to shape shift. Startled, she realized she couldn't. She dug deeper than ever before, coming close to tapping into the energy force that Ke-Hern had warned her about. She quickly pulled back.

The morning air was spilt with a scream of her outrage. She was truly trapped. It wasn't just Broan's deft, calculated move that had entrapped her, but her loyalty and belief in Ke-Hern that had allowed her to let her guard down. It was a heavy price to pay for trust. She screamed again and then glared at Broan from over her shoulder.

Broan watched her closely. "You now have no power and no freedom. Only the person who puts it on can remove the Faery Binding Cord. And don't even think of calling your friends for help. They'll just find themselves in the same spot as you."

"BUT…Ke H…"

He cut short her words and grabbed her arm, then pushed her through the door of the tower. Eirian tried again to pull free from Broan's grip. Instantly his hand tightened. In a huff she turned her face away from him. There was not much else to do but allow this manhandling…for now.

"Let her go! What she said is true!" anxiously the boys bellowed. "Ke-Hern did ask her to bring us home."

Broan looked at Leif and Jelen. He marveled that they still had that dangerous aura of youthful invincibility. This was going to be a hard lesson for the both of them.

"Sit!" he barked, with a stare that held them. "You can't imagine the worry you both caused your mothers. You can't understand the upheaval you caused here in Solveig by your little adventure." He leaned over them both. "BUT you will feel the pain of your ill judgment."

Jelen and Leif slouched low while sitting on the bench by the stairs. "But Uncle Broan we didn't mean to get lost."

"Quiet!" he sharply commanded.

Jelen squirmed in his seat, already feeling the discomfort he knew he would be feeling before sunset. "We'll never do anything like this again. We already learned our lesson. Ke-Hern made sure of that."

Broan motioned to Laeg to lead the way with the boys as he fell in behind, pulling Eirian along. He gave no notice to her reluctance as he continued down the stairs and out into Solveig's bailey.

News traveled fast and it didn't take long before there was a crowd around Laeg and the boys. Leif and Jelen were greeted with love and attention until the crowd saw ... her. Hushed whispers spread with lightening speed, and then silence took over. Eirian cringed and a shiver passed through her. She had never been so close to so many Mortals before. Unconsciously, she tucked in closer to Broan.

Suddenly four enormous warriors pushed their way to the front of the crowd. Raising her eyes, Eirian peeked out and looked at the soldiers. She recognized them from the many times she had secretly watched them in practice. Eirian suppressed a tremor, having to admit they were much more ferocious up close.

BroMac was by far the biggest, making him the easiest for her to always pick out, even at a great distance. Six feet five inches tall and well over two hundred pounds, he now stood legs apart braced for action. Next to BroMac, V-Tor stood quietly with sword in hand. His shaven head, broad shoulders and intense stare never failed to intimidate anyone. RohDin, brother to BroMac, was the third one of the group. He was almost as tall as his brother but so much different in character. He was the true maverick of the bunch. Last but not least was Ardis. He was Elftan like Laeg but slightly smaller than the rest. He preferred to stay in the background, always keeping his Elftan ears and eyes busy, and Eirian on her toes whenever she stopped by for a look.

Broan motioned for a path to be cleared by the men and started out right after them. Jarred into motion, she wished Broan would consider the fact that his legs were much longer than hers and slow his pace down a bit, but she dare not open her mouth.

Eirian could feel the panic start when the Keep loomed ahead of her. She had never been in a Mortal made building before and her fear mobilized an endless array of bad outcomes in her mind. She tried to snatch free but Broan didn't let go, pulling her along as he marched to the Keep's front stairs.

Wild-eye hysterics were about to overtake Eirian and she tensed and pulled back at the bottom step. Broan just jerked her harder. She pulled back harder, locking her feet against the rise of the step. Broan looked back at her. His blue eyes cut like a crisp winter wind. "Do I have to carry you?" he said with a rueful smile.

"NO!" She stared at him with stately indignation. She quickly rallied, straightening herself. Without farther pause Broan pulled her into the oppressive structure then into a large room. The thought of being inside this stone structure left her feeling squeamish. She sucked in what air she could while silently cursing Ke-Hern. He knew how dreadfully dangerous coming here was BUT he defiantly ignored it. "*Start…It's time to start…*" Ke-Hern's voice echoed in her head, jolting her back to the task at hand.

"Clear everyone out," Broan commanded and then pointed to the two boys. "Sit, until I tell you to move."

Hargrave had barely started to eat when Broan and his captive entered the room. Shocked, he stood up so fast he knocked over the bench he was sitting on. "Broan I have something to tell you."

"Later," Broan answered, dismissing Hargrave without a second thought.

Eirian's eyes grew large at the sight of this Manliken and she swiftly stepped behind Broan. Of all her luck!

"But…"

"Later. Go and I'll come find you after I handle this."

"No!" Hargrave countered firm and intense. "You need to hear this. NOW!"

Broan paused as he studied Hargrave. "She cannot do us any harm as she's bound by the cord. Is there more danger here than you think we can handle?"

Hargrave shook his head as he stared at Eirian.

"Good."

Slowly Hargrave left with the others, cursing himself for not going straight to Broan upon his return. Nothing good was going to come of this. He could feel it in his bones.

Satisfied that BroMac and RohDin would be ready for anything, Broan finally let go of Eirian's arm. She immediately stepped away from him, rubbing her upper arm where his offending hand had been. Suddenly her olfactory senses kicked into overdrive. There was a confusing array of smells derived from the past and present, old and new, stagnant and fresh. All of which added to weaken her resolve. She wrinkled her nose and swallowed hard.

"Let them in," Broan's voice boomed, getting Eirian's attention. She quickly stepped back from the women who rushed in, and watched. She couldn't help it. She stared at as the mothers' faces lit with happiness as they ran toward their children and enveloped them in their arms. There was laughter and tears everywhere. Never before had she witnessed such closeness between Mortals. Her stomach shivered oddly. She felt a warm fluttering in the pit of her being. It traveled up her spine, into her neck and lit her mouth with a sudden grin. And…it felt… Eirian looked down at herself and ran her fingers over her midsection. *"What is this…feeling? A Mortal thing?"* she wondered. She had heard Faeries whisper of such closeness but she had never had the opportunity to see it for herself.

"Enough!" Broan barked. "You can go with your mothers for now. We will talk about what kind of punishment you'll get later."

Eirian observed the hall once again clear out while she played absent-mindedly with the cord on her wrist. It had already begun to hurt and press into her flesh. It was not like Ke-Hern to put her in harm's way, so there must be a good reason why Broan had done this to her.

Broan had observed Eirian as the room had filled and emptied. Her willowy, coltish form always seemed in motion, her eyes always searching. He wondered what she was thinking of when she smiled at Leif and Jelen's family reunion. He knew that all Faeries had at one time been Mortal, yet Eirian seemed bewildered, and more importantly she seemed unfazed by the position she truly was in and that really worried him. He had all of Solveig and its people to keep safe and everyone knew how dangerous a Faery could be.

"Take your tunic and boots off," Broan demanded.

"What?" Eirian asked.

"NOW."

"Fine," she said as she bent down and pulled off one boot and then the other. In one smooth movement she pulled her tunic over her head. Her leggings and shirt clung to her body as if they were a thin coating of liquid, gliding over her skin as she moved.

Broan settled in a chair by the fireplace. He stretched out his long legs, lazily crossed his arms over his chest then nodded to V-Tor.

V-Tor stepped in behind Eirian and roughly took hold of her wrists raising them over her head. Instinctively Eirian tried to pull away and elbow the warrior. V-Tor's grip tightened and he yanked her up onto her toes. He waited until she stopped struggling and then waited some more. Finally lowering her to her feet, he barked, "Keep your arms up."

V-Tor let go of her wrists and ran his hands down her arms and onto her rib cage. His hands moved to the front of her, just under her breasts and down her hips. From the start, it was obvious that this Faery had no weapons; her clothing barely hid her womanly form, but V-Tor was not going to challenge Broan's orders. He squatted behind her as his hands ran down the inner and outer portions of each of her legs, causing the material of her clothing to shimmer and shift with each movement. It took everything in him not reveal how this was affecting him. Flushed, he finished and stood up, nodding to Broan, "No weapons."

Eirian lowered her arms and sighed in relief, thankful that V-Tor had missed the ring hidden between her breasts. "I am unarmed, powerless and alone. You have your men, your weapons and your freedom. Well, this may not be a great way to start things off but it'll have to do," she calmly stated.

"Start things off? All run-ins with Faeries have never started nor ended well." Broan studied her for a moment. "Besides, I am only protecting my people"

"You don't need to do that."

"Is that right?" Broan raised an eyebrow. "Are you going to tell me that all the families that were slaughtered and violated by Faeries never happened? Are you insinuating that the wave of killings that swept over the land was only a bad dream?"

BroMac toyed with his knife, waiting for her response. Some of his family was among those unfortunate Mortals that had died. Like so many other Mortals, his relatives never saw it coming.

Eirian held her chin level. "And Mortals have pure clean hands? Are you forgetting the horrific actions you Mortals have taken against us? You trapped us with enchanted cords then nailed us to trees, leaving us to slow agonizing deaths, to be eaten alive by birds and insects. That is of course, if you didn't first kill us outright."

"STOP!" RohDin yelled. "We were only countering your attacks. Even Ke-Hern was on our side. He's the one that gave us the Faery Binding Cord. It was the only way that we could capture you in the first place."

"The binding cord wasn't given to you for that reason. It was supposed to stop violence at the source of the problem."

"Which was what - that you were all unhappy with your lot in life so you decided to make our lives just as bad?" V-Tor cut in.

Eirian glanced at him. "NO! The Faeries didn't know at first."

"Didn't know what? That we didn't enjoy dying?" The room echoed with snickering.

Eirian shook her head. How could things have gotten so out of hand and had been so wrongly understood "Faeries mirror what they encounter from within a Mortal. When they look into a Mortal's eye, Manliken or Elftan, in that single heartbeat, they become whatever that person is. All the selfish, hateful, fearful motives are instantly picked up and reflected back. Deceit breeds deceit."

"You say." V-Tor muttered angrily.

"But it is true!"

"Then why didn't Ke-Hern ever mention it? You can't so easily escape your past."

"He most likely didn't tell you because it wouldn't have made a difference to you Mortal idiots. Mortals always twist the truth to suit their own needs."

BroMac had heard enough. "Our actions have always been based on facts!" His deep-rooted distain for Faeries came through loud and clear.

Eirian swiftly turned and glared at him. "Old facts. When was the last Mortal killed? Years ago? Decades? When was the last Faery killed? Last evening? This morning?"

"Soon I hope," he hissed while he eyed Broan.

Eirian scanned the group of men. "Can't you understand what a wild passage it was for us - to be plucked out of a normal, Mortal life and placed into this empty and bare existence? Can you guarantee that any Mortal today would not go crazy under such pressure?"

"You spin a good tale Faery," RohDin shook his head wondering if she was really that dimwitted. "Year after year it's the same. The facts are the facts and we cannot so easily divorce them from our minds and hearts."

Eirian looked at the others in the room and was saddened. This was hopeless. Ke-Hern was mad if he thought unifying the two races was going to work! Closing her eyes and attempting to center herself,

Eirian spoke from the heart. "There is a connection between us which is curiously strong and good."

Broan head tilted. "And what is that?"

"We all want a normal peaceful life."

"Then why don't you give it to us? Why not just leave us be?" RohDin muttered loudly.

"After Duronyk was destroyed, our lives as we knew it - our families, our homes, and our possessions - were lost. The loss drove many to the brink of insanity and that in turn, led many to lash out."

"Which is still at play today," BroMac said.

Broan raised his hand, stilling BroMac. He wanted to hear this.

"We were metaphorically dying."

"Too bad it was only metaphorically," BroMac muttered, ignoring Broan's silent warning.

Eirian focused solely on Broan. "This anger and hatred runs deep on both sides. If there's any hope of changing the futures of both our kith and kin, delve into the truth of your soul, not mind and memories. Look to the present for the truth."

"Soul, heart, minds? Your talk is baffling. Can you deny that the Faeries started the killings?" Broan asked.

"No."

"Can you deny that even to this day, that Faeries go out of their way to dry up cows, sour milk, make crops to fail?"

Eirian's head shot back, anger flaring. "That I will deny because it's not true. That's but gossip and is very dangerous, only adding to the tension already here. Faeries do not have that ability." She glared at him; "Mortals have always taken the easy route, blaming Faeries for everything that goes wrong."

Broan's eyes barely narrowed at the insult. Other than the use of a sharp tongue and blameless thinking, he wondered just what these creatures could do once their powers where subdued by the cord. He flicked his hand in the slightest of movement and RohDin quickly moved in. Eirian was not to be fooled. She quickly ducked RohDin's fist. Anticipation allowed her extraordinary speed. With supple grace, her energy balanced his. Her swaying dance of intense, precise turns and rhythmic moves, countered all of his aggressive advances.

RohDin's anger boiled over. He frantically jumped at her, hoping to tackle her to the ground. The sudden lowering of his massive body left Eirian with only one choice. She raised two fingers and drove them into the middle of his chest, causing him to drop to his knees, unable to breathe. She stood over him with hands on hips, satisfied with her fighting demonstration.

Eirian saw only a blur of motion as BroMac's fist grazed off of the side of her face, causing her to bite the inside of her cheek. The sudden pain of the blow caused her to lower her defenses. As she brought up her hand to her cheek, Laeg grabbed her and tossed her to the floor. He pinned her arms and body in the tightly restricted space between his knees.

"Your welcoming wears thin quickly," Eirian said. She focused her energy, relaxed and quickly slid out of Laeg's hold and then up onto her feet behind him.

BroMac saw red and drew his long knife. How could this wisp of a female out-maneuver two warriors? His face darkened with anger as the blade in his hand sliced upward, coming within a fraction of an inch from the artery in her neck. "On your knees!" he yelled with a lip-curling sneer.

Eirian lowered herself to one knee, and BroMac gripped her skullcap. He made sure his knife was pressed very firmly to the side of her neck. "What did you do to RohDin?" he growled.

"Have you ever fallen and had the air pushed out of you? Remember how it took a few moments to get back the rhythm of breath? Well, I simply worked with his aggressive attack. He lunged forward and I pressed back, knocking the wind out of him. I could teach you." Eirian offered.

"Teach us!" An eruption of jeers and hostile laughing mocked her offer.

"Exceedingly clever," Broan said unmoved by the commotion. "How quickly you go from innocent to rebel. You've taught me a lot."

Eirian had a hard time concealing her disappointment. "What I've shown you is…."

"You've shown me nothing more than that you are Faery, full of tricks and with much to mistrust."

Eirian raised her eyes to Broan. His view of her was as sparse and simple as BroMac's and the others. She had been right all along about him. Now what was she to do?

Broan tilted his head as he studied her. "What is Ke-Hern's message?"

"I was told to tell only you. We'll need privacy." She said trying to buy time.

"This is all the privacy you'll get. What's his message? I won't ask again."

BroMac gave her a little shake letting her know he was more than willing to slice through her neck if she didn't do as she was told. Eirian lowered her eyes and forced herself not to touch the ring and give away its hiding place. "I am his message. We are the unfolding future. We are to deliver…"

"Right!" Broan interrupted her, "well, until the unfolding future delivers Ke-Hern, you will remain here."

"That's not what he meant! There'll come a time where we'll have to count on each other."

"Count on a Faery? Now I'm certain this is nothing more than a trick. Ke-Hern would never tell me to trust a Faery!"

"Really?" Eirian looked at him stunned. "Are you sure? Nowhere in your past did he tell you of a future that was going to challenge everything you once believed."

Broan sat back and studied her.

"Broaaan?" BroMac questioned.

Broan straightened in his chair. "Until Ke-Hern arrives you will remain my prisoner."

Eirian narrowed her eyes. "I'm not a prisoner!"

"That Faery Binding Cord says you are…. unless you are a slave, a gift for my birthday. How nice of Ke-Hern."

"Your birthday is months away. What Ke-Hern sees in you I'll never understand! You're such an idiot; you couldn't even be born on the same day as your twin sister."

"What?"

Eirian instantly regretted saying that.

BroMac shook her once again, as he asked the question on everyone's mind. "How do you know that?"

"Ke-Hern told me, of course. Although he didn't add the idiot part, I did, but you can't blame me," she stated coolly as she slowly began to shift her weight. The position BroMac was forcing her to keep was getting very uncomfortable. This, of course, only caused BroMac's knife to press harder into the tender flesh of her neck.

"Now what?" she muttered to herself. "The patient war of trust requires time," Ke-Hern's words reminded her. "Thanks," she said out loud to her memory.

"Thanks for what?" Broan asked.

"Thanks for proving me right and Ke-Hern wrong. I told him you wouldn't be smart enough to be open to the truth. He has more faith in you than wisdom I fear. He said you would be grateful and welcoming. He said you would be…"

"You can say all you want but until Ke-Hern comes to vouch for your words, you're a prisoner and are here to stay. Oh, and by the way, you asked earlier when was the last time the Faeries killed, it was two nights ago. A small farm just north of here; only the children were left."

"That's a lie!" Eirian yelled.

BroMac pressed his knife into the skin of her neck. Its sharp edge cut into the whiteness of her flesh and it quickly beaded with blood. "Watch who you call a liar."

"Our punishment is too great. Are you sure it was Faeries?"

"Who else would've it been?" Laeg asked.

"Anyone else: Ny-dick, Shadow Dwellers, or other Mortals using the cover of Faery hatred to do their evil deeds and get away with it."

"You're stupid if you think we'll believe that one." RohDin yelled. "Besides, Shadow Dwellers and Faeries are all the same. You're all blight on this land, just like the Ny-dick." He leaned into her. "Some are just uglier than others."

"Shadow Dwellers may be from Duronyk, like Faeries were, but we are very different. They kill without mercy and live to tell the story. We on the other hand…"

"It doesn't matter. Shadow Dweller or Faery, you still bring nothing but pain and torment to us," BroMac cut in. He gripped her head more fiercely forcing her head back.

Eirian looked at Broan, saddened by the hatred that had such a hard, cold hold on these Mortal's minds. She strained to speak. "Do you… Lord… Broan know everything…what every… Mortal is doing right now?"

BroMac's knife pressed in harder. It would be so easy to end this all. He looked at Broan ready for the nod. "Brrooan?"

"BroMac let her go."

"WHAT?" yelled BroMac, staring in disbelief at Broan, "She uses words as her spells, twisting what is true and turning them into something that's evil. She moves like air making her hard to control. Kill her now and handle Ke-Hern later."

"No. I think keeping her bound and unable to use any of her powers until Ke-Hern comes, will be enough."

"But she can still speak!" BroMac grunted his disapproval and shoved Eirian away.

"You're right." RohDin hissed. "Maybe we should just gag her and lock her up in the dungeon and she can hope Ke-Hern comes before she slowly dies."

Broan missed nothing. Eirian was visibly shaken as she stood up. There was a sudden shift of skin tone and a slight stitch in her breathing. Her eyes briefly unfocused and there was a slight tremor in her body that she tried hard to hide. He leaned forward in his chair and smiled. She was a contradiction, bold and tough on one hand, quite vulnerable on the other. "So is it the threat of the dungeon or knowing that Ke-Hern won't be showing up that has you so frightened?"

That's it. Eirian had had enough of this bullying. These Mortals had no redeeming features as far as she was concerned. They were all the same: arrogant, wasteful, and dogmatic. She was mad enough to... "You don't get it. I am only a Faery, who out of loyalty to a friend risked her life to bring back your two boys. The two boys that you let slip through your fingers. KE-HERN DID SEND ME. HE DID!" she shouted as she threw up her hands, "I can't believe you Mortals are so daft!"

The immediate response was no more than a murmur but loud enough to show the distain everyone had for her. Broan raised his hand and everyone quieted. Eirian was articulate, animated and truly believed what she said. It was not something he had expected coming from a Faery, yet she was Faery. Everything in his past experience told him not to trust her. He gave her a mocking smile. He was looking forward to having time to discover more about her and her kind. Perhaps he would be able to find a way to rid Faeries permanently from the land.

Eirian shifted slightly under Broan's strange smile. "You truly think I am the enemy! Then kill me now and get it over with as your men suggest. You may regret it when Ke-Hern comes and even more as the season passes."

"Ah, the future again. What do you know of the future?"

Pushed to the end of her patience, Eirian glared at Broan. "I know a lot more of the future than you by what I can tell. But what does it matter. You wouldn't believe me anyway. So it'll have to be Ke-Hern you'll need to talk to. I'm only his messenger, one that no one wishes to hear."

"Why do I get the feeling you're more than a simple messenger?"

"Maybe you're smarter than an idiot after all."

"She stays." He paused a moment, his blue eyes clouding, "but I will appoint someone to watch her at all times. If she causes any trouble I'll lock her up."

"Babysitting! You want us to babysit her?" V-Tor chocked. "Lock her up. Don't waste any more time on this thing."

Outside, Bronagh bristled at their cruel words. She couldn't hold back any longer. "Stop this!" Bronagh demanded as she burst past the guard and into the room, dragging Leif with her.

Broan nodded his head to Ardis, allowing this intrusion. His sister was in one of her tough-as-nails moods, the one that got her through most things, even his temper. He watched as Bronagh stopped beside Eirian.

"Seeing as you are all so frightened of her, I'll take her under my charge. It's the least I can do to repay her for bringing back my son," Bronagh said as she handed Eirian a clean cloth to wipe the blood from her mouth and neck. She waited for Broan's burst of anger ready to stand her ground. If no one was going to trust this savior, she was.

"Fine, but you know that means if she gets into any mischief there will be a heavy toll to pay." Broan paused briefly. "I guess she could help you around the Keep, but at night she will sleep in here, under guard."

"I willingly take on your challenge. AND she can sleep in my quarters with Leif and I." Bronagh eyed the other men in the room. "I'll happily do it. Is there anything more brother?"

Broan paused as he studied Eirian. She dressed too much like a man, or a young boy. Her hosed covered legs were always exposed; her tunic was shorter than his warriors and the shirt hid none of her womanly form. "Get her some decent clothes! I'll not have people insulted by her attire."

"What's wrong with my clothes?" Eirian asked confused. "They're comfortable and very practical for living in the woods. Besides they are that of my heritage."

"You're not living in the woods at the moment. You will do as you are told." He paused briefly, "or there's a hole in the ground you can live in for awhile."

Eirian dug in her heels and straightened her stance. She glared at him in silence and he glowered back.

Bronagh bent down and scooped up Eirian's boots and tunic. She looked at Eirian and nodded towards the door. "Come on, I have some clothes you can change into." With a gentle touch of her hand Bronagh was finally able to separate Eirian from Broan's steely gaze.

"My name is Bronagh. What's yours?"

"Eirian."

"I'm Leif but you already knew that," Leif said, as he moved around his mother so he could walk next to Eirian. "Thank you for flying us home. I was getting tired of Ke-Hern's meals." He proudly looked up at his mother. "He doesn't cook like you."

Bronagh smiled at him and then glared at the warriors now standing in the doorway of the Main Hall. "Come, let's check out that bruise on your cheek and get you settled in. My quarters are on the third floor."

Eirian hesitated at the bottom of the staircase. The trepidation of going deeper into this building unnerved her. She turned to Leif and spoke sweetly, hoping to build some courage. "I bet your father will be happy to see you again, Leif."

Bronagh suddenly stopped and turned to Eirian. "His father isn't with us. He died before Leif was born."

"Sorry." Eirian whispered. She looked away briefly, caught in her own life story, until Leif tugged on her sleeve.

"It's okay," He said. "This way I have more than one father. Broan's my father and BroMac and RohDin and Laeg and V-Tor...."

Eirian was beginning to wonder if young Leif was going to name every male in Solveig or even every male in all of Remdor, when Bronagh laughed. "Resourceful isn't he?"

Eirian could still feel the angry stares of Broan's men on her back. So with head held high, back straight, she took the first step. Hesitating slightly she then took the next one. What choice did she have? With as much confidence as she could muster, she continued up the stairs after Bronagh.

Off to the left on the third landing, was a large hallway with doors to Bronagh's family quarters, and various rooms. Bronagh opened a single oak door and led Eirian into a spacious room that emanated an air of elegance and tranquility. The high ceiling was beamed and plastered. The walls were of the original stone of the Keep.

"What is that?" Eirian asked as she pointed to the largest item in the room.

Leif almost wanted to laugh. "That's a bed. You sleep in it. Don't you have beds?"

Eirian walked over to the breast high, four-poster bed. She glided her hand over the wooden posts. "Hmmm. It appears we both sleep among the trees, only yours are dead."

"So you sleep in the forest? Out in the open? Not even in caves?" Leif's eyes sparkled, "But what do you do in the winter, or if there's a rainstorm? I mean..."

"Leif!" Bronagh called out sternly. "Give Eirian time to think and adjust." She smiled at Eirian. "This must all be so new for you. I can only imagine what you're feeling. Take your time. I'll answer as many questions as I can."

Eirian nodded her agreement as she played with the binding cord once again. When she spotted an open window, she rushed to it. Happily Eirian leaned on the open window frame and raised her face to the sun. Closing her eyes she took in a big breath of fresh air. Once she was calmer she opened her eyes and took in all of Solveig. "Why do you live all cramped together?" Eirian asked.

Bronagh shrugged her shoulders. "Safety in numbers I guess. Why do you ask?"

"We have no safety in numbers. In fact we have no safety at all." The smell of hot bread wafted through the air and Eirian breathed deeply. "Aaahhh…Now there is a luxury, bread!"

Bronagh looked at Leif. "Go and fetch a plate of fresh bread and milk for all of us. With all the excitement this morning I believe no one's eaten yet." She gently pushed him out the door and then went to her trunks to search out clothes for Eirian.

Eirian couldn't believe that Ke-Hern had been so remiss in teaching Broan about his role in the upcoming events, especially when Ke-Hern spent almost every waking moment teaching her about hers. Even her earliest childhood memories were tainted with Ke-Hern lectures on what would be asked of her. This was a huge setback and there was no turning back from this path she had boldly committed to. She had no other choice now but to find some way to make Broan see reason, and she only had so much time to do it in. Somewhere in that stubborn Manliken was something Ke-Hern respected and had faith in. All she had to do was find it.

Standing a little taller, Eirian looked with new eyes at Solveig. If this was to be her new home for a while, she may as well learn about it. *"It can't be that hard. Now can it?"* Scanning the area before her, an odd thing caught her eye. Near the back of the inner bailey was a set of large double wooden doors, which were mounted at the top of five steps. From where she stood, it looked like the doors were a gateway into the mountain itself. There were no windows or carvings to establish it as part of the Keep. "What's over there?" Eirian asked.

Bronagh got up and joined Eirian at the window. "Oh that's the Back-Hall. It's cut right out of the mountain face. It's used when the villagers come into Solveig for protection. I'll show it to you later if you want." She shook out the gown and shift she had picked for Eirian. "This should fit," she said holding it up to Eirian.

Eirian looked down at the shift. It was made of heavy cotton and dyed a deep brown color. Lace ties ran down from under the arms to just under the bust. It had a deep square neck and was sleeveless. Over Bronagh's arm was a white linen gown that had long flowing sleeves. They looked like they tied at the elbow. It may have been the common clothing of Mortal women but it held no appeal to Eirian. She made a face of disgust.

"Well let's get started," Bronagh announced. She directed Eirian out of her room, down the hall, and into a much smaller room. "You can bath and change in here."

Eirian had never seen anything like it. Against the side wall in the small room there was a very large, deep hollowed out stone. Protruding out of the wall were two pipes that hovered over one end of this giant bowl thing.

"What is this?" she asked as she ran her hand over the smooth stone.

"This is a tub where you can bath. Once you fill it with water...." Bronagh shrugged her shoulders, "you get in and wash. When you're finished, you unplug the hole in the bottom and the water drains out. It's very simple. Have you never bathed before?"

"Of course," Eirian answered indigently, "in rivers, creeks and lakes but NEVER in something like this!"

Bronagh smiled at a confused Eirian. She opened the taps. "There's a hot spring between here and the village. Broan came up with the idea to pipe the water in so we could bathe whenever we wanted to without having the trouble of heating the water. There is a chamber pot over here. You do know what a chamber pot is?"

"I'll figure it out."

"Good." Bronagh turned and looked over to her left and pointed, "That trunk holds the towels to dry yourself with." She turned the levers on the pipes once again, stopping the flow of water. "When you're finished come back to my room, I'll be waiting." Bronagh turned and headed for the door, "Are you going to be alright?"

Eirian could do nothing but nod her head. Everything she saw had left her speechless. She never knew that life in a fortress was so strangely effortless. She slowly bent down and touched the hot water. She raised an eyebrow. This was all too new for her. It wasn't that she was fearful; it just felt too strange for right now. She turned her attention to the clothes that Bronagh had left her. She quickly pulled the shift on over her undershirt and tights; satisfied, she walked out the door, down the hallway and into Bronagh's quarters.

Surprised to see Eirian enter the room so quickly, Bronagh stood up and stared at her. "Eirian you're supposed to wear the white gown under the shift. Here I'll help."

"No, this is fine. If he wants my legs covered I'll cover my legs, but I refuse to fully dress in your fashion." She walked towards Bronagh so she could give her back the under gown. The shift clung to her leggings and quickly trapped her legs, almost tripping her. Eirian pulled at the offending clothes. "How am I supposed to walk let alone help in this thing when it weighs me down and hampers my step?"

"Well, if you take off your leggings and wear the linen gown underneath the shift it won't cling to you." Bronagh then lifted her gown and shift slightly to show Eirian that other than ankle boots; she wore nothing on her legs. "The gown and shift will glide off your legs as you walk. It actually feels nice on hot days."

"I am not going to take my clothes off and walk around with only this on!" She crossed her arms in defiance.

"Don't get angry with me. I'm trying to help you!"

Eirian was ashamed at her outburst. Bronagh was the only friendly Mortal so far and her words had come out harshly. "I'm sorry. Anger is one of the few emotions I've come to know. When you live day to day fighting for survival you learn to live without most other feelings." She looked back at Bronagh. "Along with anger, fear keeps you moving, together they keep you alive."

"That sounds so sad. It can't always be like that. Surely there are times that you enjoy; the laughter of children playing, the happiness of old friends meeting, or just the pleasure in companionship."

Eirian turned her head away and went to the window again. "There are no children left, there are no families, and gatherings of any type are not allowed."

Broan had always allowed open discussion and differences of opinions amongst his warriors. They often spoke with great impunity and he didn't have to wait long. Hearing some low mutterings to his side, Broan turned and looked at BroMac, "What's the problem?"

He stood with his arms across his chest. "I think you're making a big mistake."

"Perhaps, but with the growing unrest that plagues this land..."

Laeg's eyes narrowed as he looked at Broan. "You've talked before about a war with Faeries. Do you think this is it?"

"Could be and that's what I need to find out. Had any of you thought that could be why Ke-Hern sent her here?"

"What?"

"Perhaps he wants us to use her to our advantage, to find ways to fight against our enemy." Broan said with the faintest of smiles. "I want to find out if there is any truth to my thoughts. I also want to learn as much as possible. There's not enough Faery Binding Cord to trap every Faery in the land. We may need to become very resourceful in the near future."

V-Tor elbowed BroMac. "Out with it man," he teased. "You always have a way of making even silence sarcastic, so spit it out."

"I think this is a waste of time. I doubt very much that she will let her guard down. She's shown us that Faeries are swift and agile and if you think Faeries are the cause of this ill time, isn't it wiser to kill or imprison her at least?"

"It's not that cut and dried. There's a possibility that Ke-Hern sent her to do exactly as she claims. She did know something that she should not have known. Only he could have imparted that knowledge to her. I trust Ke-Hern." Broan eyed his group of warriors. "Besides, if she really gets into any trouble, you have my permission to kill her... only know that when Ke-Hern comes it will be you facing him. So I wouldn't be too quick to end her life. Look, we need to use this time he has offered us for good purpose, just remember that."

"So you really think…"

"I think I'll enjoy the next few days until Ke-Hern arrives." Broan's smiled. "I agree with you that she'll not willingly let down her guard, that's why two of you will befriend her while the others will remain as their untrusting selves."

BroMac shook his head. "THIS IS A NIGHTMARE!"

"Not if we work together. Everyone has to make a conscious effort to observe her, take mental notes. Let's see if there is more here than what meets the eye. There is a coming war BroMac, and one I wish to be ready for." He smiled at BroMac's stiff defiant form. "My good friend, you don't have to worry. You will not have to be one of the welcoming few. You already have the role down pat as the angry, unwelcoming warrior." Broan turned and looked at Laeg and V-Tor. "I think perhaps the two of you will be able to make some headway with her."

"ME!" V-Tor moaned.

"Yes." Broan answered as he started out the door.

"Where are you going now?" V-Tor asked.

"I have to talk with Hargrave. He may know more about this situation than anyone else here."

"You sent a Faery into Solveig!" the Off-World Queen DaNann screamed. *"You know why there's the law forbidding it and you still sent her there! In fact you helped make the law to protect the Faeries, the very life you sent into Solveig."* There was a slight pause in her yelling. *"And who is this Eirian anyway. Why haven't I heard about her before?"*

Ke-Hern tried to tone down the volume of her voice in his head. He had known this was going to happen and he had decided he could not avoid it any longer. He had barely escaped the Ny-dick attack and now stood on a hill just outside the Walled City.

"*Ke-Hern! WAKE UP!*" The Queen bellowed into his mind. "*Tell me what possessed you to do something so dangerous?*"

"I'll tell you as soon as you stop screaming at me." Ke-Hern dropped himself to the ground. He crossed his arms over his chest and waited for reason to come to Queen DaNann.

"*All right!*" She paused and with a lower tone asked, "*Why? Why did you do it?*"

"Eirian carries Cian's ring."

"*So why send her into Solveig? You know what could happen.*"

Ke-Hern closed his eyes and shivered. Yes, he knew what could happen. He had to hold onto the belief that it wouldn't and that Eirian would be safe. "There was no other choice." He told only a half-truth. "I had to get her to safety to prevent the Ny-dick from capturing her. Solveig was the closest fortress, and because of where it's built, I knew it would truly keep her out of Sobus' grip."

"*But what if she is seen?*"

"Oh I'm sure she will be seen. I told her to meet with Lord Broan."

"*WHAT!*"

Ke-Hern drove his large black fingers into his ears and then chided himself for doing it. Nothing was going to block out her voice. Fingers had no power over the volume she wished to speak at. "STOP yelling! You'll destroy what remaining sense I have. I did what I felt was right. Broan and Eirian need to meet for this to work."

"*You truly believe this is the war to break the curse!*"

"Yes."

"*Well I don't…*" She paused for a moment. "*Do you realize what's in store for her, if this is not the war you are hoping for?*"

"Yes," Ke-Hern said, shoulders slumping.

"*And what of the others? If this isn't what you dreamt of, you'll have condemned all the Faeries to the void. Are you willing to take on that responsibility?*"

"Yes," he whispered. "But that's not what's really bothering you…right?"

"*I…I,*" Queen DaNann stepped back from the window. "*I fear she could stir the Ancients if she stays too long.*"

"She won't be there long enough to do that."

"*I hope you're right Ke-Hern. If she wakes the Ancients it will be very difficult to return them to stasis.*"

"I know. But if this is the time of the foretelling and we don't respond, we have not only failed the Faeries, but all the life in the land."

The Queen spoke in soft tones so low that Ke-Hern had a hard time hearing her. *"I feel a very long way from everything out here on this island. I wish I could join you."*

"I know but..." Ke-Hern wished he could be there in person to assure her and calm her worries. "You know that's not wise. If Sobus is involved with the Ny-dick, he's waiting for you to make such an error. There is nothing easy about wanting to help but know you must wait. Your time will come. You must be patient."

There was silence between them as they both took to their own thoughts. The path to freedom drew its own course and all anyone could do was save it from falling and going over the edge of this land, out of sight, out of reach. Unwillingly, they had accepted that.

"Rest." Ke-Hern suggested. "I'll talk to you as soon as I have any more news."

"Alright." The Queen said as she walked away from the window. Lies were easy for her to pick up. The internal energy shifts gave it away. Like a fog, a cloudy hue of gray always crept into people's words. It was as if the fog tried to hide the truth. Lies were easy. Secrets were a bit more difficult. They are unspoken and therefore there is no fog of concealment, no gray, no imbalance, and no sign of what was really there. Ke-Hern had the remarkable ability to shield her from most small hurts and needless worries, but this time his internal misgivings had crept through and she knew she had much to worry about.

Chapter 3

"Sometimes you have to shake a tree to get the best fruit."

- Old woman, Tellos

As Broan and Laeg rode out to the village of Ezek, Broan turned and looked back at his fortress. He was very proud of Solveig with its five towers, high outer wall and unique fortifications. He especially liked that it was tucked away from the village, backing onto the steep mountain face. This insured the isolated ambience he enjoyed. *"But for how long?"* He wondered. The meeting with Hargrave had left him concerned.

If an all out battle with the Faeries was coming, they were ill prepared for it. He had a great army of strong and fearless warriors but not one of them could fight on the mystical plane of Faery. Broan leaned over and patted the neck of his horse. He wondered what Ke-Hern was up to. Why had he sent the meddlesome chit?

"Next time write a note," Broan muttered under his breath.

"What?" Laeg asked.

"Nothing. I'm just cursing that old black Wizard and his riddles." Broan turned his horse and started out again. It was about a half an hour ride to Ezek from Solveig, one he had often rode and most times enjoyed.

"When the search parties come back I want to talk with them."

"They should be back by late afternoon."

"Good…I saw BroMac ride off, where was he headed?" Broan asked quietly

"Gone hunting. So you don't have to worry, Solveig will still be standing when we get back," Laeg answered.

"It's not Solveig I'm worried about, it's BroMac. He's a hard-working, hard-drinking, tough warrior that at times can be just a little too recklessness, which makes him…"

"…the type of warrior you like to have with you. BroMac may not agree with what you have decided but he's not going to do anything without thinking it through."

Broan grunted, sighed heavily, twisted in his saddle, and looked back at Solveig one more time. He was worried that the hatred and fear that bubbled below its surface could too easily boil over, especially where BroMac was concerned. What was he was going to do, if and when that happened? Those times rarely ended well for anyone involved.

Continuing along the main road, Broan and Laeg quietly passed the abundant Ancient tombstones and monoliths. The stones were all adorned with odd, half-worn symbols, which attested to the long history of life in this area. The road soon turned away from the river, skirting the edge of a meadow and then cut directly through some terraced fields on the side of a steep hill.

When Broan and Laeg crested the last hill they paused. The heart of Ezek lay before them. At its center, displayed proudly, was a large water fountain surrounded by a wide and open space. This was where the daily influx of merchants hawked their wares. One and two story buildings, with thatched roofs and whitewashed walls, circled the outer rim of the square. They helped to hide rows of smaller huts made of stone and mud caulking. These were homes to Mortals of various trades.

The back lane on the far side of the village was where Broan needed to go. Perched on the seedy edge of town, there was a pub where men who sold secrets and smuggled goods could be found. It was a crude structure with exposed stone and wood. The mud caulking was gray, cracked, and weather-beaten from years of sun and storm. Broan and Laeg dismounted and tied their horses up to the hitching post.

Together they pushed open the bare boarded door. Instantly they were greeted with the smells of old ale and years of accumulative pipe smoke. Two serving women darted between the small tables and chairs that dotted the floor space. A ladder made of thick tree branches led up to the loft where doves once cooed and laid their eggs. Now it was an exclusive meeting place for those times when you didn't want too many eyes and ears knowing your business. Broan headed towards it.

"Usual business?" Laeg asked as he smiled at a barmaid. He quickly snatched one of the mugs of ale out of her hand. The customer to his right started to protest until he saw who the thief was.

"And mo..re…" Broan stopped cold then called out. "KapLar, where did you get that vest? It has a familiar stitching on it." He turned to Laeg. "Don't you agree?"

Laeg nodded his head as he gave Broan the stolen mug of ale. "I've seen that pattern before on a skullcap not that long ago. Where is the vest from?"

"My family," KapLar answered as he rubbed his greasy hands over the filthy old vest. "Tellos made it for my great-grandfather. NO… that can't be right; it must have been my…no. Oh damn it; ask her, she'll know who she made it for." He eyed Broan, not sure what to make of his interest in the old vest. "You're not wanting to buy it are you, because it's not for sale!"

"No, I'd hate to part you from such a treasured family heirloom."

Bronagh was actually happy to see that Broan had left Solveig for the morning. There was much to do before the evening meal and she was already behind. She looked back at Eirian who trailed behind her. "The inner bailey houses the stable, barn, storage huts, and dog shed," Bronagh said as she pointed to each building. She turned to her left and walked around the Keep. "On this side is the kitchen, bakery and the textile cabin - where weaving and washing happens. Ahead of us is the Back-Hall."

Bronagh paused and pointed to her right. "Beyond the inner bailey wall is the training field, smith's forge, barracks, and the bathhouse for the soldiers. There are four wells in Solveig – one inside the outer bailey, another near the training field, one inside the Back-Hall and the last one is over there by the kitchen."

Eirian's head buzzed with all this new information, and the congestion and bombardment of noise made her senses reel. Chickens and goats wandered about the inner bailey clucking and bleating, horses neighed in the corral and pigs grunted as they ate their morning slop. Children raced at top speed, chasing each other laughing and screaming. Eirian was used to coyotes and wolves calling to the moon in the evening light, the mating calls of elk and moose, or the deep sound of wild boars rooting around the banks of rivers and creeks, but not this.

Eirian almost bumped into a plump woman that carried a basket filled with fresh bread. Following her was a child carrying a jar of milk and a toddler who ran along behind them, its small fist clutching a half-eaten bun, now squished between little fingers. Eirian felt trapped in the confines of stone, buildings, people and this cacophony of Mortal noise.

Overwhelmed, Eirian began to slow down. She turned and looked over to a group of women who were busy fetching water from the well. They filled their pitchers and walked away from the well, all the while chatting and laughing until they noticed who followed Bronagh.

It didn't take long for the rest to notice that it was "her" the "Faery". Many passed and abruptly sidestepped, loudly snorting their disapproval. Eirian was glad Bronagh was with her. She stopped and looked up at the outer wall and the various towers that surrounded Solveig. She looked from guard to guard - all eyes were on her. She knew they were there to keep the "peace". Maybe…just maybe…that included her wellbeing too.

Both Eirian and Bronagh had to get out of the way of a plodding ox cart that was bearing a huge load of freshly cut wood. The old driver appeared oblivious to them at first. "Keep an eye on that one Lady Bronagh," he said just as he passed them, "Faeries will steal anything they can, from babies to a bowl of soaking peas!"

Just then a tall whippet-thin man with grey eyes sneered at her, "How could Lord Broan allow you your freedom when the ground is still stained with our blood?"

Eirian quickly stepped back and away, raising her hand to her chest and the hidden ring. The gathering crowds jeered loudly as the man began to strut around like a rooster, thoroughly enjoying the attention. Eirian glanced upwards. The guards said nothing and did nothing.

After a few more nasty sentences Bronagh cut in. "Are you finished?" she asked boldly, "Like it or not Eirian is here to stay until Wizard Ke-Hern arrives. This is by order from my brother Broan." The new silence was almost harder for Eirian to take than the noise these Mortals made in their daily lives.

It wasn't long before V-Tor materialized at the edge of the Keep, standing tall, his body solid muscle, broad and thick. He stared at the gathering not saying a word, watching and waiting. RohDin grinded around another corner of the Keep, his hand firmly planted on his sword, panting from the exertion of running. He glared at the group. It didn't take long for people to move on to their daily duties.

"Are you going to tell Broan when he returns?" RohDin asked coming up to V-Tor.

"No. Why add fuel to the fire. Ke-Hern will arrive soon enough and take this Faery off our hands. Until then we have our orders."

Puzzled, RohDin looked at V-Tor. "I thought you wanted her locked up."

"I did but she's not bad to look at and besides, maybe Broan is right. There may be a lot we could learn about Faeries by observing her."

RohDin looked back at Eirian and Bronagh, unsure if he agreed or not. Keeping Eirian and the people of Solveig safe from each other was going to be a daunting task, "I still think we should inform Broan. This idea of his is breeding contempt and it could easily turn to tragedy."

V-Tor smiled at his friend and then pointed to the man who started the whole thing. "Why be the bearer of bad news when he will be."

Bronagh took hold of Eirian's arm. "Come on, there really is nothing to worry about. They fear breaking Broan's decree more than they fear you. Besides V-Tor and RohDin won't let anything happen.

Eirian tried to keep step with Bronagh but with every two or three steps she had to grab the shift from around her legs and pull it loose. "OH! This thing is terrible to walk in!"

"I told you so," said Bronagh.

Not wishing to argue, Eirian changed the subject. "Do just you, Leif and Broan live in the manor?" she asked.

"Yes, most times. When we get guests, they stay with us. Broan has allowed small huts to be built near the barracks for married soldiers and their families. That's where Jelen lives."

"From your window I noticed a garden in the courtyard attached to the Keep. Can we get to it from out here?"

"No it's only accessible from the main floor of the Keep. Broan built it for Leif to keep him safe and out of trouble when he was little. He was one of those children that always wanted to play outside and he had such a temper if he didn't get his way."

Bronagh paused in mid-step and shook her head, "I was so scared I'd never see him again. I...I want to thank you again for bringing him home." Bronagh walked on as she brushed a tear from her eye. She cleared her throat, "I think the best place to start is in the kitchen."

A very old woman tottered along towards Eirian and Bronagh. "You've come back from the grave I see," she said with a shrill, crackling voice.

Bronagh stepped in front of Eirian, making sure she stood between her and the elderly woman. The woman smiled at Bronagh and then leaned to one side to look at Eirian again. "It's good to see you once again."

"Mama!" a woman with a child on her hip called out. "No Mama. That's a Faery, not someone you once knew. Come on…come home and have some tea."

The older woman looked at Bronagh. "She's from the north. Survived the curse she did. Did you know that?"

"Mama NO. Please come with me."

The elderly woman would not be put off. She smiled at Eirian. "I know…do you?" She then pointed a boney finger at those who had stopped to watch this exchange. "It would be wise to show some respect or suffer the Ancient's displeasure. I know the prophecy," she said smiling back at Eirian, "but you will live it."

The younger woman looked sheepishly at everyone and gently took hold of her mother's arm again. "Come this way, mama. I'll make you tea while you rest." She gave Eirian and Bronagh one last apologetic look and then guided her elderly mother away.

"Who was that lady?" Eirian asked quietly.

"That's Tellos. She moved here to live with her daughter and Hargrave when her husband died seasons back. She's harmless and a little crazy I fear."

Eirian wasn't ready for the sight that greeted her at the kitchen door. BroMac was hunched over a large table and a partially skinned deer. He was in elbow deep as he worked at separating hide from flesh. The animal was a large buck with a four-point antler and it was staring off into nothingness - and it wounded her. She stepped back, covering her mouth.

"What's wrong with her?" BroMac asked as he caught a glimpse of Eirian.

"Eirian?" Bronagh asked as she reached for her, "Are you alright?"

"NO. I am not alright!" Eirian said as she pointed to the deer. "That's Guine! He had much to care for in the forest. He never would have given his life willingly. I bet you never even bothered to ask his permission, did you?"

BroMac glared at her. "This animal walked into my sight and paid for it. If you think that was wrong, I don't want to hear it. We have families to feed."

Eirian glared at BroMac. "Guine also had a family, I'll have you know."

She wasn't against hunting when it was necessary, but lately it had become too common, the herds were losing their numbers. Her temper quickly flared into outrage. These Mortals had more than enough to eat and it certainly didn't look like they were starving.

"And you never killed to feed your kind?"

"Never! I would never harm another animal."

"Yeah right." He looked up to the ceiling, rolling his eyes.

"You're evil," she hissed.

BroMac pointed his blood-coated knife at her as he stepped closer. He glared at her, his rancor very evident. "You know, I really don't like your righteous attitude."

Eirian firmly planted her feet to the floor. "And I don't like your ignorance!"

BroMac leaned towards her, knife still in hand. "It's you that's ignorant."

"Oh no..." Bronagh frowned and grabbed for Eirian. "Let's leave BroMac to his work. We can help with the washing."

BroMac stood quietly staring at Eirian. Then turned back to the animal and began to work again, dismissing her coldly. Once he was alone, he let a chuckle out, "She was right, this kill wasn't for food. It was for something far more important."

He had felt that Broan was too hasty and inadequately attentive to the security of Solveig's people by allowing a Faery to walk among them. He had gotten nowhere with Broan about his grievances and concerns, so he set out to save the lot of them himself.

He was intent on doing his own type of magic. He had ridden out as soon as Broan had left the Main-Hall, and in the darker side of a valley he gathered the things he would need; eight dark grey stones from the creek bed and some bark stripped off a living tree. It had taken a great deal of patience for him to wait and kill the deer.

After gutting the animal, BroMac cut a large chunk of hide and flesh from the deer's side. He tossed it to the ground alongside the other items. With his bloody knife in hand, he took up the bark and cut deep into it, carving some simple symbols. When he was done he stood back and looked at it, making sure it emphasized the strong warning he wanted it to convey.

Picking up the eight stones, BroMac made his way over to an oak tree that stood just outside the edge of the shadows. This tree was perfect. Both morning light and the sunset would catch it. With great care, he placed the eight stones around the tree about a hand span away from it. The first was placed facing true north; the second at the southern point and the others followed suit each for a point on a compass. "North, north-west, west, south west, south..." BroMac smiled to himself, "Yes, all points covered. Now for the most important part..."

BroMac picked up both the bark and the bloody deer tissue and with one swift jab of his knife, pinned both of them to the tree. After tying his Faery binding cord to the knife, he turned and left. "The message is clear," he said to himself as he hoisted the deer onto the back of his horse and headed back to Solveig.

V-Tor elbowed Laeg. "There she is," he nodded as Eirian walked out of the Keep. "You go first. I'm still too angry to be nice," he growled.

"Oh thanks!" Laeg answered back. "And that excuse is suppose to make me jump to your demands? You're much more cunning than I. You go."

"But you're better at socializing, you're Elftan."

Laeg pushed himself off the wall. "She's affected you, hasn't she? That's why you want to keep your distance." He chuckled out loud. "I knew it. I've never seen you smile so much."

"Well I've never run my hands over a Faery's body before." V-Tor dropped his shoulders and looked back at Laeg. "Look, the sooner we get what Broan is looking for the quicker we can get rid of her. We've already been at this for three days. Besides you're much more diplomatic than I." With that, V-Tor bent low into a grand bow. "After all, you do come from the City of Bridges and are one of an honored line of learned families."

Laeg snickered and shook his head. "The things I put up with from you. All right, I'll take her up to the outer wall. You make sure you keep the others away."

"The outer wall! Broan said to get information from her, not set her free!"

"Give me come credit and just do as I say. She's not going anywhere and this will appear to be a gesture of goodwill. It may help to open her up." He raised an eyebrow. "You do want this over as quickly as possible, don't you?"

"Me and everyone else here. You go. I'll watch your back."

Laeg approached Eirian and smiled. He shielded his eyes from the bright sunlight and looked up at the sky. "It's going to be a great day, don't you think?"

Eirian stepped back a little from him and warily nodded her head.

"I have the perfect place to get some peace and quiet." Laeg reached out and took her hand. "Come on."

She yanked her hand away from him, unsure about trusting him. So far it appeared that it was impossible for Mortals to even be remotely decent to her.

"I know it hasn't been easy to be here." Laeg dropped his shoulders, and looked severely rejected. "I'm just offering you a little quiet. It's not much, but hopefully it will help. I'm trying to...." He looked down at Eirian. "I know that you have no reason to trust me, but we do have to start somewhere. Will you grant me a few minutes of your time away from all of this? Perhaps we can start over."

She deliberated carefully before smiling, "I guess it wouldn't hurt."

"Come on. Let's go up to the outer wall."

Eirian eyes grew big, alarm crystallized between heartbeats.

Laeg gently put her hand into his and smiled, "It is okay. If you wanted to escape you would have done it long ago." His smile deepened, "seeing as you sneak up there every sunrise and sunset."

Eirian paled. "You knew and didn't tell Broan?"

Laeg shrugged his shoulders. "Why? You always came back down the stairs." His smile deepened, "Look, V-Tor promised to keep the wolves at bay for as long as possible. So let's go." Amused by her silence, Laeg gently guided her across the bailey and up the stairs.

Laeg and Eirian looked beyond the edge of the wall. High above them, two hawks floated on the air currents. Occasionally, one would dart off to capture an interesting prey to feast on. The other would catch the draft and float upward while biding its time. That was how Laeg felt right then. He was darting off to catch Eirian while Broan was biding his time, and all the while she was unaware. He sat, bracing his back against the stones of the wall.

Eirian smiled and joined him there. This was the most enjoyable moment she had experienced since coming to Solveig. The open air was a strong reminder of her world out there, beyond this prison. "*But once it's done,*" she thought to herself. "*Once it's...*" Eirian stopped herself from tripping over her desire for freedom. She knew deep down inside that she would never see that life again. This was just the beginning of a succession of losses yet to come.

"So what's so special about sunrise and sunset?"

Eirian remained silent.

"You don't need to tell me, I was just wondering. I like the evening sun the most. The colors, the mystery of it all," Laeg said.

"Do you know that for a brief moment in that balance between day and night you can actually look at the sun? It fills me with strength."

"I didn't know that. So you come up here to look at the sun and get recharged. I guess that's why you fear being locked up in the dungeon."

That's part of it." Eirian looked down at her shaking hands and watched as they played with the ties on her shift. "*Why was it so important for him to know these things?*" She wondered.

Nothing was lost to Laeg as he watched her. Graciously, he looked up at the sky and the birds again, "Aren't they beautiful?"

Eirian nodded her head.

"I've always wanted to know why Faeries are so protective of animals."

Eirian shrugged her shoulders as if everyone should know the reason. "When something dies while under our care, their spirits take up residence inside of us."

He frowned. It was a surprise to hear the heaviness in her voice. "That's impossible. If you carried the spirit of everything that died, the burden would be immense."

"Trust me. I know what happens. This burden was added to our punishments."

"It still doesn't make sense."

"Actually, you Mortals do the same thing. When someone you love dies, you carry them in your heart. The only difference is that we do it on a grander scale." She paused and then whispered, "It hurts very deeply and never seems to go away."

"I had no idea," Laeg shook his head. It was beyond his Mortal understanding. He paused and looked at her, "So where did you get the notion that Faeries are immortal?"

"We are."

"Come now. Just because you don't age doesn't mean you live forever."

"We are more than our physical forms. That is one of the reasons why we can shape-shift."

Laeg leaned over and pinched her on the arm, which of course got a yelp from Eirian. She rubbed the area of skin and scowled at him.

"See you're as physical as I am. I know that Faeries are Mortal, I've dispatched enough of you."

"You may dispatch us but to where? Do you know?"

"Eirian!" GaHan's voice boomed up the wall from the outer bailey. "Down here. NOW! BroMac's calling for you!"

Outwardly Eirian appeared calm as she slowly walked down the stairs of the tower. Inside she was fuming at BroMac. He enjoyed needling and aggravating her and she was in no rush to see him. As she exited the tower GaHan roughly grabbed her by the arm and dragged her quickly to the Keep and up the stairs. She complied passively, knowing how useless it was to do otherwise. Once inside she was pushed into the Main-Hall and up to the seating area in front of the hearth. She watched BroMac take his place on Broan's sturdy wooden chair.

"Eirian." BroMac's voice may have been controlled but it hid none of his rage. "It's been brought to my attention that you've been hanging around the stables a lot lately."

She almost wanted to laugh. "I overheard others talking about one of the mares having problems with her colt. I wanted to see if I could help."

"You're not allowed near the stables, barns, and pigpen and for that matter even the henhouse."

She looked at him totally confused. "You think I will escape on a chicken?"

BroMac scowled and straightened himself in the chair. "If you're found near any of them you will be locked up. Is that clear?" Smiling, BroMac lied, "This order is from Lord Broan and it will be obeyed. Do you understand?"

"Yes," she hissed. "Anything else?"

"No."

As Eirian turned on her heels to walk out of the Main-Hall, her shift caught her legs yet again and she almost fell on her face. Angrily she grabbed the shift and yanked it away from her legs. "That's it," she seethed.

Eirian marched out the doors of the Keep and went straight to the kitchen hut. She pushed a woman out of her way and grabbed the butcher knife off the table, causing the innocent Manliken to run from the hut screaming. Eirian drove the tip of the knife through the front of her shift. Swiftly she pulled the knife down, all the way to the bottom and then forced it through the thick hem. Satisfied, she put the knife on the table and walked out of the hut feeling freer than ever.

Upon hearing all the commotion, BroMac rushed out of the Keep. He stopped dead in his tracks when he saw Eirian with the front of her shift spilt down the center. It opened as she walked and exposed her tight shimmering Faery leggings.

"What was Broan thinking?" He didn't run or even march, but stalked her. Silently he came up behind her, took hold of her arm, and spun her around.

"BroMac!" she screeched.

47

"It appears you can't follow orders…" He tightened his grip on her arm.

"I've done nothing wrong! Let go of me!" she screamed. Pushing and pulling against BroMac's steely grip was desperately futile.

Anger flashed in BroMac's brown eyes. Seething with hot emotions he swung his hand downward. The pain was instantaneous and intense. The impact sent a shock wave through Eirian. With every ounce of effort Eirian drove her fingers hard under BroMac's ribs.

BroMac shook off the urge to drop to his knees. He gritted his teeth as he glared at her. "Once a Faery, always a Faery. Binding cord or not, you are still deadly." He raised his hand again.

"*Oh crap!*" Laeg knew he had to seize control of the situation before BroMac totally lost it. Laeg rushed up to BroMac and took hold of his raised hand.

"Let go of her BroMac. This isn't the way to handle this."

BroMac scowled back at Laeg.

"Let… her… go…" The words were calm but firm. "Now!"

"BUT SHE'S NOT DRESS PROPERLY!" BroMac replied heatedly.

"It's just clothing."

"NO… no…It's more than that!" BroMac spat vindictively.

"Maybe so, but Broan has other thoughts about this. Besides, we have our orders…ORDERS…remember?" Laeg murmured.

BroMac glared at Eirian. Her face was red and already starting to swell and bruise. Then, reason suddenly kicked in. His brows flinched as he regarded her.

"It is only clothing, plain and simple." Broan's voice carried over the tension. He motioned to V-Tor to move Eirian away from the area.

"Give her to me," V-Tor said as he came up beside BroMac. "I'm sure Bronagh will have a few words to say to her for ruining her shift." V-Tor took hold of Eirian's other arm and patiently waited for BroMac's response. Slowly BroMac uncoiled his fingers around Eirian's upper arm.

"Come on," V-Tor said to Eirian as he led her away. "Take my advice. You'd be wise to not walk around like this again. Next time there may be no one around to save you. Your kind has done much harm to these people, including Broan, and revenge is sweet."

It took a long while before Eirian realized that V-Tor was right. These Mortals forgot nothing and loved their revenge. Even with a fully undamaged shift on, Eirian had endured a constant onslaught of cold stares, doors slamming in her face, people spitting at her, tripping whenever possible, and verbal abuse when they thought no one was watching.

The only people that allowed her any peace were Leif, Jelen, Laeg, and Bronagh. However, even their company couldn't relieve the stress of being forced by the binding cord to remain in Elftan form. Being Elftan was not natural to her and Eirian was finding it difficult to adjust. Her body was heavy and she found that her movements were not as fluid as she was used to. Sometimes she was forced to gasp for air. It was as though her lungs couldn't fill properly. Not only could she not stomach the food they offered her, but also her sleep had been restless at best. She was forced to sleep inside a room that was way too hot and smelled of wood fire and Bronagh's scented candles. She missed the fresh clean air of the woods. She was beginning to wonder if she would die before she ever adapted.

During the evening meal, Broan sat at the head table and listened to the sounds of the inhabitants of Solveig. It was music to his ears. There was laughter and good conversation, friendship and unity, and it warmed his soul. He sipped his ale as he looked out at the crowd. It wasn't long before his eyes fell upon Eirian. She stood so far apart from everyone; so distant and so obviously not part of the life in this room.

Eirian could feel the stare of Broan's icy blue eyes. It made her so uncomfortable that she moved. She began to clear empty platters and baskets from the table in an attempt to forget he was there, but she could still feel his eyes boring into her. He had a laid-back demeanor this evening, one that she had quickly learned not to trust.

Broan continued to watch Eirian as she moved around the tables, her arms darting in and out, retrieving plates and dirty dishes. Her movements were fine - until she walked. Then she was clumsy and ponderous at best as she kicked and tugged at her shift. He smiled inwardly.

V-Tor followed Broan's stare and laughed, "You know Broan, I think Ke-Hern will probably thank us for such fine schooling of Eirian. We may just make a lady out of her yet."

Eirian glared at the two. As she turned to leave the Main-Hall, her arms full of dirty platters, she managed to land her foot on the hem of her shift. Quickly adjusting to the error she accidentally bumped against Conn while he ate. He growled and gave her a fierce look.

"Perhaps it takes longer for Faeries to learn the graces of a lady," V-Tor teased.

That was it! Now totally embarrassed, she tossed the platters right into Conn's startled hands, picked up the hem of her shift and wrapped it around her arm, fully exposing her Faery clad legs. She took back the dirty dishes and she started to walk away.

"WHAT are you doing?" BroMac yelled as his stood up from his seat, not more than a few inches from Eirian.

"Clearing away the dishes, why?"

"Not with your gown half way up to your neck. Let it go!"

How dare he? She dropped the dishes onto the floor and with one pull of her hands removed the entire shift. "If you like this attire so much, YOU WEAR IT!" she yelled as she threw it at him.

"ENOUGH!" Broan commanded as he shot up and stomped his way towards the two of them. Frightened Eirian turned and quickly dashed out of the room.

Eirian ran across the foyer and down the stairs, but Broan's hands were on her before she was even half way to the inner wall. With a grip like a vise, he picked her up, tucked her under his arm, and walked back into the Keep. Broan walked past the open door into the Main-Hall and into his private office. He placed her back onto her feet and then quickly spun her around to face him. "Don't you ever run from me again," he said with as much restraint as he was capable of. "Do I make myself clear?"

Eirian not only refused to look up at him but she also refused to answer him. She huffed and crossed her arms in defiance.

Broan would not let go nor would he drop his gaze. "I'm only trying to keep you alive until Ke-Hern arrives. I trust Ke-Hern and that is the only reason I didn't kill you at the beginning of all of this."

"Wrong. You didn't kill me because I brought back the boys, unharmed."

He paused for a moment, "Agreed. It did buy you some time, but when I realized that you knew Ke-Hern and that there was a possibility that he did in fact send you, I decided to allow you more than just the taste of BroMac's knife. I'm trying to make this work Eirian. Do you understand?"

Eirian refused to look up at him again but this time she nodded her head slightly.

Broan finally let go of her arms but readied himself to catch her if she darted off again. When she didn't, he relaxed a little. She gave no vigorous resistance, but he knew better. "I still don't know for sure that Ke-Hern sent you. Knowing him and being sent by him are two different things." He paused wishing she would look up at him. He preferred to look into the eyes of his opponent when in battle, even if it was a battle of wills.

Eirian gave nothing and remained silent. Shaking his head slightly Broan decided to shift the focus a little. "So now that we're alone as you once requested, can you tell me Ke-Hern's message without the usual riddles?"

Eirian looked up at him, her eyes bright, "I did but you won't listen."

"I'm listening now."

"He sent me here to begin working with you to bridge the vast gap between Mortal and Faery."

Broan's eyes locked on her. He watched every movement, taking in everything from the rhythm of her speech, the tone, the color of her complexion, how she held her body, everything. Like a hawk, he scrutinized her. "Why is this so important?"

"Soon Faery and Mortals will need to trust each other."

"Trust? To trust a Faery is to gamble with one's life. Perhaps if I was alone and knew of this connection you have with Ke-Hern I might chance it, but I will not gamble with the very lives of those around me. I am a Warlord, sworn to protect."

"I know that," she quietly whispered.

"Look Eirian, win them and you win me."

"Why not win you and they follow. You are their leader. You said it yourself." Her words were sweet but somber.

"It doesn't work that way. I may be their leader, but I am not a leader of fools. How long would it take for their loyalties to switch if they feel I have really endangered them?"

"But I just need your trust not theirs."

"You are so wrong in this. I'm beginning to wonder the wisdom of all of this."

"Me too," she bowed her head once again and refused to look at him.

"Where did you get that skullcap?" Broan said as he examined it, "The stitching on it is interesting."

She chanced a quick glance at him. "It was a gift from Ke-Hern," she lied. "He will be very upset by the way you are treating me, and more so if you force me to remove it." She raised her hand to it, ready for a tug of war if it came to that.

"I've not heard of other Faeries having skullcaps. Are they common?"

"No" Eirian replied quickly and firmly.

Broan smiled and stepped back, glad for this little gem of knowledge. "It is very pretty; although I'm not sure I like it covering all your hair. Or is it that you have no hair?"

Eirian stared at him through hooded eyes, "You'll never know now, will you? May I leave now?"

"Yes. Go put your shift back on and get back to work."

"Young Broan. I need to talk with you," Tellos called out as Broan exited the Keep. He stopped and watched her shuffle along towards him with great determination. Pia leaned forward as she ran after her. "It's Lord Broan, mama."

Tellos ignored her daughter and continued to toddle over to where Broan was standing, "But he is young."

"All people here are young compared to you," Pia muttered as she looked beseechingly at Broan. She knew Broan would have his normal patience with Tellos, but lately her mother had become obsessive and no amount of reasoning or patience seemed to help.

"Hello Lady Tellos. Out for your daily walk?"

"Out looking for you. My daughter and her husband have been working overtime to keep me from my appointed duty."

"What duty is that?"

Tellos quickly grabbed his arm. "Your future is coming, but it is not in here."

"Mama, please!" Pia said as she placed her arm around the old women's shoulder. She looked up at Broan. "I am sorry Lord Broan."

"Don't be sorry Pia. Your mother has had many more years of living than the rest of us. We could all learn from her." He looked back to Tellos, "So sweet Lady that was some statement. What does it mean?"

Tellos smiled like a 'young girl' at Broan's compliments. She tilted her head to one side, "You always had a way about you. Too bad you're too young for me."

"MAMA!"

Broan coughed to cover his mouth in attempt to conceal his smile.

"Pleaaase mother lets go get some tea," Pia pleaded.

"Don't be so silly." Tellos closed her eyes and hugged herself, "I may have lost your father, but I have not lost the memories." Tellos opened her eyes and suddenly she was serious. "You are a good Warlord AND even though your soldiers are observant, they can often be blind. They may be principled, but they are also arrogant. They appear to you to be well meaning, but actually they are selfish."

"So what is a Warlord to do?" Broan teased.

"Don't listen to them. Know that your future lies on a path other than as Warlord. Many will expect you to do one thing but you will need to do the right thing." Her eyes narrowed and she stared at him. "You will face your moment of truth and it will be hard."

Tellos straightened up as much as she could. She beckoned Broan to bend over so she could whisper in his ear. "Don't worry, the Ancients know what they are doing. There will be quiet blessings of hope out there in the land for you. Your time is coming."

Broan simply nodded his head as he stood up, "I see. I'll remember that."

A strange glow emanated from Tellos. Her eyes half closed and her face blushed. "Two breaths by fate, one destiny… out of the abyss an army once hidden comes forth…."

"Out of the dragon's roar comes hope," Broan whispered finishing the verse of the Prophecy. The look of incomprehension played on his features. "How do you know the poem of Prophecy?"

Tellos smiled deeply, "Oh I remember what I'm supposed to, young Broan. I've waited a LONG time for this moment. Do you remember Ke-Hern bringing you to visit me long ago? You were about two or three. I wasn't sure at the time if it was you that the prophecy talked about but then SHE arrived."

Broan nodded hesitatingly. Tellos had conjured up something unexpected inside of him, something he was not sure he wanted to look at. He looked down at Tellos, at her lined and craggy face.

"How old are you Tellos?" he asked.

Tellos' smile deepened and her eyes sparkled, "Older than Ke-Hern. My life has been supported by the makers of the Prophecy and now that it has begun, we'll see just how much longer I'll breathe."

"Mother you are confused and spinning tales again. It is impossible to be that old. I am only two decades and three full runs of the seasons. There is no way you could be my mother if you are older than Ke-Hern," Pia said sternly.

"Child, anything can happen in this time of our history. Each of us is nothing more than a shard of history, a small piece in the gem called life." Tellos said as she turned away from Broan satisfied her duty done.

Broan watched Tellos and Pia leave. Tellos was as confusing as Ke-Hern at times. Perhaps she was from a time before Ke-Hern and they just never realized it. He started out again but stopped suddenly, remembering he wanted to ask Tellos about the bar keeper's vest. He turned, but seeing Tellos' frail body was being helped away, he decided to wait until another time.

Broan suddenly noticed a group of older boys egging on a young boy name NeLar. He knew something was up. When the young boy started to make his way across the inner bailey and got close enough Broan made his move and scooped up NeLar. "So what are you up to?"

"Nothing."

"Nothing?" Broan questioned patiently.

"OH…Umm…"

"Umm?"

"OH! I…I should go," NeLar said.

"Go?"

"They'll be so mad at me."

Suddenly Broan shifted his shoulders. "I think you lost your bug friend."

"OH NO!" NeLar moaned. "I was…suppose to put it down…give it to…"

"So you were told to scare someone with it?"

Tears started to form in his eyes. He nodded shamefully. "Are you going to punish me?"

Broan could feel the small invader under his shirt crawling about his shoulder. "Not if you never do this again." He put the boy down and loosened his shirt from his belt. He began to fan it, hoping to dislodge the insect.

Eirian came up behind Broan and slipped her hands under his shirt. He couldn't help but shiver when her warm hands glided up his back. He felt the sunny sparkling energy of her fingertips, beautiful, potent and… so very worrisome right then.

Finding the spider, Eirian pulled it out. "I think this was meant for me." She opened her palms and smiled at the young boy. "It's beautiful. What a nice gift, a big orb spider. Do you see these markings?"

NeLar stepped closer to Eirian to look at the bug.

"See these two bumps on the body?" The boy nodded. "Well if you look on the spider's head, you'll see it looks like the face of a kitten."

He inched even closer and peered intently at the spider.

"This spider is very shy and needs to make its web to eat." She smiled at NeLar. "Where did you find it?"

"I didn't find it. The others gave it to me. They told me to…." His eyes suddenly grew big and he paled.

"No worries," Eirian shrugged. "Let's find it a new home then." She stood up and took the boy's hand.

"So you like spiders," NeLar asked

"Yes. I do."

"But you don't like us."

"Who says that?" Eirian frowned.

"They did. You are Faery and Faeries kill us."

"Not all Faeries kill. In fact, far less do than anyone knows. Besides how can I do any harm here when Lord Broan trapped me with the binding cord?" She half smiled at Broan.

"I don't know," NeLar answered shyly.

"Come on. This little spider wants to eat... unless you want to give it back to the boys?"

"No. They can find another spider if they want."

"Be careful Broan. If others feel she's gotten under your skin rather than just your shirt, they will say she's put a spell on you," BroMac said from behind him. Broan turned around swiftly causing BroMac to step back. "I'm only thinking about you. I know these are harsh words but someone has to say them."

Slowly, Broan tucked his shirt back in. He looked up at BroMac as he adjusted his belt and long knife, "I think your fears have been amplified by common...."

"Common sense, which I think everyone else has lost lately."

"It's more like common stupidity," Broan declared. BroMac's attitude was beginning to wear on his nerves.

"Your unconscious desire is showing," BroMac muttered back.

"My only desire is to uncover why Ke-Hern sent her here and to use this time to gain knowledge about Faeries...their strengths and their weaknesses."

Broan took a moment to close his eyes, rolling his shoulders in an attempt to release some of his stress. What started out to be a fine day had quickly tumbled into one hell of a day. There had been a small fire in the stables, he had to put down a mare that was unable to birth her colt and BroMac was still shadowing him and continued to vocalize at every opportunity - not only about the Faery problem but also about his views on Broan's apparent lack of leadership. It wasn't until nightfall that things had finally settled down and Broan felt he could escape to his quarters. "Now to get to some unfinished business," he muttered to himself.

"Uncle Broan?" Leif's soft questioning voice came from the doorway of Broan's chamber.

"Come in Leif," Broan answered as he began sewing the sleeve of his torn shirt.

Leif shuffled towards Broan, his head hanging low and his feelings even lower. "I have something I need to tell you."

Broan put down the shirt, needle, and thread. He looked at his nephew. "So what is it?"

Leif looked up at his uncle and frowned, "Why are you sewing your shirt?"

Broan raised an eyebrow. "I tore it, I should be the one to sew it. A warrior must first learn to take care of himself before he can be responsible to take care of others. Now, are you going to tell me what this is all about?"

Leif blushed and lowered his head once again. "I was the one who started the fire in the stable. I didn't mean to! It was an accident, a real accident."

"I see. So why did you not tell us that at the beginning?

"I…" he paused, "I also want you to know that I put Rull's hog in the shed."

Broan sighed and said, "Mmm…I thought Jelen did."

"Yeah, but I told him to."

"I kind of figured that one out."

"You did? But everyone said that you thought it was the Faeries." Broan said nothing. Leif sputtered on, "BUT I didn't have anything to do with the hens getting loose."

"No I think…"

"You think Eirian did it, don't you?"

"No." Broan considered his young nephew. "Have you been talking to Eirian?"

"A little, but the older boys are giving everyone a rough time if we do." Leif's voice and eyes had a deep sadness about them. "BUT that's not the reason I came. I'm just very sorry for causing all the trouble."

"You were just being you I guess. You're still young and impulsive. Let's hope you're not so reckless that the price at the gate of manhood doesn't cost you more than you're willing to pay."

"What does that mean?" Leif turned his head slightly, exposing a frown on his face.

"Childish pranks can haunt you as an adult if you're not careful. And if they do not let go of your soul or mind, becoming a man is never fully accomplished. It's a heavy price to pay for a little fun now." Broan's words held a pang of regret.

"Are you going to punish me?"

"No. I think your mother has punished you enough."

"She doesn't know," Leif murmured to himself.

"You only have yourself to blame, Broan. She's Faery and should be locked up, not left to run around as free as the rest of us," BroMac argued. His tirade had started before he had even cleared the door. "Conn was just doing what comes natural to Mortal warriors."

Broan rubbed his temples. He had no desire to listen to yet another round of BroMac's Faery bashing. "BroMac, I didn't call you in here to be lectured to!" Broan looked sharply at BroMac, "I want you to increase training drills."

"What... to keep us busy! Why? Because of HER?" BroMac continued to argue facetiously.

"BroMac! Everyone could use the training. Your ranting and raving and all this unsettling action from the soldiers is making her hide away, keeping to herself. You are not helping the situation. We cannot learn anything from her if she is never around."

"Lord Broan. That's why you have to start listening to her," Jelen's voice came from behind the chair.

"JELEN, OUT! NOW!" BroMac bellowed. "How many times have I told you not to sneak around and eavesdrop on other peoples conversations? When are you going start listening to me?" He shook his head. "Kids!" he muttered to himself.

Jelen rounded the chair to stand in front of Broan. "I wasn't eavesdropping! I was hiding from... the... older boys."

"When are you going to stop hiding and start fighting?"

Jelen looked up briefly to his father, saddened that he always disappointed him. "Fighting should never be the first choice for a warrior. Rule number two."

"Neither is hiding."

"Not true," Jelen countered. "Rule number...."

"He has a point BroMac," Broan said. "So how would you get information from Eirian?"

"This may help," Jelen said as he reached into his shirt. He quickly handed Broan his special stone. "I found this when Eirian was flying Leif and me back to Solveig." He paused and looked longingly at the stone in Broan's hand, "It's a good luck stone. You can feel the magic in it. Maybe if you carry it with you while Eirian's around she'll talk."

Broan smiled, trying hard not to laugh, "I see. Well, I thank you for the stone."

BroMac rolled his eyes upward and shook his head. "A stone! We'll need much more than that son. In difficult times like these, there is only one way of getting information out of an enemy. Torture!"

"BroMac! Enough." Broan looked down at Jelen and considered the youth, "You know something, don't you?"

"Yes," he whispered.

"And what is it that you found out?"

"She's here for you."

"WHAT?" BroMac howled. "Why would you say a thing like that?"

Jelen ventured a glance up at his father once again. "Ke-Hern taught me to trust the things that pop into my head more than the things I labor over. It's just a feeling but I know it's true."

Broan awoke to pounding at his bedroom door. "Lord Broan there is a messenger from your Uncle, Governor Iarnan. He said it's urgent."

Broan sat up in bed and looked over to the window. The night darkness was still heavy in the sky. The news could not be good if the messenger had come non-stop from the Walled City. "I'll be right down," he yelled.

Half dressed and in a hurry, Broan raced down the stairwell. Just before he opened the door to his private den, he stopped and looked around him. He had an eerie feeling that he was being watched. Mentally shaking himself, he entered the room, quickly closing the door behind him.

Eirian followed Broan down the stairs and when it was safe, out of the Keep. She slithered around to the window of the den. She brushed raindrops from her eyes and silently cursed the weather, as she cautiously peered in.

When Broan entered the room, Ashmor got up from his seat and waited for him to approach. He hadn't had many dealings with Lord Broan, but had heard enough to know it was unwise to be too forward with him. He was after all, a Warlord.

Broan took two mugs out of a woman's hands, dismissing her. He then motioned to the bench as he handed over a mug of ale. "Sit, please. When did you leave the Walled City?"

"Two and a half days ago."

"That quick!" Broan said in surprise.

"I took the old trade route for part of the way. Not many people remember it."

"Did you run into any trouble?"

"No, nothing," Ashmor replied politely.

"What does my uncle need to say that had you traveling day and night to get here?"

"I...well he didn't tell me what it was...he just gave me this letter and told me to be in Solveig within three days, one would be preferred and two would be acceptable, three if necessary." Ashmor handed the sealed note over to Broan. "But before you open his letter; there is a message I am to give you from the High Council of Remdor."

"So my uncle is hiding the delivery of his letter in a message from the high council. You are more loyal to my uncle than you are to the council."

Nodding his head, Ashmor looked up at Broan. "He has more sense and wisdom than all the others put together."

Broan sat on the edge of the table and smiled at the young man. "What is your name?"

"Ashmor."

"Good name...means..."

"Of good council. I know. My mother never lets me forget it."

Broan chuckled. "Well, mothers do have dreams for their children. Unfortunately, sometimes the dreams are not their destiny. So what does the high council want me to know?"

Ashmor stood. He felt better that way. It helped to separate the words from himself. "There are reports of attacks on the northern fronts of both Gearoldin and Anwel. They have reviewed the news from these areas, have talked with the governors of both regions, and have decided that you are not to take up arms. They have all agreed that this is probably a small group of Faeries and it doesn't warrant the time and effort to clear this up."

Broan raised an eyebrow as he listened to Ashmor. He was stunned by the words. "And what are the words of Ashmor on this matter?"

Ashmor paled, but stepped forward anyway, "I've heard that some of the cruelest of actions have been put upon the Mortals in those isolated areas and no one is coming to their aide."

"Those are bold words of ill news."

He leaned into Broan, "That's the reason I serve Governor Iarnan more than the council, because sometimes the right thing to do has little to do with high civil council men and their decrees."

Broan played with the letter in his hand, fingering the thickness of it. "Go and get some sleep. There will be room made for you in the barracks; Laeg will make sure of it. Tomorrow I'll need you to return to the Walled City and to my uncle." Broan walked the young man from the den, through the Main-Hall and into the care of Laeg.

Eirian ducked away from the window ledge. She felt something of great importance had been imparted to Broan, but she had been unable to discern anything. She had to devise a way of finding out what was in the letter that Broan now held in his hand.

"There you are," a crackly old voice said from behind Eirian.

Eirian jumped and spun around, her hand clutching her chest, "Tellos! What are you doing out here in the middle of the night? It's raining. Does Hargrave and Pia know you have wandered off again?"

"Oh stop your silly questions. You know I've needed to meet with you." Tellos limped closer. She pointed a boney figure at Eirian, "You cannot hide from me. It is part of the promise at my birth. I am to see the start of the prophecy before the light in my soul drifts heavenward."

"I don't know what you are talking about. Ke-Hern has sent me here to mend the wounds both Mortal and Faery have placed upon each other."

Tellos laughed at Eirian's words, "Under the guise of cooperating with Ke-Hern you have begun to put in place the pieces needed to start the prophecy..." She paused and looked deep into Eirian's shocked eyes, "Or... Ke-Hern started it all by recruiting you. Do you know your place in the poem?"

"What poem?"

"The Ancient's poem. Through it their prophecy has been handed down from one generation to another in my family. We were the Keepers of their words and I am the last one." She shook her head disapprovingly, causing her hair to scatter about her face. "Pia has not the gift, nor the time for these words. It was clear to me that I was to be the last guardian," Tellos' eyes brightened, "when you appeared from the grave, from the past, just like the Ancients foretold."

"TELLOS? TELLOS?" Hargrave's voice cut through the night rainstorm, as he called out for her. "WHERE ARE YOU?"

Tellos paid no attention to her son-in-law. She continued to stare at Eirian. "Come talk with me soon. We'll figure out their plan for you in all of this."

"There is no plan Tellos. I already told you, Ke-Hern sent me." Eirian began to slip back into the shadow of the Keep. She couldn't let Hargrave see her, he would tell Broan and then... oh she didn't want to even think about that. "I must go and so should you."

Tellos quickly reached out and tried to grab Eirian's sleeve but Eirian was too quick for her. She stumbled forward and bumped her head on the stone wall of the Keep. "Ouch!" she cried out.

"There you are! I've been looking for you everywhere. Come now," Hargrave said as he gently took hold of Tellos' elbow, "You're cold and wet, and Pia is worried sick about you once again."

"That daughter of mine worries too much. I've lived most of my life without her care. Why does she think I need it now?"

"Because you're old and sometimes don't take care of yourself. Here..." Hargrave removed his tunic and placed it over Tellos' thin shoulders. "Come on let's get you home." As he began to direct his mother-in-law back towards the huts by the barracks, he turned and looked over his shoulder. He could sense something in the deep shadows. He wished he had Ardis' eyes that saw as well in both day and night.

"Are we going or not?" Tellos questioned, now impatient with him. "I'm finished talking with her for now. When she's ready she'll come to me."

Hargrave turned and looked down at his old mother in law. "Whom are you talking about?"

"Eirian of course. You don't think I would wander out in this foul weather just for something to do now do you?"

"This is foolish. Come on."

"Foolish!" Tellos stopped dead in her tracks, "I'll have you know that the beauty of the sunrise does not care nor does it need your consent to be there every morning! Things and events do not need your blessing to happen. Silly fool. Life does, as life needs to. What kind of man has my daughter married...foolish! Hump!"

Eirian? That was not at all what he expected.

Broan could feel his ire rise. He had thought he had already handled this problem. He had come across Eirian alone outside of Bronagh's room one night and had confronted both his sister and Eirian, but they said it was a one-time thing and that Eirian had simply become disorientated and that it would never happen again. It seemed a warning wasn't good enough.

His mood was getting blacker by the minute. Long ago, his younger sister had lied to him, and it had not only cost her her life, but that of his mother's as well. He sat down behind his writing table, waiting for Bronagh and Eirian.

Broan scowled at them both as they entered the room, "I've just found out from Hargrave that you've allowed Eirian to stray about unsupervised again."

Bronagh stared at her brother. "What's so wrong with that? She needs a little free space now and then. Her life here has been filled with nothing more than hateful words, stark cold rejection and threats of physical harm.

"At night? What were you thinking?"

"That..." Bronagh looked over at Eirian. "That, she's trustworthy."

"Hargrave came across her last night outside of the Keep" Broan firmly said. "Everyone here is just watching and waiting for their fears and beliefs about Faeries to be confirmed. You're not making things any easier by allowing her to run free at night." He glared at Bronagh. "I told you there would be a price to pay if…"

"Stop! Don't blame her," Eirian said as she stepped in front of Bronagh. "She didn't know …"

"So what you're telling me is that my sister just lied to me."

"No…yes…she's only trying to help me. Being a warrior, you should understand that…helping another."

"You have a choice; it is either the dungeon or …"

"Please! I'm sorry for sneaking out. But I've done nothing wrong while on my own, now have I?"

"You've got my sister in trouble. That's a whole lot of wrong." Broan shifted in his chair and focused his stare on his sister, "I tolerated you giving her a little freedom during the day. It was fine while everyone was awake, when there were enough of us around that we could keep an eye on her, but at night! Bronagh, you know the danger… "

"I am a danger to no one!" Eirian hissed. "And if you're going to say it's my safety you're thinking of, know that I've taken care of myself all of my life. I've out-witted Ny-dick, Mortals and even Shadow Dwellers. I can take care of myself."

Broan shot up from his chair and leaned over the desk, "You are so arrogant and naïve." He glared. "This isn't just about you! I've an obligation to fulfill my duty as a Warlord, which is Overseer of ALL those who reside here, including you."

"But…" Bronagh started in.

"She is not a guest! REMEMBER!" Broan yelled, cutting Bronagh off. "I will not risk the safety of everyone under my protection simply because a Faery cannot sleep where she is suppose to. If you can't control her, I will. There is always a dungeon she can sleep in." Broan looked directly at Eirian. They locked eyes winter blue to sea green. "Maybe I should stop this all now and just put you down there!"

Overwhelmed by a mixture of unexpected and intense emotions, Eirian grasped at control. She was barely keeping her head above the avalanche of feelings and experiences among these Mortals but the threat of the dungeon just added to the problem. She did her best to cope the intense pounding of her heart but when Broan rounded his desk, she suddenly leapt off the floor, spring-boarded off Broan's desk and thrust herself towards the open window. In a sudden flash of movement, Broan stuck his arm out as she whirled past him. It caught her on the legs, throwing her off balance. She hit the wall with a sickening crunch.

Eirian caught her breath and peeked up at Broan's face through hooded eyes. His mouth had a slight smile on it. Unfortunately, that did nothing to make her feel any better. She knew it had been a crazy idea to try and escape but she had become so fearful that reason lost out to reaction.

Broan walked over to her, picked her up by the shoulders and held them tight, very tight. "Know this, there is no where you can run to that I will not find you. Not now, not ever. Remember that, Faery." He released her and looked at his sister. "She either sleeps where she is supposed to or it is to the dungeon. Don't fail me Bronagh. There is no going back."

Eirian waited for sleep's even breathing to come from Bronagh. She knew the risk she was taking but she couldn't help it. She crawled over to the window and she quietly opened it. She held her breath as she pulled herself out of it. Clinging to the wall with unconscious ease she climbed up to a small ledge half way up the wall of the Keep. Climbing was just a natural part of her life. It saved her many of times and right now it allowed her a little freedom from this Mortal prison.

The cool evening air kissed her face. She could breathe again. Smiling she listened to the night sounds of the wilderness that once was her home. The stillness, the peace and quiet, and the moonlight bathing her now made the risk all worthwhile and she smiled.

Chapter 4

Alone Ny-dick named Kibria scrutinized the fortress across the long valley. He played with his killing trophies, finger bones that hung around his neck. Absentmindedly he leaned his oversized body against a large boulder and moved up and down rubbing the fleas from his skin.

Even in the moonlight, Solveig was impressive. Darkness didn't take away the stature of the fortification - its five towers, high outer wall. His eyes narrowed in concentration.

"Ei...ri...an, Ei...RI...an, Eirian," Kibria rolled the sounds around in his mouth. "Do you hear me calling Eirian? Two can use the chanting magic and next time we meet..." he growled, "I'll be waiting Ei.Ri.An. You'll not escape me next time," he said with hideous enthusiasm.

Kibria raised his snout and sniffed the air. To Mortals, the Ny-dick's smell was rank and offensive but to the Ny-dick, it was an individual signature. He paused his ranting knowing Emm was near.

Emm crawled and stood next to Kibria. He glanced at Solveig briefly and then, with a blank look, faced Kibria, "It's not fair that we follow the Faery and young Mortals here only to be ordered to move on. Those stinking Shadow Dwellers have all the fun, while we act passive like mouse droppings."

Kibria swung out his arm, knocking Emm hard into the tree next to him.

"Why'd you do that?" Emm hissed as blood sprayed past his rotten teeth. "I came to tell you what I heard. But if you want to be left alone to drool over that Faery who out-smarted you, I'll go."

Kibria's hand moved as quickly as lightning and grabbed Emm by the throat. He dragged the younger Ny-dick close to him and glared into his eyes. "So what news travels so close to your ears that I should believe it?" He shook Emm vigorously and then spotted the filthy band around Emm's wrist. "Give me the embroidered cord."

"Why? You never so much as looked at it before." Emm slid his hand behind his back.

"Well it interests me now. The cord!"

"But I found it!" Emm pleaded.

"Who cares," Kibria growled as he shook Emm hard once again.

Emm growled knowing he wouldn't win this one. He slowly began to remove the cord around his wrist while cursing under his breath. He handed it over reluctantly making sure he didn't make eye contact.

Kibria let go of Emm with a shove and fingered the cord. Still visible under a thick layer of grime was the embroidered pattern of a certain Faery's skullcap. Kibria smiled wickedly. "So what have you heard that's so interesting that you would disturb me?" he asked, still irritated at the interruption.

Emm remained squatting on the ground. He kept his eyes lowered as he spoke, "Lija's talking about the Prophecy and that it's coming."

"That's it? You've come to tell me about a Mortal's fable. The Prophecy is nothing but a sad story of a forgotten race, a race that didn't have the intelligence to survive." Kibria kicked dirt at Emm and snarled, "The next time you disturb me, it better be for real news."

"But how…" Emm began to ask. He got a fist to the mouth for an answer.

"Get out of here. I need to plan my revenge on a Faery named Eirian."

Eirian was walking under the archway of the inner wall that divided the bailey from the training field. She wiped her sweaty palms on her shift as she mused over her last disastrous encounter with Broan.

"Never had I thought I'd be in a situation where a dungeon would be hanging over my head." She shuddered just thinking about it. Eirian wondered if Ke-Hern had taken THAT into consideration. "But why would he?" she said softly to herself. "I never told him about the nightmares."

Eirian turned her face toward the sun to drink it in and got back to business. She knew that fleeing from Broan had been wrong, but it was too late for regrets now. The fact that Broan still hadn't locked her up in the dungeon, spoke volumes to her and she feared him a little less. But BroMac was a different scenario. BroMac reminded her of a wild wounded animal. "Someone to guard against at all times," she said to herself.

Eirian scanned the training field to see if Faber, BroMac's wife, was around. Eirian enjoyed helping her in her herb garden. Faber, like Bronagh, didn't seem too upset about a Faery being held in Solveig. However Eirian's biggest problem was getting to Faber. It meant having to walk past the training soldiers, and with BroMac in charge of the training, she often had to wait until he was very busy or off the field for a few minutes.

Eirian smiled to herself. Having to wait allowed her to spy on the warriors. She specially enjoyed watching BroMac's younger brothers: RohDin, Hargrave, Aeddan, and Idwal. Being from the same family gave them a familiarity that allowed them to tease and torment each other. Through them she was starting to understand the inner workings of a family, even if it was from a distance.

Today Idwal and a young Elftan soldier were involved in sword practice. The young soldier was clashing and hacking at Idwal, trying to get him off balance. Idwal, although not fully grown, was agile and very quick on his feet. It was easy for him to avoid the trainees' assault. This of course was driving the young apprentice into a frenzy.

"Your anger makes your attack overzealous," she said pointing towards the young soldier. "In fact your frustration has you reaching for Idwal and not the other way around. Your stance is very off-balanced. In battle you would have been cut down like a sapling," she said with confidence.

Stunned both men stopped and stared at her. "Do women Faeries fight?" Idwal asked, shocked by the idea.

"Yes they do. Everyone is considered equal, therefore everyone fights."

BroMac came up from behind her. "Did I hear right? You consider yourselves equal amongst yourselves." BroMac laughed at the statement. "Well young Faery, know this." He leaned over her and glared, "you are not among them anymore. You are here, and here, like all Faeries, you will never be our equal."

Even though his voice sent a spark of anger and indignation along her nerves, Eirian refused to be bullied by him anymore. She glared back. "Why is that BroMac? Is it because we defended our lands or because we stood behind Haidee's choice to marry?

"You Faeries are all liars, making up stories to feel heroic about your plight. You were all cursed because you imprisoned Haidee."

"Answer me this if you are so sure of your Mortal logic. If Haidee hadn't wanted to stay why didn't she use her Off-World power to escape? Why didn't the Queen use hers?"

"She did," he answered dryly.

Eirian clutched her fists into tight balls. "Yes, after a full run of seasons. Why not at the start of it all?" Without pause, Eirian continued, "she stayed for a long time for someone who wanted to go home. Does it really sound like she was forced?"

She paused for a moment, wondering if he had the courage to answer her question. "It may be hard to believe, but there is a strong similarity between the Faeries and the Mortals. We are both good warriors and loyal to our warlords." She did not flinch or falter. "It may not have been wise to defy an angry Off-World Queen, but tell me, if fate had changed our two lives around would you still think the same? Would you, as a warrior, not have stood behind your warlord and not fought for your land?" Trying to breathe as normally as possible, Eirian waited for his answer.

BroMac's brows flinched in response to her questions. He was startled by her truth. What Eirian did upon blending cold words and hard facts was to cut deeper than a blade. He said nothing in reply, and watched her turn and leave.

Eirian never went back to the herb garden, that way she didn't have to go near the training field and risk running into BroMac. Although she missed Faber and the garden she simply found other places to escape to. Walking into the Keep, she smiled to herself thinking of one of the spots she had discovered where she felt she could finally relax a bit, a place where she could escape the persistent and scornful comments about her being "Faery."

Eirian began her climb up the support post of the Keep's stairs. Once at the top she pulled herself onto a crossbeam that was shrouded deep in the shadow. From up there Eirian would observe people as they came and went. She especially enjoyed the faces of the newer recruits as they walked in with Broan at the end of each day. Just a few words from him and their faces shone.

"Ah Broan," she thought to herself. It may be hell living here in Solveig but she had learned a lot about Mortals, and a lot more about him. She was beginning to see that Broan was as good a warlord as Ke-Hern had proclaimed. He commanded attention without asking for anyone's soul, he gave back as much as he took - both in loyalty and fairness - and he made sure that all of his men took responsibility for their craft and their success.

Broan often pressed the men to understand that all weapons were just pieces of metal and or wood. They held no magic powers. Their forces of destruction were solely dependent upon the warrior's ability to use them. Skills of warfare came not only from hard work, the strength of muscle and bone, but also from a deep awareness of how far they could exploit their abilities while respecting the restrictions created by their Mortal bodies. Every man had an inner gift, an affinity of sorts, with certain armaments. Once the weapon was found, the dance could begin and the real training started. Broan never judged his men's limitations, yet he was a force to be reckoned with when he thought there was just a little more the man could give.

Looking down, Eirian spotted RohDin as he entered the Keep. It was obvious that his shoulder was acting up again. He was trying to rub the pain out of it. She had been idle for too long and the restlessness had been growing for some time.

"I can fix that if you want," she called out impulsively. "I know it's an old injury, but I know how to ease the pain and stiffness enough so you can use it more comfortably."

He didn't see her at first. He had to follow her voice to find her. "How did you get up there?"

"I climbed. How do you think I got here?"

"Where is your rope then?"

"Don't need one. Now do you want me to heal your shoulder or not?"

"Yeah right. What do you know of healing?" he smiled mockingly at her.

"I know a lot more than you think." She slid her way down. "I've spent a lot of time in the woods and I know more about herbs and medicine than anyone around here."

"Really?" he raised an eyebrow at her bold statement.

"Absolutely. May I?" she asked as she approached.

RohDin stepped back, turning his shoulder away from her. "You're not going to poke me again and take my breath away, are you?"

"No," she said very calmly.

"First tell me what you intend on doing." He pulled himself to his full height making sure she wouldn't be able to touch his shoulder.

"All I want to do right now is touch and probe the shoulder. After that I'll work on correcting the imbalance as best as I can. Does that sound alright with you?" His very slow nod was not very assuring to her but at least it was a nod. Eirian smiled and slowly reached up. She ran her hand along his collarbone and then pressed deep into the space just before the shoulder joint. He flinched. She pulled back on the pressure and proceeded to approach the joint from the back of his neck. While she applied increasing pressure with one hand, with her other hand she forced his arm to roll back and forth. She stopped and stepped back. "Broken bones often ache after they heal, but muscle is another problem. Muscle is living tissue that will grow around the injured area, making it stiff and sore when you use it."

"You can heal broken bones?" He sounded so startled that it made Eirian smile.

"Yes, and with great success if I get to it early enough," Eirian replied.

He cocked his head slightly to one side, "Can you really heal my shoulder or is this just one of your tricks?"

Eirian raised her wrist with the binding cord on it. "No tricks, no spells, no magic. Just the good old healing Ke-Hern taught me. I can fix your shoulder but it's up to you."

RohDin stood in silence debating the two choices he had: trust her and possibly have a healed shoulder, or not trust her and live with a very painful shoulder. He sighed then nodded his agreement. "Where do we start?"

"Over here if you want." She pulled him away from the door, and then stopped. "Or maybe not. I don't think BroMac will like this one bit. I fear he'll take his fury out on both of us if he sees us."

"Look Eirian. Unless this entails me to strip naked, leave my brother to me. My shoulder is killing me, so if you can help, go ahead."

Eirian started to reach upward when RohDin suddenly grabbed her wrist. "Know that I am willing to trust you… this time…but it better not be ill placed or…"

Eirian dropped her gaze and nodded her head. RohDin let go of her wrist and cautiously she started to work. It wasn't long before RohDin was walking around the entrance with a big grin on his face. He began swinging an imaginary sword. He was amazed. Deep thrusts and bold swipes didn't bother him anymore.

"Does it really feel better?" Idwal whispered.

RohDin stopped and looked at his brother as if he had two heads. He tapped his shoulder hard with his fist. "It feels great," he answered as he swaggered into the Main-Hall.

Idwal glanced at Eirian. "Can you heal a weak knee?" he asked as he bent over, reaching for his left knee.

Eirian knelt down beside him. "Is it weak or just painful enough that you don't want to put all your weight on it?"

That evening BroMac studied his two very cheerful brothers. For the first time in months they were sitting next to each other and were happily engaged in a lively conversation. If that wasn't odd enough, it was even more unsettling that every once in a while the conversation would stop and they would both turn and stare at him. *"Well I've had enough of this."* He gulped down his ale and rose from the table, nodded his thanks to Broan and left the room.

Four days later, BroMac discovered the reason for his brothers' good mirth. He watched a small line of men waiting to see Eirian with all the aches and pains that come from hard training. BroMac bristled.

He was about to put a stop to all this nonsense when V-Tor got up from the chair that was in front of Eirian. Just as V-Tor passed him, BroMac pulled him aside. "What do you think you're doing? We…we're suppose to get her to lower HER guard not the other way around."

"The orders are clear; the method is up to us." V-Tor shrugged his shoulders and walked away.

Sobus lay stretched out on a padded table while tender, nervous hands massaged his pasty body. "Come…come child. Relax. My back aches from all the day's work and you are helping to release the tension," he murmured.

His conduct could make the bravest shudder, and she wasn't that brave. His overly kind voice made the young Elftan even more nervous. No longer gliding smoothly over his skin, her hands began to jerk about, nervous and unsure. She lifted her hands slightly and stared at them in an attempt to calm them down. The young Elftan never saw it coming. Sobus' fist caught her just under the chin, sending her flying.

"Fool," he growled as he slid off the table and tied his cloak shut. He grabbed her by the arm and swung at her again. He could feel the Elftan's skin tear under his knuckles. Satisfied he dragged her to the door and opened it. "Guard!" he screamed. "Take her downstairs. I'll be down soon."

Alone again, Sobus casually walked over to the basket of fruit on the table when the slowly coagulating blood caught his eye. Smiling he licked the blood off his knuckles and then picked up the grapes. He walked out onto his spacious balcony and looked out over his deprived, neglected domain that stretched into the region of Duronyk, just out of DaNann's reach, but close enough to give her grief.

BroMac hunched over the pot of boiling water and carefully rolled the eggs within it, wanting to make perfect soft-boiled eggs for Faber and Jelen. He knew his mood had been terrible lately and this was one of his ways to make up for it. He set the table and poured glasses of milk for everyone. With a large spoon, he reached in and removed each egg as if it were a newly born baby. "Breakfast is ready," he said as he placed the soft-boiled eggs on each plate.

Faber beamed as she looked at BroMac. This was a side of him not many had come to know and it was one of the reasons she had fallen in love with him. "Do you need help?" she asked

"No," he answered, his face alight with a big grin.

Jelen picked up a large knife and began cutting into the loaf of bread. "When are you going to teach me more about the rules of conduct that all warriors live by?" he asked.

BroMac took his seat at the head of their small table. "I will soon... but I do wish you had more interest in the actual fighting of a warrior rather than the theory behind it all."

Jelen's eyes dropped quickly, his smile all but vanished.

BroMac noticed and chided himself for what he just said. He brought his hand up and with a laugh, tussled Jelen's hair, "But then again, if you don't know the disciplines of character for a warrior you'll never become a knight. Anyone can fight but only a few can live the way of a knight." He picked up his fork and his egg. Tapping it gently BroMac cracked it open. "So where was I?"

"Rule five," Jelen said eagerly, his smile returning.

"Yes. Rule five. The most valuable warrior does not require, nor does he ask for validation. He knows what he must do and does it, even if others think he is wrong."

"Much like what Broan did with Eirian when she arrived," Jelen said as he stuffed some bread and egg into his mouth, "He didn't seek anyone's approval when he saw the opportunity to learn more about Faeries."

"Don't start," BroMac said harshly, his temper rising.

"But dad..."

"Don't 'but' me!"

"BroMac!" Faber said annoyed. "I don't know why you hate her so. She may be Faery, but she's done nothing wrong since she arrived. She works hard and even heals those who ask."

Taking a gulp of milk, BroMac narrowed his eyes, "That's only because she has the cord on her wrist. I know as soon as it comes off...."

"But dad," Jelen interrupted, "it's not your distrust of Eirian that's gotten you so angry, it's your distrust of Broan."

Shocked, BroMac's head shot up. A smile slowly bloomed followed quickly by a laugh. His son had just spoken a bold truth. He had been trying so hard to show Broan that his decision concerning Eirian was a mistake, when he should have supported his friend and warlord. He had forgotten the reason he trusted Broan in the first place. Broan was more than a warrior or even a warlord - he was a true knight.

"My son, you may not be a warrior but you're brilliant." BroMac then looked at Faber and took her hand into his. He leaned over the table and kissed the palm of it. He would have loved to stay and gloat over the intelligence of his son, but there was something he needed to do.

BroMac rode out of Solveig on a new mission, to correct a wrong and reverse his show of distrust. Once back in the dark shadowy valley, he jumped off his horse and walked to where he had left his ritual warning to the Faeries. He had thought himself right and of sound character, fully believing Broan was not.

"Looking for something?"

"Broan!" BroMac yelped as he spun around.

"I took it down a while ago," Broan said as rode his horse out from behind three massive trees. He lazily draped one arm over the horn of his saddle. "Didn't trust me did you?"

"I just...yes...no...well, you see I just..."

"There's no need for excuses. In a way I don't blame you."

BroMac flushed, all the more shaken by what he had done. "I'm sorry...truly I am."

"No harm done so far," Broan said. "But it did leave me a bit concerned that your ritual could have worked in another way, that rather than keeping the Faeries away it would be enough to unite them to fight."

Shamed faced, BroMac replied, "I hadn't thought of that. I just thought to scare them off."

"Here," Broan said as he threw down BroMac's knife. It lodged itself into the ground next to BroMac's feet. "You may need this in the future." He shook his head. "If you think to play in magic you know

72

little about, it would be wise to not use your own knife. It's too big a calling card."

BroMac reached down and picked it up. "How long have you known?"

"Not long after the deed. The flesh was still moist."

"And you removed it then?"

Broan nodded. Slowly, his face softened and then quietly he simply said, "Help me."

BroMac looked up, stunned.

"Help me," Broan asked once again. "Ke-Hern meant for Eirian and I to cross paths and I still do not know why. If he had wanted her dead he would have killed her himself. If he feared her, he wouldn't have sent her to us. Help me uncover the truth.

BroMac uttered no threats or taunts when he finally got his turn to get healing help from Eirian that evening. Swallowing his considerable pride and nursing a new insight on life, he sat down on the empty chair and raised the left sleeve of his shirt to expose a black and blue elbow. "I'll not be owing to you. I noticed you like berries. Faber will bring you some from our garden tomorrow," was all he said.

Eventhough the mid-day sky was cloudy, Eirian still needed to shield her eyes from the afternoon brightness. She checked the sky for any sign from Ke-hern or the other Faeries, but there was nothing. Feeling alone once again she started out towards the woodpile. The wild cats and kittens had come to be a source of comfort for her these days.

Idwal spied her from the stables and rushed to meet her. "Eirian I have a favor to ask." He kept his sweet youthful smile in place.

"A favor?" She eyed Idwal.

"Yes. I want to know if you'll teach me how to climb up a wall without using a rope or ladder." He leaned closer and whispered, "everyone knows about the high beams in the Keep you hide on, but Ardis told me about the wall climbing."

Eirian paled. "Did he tell anyone else?"

"You mean Broan. No I don't think so. Well, can you show me?"

She shook her head. "I don't think that would be wise. I'm in enough trouble right now."

"That's not what I heard. Most of the warriors..." Idwal nudged Eirian with his elbow, "like BroMac, seem very happy with your healing. Besides, like I said, no one has to know. Please," he begged. "You don't have to teach me everything today. We can do it out of sight. Please show me."

Eirian looked at him with mixed feelings. "The going up is easy. It's the coming down that's hard."

"So you'll teach me. Great!" he exclaimed. He wanted to do more than just report she could climb walls without a rope. He wanted to report HOW. *Now that's something Broan needs to know.*

"Yes but not…" That was all she could get out before being pulled off in a rush towards the inner bailey wall.

"No one will see us here," Idwal said when they came to a spot near the barn.

Still unsure, she looked around nervously. Looking up, it only took her seconds to notice the slight irregularities in the alignment of the stones. She instantly knew the path she would take. "Can you pick out the irregular stacking of the stones?" She asked.

Idwal leaned towards her and looked up at the wall. "Kind of…"

Eirian pointed at a stone block about eye level. "See here," she asked as she pointed to another stone, "and…here?" Slowly she showed Idwal the path she would be taking.

"Yes! Yes I see it now. But that's not much to hold onto."

"While most of the strength you'll need comes from your legs, it's your center of balance that matters the most and not how much stone is sticking out."

"You need to show me. I really want to understand how it's done."

She glanced at Idwal and then looked around once more. "Fine." With a slight hesitation she took off her shift leaving her in her Faery shirt, leggings, and boots, the only safe way for her to climb in Mortal form. "Watch where I place my feet, that is more important than where I place my hands."

Suddenly the voice of doom descended upon her. "What are you doing?" Broan yelled.

Eirian's response was instant and she did what came natural to her. She scampered up the wall so fast that both Idwal and Broan were shocked.

Idwal looked up at her with excitement written all over his face. "Wow! Now I really want to learn how. Can you come down and show me again," he asked without pause.

Eirian looked at Broan as he waited for her at the bottom. She shook her head. "No I think it's safer up here for now."

"Eirian, get down here before you fall!" Broan commanded.

"No." She shrank back against the small out-cropping that was more than half way up the wall. She was going to stay up here until hell froze over.

Hell froze over just minutes later. The rain began without warning, the cold droplets of water started to beat against her. She didn't have her tunic with her, or even that blasted shift, and now she wished she were wearing both. She huddled in closer to the wall hoping for more shelter while HE stood at the base of the wall, hands on hips and looking very, very annoyed.

"Enough of this! If your Faery brain holds no common sense, I'll come up and get you." Broan turned and looked at Idwal, "Get a ladder."

"No!" Eirian instantly moved sideways along the wall. She didn't want to know what he would do once he got his hands on her.

"You can't escape me. The warriors in the towers already have their arrows pointed at you, so come down," he said hoping she wouldn't call his bluff.

Eirian turned her head swiftly to the left, checking out the tower windows. It was a sudden and unexpected mistake and an impossible, incomprehensible thing that happened next. The shift in her weight caused her boot to slip from the slick stone and Eirian found herself falling.

There was an audible gasp from Idwal, as he stood there, stunned. Warriors lowered their bows as they watched her falling backwards. Broan lunged for her and with out-stretched arms, snatched her from the air.

Once Broan had her tightly in his grip, he was filled with both relief and fury – relief that she was unharmed and fury that she hadn't listened to him once again. With barely controlled emotions, he marched back to the Keep and into the Main-Hall. "Idwal get me a binding cord…a long one!" he ordered as he walked over to the dog's corner.

Eirian's face turned white. "No. Please. I'm sorry. It's just that you scared me."

"Too late!" Without any hesitation Broan grabbed the rope, tied one end to the wall, and wrestled the other end around her waist. He grabbed one of the dog's smelly blankets and tossed it to her, "Cover up and be glad it isn't the dungeon."

Eirian sat down in a huff and pulled the blanket up around her chilled body. Just as she thought things couldn't get any worse, they did. Miko, one of the squires, brought in the two hunting dogs for the evening. He stopped short when he saw Eirian tied to the wall. Not sure what to do, he looked around the hall for directions, but Broan wasn't there.

"It's okay," Eirian said without even looking at him, "They'll be fine."

Miko stared at her. "They'll be fine?" he repeated out loud. Most people worried about their own safety when it came to these brutes. All hundred and fifty pounds of muscle and fangs, most of the men backed off and gave them a wide berth.

"You needn't worry," Eirian raised her wrist, exposing the Faery binding cord. "I can't put a spell on them."

"It's not that my lady, it's what the dogs might do to you," Miko said.

Eirian looked up at him and smiled. "It's so sweet of you to be concerned, but trust me I'll be fine. You'll…"

"Chain up the dogs Miko." The order was barked from across the room. Broan had just returned from getting dried off and while he may have felt physically better, he was still in a putrid mood. "NOW Miko."

Miko quickly complied. He stole a glance over his shoulder to make sure Broan wasn't looking. "Their names are Taker and Beals, he whispered. If you talk very firmly to them they just might listen to you."

Eirian was beginning to truly like this young lad. She graced him with a smile and nodded back to him. Her eyes then shifted to Broan. He was like a sliver – under her skin and a big irritation.

The smell of roasted meat and cooked vegetables suddenly assaulted her. "Mealtime," she groaned to herself. She brought up her knees knowing that within minutes the men and women of Solveig would be charging in.

Eirian lowered her head onto her knees and closed her eyes. If she had to sit here, she may as well take the time to rest. She doubted Broan was finished with her and the evening was still young.

It didn't take long for the dogs to lose interest in her. They were standing up, pulling on their chains and dancing impatiently as they watched food being handed around and consumed. Eirian reached up and touched the nearest dog on the hindquarter. Without even raising her head, she murmured something. Taker stopped what he was doing and sat down next to her. Beals was so excited about Taker's submission that he began to jump up, striving hard to get any morsel of food.

Eirian stood up and stepped over Taker. She ignored Beals for the moment and sat on the ground between them. Once again she reached up and touched the hindquarter of Beals, and again the dog sat down. It was quiet there in her little corner of the room. All you could hear was people eating and chatting.

"If only I could…" Eirian looked up from her knees and peered at Broan through her lashes. She shook her head, "No, for some silly reason I doubt anyone could lead you, even if it was down the right path!" Eirian tossed her head up in exasperation. *"WHAT am I doing in this crazy dream of yours Ke-Hern?"*

Broan watched her from his place at the table. He was a bit surprised at Eirian's reaction to the dogs and fully surprised by Taker and Beal's reaction to her. The two dogs sat like guard dogs or statues on either side of her. Broan sipped his ale and watched. She sat on the ground between them supposedly without a care. *"How?"* he wondered.

Conn and GaHan liked to sit at the end of the long table closest to the dogs. Being big brutes themselves, they had a kinship with the dogs. They would often place small bets on which dog was the fastest, or cleverest, and tonight was no different. Conn and GaHan were well into their meal before they realized that the dogs were quiet.

"What's this?" Conn questioned. "She's put a spell on them. Look how well they sit."

GaHan smiled and shrugged, "We'll see." He then tossed a piece of meat at the dogs.

As soon as the piece of meat left GaHan's hand, Broan and V-Tor shot up from their seats. All had seen the dogs fight over food. Sometimes the fighting would get so bad that by the end, one or the other needed stitches. But the dogs remained sitting, both eyeing the piece of meat. You could see the salvia drip from their mouths as they licked their chops, wanting to eat it - yet neither moved. Taker and Beals worked hard at trying to keep their eyes both on the food and Eirian.

Conn pushed himself up from his seat. "She's done something to the dogs!" he yelled. "They've had the fight taken out of them." He moved towards Eirian as he continued his tirade. "Is this some Faery trick?" he bellowed. Taker and Beals bared their teeth at him, immediately stopping his advances.

Eirian studied the surprised look on Conn's face. "No trick, no spell, just teaching them some good manners. If you think having fighting dogs nibbling at your feet is okay, come and change places with me," she said calmly.

"Broan?" Conn called over his shoulder, without losing eye contact with the dogs.

"Fighting over a small piece of meat is very different than running down a boar. Actually, I'm enjoying the peace and quiet." He sat down as he eyed V-Tor.

Conn gave Eirian an evil look as he turned and walked away.

Eirian's hands were full. She marched behind Bronagh and Faber, carrying a load of freshly cleaned linens. Sweat was forming in places Eirian had never thought much about before being stuck in this Mortal form. In fact there was much about her body she had never been aware of. Somehow the ground was harder and pressed against her hips and shoulders when she slept, and sometimes hunger growled in her stomach as loud as Broan's booming voice.

Eirian's steps were not as quick as Bronagh and Faber's. Her heavy shift still found time to cling to her tights, which she still refused to give up. She shifted the linens into her right arm while she tried to pull the offending shift away from her legs. If this kept up, she just may have to give up wearing her Faery clothes and follow Bronagh's lead, wearing nothing but sandals on her feet and what nature gave her under the shift.

The shift caught her legs again and Eirian almost dropped the load of fresh linens. Eyeing a bench tucked along a narrow building, she started towards it, kicking the shift and shuffling her feet in order to get there without tripping again. Once she got to the bench, she put down the load and looked around her. Satisfied that she was alone and out of sight, she inched down her tights and pulled them and her boots off.

She had just finished with her discreet removal of clothing when she heard voices approaching. Turning quickly Eirian bumped into V-Tor as he rounded the corner of the building. It had been a hard, hot day on the training field for the men and most had removed their shirts as they made their way to the bathhouse. The collision caused both V-Tor and Eirian to grab at each other to stop from falling. Eirian's hands on V-Tor's bare chest awakened a new stirring within her. It was immediate and startling. Quickly she removed her hands and tried to step back, but V-Tor's grip was firm.

He slowly let her go and stepped back as well, confusion written all over his face. He was at loss for words. The sensation was not anything he had felt before. It started deep in his belly and radiated outward. It caught his breath and stilled his mind. He looked at Eirian with interest. "Sorry, I didn't see you there," he mumbled.

Eirian scooted back from V-Tor. "My... my... fault," she stammered.

"What's this?" BroMac bellowed, "Hanging out around the men's bathhouse trying to get a peek?"

"No! No!" Eirian said, inching away from BroMac and V-Tor.

"You shouldn't be here," Laeg said as he moved in next to V-Tor and BroMac.

"Right...right..." Eirian's face turned red as she realized that Laeg was also half naked. His chest was wet with sweat, adding to the definition of his muscular body. She could do nothing but stare, finding it hard to remove her eyes from his broad chest. "They just shouldn't make Elftans like that," she said under her breath.

"Really?" Another warrior said from behind her. Hastily she turned around, seeing nothing but warriors, all who were in assorted stages of undress - sweaty, muscular, and all male. Her breath caught in her chest. She dropped her eyes and wet her lips. "*What's happening to me?*" she cried inside. She wanted nothing to do with these strange feelings

V-Tor grabbed Eirian's wrist again and pulled her attention back to him. "I saw her first," he teased. He was strongly tempted to pull her away from the group and go off into the hills. Those natural thoughts of procreation came to a jarring stop when Laeg grabbed his shoulder.

"Let her go," Laeg said. "I don't think your father would like knowing you bedded a Faery, no matter how much she threw herself at you."

"I didn't throw myself at him! We merely bumped into each other," Eirian protested, "I was just..."

"Hanging out by the men's bathhouse and just happen to be taking off your leggings and boots," BroMac said, finishing her sentence as he eyed her discarded clothes.

Eirian blushed all the deeper and she scowled at him. "I was hot and my shift was trapping my legs again, making it hard to walk... LET ME GO!"

"Let her go," Laeg requested again.

V-Tor held her for just a moment more, wondering if she felt the same sensation as he did. "Another time perhaps?" he asked her.

Eirian tore from his grip. Grabbing her leggings and boots, she raced away leaving the linen and the men, but she didn't escape Broan's harsh stare, as he watched from the armory. Eirian rushed through the archway into the inner bailey. She didn't know where she was going she only knew she needed to get away. She was bewildered by the whole episode. There was no way to salvage that embarrassing moment. She was doomed by the betrayal of her own body. Her emotions had gone well beyond her experience, exploding and exposing her to something brand new, and it unnerved her. "What was Ke-Hern thinking?" she wondered miserably.

Eirian spied the Back-Hall and headed for it, hoping no one would be in there. Once inside she breathed a little easier. It was cool, quiet and thankfully deserted. Moving to a secluded area off to the side of the doorway, she lowered herself to her knees. Pressing the palms of her hands against her eyes, she wished she could forget what she had seen and forget what she felt.

Tears began to wet her hands so she pressed her palms even harder into her eyes. She was not prepared for this. She lifted her head. "I HATE THIS!" she wailed.

"Oh I don't know about that. You looked like you were enjoying yourself." Broan stood next to her, looking down.

Embarrassed even more by the state he had found her in, she cried that much harder.

Broan smiled. He wasn't sure why he enjoyed knowing she was so uncomfortable with her feelings, but he was. Her pure Mortal response was refreshing. Broan pulled her compliant form up off of the floor and stood her before him. "Eirian, no one was going to force themselves on you. You never need to fear that." He paused for a moment and then continued, "Besides V-Tor was wrong, I saw you first."

He stood close to her. Eirian refused to look up at him and instead focused her eyes on the ground.

"Eirian." Broan whispered. "Look at me."

When she finally looked up into his eyes, her breath quickened . This was so wrong in so many ways but she had lost the war in controlling the feelings she didn't understand.

Broan felt the potent force that radiated from her, a force that even he could not withstand. His own willful need roused with a furor and was suddenly let loose within him. He lowered his head to kiss her, stopping but a breath away. He smiled at her as his eyes took in the answer his pause was asking.

A bold shock, a lightning bolt of pain suddenly pierced Ke-Hern's heart. He shivered as he stood on his balcony. "Eirian?" he called out, hoping to understand what was happening. Many troubling and painful memories played in his mind. All these thoughts were like uninvited guests at a celebration. Ke-Hern shook his head. He desperately searched to find Eirian's energy print but still couldn't locate her. What magic is this that would keep Eirian hidden from him? Had the Ancients decided to imprison her there? Ke-Hern's worry deepened when he felt the tremor in the land. He forced the special power deep within himself out onto the wind. If he couldn't find Eirian, damn it, he'd find Broan!

Pity those who do not understand the fury and intensity of a Wizard on a mission. He yelled into the air once again giving direction to his power.

Broan felt like he had been kicked on the side of his head as the entrance door of the Back-Hall burst open. The power of Ke-Hern's magic reverberated throughout the room. The words "*Save her*" battered the inside of his skull. The sense of intense imminent danger woke him as if from a sleep. He looked down at Eirian, stunned to find himself in such an intimate position. Broan quickly rolled off Eirian. This was a big mistake. Then he realized this was more than a lapse in judgment, this was a lapse in memory. The time between them was missing from his mind! Broan glared fiercely at Eirian. "What did you do?" Her stunned silence enraged him even more. "Don't ever use your tricks on me again or I'll have your head, Ke-Hern or not." His voice shook with anger.

His words were cold and cruel and cut Eirian like a knife. She pulled down the hem of her shift and sprinted away from him. She was up the wall at the far end of the hall before he could even get to his feet. "You take me and then you have the nerve to put the blame on me!" She braced herself against the rock wall. "You may not be able to grab this concept but please try. Thanks to your binding cord, I cannot perform anything - not tricks, not spells, not ANYTHING."

Broan straightened his clothes and walked to the open door, away from her. She just had made his life a whole lot more perilous, and he had willingly helped her. Turning he could barely see her against the rock face. "Good and stay there!" he yelled. "You are Faery through and through and all Faeries belong in hell," he cursed at her as he slammed the door after himself. He marched across the inner bailey. His head was a storm of thoughts and emotions. "Here," he yelled to Jelen as he walked past him. "This stone may be good luck for you but it didn't do a thing for me." He tossed the smooth rock back to Jelen and kept walking towards the Keep not once breaking his stride.

Jelen caught the stone and watched Broan walk away. He looked down at his stone and rubbed it between his thumb and fingers and enjoyed its gentle tingle. He smiled. "It's nice to have you back," he said placing it back into the special little pouch he had made for it.

Eirian's eyes filled with tears. She had tried with all that she possessed to manage the energy of this new desire, this physical need of the Mortals. She had run away to find seclusion, except HE had followed her. "*Why him?*" she moaned.

Eirian tried to replay in her mind what happened but nothing was there! Only the words Broan had whispered to her when they....

Wait… they weren't of his language. She paused recalling his speech. She held them in her mouth and tasted them for what they were. The words of the Ancients! How could Broan have crossed through unhindered to a place Ke-Hern only whispered about?

Chapter 5

"There is always gracious acceptance, if fear is not there."

- Queen DaNann

Merchants usually came to the village outside of Solveig by sunrise. Arriving in donkey carts or on foot, they traveled down clay roads, which had long ago been harden by the trampling of many feet. By early morning, they were set up and ready to sell. Booths of herbs and spices, fresh meats, fruits, vegetables, cloth, and household items lined the main market square in the center of the village.

Everyone worked hard at hawking his or her wares, accepting a bartered deal, or money, if any was to be had. There was always an air of fair trade and friendliness in the village of Ezek, Broan saw to that. But unlike any morning before this a different type of visitor arrived. Wounded and tired a young boy fell against the baker's door begging for help. He came with ill news from the north, news that would change the aura of peace in Remdor to one of fear.

Ced, the young boy, was from a farm near the outpost called Khumer. Battered and worn out he looked tiredly at Broan. "So much blood! We were too late...couldn't save anyone...the whole neighboring farm was ...." His eyes watered as he stopped for a moment, "You have to help. They'll kill everyone and everything!"

"Who are they?" Broan questioned quickly.

"Some say it's the ghosts of Cian's warriors now trapped in the moving light in the night sky that have come down to have their revenge," he whispered to Broan. "Faeries with deep magic." Ced could give them no more before pain and exhaustion overtook him.

"I don't think ghosts have anything to do with this," Laeg said as he turned to face Broan, "It seems too organized for the Ny-dick to attack at night. Yet…" Laeg waited for Broan's response, and when it took longer than he thought it should, he raised his hand and put it firmly on Broan's shoulder. "You know something."

Broan looked at both V-Tor and Laeg. "There's been news that the outer regions of both Anwel and Gearoldin have been having problems like this. Interestingly enough, when uncle Iarnan heard he offered soldiers to help patrol the areas, but the other Governors kept insisting that there were too few attacks to warrant such manpower. The council sent notice to me that we weren't to get involved unless Solveig itself was under attack."

"That's stupid! Are they all blind to life outside of their cities?" V-Tor snorted.

Broan leaned into Ced one more time and gently shook him awake. "Tell me. Do you know if Khumer itself has been hit yet?"

Ced weakly shook his head. "I…I don't know but my dad told me to get to Solveig. He said you would help. PLEASE, please help them."

Broan lightly gripped the young lad's shoulder and nodded. He looked at the gathered group of soldiers and motioned for them to follow him out of the room.

"Faery?" V-Tor asked, once they were out of earshot.

"I don't think so. They've never done anything on such a grand scale. It would take a large group of them to carry off an attack like this."

"But you've always talked about the war with the Faeries. Could this be a precursor? Is this it?"

Broan shook his head, "They wouldn't waste soldiers on simple farmers."

"Then its Ny-dick."

"Perhaps." He stood up. "V-Tor, get BroMac and twenty men ready to ride out. We are not going to sit here in safety while others are in danger." He turned and addressed Laeg. "You're in charge while I'm gone. Because we don't know what we are dealing with, send word that all the locals should make their way here for protection. "

Eirian was on her way to the Keep when she got caught up in the controlled chaos. People where rushing out of warriors' way. Young soldiers hurried behind Broan, their arms full of weaponry. "What's

84

happening?" she asked Laeg, who just came rushing down the stairs of the Keep.

"Another attack…about half a day away."

"But…" her attention was suddenly diverted as Broan's roan stallion emerged from the stable. With each proud step, it snorted intently from its flared nostrils. "He likes the run and the clash of battle. He knows what's to come," Eirian said softly.

Laeg gave her a quick glance. "Even though he's ill-tempered, he's a great stallion and he will take care of Broan."

Broan mounted his horse. As soon as he was seated, the horse began rearing and sidestepping, its energy intense, its patience lacking. Broan sat him well and allowed this little tantrum. Once the horse calmed down, Broan looked at his men and with a nod to Laeg, they started out with swords glittering in the morning light. Upon clearing the gates of Solveig the warriors spurred on their horses, rapidly increasing the distance between them and the walls of safety.

The town of Khumer was situated along the high eastern slopes of the mountains, about a day's ride north of Solveig. It sat on a valley floor that once was a lake. It was a busy place with a large main square and an over-sized gathering lodge where people mingled and met for council meetings. Scattered thatched-roofed houses crowded the valley floor, where children dodged adults as they ran and played, women dried laundry while they gossiped, and men hawked produce and conversed.

It was a quiet, stable place, so Broan only visited once a year and at the moment he was regretting it. He had known all too well that things were heating up. But instead of following his own instincts, he had occupied his time with a Faery living in Solveig. And that had cost the lives of the people he was sworn to protect.

Broan lead the twenty warriors, their horses nervously racing through the pines of the shallow forest. They still had a ways to go before they reached Khumer, when they came across a thin cloud of smoke that wafted through the air. Broan signaled the group to divide in two. V-Tor led one group around the ridge while Broan rode straight over it with the other. There was an uneasy sense of dread in the air as they neared a low rise.

A farm was ablaze. What once was a wall now lay in various broken heaps. The Mortals were on the ground. Their limbs twisted at odd angles, throats slashed and gaping. It was a grotesque slaughter.

"Are you thinking what I am?" BroMac asked.

Broan said nothing as a multitude of emotions collided. He got off his horse and reached down, turning over a small child's body.

She lay by herself in the ditch, her blond hair matted with blood and dirt. His dead sister's image grew within him. He shook it off and remounted.

Conn nudged his horse forward. "By the gods …isn't this just like the slaughter of your family BroMac? This looks like the work of the Faeries."

"Be quiet Conn," BroMac hissed.

"I'm only speaking the truth. Look, none of the bodies have been ripped apart." Conn spread his arms wide. "What they couldn't burn they tore down. Ny-dick don't take the time to do such things. Just answer me BroMac, isn't this just like what was left of your family after the Faeries attacked?"

Conn was caught unaware by BroMac's fist, which quickly knocked him off his horse. Picking himself off the ground, and with blood spilling from his nose, he slowly remounted his horse. He kept his head down, his smile hidden.

"Look!" GarrRod yelled, "Smoke is rising in the east."

"Ride!" Broan ordered. "Khumer must be under attack!"

Everyone pushed their horses even harder as they crested the last hill. Clumps of dirt flew through the air as the horses dug their hooves deeper into the ground to meet the demands of their riders. They hurtled down the hillside, putting horse and rider at tremendous risk. Broan and his warriors rushed past bodies hanging upside down from trees, arms cut off and legs partially devoured. They slowed down at the gates of Khumer.

In a matter of seconds a Ny-dick bounded out of a ditch and charged towards the group. Its thick arms lifted its double-headed axe high in the air, letting it drop towards a soldier's leg. An anguish scream cut the air as the injured soldier slipped from his horse. V-Tor's arrow caught the Ny-dick in the shoulder pinning it to the horse saddle. The horse reared and kicked attempting to dislodge the Ny-dick from its side. Twisting and stomping the horse finally raced off, dragging the Ny-dick with it.

Idwal gagged. The putrid smell of Ny-dick surrounded him. There was no hiding the distinct odious smell of sweat and filth that rolled off their skin. Sensing one was near, Idwal swiftly pulled his sword in a wide arch, slicing into a Ny-dick's arm, which only managed to enrage it. He then quickly swung his sword from left to right, cutting right through the midsection of the enemy. Astonished, the Ny-dick fell to its knees, staring at the wound, and then with a heavy thud, fell over, dead.

As the group of warrior's charged into Khumer, GarrRod diverted and galloped towards a Ny-dick who was splitting a chest bone and removing the heart of its latest victim. Blood dripped from the Ny-dick's fist and mouth as it began to eat. Driven by the adrenaline coursing through his body, GarrRod gripped the handle of his sword and slashed, taking the Ny-dick's head off. His horse continued forward and GarrRod's sword sliced through the back of another Ny-dick that was running away.

A group of Ny-dick was busy throwing flares, which immediately exploded into fire when it contacted with the thatched roofs of the village. People emerged sputtering and red-eyed from the flaming huts. They floundered to distance themselves from the fires only to run into the swords and axes of the Ny-dick. It was a mad killing spree.

Hearing a child scream, Broan turned, jumped from his saddle and sprinted towards a Ny-dick fighter who had just grabbed a child by the hair and was retreating into a hut. Broan leapt over a disemboweled woman who lay dying in the blood soaked mud. He removed his bow from his back and shot two arrows, swiftly and fatally into the back of his enemy. He quickly picked up the child. Its head flopped back, its eyes open but unfocused. Bile scorched the back of his throat as Broan's stomach convulsed. He was too late.

Suddenly the hut burst into flames, forcing him to leave. He staggered out of the shelter, his lungs struggling to breathe through the thick black smoke. Broan paused briefly. Out of the corner of his eye he caught something moving and swiftly turned his head, just in time to watch a Shadow Dweller shifting into the form of a raven. "Dark Faeries and Ny-dick," he cursed. The feeling of death stomped ominously across his heart.

Seconds later, a wall of Ny-dick materialized out of the smoke filled air. Broan crouched and slapped his sword against his leg, his ice blue eyes staring at them in rage. With a wicked smile and a piecing roar, Broan attacked causing the Ny-dick to explode into a savage burst of violence. Recognizing that familiar war cry, V-Tor quickly found Broan and slashed his way towards him. Together they stood, back to back, fighting off the massive enemy. Blood soaked soil sucked at their boots, yet this did not slow them down.

BroMac fought furiously, making his way to their side. He turned to avoid a Ny-dick close on his heels, but his foot slipped and his weight shifted, pitching him forward. He tumbled headfirst to the ground. Keeping with the motion of his body, BroMac rolled back onto his feet bringing up his sword just as the Ny-dick swooped down on him. With brute force BroMac drove his weapon through the midsection of his enemy only to have the Ny-dick's swinging sword catch him on the side of the head. Ears ringing, BroMac shook off the hit, leapt up and plunged his knife into the Ny-dick's neck, ending the clash.

The battle was over. Tendrils of smoke curled from patches of rubble, as dusk settled among the survivors. The size of damage and carnage was unnerving. There were only charred and shattered remnants of houses. Nothing much was left. Khumer was now a burned-out husk.

Broan's face ran with perspiration. He used his sleeve to wipe the sweat, blood and soot from it. "How many?" he asked RohDin.

"We lost eight and two are badly injured. V-Tor is patching them up. The others are making sure no Ny-dick are left alive."

"Survivors?"

"More than I expected. About fifty, varying in ages and health."

Broan pondered his next move and then spoke to the remaining villagers. "We'll set up a night watch so the dead can be buried but that's all I can give you. We leave by morning. Solveig is now the only safe place for you."

As RohDin slipped past Broan, he pressed something into Broan's hand and then nudged his shoulder against Broan's, making him turn away from the locals. "Just found it," he whispered. "Smells of Ny-dick."

Broan opened his hand and stared at the filthy band of cloth, its intricate stitching very familiar to him. "Time to go home," he hissed.

The first rays of sun filtered down to BroMac as he stood watch. Even though it was summer, the morning coolness plagued his worn out body. He pulled his tunic a little closer to his body, his hand brushing against an odd lump. Digging into his pocket he removed Jelen's stone. He had forgotten about the damn thing. He hadn't really wanted to bring it with him but who was he to question a son's love.

Hargrave came up and stood beside BroMac as he finished retying the bandage on his neck. "Even if we travel both night and day, with so many walking wounded it will take us at least two full days to get back," he said.

BroMac nodded his agreement. He looked back over his shoulder. Mounds of graves and dying embers were all that remained of Khumer. This was one of those harsh moments in life that reminded him that death waited for all of them. BroMac turned back to look at his brother, "Let's get going."

The horns from the watchtower suddenly blew, announcing the return of Broan and the people of Khumer. All of the locals from Ezec, now safe inside the walls of Solveig, rushed towards the gate to help as terrified and exhausted people spilled into the fortress. From his horse, Broan surveyed the growing cluster of people now housed in Solveig. Within days the numbers had moved into the hundreds and who knew how many more were still on their way.

"What happened?" Laeg asked as he approached Broan.

Broan looked out passed the closing gate, "The Ny-dick are back. They've returned in full force and are more malicious than ever. It seems they are intent on eradicating us this time. Not only are they massacring anyone in sight, they are also destroying any livestock and burning everything in their path."

"So there is a good chance we'll soon be under siege."

"Yes," Broan said as he got off his horse, "And we better be ready. We start today at uniting everyone, warrior and civilian."

"And Faery?" Laeg questioned.

Eirian and Bronagh were knee-deep in injured and sick people. The amount of carnage to the flesh was immense. It seemed like no one had been spared injury. The sheer numbers that needed attention was overwhelming.

"I'll take the group over there," Eirian said to Bronagh as she shifted the load of clean bandages to her other hand. She lifted the hem of her shift and started over to a small group near the sidewall.

"Get away from here!" a voice from beside her hissed.

"No," Eirian said as she stepped forward in an attempt to help a child that was bleeding from a head wound.

"We don't need your help. Get away from us, FAERY!" a short stocky man growled.

Eirian looked at the man. He was dirty and tired. His blood stained clothes spoke loudly about his ordeal. "Yes I'm a Faery - with a binding cord on," Eirian said. "So stop worrying," she said moving towards the now whimpering child.

"Don't touch her!" he screamed. "Get away," he yelled and violently pushed her.

"I can help. Ke-Hern taught me how to heal."

Speaking from his bottomless hatred, "LEAVE," was all he said as he stood between her and the young child.

She looked around at the injured and their loved ones. No one was willing to look her in the eye. "No! I won't leave. Tell me, did you always hate the people of Duronyk, your neighbors?" No one would answer her. Nothing, no response, even the groans and crying stopped. The silence spoke volumes.

Eirian stood her ground. "Answer me," she yelled.

"It's not the Duronykians that we hate, it's Faeries. You cursed demons!"

She glanced at each of the surrounding survivors. "Lord Broan has allowed me to live for a good reason. Maybe you need to trust in him and in Ke-Hern who sent me."

"Faeries have kept food from our tables and have made our children cry with hunger. We don't trust you because WE know what Faeries do! Faeries have never done anything good for us," someone yelled.

"We DO NOT have that kind of power. Do you really think the Queen would punish us and then give us powers that would aid us?" Eirian paused as she scanned the Mortals around her. "Lord Broan trusts me, why can't you?" The silence that followed was bitter and harsh. Sadly, Eirian realized the situation was at a standstill. The people would rather suffer and die than trust in her. She turned to go.

"Wait!" Thidor said, standing up. In his arms was a young boy. "I work in the tannery here at Solveig," he broadcasted to the group. "And I've watched her heal the soldiers. If they can trust her, I can too." He handed the young boy over to her. "Please help him. He's been burned by the flameless fire, can you heal him?"

Eirian removed the blanket that was draped over the young body and gasped. "I've seen this before and yes, I can help. I'll need to gather some ingredients to make a cream. Do you think you can get them for me?"

"What do you need?" Bronagh's voice rang out.

Eirian smiled at her, thankful for the support. "I'll need the bone marrow from the game they cooked last meal, as much as you can get. I'll also need goat's milk and a large bowl to mix things in."

"Who's the mother of this child?" Eirian asked.

"She's not here. I've been told my daughter died from her burns on the way here," Thidor answered, deep sorrow hanging in each word.

"I'm so sorry." She paused, compassion taking over. "Let's make sure that doesn't happen to him. I need to go and get some herbs, and I have a need of your services as well. Is there anyone here who can hold the boy until I came back?"

"I will." Everyone turned to the voice at the front of the room. Laeg quickly moved through the mass of people. He gently took the child from Eirian and sat down on the ground. "Is there anything I should be doing?"

"No, I'll be right back." Taking hold of Thidor's hand, she quickly pulled him along with her. She picked up a large pitcher as they left the hall.

"I need you to ask BroMac to pass his water into this and bring it to me. Don't say a word to anyone. They already think I'm up to no good."

"BroMac?"

"Yes. He's the biggest, and he drinks much ale. I'm sure he's already started on a pint after all that's happened. Tell him it's very important."

Thidor paused for a moment as he looked at the quart in his hands. "You're sure about this?" he asked quiet as a mouse.

"Yes, I'm very sure."

BroMac was with the other soldiers in the Main-Hall, and just as Eirian had predicted, he was already drinking and eating. On the way back to Solveig, Broan made sure that what the little food they had was given to those who needed it most. BroMac and the others had gone without. It was only now that he would allow himself to fill his stomach and reward himself with good ale.

Thidor walked up to him and whispered something into his ear.

"You want me to do what?" he bellowed.

Thidor's face turned red with embarrassment. He leaned in and whispered. "It's for my grandson. Please. Eirian said she needs it to save him. I've already lost my daughter to the black fire. I don't want to lose Wiltam as well." Thidor sternly looked at BroMac and then shoved the vessel at him.

BroMac stood up and hastily went out the door of the Main-Hall. Outside the Keep, BroMac stopped, filled the jug, but refused to hand it over to Thidor, insisting that he deliver it himself. Thidor kept on BroMac's heels, his worry increasing with every drop that sloshed over the jug's edge. "Please BroMac, be careful. I don't know how much she needs."

"Don't worry there's lots more where that came from."

BroMac entered the Back-Hall and didn't find it hard to spot Eirian. He marched right over to her and scornfully looked down at her as he held the jug just out of her reach. "Why me?"

"ALE! You drink lots of ale. Besides your breath is often sweet which means your body doesn't purify it as others do," she answered. She narrowed her eyes and placed her hands on her hips. "Look

BroMac, you can take your embarrassment out of my hide later but right now this child is suffering! Now give me the jug."

BroMac handed over the jug and as he walked away, he began to laugh. Eirian gave a sigh of relief when BroMac disappeared out the door, although she did wonder if BroMac's mirth was because he planned to take her up on her offer later.

Once she made her emulsion she nodded to Laeg and started caring for her only patient. As Eirian worked on spreading the balm over Wiltam's skin, his grandfather held his hand, watching the boy's face for any signs of added pain. At even the slightest wince, Thidor would caution Eirian, asking her to be careful, to which she would always nod back. Soon others asked for help and it took all the cream she had made and hours to get to everyone.

Sobus barely looked up when Lija entered his private quarters. "Would you like some grapes?" he said as he held out a bunch in his hand. "A gift from Tybalt the Governor of Gearoldin. Even in the Queen's perfect world there is always someone who's looking out for himself."

Lija stepped forward and took the grapes. Sobus was the most self-imposing man he had ever known. One of his many weaknesses was his obsessive need for recognition and approval. This manic drive ate away at any redeeming qualities the man might have had. It ate away at Sobus' heart and soul like carpenter ants eating wood, leaving no good character behind only a writhing undulated mass of black cancerous desire.

Sobus eyed Lija from the corner of his eye. "This is such a dull, thankless world," he complained. "I'd leave you all to the fate of the DaNann but…" he smiled at Lija, "But why go, when here I can be a god!" Sobus was sorely disappointed when Lija didn't react. With a mock sigh, he continued, "You're no more fun Lija." He tossed another grape into his mouth while studying Lija carefully, "The Shadow Dwellers have told me that the Faery's name is Eirian. Do you know anything about her?"

"No."

"I would think you'd have known something of this fool."

Lija shook his head, "I'm sorry but I don't."

"Fine!" Sobus hissed. "But if I find out that you did and withheld information...well, you know the punishment."

"Yes. We all know the cost of lying to you."

Frustrated Sobus motioned for Lija to leave. He glared at the Wizard's back as he turned away. "Stop!" Sobus bellowed. "I almost forgot. I've also heard from my Shadow Dwellers that this Eirian is still in Solveig." When he saw a slight shift in Lija's back he declared. "I want to you lead an attack on Solveig, and I expect results. I want that Faery!"

Lija nodded his head slowly, "I'll gather the forces and leave tomorrow."

"You'll leave today!" Sobus yelled and then quietly changed his mind, "No, wait. You can leave tomorrow. I think I'll help you a little. The Sulpets haven't eaten in a while. I'm sure there's some good meat at Solveig for them."

V-Tor slunk back into the shadow of the inner wall where he could better observe Eirian unfettered. Even from this distance he could pick up the inimitable odor of rose and sage that emanated from her skin. She was of the woods and its scent still clung to her like a protective cloak.

"You like her," a squeaky voice said.

He spun around to see old Tellos standing near him. Her faded blue eyes were peering deep into him. He shifted uneasily and grunted a firm "NO!"

Tellos narrowed her eyes and pointed a bony finger at him. "Don't lie to an old lady. It's rude and useless!"

"It's not that I like her, it's more like curiosity." He glanced back at Eirian once again.

The wrinkles on Tellos' face deepened, "Perhaps I'm wrong, and you're the one."

"One for what?"

"The Prophecy!" she said firmly.

"What Prophecy?"

Tellos leaned into him and intently watched him. "Crushed by what is held, re-shaping the future...?" She waited to see if V-Tor knew the next verse of the poem.

V-Tor looked at her blankly.

Tellos straightened up, but continued to study V-Tor. She then took a sideways glance in the direction of Eirian. "I don't know what the Ancients have planned, but it should be interesting."

"Ancients? You think Eirian's coming here is about the Ancients?"

"I don't think, I know." She smiled up at him. "It's clear that Broan needs something more than just Eirian... As usual trust cannot grow when understanding is far and few between the words spoken. Maybe...maybe that will be your course in all of this. Maybe..."

Tellos paused and raised her hand to her forehead, "Maybe I better sit down…"

"You don't look well. Are you alright?"

Tellos reached out for V-Tor as she swayed. "Could…could I ask you to help me back to my hut? Too much excitement I think."

V-Tor jumped to her side and wrapped his arm around the frail Tellos. His right hand was solidly under her right arm, while the other held on to her two hands offering what support she needed.

As they shuffled along, V-Tor was careful not to make his steps too big, his eyes never leaving Tellos' pale face. "You're out of breath. Do you want me to carry you?"

"No don't be silly…" Tellos' eyes rolled back and her head suddenly flopped forward.

V-Tor scooped down and picked her up. He called out to those around him to go find Hargrave and Pia. Cradling the frail women to his chest, he made his way quickly to her hut. Without hesitation he used the heel of his boot to open the wooden door and with not much more than three steps had Tellos lying on her cot.

Pia felt panic when she rushed into the hut and saw her mother lying so still. "Mama?" she questioned softly running towards the bed.

Tellos opened her eyes and gave her daughter an unusually peaceful smile. "We all bear witness to life's end my child. Don't look so sad."

"You're not dying! You've just over done it again." Pia started to massage Tellos' unnaturally still, cold hands.

"No child, there's no more life in those fingers of mine. They have served me well. I've held sons and daughters and even grandchildren and I have never raised my hands in anger or rage." Then she giggled. "Now my voice is another matter. Maybe that's why it's the last to go, so I have time to say my piece and make amends for what I've spoken in haste."

"You've nothing to make amends for…besides you'll be fine. All you need is some rest."

"Hush child. This is my time. Your time will come as well. No one has power over death. Oh I'm not afraid to stand at the abyss one finds at the end of life." Tellos narrowed her eyes to see Pia more clearly and smiled weakly.

The effort was great and Pia knew what it was for. As misshaped as the smile was, she knew the good of it. This was a simple act of comforting that her mother offered her, and Pia appreciated it wholly. She turned and looked up at her husband Hargrave, "Go get Eirian. She has helped many others; maybe she can help her. We've nothing to lose." Pia turned back to her mother and tucked the blanket under her chin. She looked lovingly at her mother, wishing there was more she could do.

"Now…Pi..a. I must tell you something…important."

Pia straightened up and leaned nearer Tellos face. "What mama?"

Just at that moment Eirian ran into the hut with Hargrave right behind her. She slowed down taking in the sight of Tellos. Quietly she kneeled down near the head of the bed. "Tellos," she called sweetly into the old women's ear, "What does your heart say?"

"It says that my duty is done and that I can now go and at last visit my husband. Now that isn't so bad." She turned her head slightly and peered into Eirian's eyes, "You on the other hand have much to do and you've barely even started." Tellos then looked at Eirian's cap. "There are so few of my handworks left." She motioned Eirian to lean in. "Does Ke-Hern know of the magic it holds?"

Eirian touched her cap and then looked over her shoulder at Hargrave and Pia, "No…" she whispered.

"Good girl. Wizards shouldn't know everything… they…are too…uppity at…tim...mes," Tellos head slipped down on the pillow.

"What was that about?" Hargrave asked with suspicion.

Eirian's voice cracked with sadness. "She is in a precariously fragile state and there's no way out."

Pia shook her head in earnest and struggled with her tears. She propped her forehead against her fists and outright sobbed.

"Why do you keep bringing me back with all that howling?"

Pia wiped her tears away and tried hard to smile at her mother, "I love you."

"No regrets," Tellos said and then looked back at Eirian. Her eyes were unfocused and she blinked them a few times. She spoke slowly, trying harder to articulate her words of importance, "Tell young Broan…he… needs to… remem…ber…"

Moment to endless moment, Pia and Hargrave watched Tellos weaken before their eyes. Her speech had become garbled and the side of her face sagged as gravity won the war. It was as though the weight of the world was pulling her body down. Tellos' breathing was becoming more shallow and laborious. And then it happened - complete stillness - no breath, no movement. Tellos' shell lay upon the bed in that special stillness of captured inner peace. Pia kissed her mother's cheek and whispered her blessing, her good-bye, "No more time upon this land. Gone are your light and bountiful days. Say hi to dad."

Hargrave stepped out of the hut, unable to watch as Tellos' body was prepared for the burial. There was so much silence, too much for him. He knew that Pia's heart ached and there was little he could do to ease her grief. He walked towards the barracks, lost in his own thoughts and sorrow.

"I wouldn't have let THAT Faery into my hut. She killed Tellos right under your nose. You were so stupid to trust her," Conn said.

Hargrave glared at Conn. He was in no mood for this. Eirian was in HIS hut because Pia wanted her there.

Conn shook off Hargrave's stare. "Don't you get angry with me. You know I'm only speaking the truth. That Faery should have died a long time ago. You said so yourself. Or has she wormed her way into your good senses?"

"Shut up," Hargrave growled. "You know nothing."

"I know that you were stupid to let her in. What'll be next, your infant son?"

"Enough! She had nothing to do with Tellos death. Go ask V-Tor. He was with her when she fell ill. Stop using the death to feed your own anger."

Conn simply shrugged his shoulders, "You'll see in the end. That Faery is trouble."

Hargrave wondered what impulse drove Conn to speak his mind at a time like this. "I think its best you leave Pia and me alone for a while. Your words are not comforting in this time of sadness."

"There are never any words of comfort when Faeries are around." Conn was not about to be put off. "She'll kill again. You'll see. Maybe Pia, maybe your son…maybe you, it doesn't matter to a Faery. You were stupid enough to invite her in and now you'll pay the price. Fool, bloody Fool."

Dizzy with raw emotions, Hargrave leapt towards Conn. A left jab and Conn staggered sideways. Another punch and Conn was on the ground. Hargrave pounced on him, driving his fists into Conn's face and body.

Broan and BroMac raced towards the two fighting men, "Stop! Stop this now!" Broan commanded pulling them apart. Hargrave watched and when Conn was on his feet, he lunged forward - but BroMac stepped in the way.

Conn smiled wickedly as he wiped blood away. "Faery fool," he growled. He continued to taunt Hargrave, "Can't take the truth can you? Faery lover!"

Not surprisingly Hargrave rushed at Conn but Broan held him back. "Get him out of here," Broan demanded as he motioned for BroMac to remove Conn.

"Come on Hargrave," Broan said in a softer tone. "There's enough pain for today. We don't need to add to it."

"That idiot!" Hargrave replied shaking his head. "How can I feel both sympathy and loathing at the same time?" He broke free of Broan's grip. "I'm beginning to hate Conn's hunger to make trouble." Broan placed his hand on Hargrave's shoulder in a sympathetic gesture. "Tellos was always straight-forward and her principles were unbending. She would have made a good warlord."

Silhouettes of ravens merged in the dim, cold recess of a coulee. The Shadow Dwellers huddled around a large flat stone. The glow from the flame of a single candle graced their odd shaped bodies with soft light.

Each Shadow Dweller was unique. The largest in this group of six was Bacot the ox. He was the most disfigured and the strongest. The beast part of him ran from his feet through his thick legs and solid hips. The ox form then seemed to miss his torso, which was of a normal broad and muscular man. It then cruelly continued upward through his thick neck and face, which was ox like with a wide nose and ridged forehead. He was enormously fearsome and the only one with fully disfigured face. Deeply aware of that and dreadfully self-conscious, Bacot was often the most silent.

Larden was part eagle and a skillful predator, often striking out in fights with the hooked talons on his feet. Built for quick maneuvering, he had a solid breastbone for the attachment of enormous muscles. Broad in the shoulder, tapering at the hips, his body was covered with golden feathers except for his head and hands. As with all birdlike creatures, Larden's eyes had eight times more acuity then his counterparts, which he used to his advantage.

Marcoff was half wolf, and efficient in attack and defense. He used his wolf abilities of heightened sense of smell, sharp vision, and powerful legs to bring down the enemy swiftly and proficiently. Only his back and lower part of his long muscular body was covered with fur. Out of all the Shadow Dwellers, Marcoff had the most animal emotions. He growled and bared his teeth if threatened, even though he too had a normal Mortal face.

Flazon was half ape and cruelly deformed. His upper ape body was much too broad and heavy for his normal lower half. He physically suffered his curse more than the others and his temperament showed it. Yet his deformity made it easy for him to catch and trap anyone in his viselike grip. Crushing the enemy was considerably easy. It also aided in charging through trees and underbrush.

Kuiper was lizard-like and Flazon's brother. Where Falzon was large and out of proportion with his ape physique, Kuiper was long and lean. With his sprawling gait, he was quick and agile, a most perfectly efficient predator. He often used the clinging pads on the underside of his fingers and toes to scurry about at breakneck speed. His flexible spine added to his swift, lithe movements but it also caused his back to curve badly to the left when he stood upright. The one thing he hated the most was his lizard eyes with their superb night vision because they glowed blood red even in the dullest of light due to the reflective pigment in them.

Then there was DeSpon, the leader of the group. Lion on the lower part of his body with retractable claws in his feet and massive leg muscles, he ruled with fierce physical power. His stealth ability and power of acceleration to exceptional speeds made him deadly to his enemies. His face was untouched by the curse except for his eyes that were gold and cat like. DeSpon had a golden mass of hair that blended quickly into a lion's mane, which ran down his back to narrow hips then continued to the very end of his paws. A bare, broad muscular chest and strong well-muscled arms balanced the one thing that was not lion or Elftan, his leather wings which protruded from his back. They were a gift from Sobus, a sign of leadership among the Shadow Dwellers. He was the only one who did not need to shape-shift into a raven to take flight.

The Shadow Dwellers had gathered because they had felt something, something they had not expected. DeSpon raised his hand and hushed them all. "For now we keep this to ourselves. Sobus is not to know what we felt. It's not good to let a man with a whip know every secret." His golden lion eyes bore down on the other Shadow Dwellers. "I'll talk to the 'Seer' and find out what will come of this, and then if we need to… we'll make plans."

"How do we know for sure he hasn't felt the movement already? And what if this is the war we've been waiting for?" Kuiper asked, standing as straight as he could. "What then? Do we just wait to see if we are forgiven or condemned?" He glared at DeSpon. "We too were Duronykians once. We too had been changed into Faeries with the possibility of freedom but thanks to your ill-advised rebellion against Ke-Hern, we are now locked into servitude to Sobus. I'm tired of listening to you."

DeSpon rushed at Kuiper knocking the lesser one over. "We'll do as I say. For now, nothing will happen." DeSpon glared at Kuiper, "Sobus' is focused on creating chaos and nothing more. And since he hasn't said anything yet, I don't believe he knows what's happening out here beyond his private world."

Kuiper rolled onto his side and hissed, refusing to adopt an expression of submission. "We were equal once, before we followed you down this path of regret, before the curse."

DeSpon rushed at Kuiper again, "Once!" he yelled, his animalistic powers over-taking him. He pressed Kuiper's lizard body hard against the ground. "Once! It's always a honey coated past for you, Kuiper. Remember that Sobus offered us more than what the Queen had left us with. Be glad you had a choice!"

Falzon came to his brother's rescue. He wrapped his large ape arms around DeSpon and tossed him backwards. "Enough of this, we waste energy fighting one another. It's agreed that we'll not tell Sobus."

DeSpon glared at him as he stood. He then eyed the others, challenging them one-by-one with his stare. When his instincts told him that they understood he was in charge, he nodded. Once everyone was gone, he allowed his form to slump down on a rock. He hated the way his animal tension always got the better of him. It didn't matter how brief their gatherings were, they were always at each other's throats, fighting for supremacy.

In changing their form Sobus had not only given them special powers but also made sure they would always remain totally isolated. They could no longer blend in with other Faeries and when they were too close to each other, their animal instincts would emerge and they would fight each other for dominance. He made sure they were his to keep and his to control.

"But," leather wings flared in anticipation as DeSpon looked up at the sky. "But we have united and we will fight you. Your curse isn't as perfect as you think."

Chapter 6

"Understanding that life is uncontrollable is common sense, even
for Faeries."

- Eirian

Eirian lay nestled beneath a spectacular tree in a lush valley.
She could hear the echoing of birdcalls and a bubbling brook nearby.
She stretched out her curled up body and smiled. It was a good dream,
she thought to herself. She tried hard to hold on to the image of the
tree, blue sky and rolling hills, but reality had other plans. Eirian's eyes
shot open as an ill sense filled her being.

The wind carried a sound, one she had hoped to never experience again. Quickly, Eirian got up and looked out the window,
nothing. Taking no time to pull the shift over Faery clothes, she ran out
the door of Bronagh's quarters and up the stairs to the top floor. She
hopped up onto the stile and leaned out, scanning the horizon to try
and locate where the noise was coming from. It only took one encounter to forever imprint her brain with the sound that the Sulpets made.

When in flight, their wings spanked the air on their downward
thrust, and then rubbed against the saw-toothed edges of their hard-
shelled bodies on the upward thrust, causing a pounding beat followed
by a high-pitched hum. This is what she was hearing, she was sure
of it. She leaned out even more and was beginning to think about

climbing up to the roof for a better look when she suddenly spotted a dark and churning cloud to the north. A chill passed through her.

Sulpets were nasty bugs from a bog well inside the boarder of Duronyk. The Sulpets were not natural. They were created from pure evil. Twice the size of a Faery, their green and brown sickle-shaped mandibles could penetrate even the most protected skin. If you were in Faery form they ate you, if you were in Mortal form, they chewed at your flesh without pause.

Eirian shook her head refusing to let the images of what the bugs had done to the Faeries take hold. She rushed out the door and down the stairs in seconds. "Damn! My shift!" She paused briefly until high levels of adrenalin pushed her on. "Broan's wrath would just have to wait." She sprinted towards the bell tower. They had to get everyone indoors and there was no time to waste. She sped past everyone and kept up her blistering pace all the way up the stairs and through the door.

"What the hell!" Conn yelled at her as he tried to stop her. It had been Conn's watch that night which was almost over and Eirian was the last person he had expected to come through the door. "You're not allowed up here!" he yelled.

She scooted past him and grabbed the bell rope. She got in one pull before Conn was on her, pulling her away from the bell rope and towards the stairs.

"Conn wait! You've got to ring the bell and warn people. Bugs… bugs from the darkest hell will be here soon and they kill Mortals just like you." She pushed at him with everything she had trying to get to the bell rope again. "Conn, please. You've got to warn everyone."

It didn't make a difference. He easily dragged her back away from the bell, finally releasing her by the top of the stairs. "And how do you know these bugs are coming?"

"If you can't hear them look to the north you'll see them."

"Stay there!" he barked and he went to the north end of the tower. He scanned the horizon. "There's nothing there; just a storm brewing." He looked back at her. "Go find someone else to play your tricks on. Now get out of here."

"Stupid Manliken," she said to herself as she rushed down the stairs almost as fast as she had going up.

The sound from the cold-blooded insects was growing louder and her panic rose dramatically. In her mad dash to find Broan, Eirian passed Miko who was working hard at fencing in some unruly pigs. "Get the animals inside. Get them all inside," she screamed at him, her voice brittle and harsh.

The livestock were becoming more agitated. She could hear horses' high pitch cries coming from the enclosure behind the stables. The red-coned rooster was chasing the hens and Taker and Beals started to howl. "You can hear them coming too, can't you," she said.

Bronagh and Leif were coming out of the Keep as Eirian ran past the stable. She charged at them. She grabbed both of them and pushed them back into the entrance of the Keep. "Get inside! Get everyone inside! There are flesh-eating Sulpets coming!"

"What?" Bronagh looked at her, unsure if she heard right.

Eirian forced them farther back from the door. "Sulpets, bugs that chew up flesh like its rice paper!" She quickly glanced over her shoulder. It was an eerie feeling knowing that the rising black wave of bugs were rapidly coming their way and she was the only one who knew what was about to happen. "Trust me! Please just trust me!"

It didn't take long for Bronagh to drag Leif into the Main-Hall. "YOU stay here." She looked at Eirian, "I'll spread the warning."

"Where's Broan?" Eirian asked, while bouncing on her toes ready to race off again.

"On the training field."

Eirian was off again. She needed to find Broan. She left the front entrance of the Keep and ran down the stairs. It didn't take long before she was elbowing her way through a crowd of people out in the bailey - all unaware, all just starting their busy day. Relentlessly she screamed at anyone who would listen to go back inside. As she neared the inner bailey wall she decided that these people were slowing her pace too much. She jumped and climbed the wall all the way to the top. She turned quickly scanning the horizon, checking the Sulpets progress.

This army of huge, lethal bugs was advancing quicker then she feared. What once was a dark churning cloud was now a visible canopy of red and brown that was thick enough to block out the sunlight to the ground below. Layers and layers of interspersed Sulpets were leapfrogging over each other trying to get to the front of the soon to be 'feeding line'.

Eirian pushed herself faster, running along the top of the wall towards the field, realizing, as she got closer that there was no one there. "Where is he? Where is he?" she cried. She soon spotted Broan and a group of soldiers coming out of the armory. She yelled his name and started to climb down.

Broan had just finished looking over the weapons they had in storage and was reviewing what they would need for the coming battle when he heard his name called. The sight of Eirian on top of the wall made him angry. "Damn it! As if I don't have enough to concern myself with." Annoyed he stormed towards her with V-Tor, Laeg and BroMac trailing behind him.

Eirian began waving her arms at them, motioning them to get back. "Get back inside!" she screamed. "RUN!"

Without warning the sunny, lazy day erupted with a thunderous noise as the Sulpets flew over Solveig, attacking at will. As some of the bugs bridged the inner bailey wall behind Eirian, Broan and the others froze. The sheer volume of the bugs left them breathless. Broan watched in horror as the wave of bugs dropped down and crashed into Eirian. The force was so ferocious it lifted her off the ground and flipped her over. She hit the ground hard, half twisted on her side.

Broan rushed back into the armory and grabbed a few shields, tossing one to Laeg as he exited. Hunching under the raised shields, they made their way towards Eirian, while the Sulpets dove at them with increase ferocity.

Taking up the rear, BroMac and V-Tor swung their swords as they rushed forward. V-Tor sliced through a couple of Sulpets, while BroMac grabbed one off his arm. It was as large has his broad hand. He growled at it as he tried to crush it, but the external skeleton of these bugs had been harden over time by secretions, making it a protective armor, resistant to pressure. BroMac tossed it into the air and sliced it in two.

Broan and his warriors quickly found themselves having to negotiate their way through a deep soup of bugs, which slowed down their progress. Broan looked over at Eirian who was trying to get up. Worried, he pressed harder into the wall of bugs. Once there, Broan collected her under one arm and the four of them fled back to the armory, shutting the door and shutters behind them as fast as they could.

The bugs hit the armory walls like shock waves, over and over again. The sound was deafening as everyone collapsed to the floor. Eirian crawled out of Broan's arm and quickly made her way to a pail of water. Swiftly she dumped it on the dirt floor. She lunged at a knife on the table and started to scrape at the wet ground.

"What are you doing?" BroMac asked, forcing his way up by grabbing onto the side of the table.

"We have to smear mud on the bites. The bite was just to distract you while the bug planted fertilized eggs under your skin." She grabbed his hand and then picked up a gob of newly made muck and slapped it into BroMac's hand. "Once the eggs reach body temperature they quickly change into larva. Once it's a larva, it will twist around and then plant a spear like air-tube through your skin, which allows it to breath. The mud will plug the breathing tube and force the larva out. "

She took some of the mud and crawled back to Broan and Laeg. "If we don't succeed in removing the larva, it'll bury its head deeper into the flesh, spewing acid as it goes. The acid melts muscle, tendon and even bone and turns it into a frothy liquid, which it then consumes." She smeared the mud on Broan where sharp mandibles had torn into his skin and when she ran out of the visible bites, she frantically searched him for hidden bites.

"Shit!" Broan whispered, as he grabbed Eirian's hand. He took some of the mud and smeared it onto her face, covering two big bites that were already oozing blood and a clear fluid. Then he took some more and covered the one on her thigh. Suddenly Broan's head shot up. "Damn! What about everyone else?"

Just then, out beyond the safety of the armory a new sound arose. Adult heron birds, royal terns, and falcons were bringing their scattered flocks together to feast. Eirian heard the distinctive sounds of the birds regimented assembly signals and scurried to the door.

Swiftly, V-Tor slammed himself against the door, preventing Eirian from opening it. "It's okay," she said. "The birds are the only enemy the bugs have. I've got to get out and help those that were bitten." Unmoved, he pushed her back into Broan's arms and then opened the door a crack.

The sight before V-Tor was chaotic. Birds were darting through thick blankets of large bugs, pecking and gulping as they went. They were everywhere. Some were cocking their heads as they viewed the carcasses on the ground. They swiftly dove at anything that moved. Some birds clung to the rock walls with their claws, their heads darting in and out of cracks as they attacked the few smaller bugs that tried to hide. It seemed like it was over as quickly as it had started.

Broan released Eirian from his iron grip and walked over and stood in the doorway gazing out at the welcomed carnage, a canvas of red-brown carcasses that stretched out before him. "What do you need?" he asked Eirian quietly.

"I need to get pails of mud, enough to cover everyone's bites. I'll also need to make a cream. Once the larval have vacated the body the mud should be washed off and the ointment applied. It'll stop any infection."

"And what'll happen if we miss a bite?" Laeg asked.

"Don't." She turned and looked up at them, "Treat every bite—this isn't a death you'd want to watch."

104

Broan looked at the group. "Ok then, let's go. Laeg if you are you well enough, start making mud. BroMac and I will handle the injured in this area. V-Tor, you gather anyone who's well enough to help." He looked down at Eirian. "I think you better go to the Back-Hall and take care of any injured there."

Eirian limped to the hall with mud on her face. She had no time to get her shift and it was stupid to even think of putting it on right then. She had work to do.

The volume of crying and screaming that greeted her at the door almost forced her back. She slipped in and spotted Bronagh near a group of frighten parents all holding children with oozing bites. Eirian went to the well and drew up water. She poured it onto the floor and started making the mud. She scooped some up in her hands and walked forward towards the mothers, who instinctively stepped back.

"Ke-Hern told me that love heals everything. I need you to spit in the mud and mix it up, then put it on your child's or loved ones bites. It'll draw out the evil." She held out the mud. It didn't take long before everyone was filling their hands with mud and spitting into it. "*Oh thank the stars,*" she thought.

Eirian looked at Bronagh, "Is Leif okay?"

"Yes. For once he listened and stayed in the Main-Hall."

"Good. I'll retrieve my shift from your room and start making a salve for everyone. Do you think you can handle those in here for now?"

Bronagh nodded. The sounds of spitting filled the air. "Does the spit really help?" she asked in a whisper.

"No, well… at least not the bites. There's nothing worse than parents who're feeling powerless. I just wanted them to feel that they were helping their children." She smiled cheekily at Bronagh. "Guess you can officially call it a Faery trick."

Conn awoke from his nightmare and entered another one. He raised his head and looked around. There were so many people, so many crying, and so many in pain. "It's all her fault," he cursed under her breath. He worked his way up onto his elbows. He noticed patches of mud dotting his hands and chest. The mud was dry now and pulled at his skin. He started to remove it by putting his fingernails in the cracks and lifting.

"Don't!" screamed Vlad as he rushed towards Conn, "Eirian says it has to stay on until the emulsion is applied."

Conn continued picking at the mud. "What does she know about anything?"

"She knew they were coming. The Faeries had been attacked before by these evil bugs."

Roughly brushing dried mud off his chest, Conn said, "Sure, she knew they were coming, she called to them. I caught her up in the tower singing to them. It's a trick to make it look like she saved us, so we'll drop our defenses."

Vlad looked at Conn. "Are you sure? I mean we're all trus...t...ing...her."

"Just what she wants," Conn hissed. "But I'm not going to be her fool and if you're smart neither should you."

Batch after batch, Eirian worked nonstop in front of the fire, mixing the boiling pots. It took hours to make enough cream for everyone.

"We're just about done," Bronagh said as she walked into a wall of heat. "Why not take a breather from this hot kitchen and come and see."

Eirian wiped her hands on her shift and arched her back, stretching out the kinks and brushed away a few long strands of hair from her face. "Are you sure there's enough cream for now?"

Bronagh nodded and took Eirian's hand, "Come, if nothing else, the fresh air will be a nice reprieve for you."

They walked together in the coolness of the evening air. Eirian paused briefly and looked up at the night sky. She loved twilight the most. The stars were just starting to come to life. Hushed and still, life rested after the day's endeavors. Suddenly Eirian heard "STAY AWAY FROM US." which instantly dissolved her pleasant moment.

"You've caused enough problems with your evil today," Vlad hissed.

"What evil. I didn't do this."

Vlad charged at her, pinning her to the wall. His forearm pressed hard against her throat. "Don't try and trick me. If you hadn't been here, they would not have come to your calling and none of this would've happened."

Eirian paled then looked away from him. Maybe, just maybe, he spoke the truth. She hadn't stopped to consider that she might have attracted the bugs here. "I...I..."

Vlad shoved Eirian away. "Get out of here, Faery! And don't come back."

Eirian rushed back to the kitchen. Tears ran down her cheeks. Was she responsible for all this misery? Did the Sulpets attack because she was here? Did they somehow know she was trapped in Elftan form and more vulnerable, an easy target? As she sat down on the kitchen step, she looked up into the night sky. "Where are you Ke-Hern? I need you... if this is because of me... I can't put them in any more danger. I have to leave."

Eirian was so consumed by her thoughts she didn't hear Bronagh approaching. "Ignore them Eirian, they are just stupid."

She quietly nodded as she dried her eyes. Then she hesitantly asked a question. "Why do you treat me differently? Why does my being Faery not threaten you?"

As Bronagh sat down, she smiled to herself. "I've had a few meetings with Faeries over the years and I have never been given a reason to not like them or trust them."

"You know other Faeries...But the risk... do the others know?"

"Everyone knows my feelings about Faeries." Bronagh stated firmly. She then smiled deeply, held her knees and gently rested back against the step. "A Faery once saved me from a watery death. He made a fire and kept me company until help arrived. Everyone knows the story. But..." she looked at Eirian, "there is one small secret I've kept from them."

Eirian leaned closer, "What secret?"

"I fell in love."

RohDin came out of the kitchen and walked up behind them. "There you are. I was just about to start checking for you in all the rafters and walls."

Looking over her shoulder at him, Eirian asked, "Need more ointment?"

"No. Broan wants to talk to you. He's in the Main-Hall." He lowered his hand towards Eirian, waiting to help her up.

Instead, Bronagh took RohDin's hand and stood up with a huff. "Why?"

RohDin ignored her question and dropped his hand again. "He didn't ask for you, Bronagh. He only asked for Eirian."

"Can't this wait until morning? Eirian's exhausted." Bronagh protested loudly.

RohDin simply turned on his heels and began walking towards the Keep. "Come on Eirian," he called. "Let's go."

Bronagh quickly moved to stand in front of RohDin. "Oh, no you don't! This isn't right. Why does he want to talk to her?"

RohDin chaff at the interruption, "Eirian, NOW!" He barked as he moved Bronagh aside. "Stay!" he demanded as he gave Bronagh a harsh look.

"This is crazy! NO Broan's crazy?" Bronagh yelled at RohDin's back.

RohDin spun on his heels. "Yeah, he's crazy. You have to be a little crazy to be a Warlord and battle Ny-dick and bugs. You have to be a touch crazy to allow a Faery to live among us. Now hurry Eirian, before Bronagh drives me crazy."

Eirian walked into the room and looked at those who were assembled. She felt uncomfortable with the looks Broan gave her, and quickly became aware of the state she was in. She was worn, haggard and dirty. She dropped her gaze and with a self-conscious tug, adjusted her shift, and dusted off some of the dirt from her clothing. She suddenly realized that she was barefoot which only added to her embarrassment. She had tossed aside her tights and boots in the hot kitchen - along with her cap.

Her CAP! Eirian's hand shot up and touched her hair. It was a mess. Some strands had escaped the long braid that wrapped around her head. They clung to her sweaty face and drooped down past her shoulders. She started to weave them back up into the braid, and then stopped. "*What does it matter?*" she said to herself. She still had traces of mud on her face. Sweat stained her Faery undergarment. Her shift was spotted with various things, and yes, she was barefoot.

"Where are those bugs from and why did they attack us? The TRUTH this time!" Broan barked coldly as he stood with feet apart, arms crossed over his chest.

Eirian didn't know how to start. By the tone of his voice and the way he stood she knew right away that he had already blamed her. She looked at him sadly, "Just let me go, Broan."

"Or what? You'll cause us more harm?"

"No! I'd never…"

He stared at her. "Did you cause this? The truth, no more lies or tricks!"

Eirian worked hard at containing her tears. "I don't know. The Sulpets could have sensed me since I've been in this form for a long time, they could have just been out hunting for new victims, or the Queen could have sent them. I don't know"

"Or you could have called them," Conn's voice rang out.

Eirian looked at Conn as he stood partially behind BroMac, looking every part the weasel that he was.

"I never did such a thing," she retorted.

"I heard you up in the bell tower," he sneered at her.

"I can't call them!" She addressed everyone in the room. "Why do you keep insisting that I have the power of Wizards and Off-World Queens?"

"Everyone knows Faeries also have power. You just want to dull our good senses, so we don't see the truth," Conn hissed.

"That's not true," she yelled.

"Really? Ask her if the villagers trust her. I heard they barred her from the Back-Hall." Conn's voice was loaded with hatred as he stepped away from BroMac. Raising his fists he continued. "Someone needs to show you how Faeries are suppose to be treated."

"Enough Conn!" Broan bellowed. "Leave now!"

"But!.." Conn hesitated for a moment then glared at Eirian. "It's not over Faery," he whispered to her as he left the room.

Once Conn slammed the door behind himself, Broan stared at Eirian. "Now, answer me. Where did those bugs come from and how did you know they were coming?"

Eirian briefly studied the others in the room. V-Tor, Laeg, RohDin stood near Broan, while Hargrave hung back, leaning on the wall behind Broan's desk. They all looked so angry with her. It was obvious they had deemed her guilty before hearing what she had to say. She took in a deep breath. "The Sulpets were created by Off-World powers, is what Ke-Hern told us. The bugs successfully attacked us and drove us out of Duronyk long ago. They continued to attack us whenever we ventured close to our homeland, but they have never come out this far before." She paused briefly and then rushed ahead. "As for how I knew they were coming, I'm sure you'll all agree that after hearing them once, you'll never forget that sound. I simply heard them." Eirian chanced a brief look at the assembled group. "Ke-Hern taught all of us how to heal the bites. He wanted us to survive."

Broan truly wanted to believe her. He rubbed the filthy embroider band found in Khumer. He was tired, angry and the bites were still very painful "I have no choice."

"No!" Eirian started backing up. "Not the dungeon!"

V-Tor straightened up. "Broan…She did make the ointment… and…"

Broan raised his hand, stopping V-Tor cold. "For tonight you'll sleep in the room next door. Hargrave can stand guard. After that you'll be locked in the tower each evening." Broan leaned towards her. "So you can't climb out onto the wall and escape, Idwal will block up the window. I've wasted enough manpower on you all ready."

Feeling Broan's distrust to the bone, Eirian followed Hargrave without a word. In the other room, she moved to a corner away from the door and curled up. She thought of Ke-Hern. He had always told her wisdom was a by-product of courage but right now she felt she had neither and wished he where here.

Hargrave settled in a nearby chair and looked down at Eirian, "I have a question for you. So which was it?"

Eirian sat up, "Was what?"

"The first time we met, were you saving me or collaborating with the Ny-dick?"

Eirian shoulders slumped. "What do you think?"

"Answer ME!" Hargrave demanded coldly.

"You're here aren't you?"

"That's not an answer!"

"Don't start yelling at me. What I've come to understand about you Mortals is that no matter what I answer, you will still believe what you've already decided. If I had said I saved you, you would have screamed at me that it was a lie. Your being here is the reality. Be glad it worked out that way." She glared at him. "I'm tired. Can I go to sleep now?"

Hargrave huffed when she turned her back to him. "All you Faeries are tricksters. Can't get a straight answer out of any of you."

"Then stop asking questions and start accepting reality as truth."

Silence lay heavily over both of them for some time, until Eirian whispered, "Not all of us are bad you know."

DeSpon stood hidden in the deep shadows of a small alley in the Walled City, while Council Member Mohr stood just around the corner in the bright of day. Mohr would pass on what news there was for Sobus and then walked away, not giving DeSpon a second glance. It bothered DeSpon some but not this time. He turned, shape-shifted into a raven and took flight, heading to the Queen's Island. He needed to see Aillil, the 'Seer,' again. He hoped she would be able to put meaning to the disturbance the Shadow Dwellers felt, the quickening in the land itself.

Aillil walked in her slow and comfortable way with her hands slightly outstretched. She used them to "see" the land she walked on. Her heart quickened with the knowledge that DeSpon was near. She had missed him and was not embarrassed to show it.

DeSpon landed next to her and took her hand. "It's good to see you Aillil. Has the Queen been treating you well?"

"She has. Are you sure she can't sense you?"

DeSpon's laugh was rich and clear. "She didn't when you and I first met, so why would she now? Besides, even if she knew we were meeting, she couldn't come out here. Only you can walk through walls and only you can sense me when I'm near." He patted Aillil's hand as he continued; "I've something to ask you about a Faery named Eirian."

Aillil pulled her hand free in great haste. "I'm beginning to dislike that Faery without ever having met her. Everyone is so concerned about what powers she has and if she provoked the Ancients' corpses to awake."

"So the Queen has mentioned it as well," he mused. "I'm sorry Aillil. I didn't mean to upset you. There's so much happening surrounding the coming war. You do want me to keep safe don't you and it's only through information that I can."

Aillil leaned into him and rested against his bare chest, a closeness that had never happened before. DeSpon tensed, fearing her reaction. Would she have a clearer picture of his misshaped body, the beast, the monster he looked like?

"It's I who should say sorry. You know I'll aid you in anything," Aillil said. She pressed her hands against DeSpon's chest and slowly pushed herself away. She stopped when she heard him draw in his breath. She left her hands resting on his chest and smiled to herself. "I don't understand why everyone fears the Ancients? They're really not as bad as the Queen professes."

DeSpon placed his hands over hers. He was enjoying the feeling of flesh against flesh. It had been so long since he felt this pleasure. "And you know this how?" he urged.

Aillil's smiled warmed. She was enjoying this newfound intimacy. "I talk to them…well actually they talk to me."

DeSpon hands tightened around hers. This was too good to be true. She was actually communicating with the Ancients. "Does this happen often?"

"Yes, I guess. The Queen worries that tapping into the Ancients' energy will take on a life of its own and kill me."

"If it's risky, then you should not do it."

Aillil laughed out loud. "It's not always that way. There are two Ancients that talk to me. When Kurtz talks, I'm totally overpowered, but when the misty voice of the deep calls, I'm fine. In fact, I'm my usual self."

"You told me the name of one. Is there a name for the other?"

"No," she said with a sigh. "There's something different about…."

Now that nervous weeks of chaos had given way to order and preparations for war, Broan finally had time to ponder about the situation with Eirian. On his way to the noon meal, he tried to recall the sexual intimacy that had happened between them. "Still nothing," he cursed to himself. "And who the hell had those shifting and flickering eyes of flame?" They couldn't have been Eirian's because she was safe in his arms while they…whirled through…the… through the. "There was more than just attraction there," he stated to himself. "So…magic, but whose magic?"

Broan shook his head as he looked at the tower, Eirian's nightly prison. He did not know much of the world of Faery. It was a reality beyond his, but there was one way he could possibly get answers. He walked into the Main-Hall and gathered some food for the mid-day meal - bread, cheese and a jug of milk. He paused over the fruit, picking only the best out of the bunch of apples. Satisfied, Broan tucked everything into his arms and headed to where Eirian was.

Broan froze at the sight of Hargrave walking away with Eirian. He also had a loaf of bread tucked under one arm and a mug in each hand. It seemed that Hargrave had the same idea. Broan watched them as they made their way toward a small grouping of birch trees, up against the interior wall. He was just about to turn back to the Keep when he stopped, nonchalantly looked up at the blue summer sky, and smiled.

"What made you change your mind?" Eirian asked as she lowered herself to the shaded ground. She took the bread and the mug Hargrave handed her. She paused, looked into it, and smiled. "Thanks for the milk. I was worried it might be wine or ale."

"I'm aware of what you drink. Is it the taste or the after effects that you dislike?"

"I don't know I've never tasted it. Now back to my question. What changed your mind about me?"

Hargrave shrugged his shoulders. "You were right. I had already made up my mind that you and the Ny-dick where collaborating."

"And?"

"Like you said, I am alive. The truth speaks for itself."

Eirian smiled at him as she sipped the cool milk. "Now what?"

"Let's just eat and talk."

"Talk! Why does everyone always want to talk?"

"Because we know little about Faeries. Well any of the good stuff that is."

Eirian dropped her eyes and pulled at the chunk of bread in her lap. "Sorry. It's just that most of my life has been spent alone.

Conversation wasn't even a daily thing." She looked at Hargrave, "I'm truly amazed at just how much Mortals talk and how loud they can be!"

Hargrave relaxed and laughed, "It is part of our social structure. It brings us together even if it does cause a fight or two." He stuffed a large piece of bread into his mouth. "So, what do you think of life in Solveig so far?"

"It's okay I guess. Once you get use to all the noise and all the rules."

Hargrave shook his head. "I won't accept that as an answer. You've been here long enough to form an opinion. In truth, what do you think?"

Eirian sat up straighter and squared her shoulders. "You want the truth? Well for starters there are too many rules. Many of you are rude, the food is horrible, the noise is intense, the beds are too soft, the rooms are too hot and smelly, and Solveig itself is too crowded with too few places to slip away for some peace and quiet."

Hargrave couldn't help himself. He burst out laughing.

"Actually it's frightening," Eirian continued, "but I have learned about communal living and a bit about what it's like being Mortal. More importantly I've come to understand that there is a common thread that runs through both Mortal and Faery."

"And what's that?" Hargrave asked gulping his milk.

"The concern and care for one another. We all have that need to help."

"Mmm…well, other than you, I've not met one Faery that had the need to help. Sorry."

"Did you give them a chance?"

Hargrave wasn't sure how to answer that so he didn't. "So tell me something about Faeries if that's not too personal?"

"Like what?"

"Anything."

"Well, there's no communal living for us, even families have been scattered. We can do little outside of what's been decreed. It's as though we live in an invisible prison of isolation, sitting and watching life around us, lamenting over what was lost."

"I see…" Hargrave paused in thought briefly, "But just so you know, Mortal life is not all roses. There are many battles, both on personal and social fronts. There's illness, hunger and a lot of hard work."

"Yes, but try to imagine," Eirian exclaimed, "knowing you have a family, but you can never see them. Imagine having a talent, but never being able to use it or express it; dream of a better way, but never see it unfold; or wish for an end when there is no end in sight."

"Think about two older brothers called BroMac and RohDin!"

Eirian started to laugh, "I guess you're right. Both have room for improvement."

"Tell me of the Ny-dick." Hargrave ventured.

"Hmm," she said.

"It's okay if you don't want to. Seeing that you saved me from one not that long ago, I wanted to see if your opinion matches mine."

"They're vile creatures. They come from the land beyond the known mountains to the west and north of here. They're not primitive even though they look it. But you already know that." She eyed Hargrave and then continued. "Here's something for you. They're an enemy to both of us. They like eating Faeries like one eats a bird. After picking off our wings, they slowly roast us over a fire. As for Mortals, they prefer to eat you quickly before the blood clots."

Hargrave choked on his food. Finally, in a soft voice he asked, "Did you use a spell on that Ny-dick?"

"Yes I did. They're large and smart and their brains do not missing anything. But their weakness is their hearing. Their brains are tuned to a particular frequency. Faery song mesmerizes them, but we can only do it one-on-one and when in Mortal shape. Ke-Hern gave us the gift to tap into it awhile back."

"And us Mortals?"

Eirian smiled and shook her head. "I only wish. Actually Mortals' hearing is not as sensitive. As Faery we can confuse you, but it doesn't last long."

"Can you show me?"

"Sure…. if you can get Broan to take the binding cord off."

"Ahh, well that's not happening anytime soon."

Eirian dropped her head once again and looked away from Hargrave. Even though the words had been spoken lightly in humor, there was heaviness to his answer that hurt.

Hargrave cleared his throat. "How do you heal?"

"Questions, questions, questions, I already told Laeg how - Ke-Hern taught me." Eirian paused, and then suddenly called out, "Leif and Jelen, you can come join us if you wish." She turned her head towards the clump of birch trees and instead of a couple of boys, caught sight of Broan resting against a tree.

"OH!" she said as she jumped up. "Sorry. I'm just so used to having the boys spy on me, I thought it was them making all that noise!"

"Noise? I was as quiet as a mouse."

"More like a rat." Eirian huffed.

Broan smiled at her then took a bite of his apple. "So life in here is very different from life out there?"

"Like a fish out of water. I'm just amazed I can still breathe." With that Eirian turned and walked away.

Hargrave gathered the rest of his lunch and went and joined Broan under the trees. "Do you think she spoke the truth about the Ny-dick?"

"Time will tell."

Conn's erratic behavior was even starting to get on Vlad's nerves. He was grateful for Conn's help in gathering them together in their stand against Eirian. But what had started as help had soon became a curse. The ailing warrior spent all day in the Back-Hall now, sitting around complaining to anyone who would listen.

"Conn, are you alright? Your color's not great," Vlad proclaimed as he approached.

"I'm not well! I feel terrible. It's that Eirian. She cursed me you know, for going to Broan with the truth." He grabbed Vlad's hand. "But don't worry I won't give in to her evil."

"I'm glad," Vlad answered, uneasiness rising within him.

"I've not been well enough to spy on her lately. What has she been up to?" Conn whispered, his clammy and cold hand still holding Vlads.

Vlad pulled his hand away and brushed it off on his tunic. "Not much. She's been mostly keeping to herself since Broan talked with her."

"I heard she made some tea for the sick. I hope you're smart enough to refuse." Conn spat as he spoke, spraying Vlad in the face.

"Of course," Vlad answered moving slightly away from Conn. Vlad sighed heavily in an effort to build up his courage. "Look Conn, we're all grateful for what you've done for us, but everyone is uncomfortable with you hanging around here all the time."

"What…What! Is this all the thanks I get for saving them?" Conn grabbed Vlad's shirt and pulled him near. "I'm not the enemy here. Has that witch put a spell on everyone?"

"Conn, there is no spell. Look, I'm sure you have other important things to do."

"Saving the Mortals of Solveig is very important to me." He glared at Vlad and pointed his finger towards the door. "She… she has fooled you all!"

"No! Conn we just want you to leave. You're not well."

"LEAVE! She should leave, NOT me." Slowly and with great effort, Conn staggered to his feet. "Well she can have the lot of you." He paused and stared at Vlad. "You'll…" He poked his finger into Vlad's chest. "You'll be sorry. You'll see…" He turned and like a drunken man, staggered out the door.

Once outside Conn found it difficult to navigate his way. The sun was too bright, the wind too strong, the ground too uneven. Suddenly Conn bumped into young Jelen coming around the corner. "Watch where you are going, you've no respect for your elders." he barked.

"I'm sorry, Conn. I didn't see you there." Jelen answered as he fumbled with his stone. He tucked it back into his pocket. "Do you need help?"

"Help, yes, help. That would be nice." He grabbed Jelen as he began to fall forward. "I need some space to be alone…can you help me to the stables?" He spat out the last word. "You're a good boy, Jelen, better than some around here." He leaned heavily on Jelen's shoulder and as they passed the Back-Hall he glared at it.

They almost made it to the stable when suddenly Jelen started turning them around. "You're very sick Conn. I think it would be better if I take you to Eirian. She's helped lots of people so far."

Enraged Conn pushed Jelen away from him. "NO ONE IS GOING TO HAND ME OVER TO THAT BITCH." Quickly Conn pulled a knife out of his boot and pointed it at Jelen. "Not even you!" He lunged at Jelen, cutting him on the arm. "That's for trusting her."

Jelen quickly grabbed his arm to stop the bleeding and backed away from Conn, staring at him in shock. He had known Conn all of his life. And Conn had never, ever hurt him. He turned quickly and ran.

"Go," Conn screamed. "Go run away you Faery fool."

Blood gushed from Jelen's arm leaving a trail of red behind him. It didn't take long for Eirian to catch up to him. "What happen?" She asked as she tried to slow him down.

"I want my father," Jelen yelled. He looked down at his arm and his eyes grew big with fear. "I want my dad!"

"Okay. I'll go get him, but first let me look at it."

"NO!"

"Okay…Okay! Then sit down before you fall down." Eirian forced him onto the bottom step of the Keep. Quickly she rushed into the Keep looking for help. For the first time ever Eirian was actually relieved to find BroMac there, talking with Broan and V-Tor. "Come quick!" she yelled. "Jelen's hurt!"

With worried furrows on his face, BroMac knelt down beside his son. "What happened?" he asked, calmly taking hold of Jelen's arm. Jelen paled even more as he watched what his father rip a piece of cloth from his shirt. "Conn asked me to help him to the stables - and then he went crazy." Jelen looked at Eirian. "He said it was punishment for trusting…Eirian."

"That's it." BroMac said as he finished tying the strip of material around Jelen's arm. Swiftly he picked his son up. "I'm going to kill him," he hissed.

"Just take care of Jelen. We'll handle this." Broan said as he started out the Keep.

Broan slowly opened the door to the stable and listened. Everything was still and quiet, too quiet for Broan's liking. In the dim light of the stable, he and V-Tor began their searched for Conn. They inched forward moving slowly from one stall to another, hands on their knives, unsure as to what to expect. Conn may have been stubborn and crusty, but for him to even raise a finger at Jelen was unheard of.

"Maybe he fled?" V-Tor questioned. "I don't even hear the sound of him breathing."

Broan shook his head, "Conn may not be well right now, but he wouldn't run and hide from us, even after what he did."

A few more stalls down Broan and V-Tor understood why things were so quiet. They came across Conn's body. It lay in a heap near the back of a stall; he was face down on a pile of straw that had turned a deep red color.

"What the hell!" Broan said, quickly, turning Conn over. The last of Conn's blood seeped past the hilt of a knife that was buried deep in his chest and onto Broan's boot.

"He's killed himself," V-Tor said in a hushed tone. He glanced around to see if anyone had entered behind them. "This'll not be good if the villagers find out. It's bad enough that they will all be talking about Jelen's attack. But the fact he was crazy enough to kill himself… everyone will think dark magic did it."

"Here help me," Broan said standing up still holding Conn's body. "We'll bury him quickly and clean up the mess. We'll tell everyone that he died. Hopefully they'll believe it was from the bugs."

That evening, Broan barely acknowledged Eirian when she walked in to his den.

"I need to ask you a question," she said. Broan grunted his agreement, but still didn't look up. "I need to know what you did with Conn's body."

"We buried it. Why?"

"Just wondering," she looked intently at Broan for a second. "Was there any blood?"

"WHAT?" Broan sharply barked. "Why would you ask that?"

"You and V-Tor were very mad at Conn. You could have run him through with your knife or sword. Look, I'm just concerned, that's all."

"Well don't be. V-Tor and I found him dead and we buried him quietly. Had I known you had such deep feeling for him, I would've invited you to the funeral." Broan rose from his chair. "NOW LEAVE."

Eirian nodded her head slightly and turned to go then suddenly spoke again. "I'm not questioning your leadership. I am asking hard questions because I need to know. The safety of all of us depends on it."

"LEAVE Eirian, my patience is running very thin, too thin to play mind games with you!"

Eirian nodded her head slowly and quietly left.

Chapter 7

I t was a bloody day for Lija. He stood watching Sobus' army attempt to attack Solveig, whose well-planned defenses hindered the Ny-dick mightily. He watched as the Ny-dick waded across the 'Blue River of the West' and then through the buttress and into range for the archers. A few tried to retreat but found it difficult to transverse the bolder formation. It had been constructed with a reverse slop and it took much time and effort to maneuver. It exposed the Ny-dick's backs to arrows launched from the walls of Solveig. Lija closed his eyes to the slaughter and tried to close his ears to the screams of the dying.

"*Don't worry so, Lija. Things will work out in the end,*" Sobus said telepathically. "*Now did you get the other things I wanted?*"

Lija nodded his head briefly. Pain shot through his head instantly.

"*SPEAK to me, you fool. You know how limited your power is for communicating through thought.*"

Lija grabbed his head, trying to press out the pain. "Yes. Yes," he screamed. "Most of what you asked for is here. The rest will be here within the week," he gasped.

"Good...Good. Now call the Ny-dick back, we've wasted enough of them. You know what to do next. Once we've finished playing with them, I want you to send Solveig a message letting them know my demands."

"And once they hand over the Faery?"

"Kill them."

It was a quiet evening meal in the alcove of the Main-Hall. The refugees were all tucked away in the Back-Hall and Broan sat with only his best. It was a great relief to not have the masses under foot. This evening more than ever Broan needed a small spot of calmness.

"I'd say the Ny-dick are off to a rocky start. How many do you think died today?" V-Tor asked, pushing away his uneaten meal. He raised the mug of mead to his lips, but the smell was more than he could handle. He plopped his mug down on the table and looked over to Broan. He wondered if Broan was feeling ill like he was. "You know Governor Iarnan wouldn't be happy to hear how well your ideas on the defense system of Solveig have stood up."

Broan noted the tightness between his eyes was beginning again. He rolled his shoulders hoping that some of the aching pain in his joints would let up. "It's not an assault we have to be worried about. It's what's to come next. There are larger forces at play here - Wizard magic. Who knows what tricks the Ny-dick or their master will come up with?"

"You saw Lija?" Idwal asked and Broan simply nodded.

BroMac leaned in. "So the lost Wizard has gotten himself an army."

"Of Ny-dick no less..." V-Tor muttered.

"And Shadow Dwellers," Broan added coolly.

"What?"

Broan nodded again, "I saw one with the Ny-dick in Khumer during the fighting."

"But Shadow Dwellers are Faery!" BroMac barked.

"Faery or not, they're under Lija's control along with the Ny-dick."

"So it'll take more than muscle and brains to get from one end of this war to the other," BroMac said as he pounded the table. "You may be right Broan. This could be the Faery war coming."

"Perhaps that's where Eirian comes in. She's Faery also..." Idwal muttered, thinking out loud.

"Perhaps," Broan nodded. He flexed his right hand under the table. The twitching had started in the middle finger that morning and had slowly worked its way up the right arm. Now that it was evening, he found the twitching had stopped, but weakness had developed in its place.

"I mean it makes sense now…why Wizard Ke-Hern sent her here." Idwal grunted when BroMac's elbow caught him in the ribs. He glared at his brother. "Maybe he knew this would happen and sent Eirian…a Faery to help us." Raising his chin, Idwal continued, "at least I'm willing to consider that there is a positive reason that she is here."

"Or," V-Tor cut in, "he had no idea that the Ny-dick and Shadow Dwellers have joined forces and Eirian has nothing to do this. There is no telling why Ke-Hern sent her here."

BroMac sipped his ale, "I agree…never liked the whole idea to start with."

Broan studied his group of warriors. "It's the joined forces of Ny-dick and Shadow Dweller we need to worry about now, not a single Faery that is paralyzed by a binding cord. I want a double watch on the outer wall. If anything changes, even in the slightest, I want to know."

"If you're worried about a siege Broan, Solveig is well stocked. You saw to everything yourself. We could hold up for a long time," V-Tor said. He tried once more to drink, only to have his stomach rebel again.

"With the influx of villagers we can hold on for a while, but not forever." Broan said matter of factly and the table fell to an eerie glum silence.

The sound of flapping wings shifting quickly to that of stomping footsteps made GaHan turned abruptly. He peered deeper into the shadows of the parapet. "Who goes there?" he yelled than waited for a moment. "I said who goes there?" A rumbling sound from deep within the throat of the intruder was all he got for an answer.

"LansRo," GaHan called over his shoulder, "take position here while I check something out."

"Send him away," whispered a voice. "I only wish to speak with just one of you Mortals."

GaHan raised his hand to stop LansRo while keeping his eyes on the shadows. "Show yourself," he called out. "I'll not be talking with anyone who's not able to face me in the light."

"Ahh, good, a very wise warrior, just the one I've been looking for. I do fear though that the sight of me may stop the conversation before it has even started and there's something very important I need to discuss."

GaHan stepped forward with his hand on the hilt of his knife and the other on his sword. He stopped abruptly at the edge of the light. His head jarred back when he saw flashing red eyes peering at him. "Who….who are you?"

"Shut up and listen. You already know what I am and that if I had wanted to kill you and the other night watchman you'd be already dead. I come with a simple demand that will be beneficial to you and those whom you guard."

GaHan's curiosity was tweaked and he stepped a little closer.

"Wizard Lija sent me. He wants Broan to know that the sole purpose of this siege is to recover the Faery he's been holding. All he has to do is hand her over and we'll leave."

GaHan stared at the dim outline of the Shadow Dweller, and looked away. "Why does Lija want her?"

"She has spent her life hiding from him. He only wants to stop her mad plan."

"What plan?"

"She leads a Faery army. If you don't believe me, ask her yourself and watch her eyes shift about as she lies. You'll see."

"How did she become the leader of a Faery army? She's but a woman and also a friend of Ke-Hern's."

"A friend of Ke-Hern's?" The Shadow Dweller laughed loudly. "Now that is rich. He's been trying to capture her as well. She'll tell you anything you want to hear to hide her true purpose." The creature tired of standing and shifted its weight. "Of course it's too bad that Broan has feelings for her. I'm sure his affair with her weighs heavily on him now that it's brought such chaos to..."

"What? What the hell are you talking about?"

The Shadow Dweller smiled to himself. "How else can you explain that she is still here and still alive…for this long? Go ahead… watch the two of them. Trust your own eyes."

The creature lingered a moment longer watching GaHan. "Give Broan the message. He has one day to respond."

"Well, there certainly is truth to your story, GaHan. The stench of Ny-dick and Shadow Dweller is all over you," Broan said. "How long did it stay?"

GaHan's eyes widened and he sniffed himself. "Only a few minutes, just long enough to give me the message." He looked at Broan. "So what are you going to do?"

"Nothing."

The single word silenced the room. GaHan's face swiftly changed from concern to annoyance in seconds. "What? But they're offering us a way out of this mess. Why? Why not take them up on their offer?"

Broan smiled. "You're a good soldier GaHan and I thank you for your concern, but I'll not play their game. This is nothing but a ruse."

"But there's a benefit. It's that Faery isn't it? The Shadow Dweller said she…"

Broan raised his hand stopping GaHan short, "Go back to your post, GaHan. Let's watch and see what their next move is."

With a curt nod GaHan turned and left the private room. He muttered and cursed all the way back to his post, unhappy with the way things were looking.

When Eirian woke, it was still dark inside her tower prison. She had a sick feeling in her stomach. She placed her hand over her abdomen and took in a few deep breaths. It wasn't from lack of food or too much food, or even the type of food she ate; it wasn't the feeling of a sour stomach. Eirian closed her eyes and relaxed, scanning her body, searching for what was causing this illness.

Eirian pulled her hand away in shock. She was stunned. There was a growing source of individual energy, separate from her, and yet within her. "Can't be! Faeries do not get pregnant! They don't have…" But Eirian could feel its essence. She couldn't discount the fact. Apprehension seized her. "No, not now! Not Broan!"

Her world suddenly tilted. She was shamed and confused and close to tears. She hugged her knees and started to rock herself. This could NOT possibly be in Ke-Hern's plan, and it definitely was not in hers. She frantically considered and rejected options as they popped into her mind until one made sense. Alone and trembling Eirian felt the enormity of what she now had to do.

After a few sleepless hours, Idwal finally arrived with the key to her freedom and let her out of her prison. In great haste she rushed down the steps of the tower, out into the inner bailey, and into the half-light of dawn. Harsh rapid breathing echoed loudly in her ears as she ran all the way to Faber's small garden.

Eirian thought of what she was about to do and bile rose into her mouth. She shuddered and tried to calm herself. Lack of sleep and tension had left her balancing precariously on the edge. She gripped the little wooden gate to a very small but very useful garden full of edible flowers, herbs…and Merlion.

Merlion had been known to cause the separation of life from life. This translucent, bitter tasting plant had powerful cleansing abilities that many used to inhibit or stop the progression of a pregnancy, and Eirian intended to use it.

Pushing the gate open, she stepped inside the wee garden and frantically searched for the plant. Anger and fear fueled her on. *"There!"* The pungent, decidedly sweet smell of Merlion called to her. Her legs shook as she slowly lowered herself to her knees. She dug with clawed fingers till finally the damp soil gave way, freeing the plant.

Suddenly overwhelmed with the reality of being a Faery, she let the plant slip from her hand. She couldn't chance it and be pulled into the void. A decision like this could trick her into ending all hope for the Faeries. There was no turning away from her appointed destiny even with this new life inside of her and she knew it. Tears streamed down her face. She rose and walked out of the garden, paying no mind to the hidden form that watched her from the side of the hut.

No time for the morning meal and no stomach for it either, Broan was just about to exit the Keep when Laeg approached him. "There's trouble brewing. I think Wizard Lija isn't happy with your response to his request."

Broan and Laeg climbed the stairs to the nearest tower. There was only a small arch of the sun showing that dawn but it gave enough light for them to see a group of Ny-dick hastily digging with their bare hands. They were ripping up clumps of earth in an attempt to form pits just beyond the ditch. "What do you think they're doing?"

"I don't know." Broan stepped back. "But if they come any closer, fire on them." Half way down the stairs Broan stumbled. His stomach turned and a strange dizziness briefly washed through him. He shook it off and continued down.

Noon gave them their answer. Chaos came on a current of air this time. The prevailing westerly winds were unusually strong that day. They blew cool and furiously as they hastened over the forest and river picking up the black smoke from the newly made pits. The smoke traveled jarringly over the field and the last rubble fortification, dragging the caustic haze along as it hit the outer wall and rose over it.

The cloud of black toxic fumes surrounded those in the tower and up on the parapet. The alarms were sounded, as the guards gasped and choked. Several of the young soldiers on the wall broke from their posts and ran down the stairs, trying to get away but it was no use. The smoke quickly settled lower into Solveig. Frightened and scared, panic quickly overcame the crowd. Children cried and screamed as they were yanked up into their parent's arms. Elbowing one another, people rushed towards the Back-Hall and hopefully salvation.

The thick dark curtain hung over Solveig for days, blocking out most of the sun. A pungent sulfur smell that was produced by the constant fires filled the air, burning the lungs of those who needed to be outdoors. This was the beginning of the thing that Broan had feared the most - magic.

"Does it ever end?" one soldier asked Broan as he entered the tower. "I don't know what they burn, but let's hope it's hard to get and that they run out soon."

Broan nodded in agreement while he scanned the area. It was hard to see through the darkness. "What we need is rain," he said walking away, keeping his foul mood to himself, "a good long storm, a storm to wash this all away."

The rains Broan wished for came two days later. Moisture laden winds from the east arrived in torrential sheets of cleansing water and everyone cheered. Even the thunder and lightning didn't stop anyone from venturing out into the bailey. Many raised their faces to the gray sky and laughed.

Jelen woke up in a foul mood. He could not shake this flu feeling. Even though the smoke had finally cleared and everyone was allowed outside, nothing felt right. The seams in his leggings cut into his sensitive skin. The smallest effort caused his heart to pound in his ears. Jelen tossed down the basket of eggs onto the table. He didn't care that a few had broken. "Here are your dumb eggs," he growled.

"Jelen! Be careful!" Faber said picking out the undamaged ones. "I don't know what's gotten into you lately!"

"I told you. But you won't listen to me. You NEVER listen to me. You and father only hear what you want to hear, and I'M SICK OF IT!" He turned, grabbed his bag and stomped out the door.

Faber was stunned at first and then just plain annoyed. She rushed after him. "Jelen get back in here!"

Jelen spun on his heels and glared at her. "NO! Just leave me alone!" Then as quick as a rabbit, he ran off.

"Let him go," BroMac said as he came up next to her. "He's finally showing some fight in him."

"He's becoming a child tyrant!"

"He's growing up."

"He's disrespectful. NOT a knight in the making, I'd say!"

BroMac held back his smile and simply nodded his agreement. "I'll talk to him."

"And I'll take the spoon to him if this continues much longer."

BroMac scowled, "Now Faber, I know that this is different from his normal behavior, but you must agree that at least he's showing some spirit."

"Spirit is fine. It's where he applies it that angers me."

BroMac reached out, pulled Faber into his arms and nuzzled her neck. "I'll talk to him. Leave it to me, okay?"

V-Tor sat down and closed his eyes. "*This is beyond the effects of that damn smoke*," he lamented to himself. It had been one rough day so far. He was glad the slight tremor in his legs had gone, but he didn't enjoy the heaviness that replaced it. He wiped his forehead again. He had been perspiring profusely all day. "It may be summer, but this is silly. I've never felt like this before."

Shifting his weight, V-Tor tried to find a more comfortable spot to lean on. It wasn't working. His skin was over sensitive and every time he moved, his clothes rubbed against his skin causing it to tingle and ignite with burning. He shifted again and then just gave up. Nothing was going to make him feel better.

"No resting now," Laeg said as he came up to V-Tor. "Broan wants to meet with us in the private room."

V-Tor got up without complaint, and fell in behind Laeg.

Eirian had kept out of Broan's way as best as she could. She didn't need her little secret to complicate things even more. However she had realized that her healing supplies were almost gone. Soon she would need things that were only found out beyond the walls of Solveig. There was no way around it. She had to get her courage up and speak to Broan before she totally ran out of herbs.

Patiently, Eirian waited for him on the steps of the Keep. It didn't take long before she heard the echo of his boot heels on the stone floor. She quickly stood tall keeping her head down and her eyes on the ground and just when she was about to approach him, he grabbed her arm, pulling her along with him.

Eirian needed to take double steps to keep up with Broan's long, fast stride. She looked over her shoulder to see not only Laeg, but also V-Tor and BroMac coming up behind them. Eirian looked up at Broan. "I guess this is a bad time to ask to have my binding cord taken off," she said.

Broan froze. He pulled her around and glared at her.

Uneasy with his stare, she struggled trying to free herself. "I need to get some herbs and plants. It'll be hard to treat the injured without them."

"You want me to take off the one thing that controls you!" Broan almost laughed. "You want me to believe that you'd fly away, gather what you need and come back."

Eirian felt it was better to keep her mouth closed. She simply nodded her head.

"Are all Faeries so stupid or is it just you?"

Eirian stopped nodding. She went to open her mouth, but slammed it shut, refusing to give into the temptation.

Broan shook her. "I'll not take that blasted thing off, not now, not ever! Lija provides the Ny-dick with enough help. They certainly don't need yours!"

"Help! All I want to do is help YOU! Not them!" she screamed.

"The answer is NO," Broan barked, "and don't ever ask again." His grip on her arm was fierce as he dragged her up the stairs of one of the guard towers. Once they reached the top of the stairs she was thrust up against the window.

"You, more than anyone, know what the forest holds. What do you think that is?" Broan raised his hand and pointed. "Do you see it? Trees are parting. Something's moving them aside to make its way through. What would be that large to make the trees sway as they do?"

Eirian stood on her tiptoes, looking in the direction Broan was pointing. She looked back at him from the corner of her eye, and then started to ease her way up onto the ledge of the embrasure. His hand lashed out, grabbing her. "Now is not the time to try an escape. Just tell me if you know what it could be."

Eirian looked at him angrily. "I wasn't trying to escape! I just need a better look." She turned and looked back at the forest. There definitely was something down there. Birds were taking flight. Animals were rushing out into the opening between the forest and the first fortification. One could hear the limbs of trees break, too old to bend or too stubborn to move. This was not something that normally lived in these woods.

Broan's impatience got the better of him. He pulled her near. "Just tell me if you know what it is!" he yelled. "If you don't know, that's fine. We have no time to waste on little games!"

"I am not playing games. I just need to be sure before I tell you what I think. Since I'm sure you'll not let me climb to the roof to get a better look."

Laeg stepped forward, touching Broan on the arm, trying to get things back on course. "So Eirian, what is it?"

"It's human formed, not animal, and the only things that are human formed and that big are... Giants."

Broan let go of her arm and moved her aside as he went to look out of the window. "Giants?"

V-Tor looked at Eirian. "That can't be possible. Everyone knows Giants live only in their valley, if they live at all. No one has ever seen one outside of it."

Eirian crossed her arms over her chest and glared at V-Tor. "Broan asked what was out there and I told him what I think. Why do you condemn me for telling you the truth?"

"Because you're Faery," V-Tor answered pushing past her as he joined Broan at the embrasure.

Eirian was puzzled. What was happening to these Mortals?

Broan continued to watch the parting of the trees. "And I can just image what drew them here," Broan barked as he looked at her. "There's more! You know more than you're telling!"

"Stop it! Don't be an idiot." Eirian hissed back.

No sooner had she spoken, than the soft grunts turn into eerie howls. One of the Giants had come out of the forest and stood in the open, cursing Solveig. He raised his arms and pounded his chest, creating a deafening sound that echoed all around them. Then he squatted for a moment and left a pile of manure. Like an animal, he left a challenge to those in the fortress.

"Now that's a big... brute," said BroMac.

Broan turned back to Eirian. He stood in front of her with a sneer on his face. "Do you know that the Ny-dick have sent a message telling us what they want?"

"So what is it they are after?"

"YOU."

V-Tor picked at his shirt trying to ease his irritated skin. "I say let's hand her over and be done with it."

"You can't!" Eirian exclaimed.

"And if it is a way to save Solveig, why not?" Broan declared.

"They'll eat me alive. They're my enemy too!"

"Why did you come here?"

"I told you. The Ny-dick were coming. Ke-Hern sent me here with the boys to save us all."

"Put her through the gates," Broan hissed.

"NO! Don't! Why are you being such an IDIOT?" Eirian screamed at him.

Broan's hand came up so fast no one saw it move. It wrapped itself around her throat as he violently slammed her against the wall, pining her there.

"I am getting awfully tired of the word idiot," he growled into her ear.

"Well it's better than what I could be using," Eirian gargled out.

He seethed. "Witty until the end." His cold eyes held her. "You planned all of this didn't you?"

"Why would I do that? Think for once beyond your..." She paused trying to breathe past the continued and increasing pressure on her neck, "...limited knowledge. Ke-Hern needs you and me alive. He needs US! Both of us! He needs us to work together."

"WHY?"

Eirian closed her eyes and willingly gave up. "To conquer the second invasion of the Ny-dick, trust what I'm saying to you."

He released his hold on her neck and quickly grabbed her with both hands. He flung her against the far wall of the tower. "If you think for one minute that I'd ever trust you, then you're the idiot here."

"Yes it appears I am," Eirian sadly said as she pulled herself up. "And I guess so is Ke-Hern. He believed in you, too bad you don't believe in him or the reality around you." She stood with dignity before him. "If you don't have any more questions I'll go help Bronagh."

Guards stood frozen, unable to blink, shocked by what they were seeing. Giants were picking up dead Ny-dick from the field and tossing them at Solveig. Many hit the outer wall with a vociferous sound, shaking the foundation of the towers. The first body hit within the outer bailey and the force of air snatched Leif off his feet then flipped him hard onto his back. He quickly scrambled away from the dead Ny-dick as another corpse came flying his way.

The stench was abominable. The gas filled stomachs of the dead distended outward, ripping their clothes apart. Limbs rose ridged at odd angles from their bodies. The faces that had not exploded on impact were swollen, the skin shiny and tight as muscle putrefied underneath. Too many days out in the open, too many days left to rot, too many days to create a virulent germ.

Broan and V-Tor pushed their way through the growing crowd. "Now I know why they don't claim their dead," V-Tor said covering his nose and mouth with his hand. Suddenly another one hit the ground and people scattered.

"Get wood and fuel. We need to burn them where they've landed." Broan yelled to the crowd, setting everyone into motion.

Turning to V-Tor he growled, "Get those archers up there. I want those Giants stopped."

In total there were eleven bodies burning that night. Once V-Tor got the archers to start shooting, the Giants turned around and walked back to the forest, making disgruntled sounds and gestures.

Lost in her thoughts about forests, mountains and a familiar creek, Eirian jumped when she felt a tap on her shoulder. Startled, she spun around, coming face to face with Vlad. He glanced sheepishly at her. "I need to ask you something."

Eirian nodded, taking a step backward. Vlad followed, taking a step forward. "I... I..." He looked over his shoulder, and licking his lips turned back to her. This time a slight sneer graced his face. "I want to know how you put a spell on Lord Broan in spite of being bound by the Faery Binding Cord."

"WHAT?"

"You heard me. You put a spell on him so he'd let you stay here."

"There is no spell," she said, slowly creeping to the right. "The only thing that's kept me alive is my relationship with Ke-Hern."

Vlad matched her step and quickly reached for her. "I...We don't think so."

Eirian was surprised to see more Mortals coming up quickly behind Vlad. Eirian tried to pull free of Vlad's grip and when that didn't work she dug her nails into his hand. "Let me go!" she screamed, terror written across her face.

"We will not be doing that until you are outside the gates. Lord Broan may want to keep you here, but we don't. The Ny-dick are demanding you in exchange for peace, and we think that it's a fair trade."

Eirian drew up her right hand, with index and middle finger pointing outward and waited for the right moment. Quickly the pressure of her two fingers drove deep into Vlad's chest, forcing the air out of his lungs, causing his chest muscles to convulse. He doubled over, gasping for air as he dropped to his knees. Eirian pulled free, turned and started to run towards the inner bailey wall when two rocks hit her hard. Both struck her high on the back, causing her to stumble forward. She shook the pain off and she forced herself to gain back her stride. Another rock hit her on the back of the head. Stunned and dazed, she stumbled. Three pairs of hands instantly dragged her down to the ground. She could hear someone yell to get more rocks, but before anything else could happen, two arrows hit the ground near the group.

Now that Ardis had their attention, he threatened to launch another arrow at the Mortals closest to Eirian. The crowd froze. He stood on the steps of the kitchen hut, arrow drawn. He tossed his head up towards the guards up on the wall, they all had their bows pulled tight, waiting for Ardis' signal. The crowd parted and stepped back a few steps.

Broan ran to the inner bailey with Laeg right behind him. They slowed down when they saw Eirian laying on the ground and a mad crowd hovering over her. This was not good and Broan knew he had to be careful or his effort would all be for not. Broan looked at those who had gathered. His cold, ice blue eyes zeroed in on the few fresh-faced soldiers that were there, LansRo and Ryler included. He stared at them and their youthful cockiness, letting them see his disappointment with them. They didn't shy away.

"Ahh, young soldiers, oozing with immaturity and stupidity I'd say," V-Tor whispered quickly coming up beside Broan and Laeg.

Broan nodded his head, keeping his eyes on the crowd.

Vlad stepped forward, cleared his throat and squared his shoulders. "Lord Broan, it has come to our attention that the Ny-dick are willing to leave us in peace if we hand over this Faery."

Broan raised his chin, but said nothing. He always held an open court with his seasoned warriors and he was used to being challenged by them, but these were civilians, who knew little about military politics and posturing.

Vlad was uneasy with Broan's silence. He couldn't afford to mishandle this. Broan could just as easily turn against him, and send him out the gate instead of Eirian. "Lord Broan. We are all deeply indebted to you for saving us in Khumer and opening Solveig to all of us." He turned and looked back at those who had gathered with him. He nodded his head, hoping to get an agreement, the murmurs where positive, so he continued. "But we've waited long enough for you to resolve the Faery problem. We want you to act on the offer of peace the Ny-dick have given you."

"There was no peace offer."

Stepping forward, Vlad proclaimed loudly, "But we know that all they want is HER."

"Who told you such things?"

"Hmmm," Vlad said, a little confused and unsure as what to say. He looked back at the group.

"LOOK at me. Don't look at them! Since you wish to become a leader, start acting like one, NOW."

Vlad closed his eyes ready for a sword strike or a burst of arrows. But it didn't happen. In fact Broan actually gave him time to gather his thoughts and calm his nerves. He cleared his throat again. "Can you in all honesty, say that you received no terms to stop this siege?"

"I can and will say that demands were presented to me."

Vlad quickly pounced on the opportunity. "We all feel that the demands that were presented to you should be honored. This Faery has no worth to anyone here. Release her before this siege kills each and every one of us."

"So what you're saying, Vlad, is that you trust a Ny-dick…no actually a Shadow Dweller over me."

"NO, NO, of course not! I trust you. We all trust you. But keeping her here can only lead to disaster. How long before it's too late and everything ends in destruction, just because you fancy a Faery?"

"Fancy a Faery?" he questioned coldly.

Vlad paled and swallowed hard. Slowly nodding his head, he squeaked out the rest of his words. "You may have had good reason for keeping her alive and free among us, but you must see that it's been disaster after disaster since her arrival; Tellos death, the bug attack, the poison smoke…this very siege!"

Broan had to give Vlad credit for having the guts to stand up to him. He half smiled at Vlad. "I don't know… Perhaps Ke-Hern sent her here to keep her out of the Ny-dick's clutches, or to heal us from the Ny-dicks tricks like the smoke, the bugs…Maybe Ke-Hern sent her here to protect us and watch over our children as she did with Leif and Jelen. Maybe, just maybe, Ke-Hern knew we'd need her Faery skills against the Ny-dick's brutality and the Shadow Dwellers magic. They are both Faery, aren't they? Have any of you thought of that? Do you really think it's clever to reject her so coldly? Do you really think it wise to trust the honor of a Shadow Dweller?"

Vlad frowned "We've heard that she's a leader of an army that'll destroy us!"

Broan looked at Eirian. "Are you a leader of an army?"

"I…I…" Eirian stumbled.

"That's not too convincing, I'd say, by the looks on their faces, Eirian." A hush came over the crowd as they watched Broan approach Eirian. He drew his long knife out of his belt and looked back at Vlad. "So if you're right, what you're saying Vlad, is that you want me to set free the possible leader of that very army out there. Which makes handing her over to the enemy far too dangerous, I'd say." Broan looked over at one of the peach-faced young soldiers. He nodded his head towards the lad. "So what do you think I should do?"

"I...I..." Then the young soldier braced himself. "It's not wise to hand her over but it's also not wise to keep her here so...the only way I see out of this is to end her life. There's little mischief a dead Faery can do. They said if we hand her over, they'd leave. They didn't say she had to be alive."

Another civilian stepped up behind the young soldier and enthusiastically pushed him forward, "Yes! Yes! Ke-Hern would understand that it was us or her."

Someone else from the back spoke up, "Ke-Hern didn't send her with anything that would prove that he wanted us to protect her. I say kill her and end this now."

"Kill her! Kill her!" echoed from all around. "It's time for Lord Broan to do the right thing for all of us even if he's uncomfortable with it."

"Yes! Yes! If this offends him, we'll do it for him!"

The crowd quickly surged towards Eirian and Broan. He didn't move one inch. He didn't even blink. Every guard on the wall drew back their bows.

Bronagh couldn't believe what she was hearing. Furiously she started to rush towards Broan and Eirian when V-Tor quickly yanked her back by the scruff of her dress. He clamped one hand over her mouth and hauled Bronagh right off her feet. Pinning her to his chest, he spoke quietly in her ear. "You have to let this happen. If you want Eirian to live, Broan must get control of the civilians."

Bronagh's face paled. She watched Broan lower himself down, placing one knee on Eirian's lower back. Bronagh wanted to scream when he yanked the skullcap off and pulled hard on Eirian's hair forcing her back to arch sharply.

Eirian had to brace herself with both hands or suffer the pain of her hair being pulled out. She tried to dislodge Broan's hand with one of hers, but it didn't work. He pulled her head back even further, forcing her back into a more painful position. She refused to whimper and cry.

He looked up at the closest civilians. "Well, she has been a problem from the very beginning." He placed his knife up against the side of her stretched, bare neck. "Are you sure though, to kill her now, after waiting all this time for Ke-Hern." He pressed the tip of his blade against her neck and beads of blood formed. "But...what if... the Ny-dick need her alive? If she were dead, would there be any reason for them not to storm the castle? OR even worse, what if they WANT her dead because she is the only one that can save us from them?"

Silence.

"Now is not the time to dally, my friends. Do I kill her or not? Are you all willing, to take the chance that her being alive has been the only reason the Ny-dick have only played with our defenses and not fully attacked us?"

Still no one spoke.

Broan looked at the crowd. "Well I can't wait all day. A quick jab of the knife into the artery and then a swift pull through her neck and she'll be dead in seconds. If you're right we'll have peace, if not, then we're all dead. So which is it?"

"Let her go," Vlad whispered. "I...WE...we didn't think this...I'm...No...we're all sorry for doubting you, Bro...sorry, Warlord Broan."

"Good man," Broan said letting go of Eirian's hair. He rose. "Until we have more knowledge," his voice boomed, "I plan to keep her alive and unharmed! I'll be counting on your support! No more of this...this craziness." He said swinging his arms in a broad sweep.

Everyone nodded their heads.

Broan turned. "You, you and you, LansRo," He smiled feral, "Come with me. Now."

The alarms suddenly sounded stopping Broan mid-step. He turned and in seconds had climbed the tower staircase wondering if he should just take up residence there. V-Tor was close behind him and once up top they met BroMac. "Didn't look too good down there, need to talk about it?"

Broan shook his head as he grabbed BroMac on the shoulder and gave an assuring squeeze, "What's happening?

"Look," BroMac motioned Broan over to the open window of the watchtower. From there, Broan could see the Giants working around the river. They were hauling trees and stone, some the size of a man's body, towards its edge.

"It looks like they plan to build a bridge over the river and then who knows, maybe fill in the ditch with wood and earth," BroMac speculated. "Look over there in amongst the trees to the left. They've made a siege tower."

Broan looked away, "And most likely a battering ram." He wiped his forehead with his hand as he thought of the next course of action.

"Should we start shooting on them?" A very agitated V-Tor asked.

"No," Broan answered as he thought for a moment. "It'll be just a waste of arrows. They're too far out of range. No, this'll take something else, something as big as the Giants themselves to bring them down."

Suddenly Broan was off, running down steps two at time with BroMac and V-Tor right behind him. "Where the hell is Laeg?"

"Checking the south wall," BroMac answered from behind Broan.

Broan hit the ground of the outer bailey and started barking orders. Time was not on their side and they would have only one chance at this. "BroMac go get Laeg, GarrRod and few others. Meet me in the Main-Hall. NOW!"

V-Tor just couldn't keep up with Broan. "The man has the stride of a horse," he said to himself as he stopped to catch his breath. V-Tor bent over, placing his hands on his knees. "This just isn't right," he said to himself. He reached out his hand to let Broan and BroMac know he was in trouble, but they were long past his reach. He tried to straighten up, but weak with vertigo and shortness of breath, V-Tor's legs buckled under him.

Once inside the Keep, Broan went to his bedchamber and retrieved a roll of old plans from his trunk. He unrolled them as he rushed down the stairs towards the Main-Hall. "We need to open the dam." Broan said, looking up at the group. "If we can open the dam while they're working on the bridge, there's a good chance we'll flood them out. It may not stop them, but it'll certainly delay them."

"So who gets to run the gamut?" Laeg asked. "The Ny-dick will have archers ready for whoever tries to leave."

"Yes, but..." Broan turned his attention to BroMac, "Do you remember the fissure we used to divert some of the water when we built the dam?"

BroMac nodded. "But we filled it up with rock and debris because it now ends within the walls of Solveig."

"But not enough to seal it... if we open it up Laeg and GarrRod can get through. They would come out just up from the dam. They could work their way down and knock the supports out."

"What about Solveig? Will the foundation hold when the water rushes at her?"

Broan stood and looked at BroMac. "She'll have to."

"Laeg and GarrRod, get ready. BroMac and..." Broan suddenly realized V-Tor was not with them. "Where's V-Tor?"

Broan and the others found V-Tor passed out on the ground just inside the outer bailey. "Take him to the Keep." Broan ordered the men nearby. "Then find Eirian. She'll take care of him." Quickly he motioned for Laeg to get going, "GO!" Broan insisted. "We don't have much time."

135

"You've quite a bump and a cut on the back of your head. Do you have any cream I can put on it?" Bronagh asked as she picked through Eirian's hair.

"No. My supplies have run out. There's nothing left."

Bronagh helped Eirian up. "Broan may be seeing the light…" she paused briefly, "If he had wanted to kill you he wouldn't have hesitated."

Half smiling, Eirian shook her head. "That I doubt. He made it very clear the other day."

"Eirian come quick!" Leif's voice rang out between gulps of air. "Jelen's ill and Faber told me to get you quickly, so I ran all the way."

Eirian and Bronagh exchanged looks. "This isn't good," Eirian said to Bronagh. "Not good at all."

Upon arriving, they found Jelen in a cataleptic state and he was extremely warm to the touch. "Is anyone else in the family sick?" Eirian asked as she sat down on the edge of Jelen's cot.

"No. He's been very moody lately, but he seemed fine. Then suddenly out of the blue, he collapsed."

"You're sure you feel okay. You've been with him the most lately."

"Yes…Yes I'm fine. Eirian what could be wrong with him?" Faber couldn't hold back the tears any longer. "Please Eirian save him. He's my youngest."

Leif hung just inside the door watching Faber cry. "Will he be okay?" he asked

"Maybe with your help." She rose from Jelen's bedside. "I need you to find me some flat smooth stones." She took Leif's hand and with her index finger showed him the sizes she was looking for. "Do you think you could get your friends to help?"

"Yes. Yes of course." He started out the door, but spun around. "How many do you need?"

"About twenty."

"Okay." Leif suddenly reached into his pocket and removed a stone. He rushed back to Eirian and handed her the rock. "This is Jelen's lucky stone. I know he'd want it near him." He pressed it into her hand and ran off.

"Do you really need the stones or are you trying to keep him busy?" Bronagh asked, watching her son charge off across the training field towards the inner wall.

"I really need the stones." She put her arms around Faber to comfort her. "Faber, I need your help too, but first we must move Jelen to the Keep."

Leif came through the gate of the inner wall and nearly ran into Idwal. "Where's Eirian?" Idwal asked.

"She's at Jelen's hut." He kept running. He was on an important mission and nothing was going to detour him from it.

Idwal ran to the hut and barged in just as Eirian was picking Jelen up. He stopped quickly. "What's happened?"

"Jelen's sick. I need to get him to the Keep."

Idwal took Jelen from Eirian's arms, "V-Tor's ill too. They found him passed out on the ground. Broan asked me to find you."

BroMac and a team of strong men crashed through the pile of stones. It wasn't a big hole, but it would be enough for Laeg and GarrRod to get through. "We'll have archers up on the south side of the wall. If they see any movement from the Ny-dick, we'll start shooting. That should give you and GarrRod some cover," Broan said as he slapped Laeg on the shoulder. "Good Luck."

Laeg motioned to GarrRod and went through the narrow opening and into the dark crevice of cold granite and sandstone. Once inside, Laeg lit the torch and the two of them followed the corridor of rubble and boulders, created long ago by the land shifting.

GarrRod marched behind Laeg, carrying the two battle-axes they needed to cut through the wood supports of the dam. "I'm glad Broan didn't listen to V-Tor and put in a stone dam. I don't think we'd have enough time to take it down." He checked over his shoulder at the vanishing light of the entrance and suddenly bumped into Laeg, who stood frozen in front of him. Just beyond the dim torchlight he could see two yellow eyes staring back at them. GarrRod could hear the distinctive sound of rasping scales and the warning rattle echo off the walls. "I hate snakes," he cursed.

"Well, it's between us and the way up," Laeg whispered, slowly raising his bow and arrow. The long pull of animal gut string vibrated around them. With a sharp hiss, the snake shot forward at the offending men, only to be met with Laeg's arrow. It caught the snake just below its head and threw it against a large boulder.

Quickly, Laeg and GarrRod started to scramble up the precipitous side of the fissure. After a two hundred meter climb they finally emerged. Looking around Laeg was relieved there was no sign of the enemy. "Come on," he whispered as he hunched over and started out. Together they slipped through the trees towards the dam.

An earth shattering crash echoed throughout the area as the river began its rampage. Tons of water once held back by the dam, now rushed down past the fortress. Suddenly a thundering vortex of water slammed into Ny-dick and Giants, washing many away.

Rushing up the stairs of the tower, Broan was surprised to find that he couldn't take two stairs at a time and that his knees wobbled as he went up. He barely made it to the window and had to rest against the wall.

Eirian ran into the Main-Hall and finding no one there quickly turned and ran up the stairs. She found V-Tor on a bed in a small room just off of the second landing. A young guard was trying to ease V-Tor out of his tunic.

"I'll take over," she said as she pushed the young man away. "I need you to get a cot in here and lots of wood to burn." She didn't even look up at him to see if he was going to respond. "NOW!" she screamed. She heard him run off and she smiled. "It works. Yelling to get your way, really works. No wonder Broan always uses it."

Idwal marched in with Jelen in his arms. "Where do you want him?"

"As soon as the cot gets here I want him by the fire place." She continued to undress V-Tor. "Faber, I need you to go and get me small pieces of cedar, amber leaf and pine cones. There should be some around after the rain." She gave Bronagh a quick look as she tried to turn V-Tor over. "I'll need a large basin with water in it, string and nails, oh and also linens and towels." She stopped for a moment. "Cinnamon...cinnamon, if we have any."

Chapter 8

"Trouble has a rapacious appetite."

- BroMac

Eirian had no herbs to make teas or potions. She mentally reviewed everything Ke-Hern had taught her. She had wet the flat garden stones that Leif had brought her, and they were now warming near the fire. Although she didn't like the strange feeling Jelen's stone gave off, she hoped Leif was right and that it was lucky. She had tucked in into Jelen's hand sometime ago. She now stood looking at her two patients, Ke-Hern taught her lots about healing but never with so little resources.

Knowing she had to start somewhere she went and picked up a clean cloth and a pot of water from its warming place. She walked over to Jelen's cot and gently pulled down the sheet that covered him. "Oh no," she whispered to herself, sitting back on her heels. Purple blisters filled with blood had developed on his torso.

She quickly moved to V-Tor's bed. He was such a strong man who made people either feel safe or threatened, depending on which side of "bad" you were on. Yet right now, he was simply ill, his strength weakening and his body weary. Lowering the sheet that covered him revealed dark blisters just beginning to form. These were from the Sulpets all right, but both V-Tor's and Jelen's bites had long ago healed perfectly. It didn't make sense that they would now be infected. "Except…if..!" Eirian muttered out loud.

Eirian stood at the doorway, with one hand on the latch and the other near her heart. She tried to appear calm, but it was all she could do to keep her composure. She had to convince Broan to trust her. Two lives were at stake. "Bronagh I'm going to go talk to Broan. I need those plants for V-Tor and Jelen to make it. Chucks of wet cedar hanging from nails and warm stones won't save them."

She found Broan and the others in a somber mood, their voices nearly inaudible as they sat around anxiously waiting for any news about V-Tor and Jelen. Ignoring everyone, Eirian simply walked over to where Broan was sitting and raised her bound wrist. "I need you to remove the binding cord so I can fly and get some Simaca; it only grows in the forest under the acidic pine trees to the north." Getting no reaction she continued, "It'll save them from this illness."

The silence was deafening. She stepped forward as her words tried to fill the void. "I know I've asked you before to set me free, but this time it's different. I'm not asking for myself, I'm asking for those who lay deathly ill upstairs. I don't even care if you put the damn thing back on after I get back. Just let me go and get what I need. Let me help them."

Broan said nothing, staring at her through heavy eyes. Eirian raised her chin, "You should have told me the truth about Conn's death and that his blood was spilled. I would have been more prepared for this."

Broan's ice blue eyes narrowed in response to her reprimand.

Eirian bowed her head and got down on her knees. If she had to beg she would. "If you won't take the cord off, then let me climb down the outer wall. Hopefully I'll be able to get what I need from the rubble fortification at the base of Solveig. I noticed moss and plants growing down there."

Strange, Broan thought to himself. He had not thought Eirian would humble herself before him. This really was important to her. He continued to watch Eirian, intrigued to see what she would do next.

Eirian didn't cry, instead she let her shoulders slump as she sat back on her heels. "What are you so scared of?" she asked boldly.

One of Broan's eyebrows shot up and his head slipped back ever so slightly, but still he held his tongue.

Angrily Eirian stood and glared at Broan, "Time is wasting. I've had enough of your game. One way or another I will get my supplies." She started towards the door.

140

"STOP!" Broan yelled as he staggered to his feet. "What if I order you to either go back to taking care of V-Tor and Jelen, or go back to the locked tower?"

"Like I said, one way or another I will get those supplies. That's how much those Mortals upstairs mean to me," she said heading for the door.

Broan didn't make a sound and watched in fascination. He eyed his warriors and they were ready. Some had their hands on their long knifes while others were tense, ready to jump her. "Eirian," he called out to her. "You're sure of this? You would defy my orders for them? At any cost?"

She stopped, turned. Her eyes narrowed as she stared back at him in defiance. "It's not would I, it's I will or I'll die trying. You really are an idiot!"

"Then go," he breathed out. The pain from his body was beginning to penetrate his stoic image and Broan knew he could not hold on any longer. "OH damn…" was the start of a curse from deep within as he collapsed onto the floor.

With Broan sprawled unconscious on the floor there was no way for anyone to confirm what they all thought he said or why he had agreed to let her climb down the outer wall. BroMac and Laeg stood looking at each other while Eirian pushed her way through the group who now hovered over Broan. She eased open his shirt and just as she feared, blood filled lesions spotted his chest.

"Get him upstairs with the others and be careful not to disturb the lesions! I'll be a quick as I can!" she said as started towards the door.

Laeg grabbed her arm, abruptly stopping her exit.

"I don't have time for this," she said as she motioned towards Broan. "Distilled down to the bare truth Laeg, the question is, do you want Broan and the others to live… or not?" She paused. "So which is it?"

"Fine!" he said, "BUT there will be archers at the wall, and if you make one wrong move, they will be ordered to kill you."

Eirian nodded. "I'll need my tunic, a knife, and a pack to put the plants in."

"I have a pack you can use," Idwal offered.

"Good. Go and get it. Then meet us at the north end of the wall." She looked back at Laeg, "Shall we go?"

Eirian brought the hood of her tunic up and over her head and leaned over the edge of the parapet. She looked for the safest and most direct route down but this area of the wall still gave her pause. It would have been treacherous in the daylight. At night it was going to be deadly. She turned towards Laeg. "It's time to go," she said, quickly scanning the row of archers behind him. He was obviously still very uneasy about the situation.

"Wait up," Laeg demanded as he firmly took hold of her shoulder. "Ardis and I will be watching and waiting. Ardis will be over there," he tossed his head in Ardis' direction further down the outer wall, "and I will over there, near the tower. One step away from the fortification, and we will shoot."

From those positions Eirian knew they would have a clear and easy shot at her. She smiled at him. "That's what I'm counting on. I'd rather be killed by your arrow than be lunch for some Ny-dick."

"Ny-dick are the least of your worries," Laeg retorted sternly. "We'll be watching."

As Laeg walked away to take up his position, Eirian pulled herself up and sat on the edge of the parapet. She looked down. A myriad of boulders encircled the fortress wall. They stood, slanted steeply towards the fortress. Their shadows were deeper, twisted and blacker than the night. She prayed they held the plants she needed.

Eirian glanced at Laeg and Ardis. Both stood with bows drawn tight. She could see the steel tips of their arrows glinting in the moonlight. She nodded to them and then eased herself over the edge and onto the wall.

It was slow going and nerve jarring. Gripping onto stone edges with tense cold fingers and toes of her boots, she moved as fast as she could. She had to get down before any Ny-dick got curious.

Eirian dropped the last five feet onto one of the larger rocks below and regretted it immediately. She slipped on the slick face of the boulder, hitting her hip and twisting her ankle. Biting back the pain from the impact Eirian gingerly scrambled to the top of the stone. She waved to those who waited up top for her, letting them know she wasn't making a run for it. She was greeted with a row of arrows, all pointing down at her.

Sucking in a deep breath, she tested her ankle and decided to slide back down the side and into the recesses between the rocks where a velvety carpet of moss, brimmed with moisture. When she stepped on it, she sank. Water flowed over the tops of her boots and within moments she was shivering violently. "Great," she cursed.

Hunched over in the cold water and rubbing her legs furiously, she realized she hadn't thought this part out carefully enough. There wasn't much light to see by. Boulders, the fortress wall, and a very narrow view of the night sky were all she had to navigate with. She knew and understood walls and cliff faces, but jumbles of stone and rock were not her specialty; that was Giants' work and care. She let out the breath lodged in her chest. This infection, which would soon command the body and mind of three Mortals, needed special herbs and a deep faith to conquer it. Their lives were in her hands. She had to get moving.

Eirian snaked between various sized boulders and down the naturally made corridors. Stumbling along, she searched all the crevices, nooks and crannies for anything that held the adaptive agents within them, healing powers that had the ability to work doubly hard at aiding the body. Spying some greenery, Eirian pulled out the small knife that Idwal had given her and quickly began to cut and gather it. Disappointed once she figured out what it was, she paused for a moment and looked up at the warriors. Their arrows were still pointed steadily at her. "If I could just get some Simaca! Damn them!"

Closing her eyes Eirian centered herself. "Think…Think…" she muttered to herself. "Mushrooms! Yes, it might work," She would be happy if she could find Reishi, and Ash-Wadanlha mushrooms, which would at least eased the convulsions that usually came with this type of infection. Peering around her, Eirian finally accepted she would have to make the things that lived at the bottom of Solveig work. She began to cut and stow various plants into her pack again.

Minutes later after reviewing what she had gotten, she scanned the area a little further away from the wall and a whole lot drier. Eirian pointed to where she needed to go, hoping Laeg would understand. Building up her courage she scuttled around the last tall boulder and onto firmer ground where the boulders were less orderly. They were scattered further apart which allowed more of the sunlight to touch the ground around them and this in turn allowed different types of plant to grow.

Feeling more exposed, she quickly checked to see if there was any movement from the enemy's camp. Nothing was moving, except the Giant, Stamas, who paced impatiently keeping vigil at the forest edge since he arrived. She wasn't sure how to let him know that for the most part, she was fine. She knew any overt movement would be taken as betrayal by those above. She sighed and although the binding cord negated magic, she chanted anyways just hoping the earth would pass her message on.

Pulling out a few spindly twigs from the ground, she studied them. Yes! This plant contained some Wizard's wart. Still not the best but it would come in handy. Greatly satisfied and brimming with newfound hope, Eirian turned and headed back towards the wall. So over-whelmed with energy, she didn't realize that the long strides her legs made were limp-free or that she felt absolutely no pain anywhere or any cold. She swiftly latched onto the stone outer wall and ascended quickly. Before she knew it, Eirian was stretching up to grab the hands that awaited her. She was instantly pulled up and over the top and into Solveig.

She turned quickly to look at Stamas, the Giant. She caught his wave and smiled, then watched him move on away from the edge of the clearing, and away from harm. She knew the other Giants would follow him. Giddy with one thing less to worry about Eirian smiled. "Well you won't have to worry about the Giants anymore."

"What?" Laeg asked.

"They're leaving," she answered quickly and started for the stairs. Rushing after her, Laeg grabbed her arm, stopping her descent. "But why?" he demanded. "What did you do?"

"Nothing!" Eirian turned and looked at him. "Look sometimes there's no answer to why. Just be glad they're leaving."

Laeg's eyes narrowed. "Sometimes why is the most important question of all!"

Eirian shrugged her shoulders and patted her backpack. "I've work to do."

Eirian's boots were still full of water as she walked across the bailey and into the Keep. They made squishy sounds on the stone floor and left a trail of water in their wake. She rushed up the stairs and into the sickroom, removed her tunic and boots and hurriedly put her on her shift.

She knew that her ability to sense what needed to be done was going to be put to the test. Ke-Hern wasn't here to guide her hand and give her encouragement. She took in a deep breath, filling her lungs. The combined odors of cedar, pine and spices, cleared her head.

Eirian quickly gave some orders. As soon as all the needed pans, utensils and other items were gathered from the Keep, it was time to get down to work. She needed to fully concentrate on her three patients, and everyone there was too personally involved. She knew she needed to clear the room.

After much begging and protesting, Faber, Bronagh and the others agreed to leave if and only if two aids - Suh, a kitchen maid and Gurnee, a young soldier - were allowed to stay. Eirian didn't like the compromise. Still, she had to agree, the extra pairs of hands and feet would be a huge help to her.

Eirian stopped BroMac just before he stepped out the door. "They have a virulent type of infection, and it will take time before we know if your son and the others are able to fight it off. Take care of Faber; the wait will be extra hard on her. Oh, please make sure that she drinks this tea…often." She paused, "And you'll need to take it as well. This infection can transfer to others when blood is…"

BroMac didn't say anything at first. Taking the tealeaves from Eirian, he turned and started towards the door. "Use the two aids well. I'll be back to check in on things from time to time. I'm not as trusting as Laeg."

Eirian nodded, turned and looked at the young girl, Suh. It didn't take long before she had Suh packing, cutting, mixing, boiling, and soaking various bits and pieces of the plants.

Once that was on its way, she looked towards Gurnee the young soldier. "Because you are a soldier I'm sure you are good with that knife of yours. I need you to carefully cut free twenty threads from my skull cap," she said as she removed her cap. "Only twenty!"

"I'm a warrior not a maid. My knife is for fighting not trimming threads."

"Stop thinking of yourself! Your skill will be fine enough and your job is worthy of a warrior, for without those threads the stones won't work." She handed him the cap. "Now get on with it or I'll ask for another aid. I've much to prepare if all is to go well."

Gurnee took the skullcap and slumped down by the fire. Thoughts of simply destroying the cap, made him smile. He took out his knife and paused. He looked over at the sick men and shook his head. "So the threads have magic? Broan won't be happy to hear this," he muttered.

"It isn't the threads that hold the magic, it's the stones. The threads just capture it like a spider's web so we can use it." Eirian stood with her hands on her hips, staring down at Gurnee. "Look, just remove the threads. If Broan makes it through you can tell him all about the threads, but for now I need your help. No actually Broan, V-Tor and Jelen need your help. So either help…or leave."

Gurnee nodded with a slight frown. Quietly, he began, using the fine tip of his knife to loosen the threads. Although he bent over his task, he still kept an eye on Eirian just like Laeg told him to.

Once the threads were removed from the now slightly damaged cap, Eirian placed it back on her head and smiled at Gurnee. "Very good, now watch." She took a single thread and wrapped it around a stone.

Gurnee felt rather odd, learning a Wizard's spell. He realized that she trusted him more than he trusted her. Slowly, picking up a rich red colored thread, he began wrapping it around a palm-sized stone. "Life gives us much to learn…"

"And often not from where you'd think it should," Eirian finished for him.

Gurnee helped Eirian turn the men over onto their sides. Then she placed the warm stones on the beds where their lower backs and their shoulder blades would lay. "I need to place these rocks just right. Think of it as a board game of war. The stones are helping the defense of areas they warm, to fight back the infection," she said, easing the men onto their backs. Then she rolled down the sheets of linen to the men's hips and rolled up the sheets from their feet. She positioned warm stones and moss at the base of their feet. "South," she said out loud. Then she placed some at the top of their heads "North," she continued as she surveyed her handy work.

Eirian was pleased for the moment. "Once we get their fever down a bit," she said, "we'll need to work on their blisters." Eirian looked through the remaining plants she had gathered and was again disappointed. She couldn't find any that were haustoria-like - able to penetrate the outer layers of its host and able to absorb water, and deadly mineral salts. She had hoped to use them to draw out the blood and infection in the blisters. She sat back on her heels. *"I'll have to do it the hard way and make a drying pack to draw the infection out."* That meant she would have to poke a hole in each blister before applying the pack. Once she opened the blisters there would be a greater chance that the illness could spread. She looked up at Suh and Gurnee and decided to hold off as long as possible. She knew she would have to be very, very careful.

"Suh, I need you to go and find me a sewing needle. A big one, not one used for embroidering."

"Oh you mean a darning needle."

"Is it big?"

"Yes," Suh said quietly.

Eirian smiled at her. "Then that would be perfect. Once you get the needle for me you can go back to your own bed and sleep. If I need you later I'll have Gurnee call for you."

Then she addressed Gurnee. "Go and get a mat to sleep on. Place it over by the window. I fear we'll be here for many sunrises."

Once both aids left to do her bidding, Eirian tore a piece from the linen on Jelen's bed. She glanced once at the closed door then began wrapping the wrist that was irritated by the binding cord. She couldn't chance getting it infected. She touched Jelen's forehead, very concerned. It wouldn't be long before the seizures would start, and the real battle for life would begin.

The transition from powerful Warlord to sick patient was bumpy. Broan's head was full of cobwebs and clouds. He felt paralyzed with pain. Each and every muscle shrieked in agony. Even the tips of his fingers burned from simply resting them on the linen sheet. He wasn't sure where that evil smell was coming from, but if it didn't go away, he was sure he was going to heave. He could hear himself challenge Eirian, but he wasn't sure why. He could feel the feathery touch of her cool hands on his body, yet he couldn't understand why she would do that. Broan could hear her plead with him to fight yet firm hands held him down. He yelled in protest again and again. It wasn't long before he slipped from semi-consciousness into a delirium. After that it was an easy short passage to another dimension of the intellect. He welcomed falling into the strange abyss.

A ripple of musical words expanded around him, forming shapes and images. Broan was completely enraptured and not at all afraid.

"You have found your way back to us."

The woman with fiery eyes from his intimate encounter with Eirian was smiling at him. He smiled back at her.

"You are lucky to have Eirian as your physician. She is very skilled."

"What do you know of Eirian?" Broan asked as he watched his own voice explode with song, lights, and color.

"There are many secrets that shroud her yet she works to save you. You would be wise to accept her gift."

"I don't know if what she offers is a gift or a trick," Broan muttered through clenched teeth.

The lady hovered over him and looked deep into his eyes and into his soul. *"There is risk in every new experience. Eirian has risked and continues to risk everything for you and the future."* She touched his face gently and his skin tightened uncomfortably under the intense heat of her fingers.

"Risk is not to be taken lightly when you are a Warlord."

"Feel what you want but you will do what we ask of you." She paused and stared at him. *"You must protect Eirian until she fulfills her duty."*

"And what is her duty?"

The lady got closer and placed her cheek against his. *"First, she must lead the Faeries into battle and then..."* she sang into his ear.

"Damn!" he cursed gruffly as he tried to push the phantom away.

"You have nothing to fear from Eirian."

Broan shook her off. "I'll be the judge of that! Why should I save someone who'll battle..."

"*You will do what we have asked of you.*"

"And if I don't?" Broan asked.

The woman with the fiery eyes stared at Broan. "*We will offer her to another for protection.*"

The words cut Broan deep. He began to shiver uncontrollably. His bones felt like ice and his flesh felt dead.

"*Do I have your commitment to keep her near and protect her?*" Her eyes narrowed, her patience running thin. "*Once the Faery curse is over you can release her. In fact we are counting on it.*"

Broan simply nodded his head. "Keeping her near, protecting her is not as easy as it looks."

"*There is always another who will do the job.*" The lady took his face between her two hands and made him look into her eyes. "*Quickly, Eirian calls you back to your world, but before you go remember this. Eirian holds more than just your future in her hands. She holds the Faeries, ours' and even the lands' so it would be wise to take care of her in this time of war.*"

"Who are you?" he whispered.

With no answer to his question, and without pause, Broan lunged for the mysterious lady. She swiftly disappeared leaving him to fight desperately against invisible arms. He screamed in frustration until he heard Eirian's voice again, distant and defiantly strong. He slowly came to realize that Eirian always knew, somehow, what it would take to make a sanctuary within the wild chaos that was his soul. Her words worked like a balm and soothed his frustration into sleep.

The early morning sun broke through the window and rested fully on Eirian. Hot and bleary eyed, she rose and dropped the drapes over it. The room had been kept as hot as possible. Eirian wanted Broan, V-Tor and Jelen to sweat because she knew it was a good way of cleansing the body. This of course meant that she, Suh, and Gurnee had to work through the humid heat.

Absentmindedly Eirian reached up, drove a finger under her skullcap and scratched. Frustrated, she loosened the one long braid from under the cap and allowed it to fall down her back. She tugged at the neck of her shift. Other than the rose colored Faery chemise, the shift was all she wore. Long gone were her Faery shirt, tights and boots, all tossed aside so she could work more comfortably at saving her charges. The freedom from all those clothes felt good to Eirian, yet she still fought with the coarse shift that now scratched at her skin and hung heavy over her body. "My Faery clothes would be a lot more comfortable. Not that you care one bit," she muttered to an unconscious Broan.

BroMac entered the room, jarring her from her unpleasant thoughts. First he walked over to Jelen and then to Broan and V-Tor. He smirked at himself, finding that her placement of the stones were similar to the ones he had placed around the tree. "So I wasn't that far off," he whispered.

"Yes you were because you forgot the threads. They are needed to draw the power out of the stones." she muttered back, absentmindedly.

"But ho…w…How?"

Eirian turned and looked at him. "How what?"

Unnerved, BroMac quickly changed the subject. "By the gods Eirian, does this room have to be so hot?"

Gurnee looked up from his mat. "It's cool compared to what we've been working in. Eirian wouldn't let me open the window even a pinch until the fevers broke." He stretched and got up, then looked over to Eirian. "I'll go and get freshened up then I'll bring you back some food."

Eirian smiled weakly at him. "Why don't you take the time and join the others for the morning meal. I still have food left over from yesterday."

Gurnee gave her a worried look. "I'll be back with food for you and this time you'll eat it."

BroMac stood back and watched this little encounter. It was not what he expected to hear from Gurnee, yet if truth were told, he was worried about Eirian as well. In the brief moments he spent when he came to check on them, he had watched Eirian work with determination and intensity. She had never let up for even a minute. It hadn't taken long for him to appreciate that his son was in the best possible hands.

Eirian stood with her back to BroMac. The slumped shoulders gave testimony to the heavy weight they had been carrying of late. He doubted if she had anything other than momentary interludes of sleep. "It's not been easy has it?" he asked. Suddenly uncomfortable with his line of question, he cleared his throat, "I've noticed much improvement in Jelen."

Eirian walked over to Jelen's side. "His fever broke before the others, and he seems to be slowly getting stronger. There's a good chance he'll pull through. How's Faber holding up? Is she still angry at me?"

BroMac chuckled. "She wanted so badly to be with Jelen. I had to hold her back twice. She was going to storm in here and fight you if she had to. This was the hardest thing she's ever had to do."

Eirian looked down at Jelen's resting body. "It's hard to watch your child lay sick and so close to death. I knew she wasn't emotionally strong enough to watch what I knew had to be done. I hope someday she'll understand."

"She already does. She may not like it, but she knows you only had Jelen's best interest in mind." He stood up a little straighter. "Have you had any sleep lately?"

She smiled at him. "Yes, in fact I was just having the most wonderful dream about bolting into a cloudless sky and feeling freer than ever before."

He raised an eyebrow. "I know that even with the archers you could have…" he paused for a moment. "Why did you return?"

Eirian let her shoulders drop even more. "I came back because I said I would." She looked BroMac in the eye. "Would you have done any less?"

"No, no less," he finally answered her. "Why do the Ny-dick want you dead?"

Eirian rolled her eyes and began to make herself busy. "They pretty much want everyone dead that they can't control."

"And Giants?"

"They're too much a part of nature. They don't want any death on their souls unless it's necessary to protect what they hold dear," Eirian answered quietly as she straightened Jelen's bed coverings. "So are you going to trust me a little more now?"

"Don't know…" BroMac smiled slightly, "Yet."

The day spilled into night once again, without much further progress. V-Tor, Jelen and Broan still lay in a slumber. Eirian had run out of ideas. Gone were the incenses and cedar strips, only the warm stones remained. Eirian sat by Broan's bed, and Gurnee slept on his mat. Suh had long ago been sent back to her family with deep thanks for all of her help. Eirian knew it was now up to her patients to win the battle.

In the night's silence, Eirian began to talk to Broan in an effort to keep awake. "You know, for many years we Faeries have lived in darkness and despair without any hope, suspended as we are between life and death." Eirian yawned and leaned more on her elbows, which were planted firmly on the edge of Broan's bed. "But now we live because we have hope."

She was so tired. She lowered her head onto her arms that were now laying flat on the soft bed. "Just for a second," she said to herself as she slipped into a deep sleep.

Broan's hand found its way to Eirian's face. It slowly ran along the edge of her skullcap and then finally came to rest, cupping her jaw.

Broan awoke to the feeling of a heartbeat against the fingers of his right hand. It took a lot of effort to open his eyes, but he wasn't disappointed. He looked down to see Eirian leaning on his bed, asleep. His hand was curled around the gentle curve of her jaw and his baby finger bounced to the rhythm of her heartbeat. Her braided auburn hair fell out from under the back of her skullcap and cascaded over her shoulder. She was alive…NO… he was alive! Eirian stirred and he smiled at her as she opened her eyes. "Good morning," he said.

"Good morning," came from familiar voice in the next bed.

Broan turned his head to look at V-Tor and smiled at him.

"What time is it?" asked Jelen.

Broan raised his head to look at Jelen. "Your father will be very pleased to hear you talk, young man." He let his head fall back and looked at Eirian again. "So, did you leave Solveig?"

She stood slowly. "YES."

He smiled at her again. Was he smiling so much because he had fought the battle of his life and won, or was it that Eirian did what she said she would do, and saved them all? He enjoyed remembering her battle cry, "*I will or die trying*." Everything else he just wanted to forget.

Eirian woke up Gurnee. "Go; get Laeg, Bronagh, BroMac, and Faber. Tell them the good news, but please be quiet, we don't need the whole Keep up here."

She checked Jelen, then went to the fireplace and made some hot honey water for them to drink. "If you feel up to it by noon you can have some thick, meaty broth."

"Broth!" V-Tor protested, "I could eat a horse!"

Eirian laughed at him. "Well, maybe in time. You have all just fought your way back from death's door. Let's just take it easy on your poor stomachs for today."

Eirian gave Jelen his sweet water first and then walked towards V-Tor.

"I know Broan told you not to wear Faery clothes, but aren't you suppose to wear something under your shift?" V-Tor asked as he stared at her bare arms and well-exposed cleavage.

Eirian blushed. "Well now I know for certain you're back to normal." She helped V-Tor take a sip of his drink and then went to help Broan.

"You're shaking! Are you all right?" Broan asked, concerned. Then he saw her bound wrist and gave her a questioning look.

151

She quickly hid it behind her back. "I'm fine. I'm just tired. I've spent a week taking care of you three."

"How long?" V-Tor asked. He was surprised at the amount of time that had passed.

"She said a week," Jelen answered. "We slept a week."

"I only wish that's all you did. I'm afraid there was a whole lot more to it than just sleep, and Gurnee and I have the bruises to prove it." She slumped down on the stool at the side of Broan's bed. She just couldn't stand up anymore. Now that the battle was over and her heightened energy had retreated, she was left with a very worn out, barely awake body.

Eirian got up from her stool, inched back against the wall, as the room crowded with people and happy energy. She watched in fascination as BroMac chuckled with delight as he hugged Jelen. Faber rubbed her son's back with a familiar, loving touch. A comfortable smile form on Jelen's face as he welcomed a much-needed connection with family.

She stared at Bronagh and Laeg as they stood around V-Tor and Broan. They were all joking and teasing each other. She stood in silence as the energy bubbled and danced upon the laughter of friends, lightening everyone's mood, everyone's but hers. All she could do at that moment was to painfully accept the cold hard fact that she was not a part of these strong bonds of blood and affection.

Mortal feelings surged, intense and still unfamiliar. She felt hurt, knowing she had been forced to live on the sidelines of this thing that all Mortals shared. This group of connected Mortals had unknowingly awakened a new truth in her, one that up until now she had never been aware of. Before the curse, the Faeries where Mortal and still to this day have memories of the closeness of kinship and love but it had never been a part of her life.

In the midst of utter exhaustion, self-doubt raised its ugly head. She felt the sting of being dismissed by all in her life, and she quickly descended into a dark emotional pit filled with loneliness. She suddenly needed to leave the room and this joyous picture frame of life that she was not a part of.

Eirian quietly walked through the doorway and didn't look back. As she walked down the stairs, anxieties and fears surfaced like a tidal wave. The emotional pain was so intense. Wishing to relieve the pain and pressure, she pressed her hand hard against her chest and whimpered with an uncontrolled sob.

She needed to get out - out of the Keep, out of Solveig, away from the harsh reality of what they had and what she never could or would have. She clawed at the binding cord. "I want to go back, back to my life and away from here and all these feelings." She cried in frustration when her efforts to remove the cord only made the cord contract even tighter around her wrist.

She pushed through the door of the Keep and ran down the front stairs. The agony gripped her harder this time. She clutched her chest and cried out at its cruelty.

RohDin watched Eirian exit from the Keep, and by the level of her distress, he felt there was nothing but bad news on the wind. He rushed up the stairs and into the Keep, taking two steps at a time. He ran into the room that housed Broan and the others, expecting the worst and froze at the laughter and cajoling that greeted him. "The way Eirian was acting, I...I thought someone died."

Everyone stopped talking and looked around. Eirian was gone. "What do you mean, the way Eirian was acting?" Laeg asked.

"She was crying."

Broan tried to get up from his bed, but Laeg pressed him back down. "We'll handle this." He motioned to BroMac and RohDin to come with him.

"You better listen to him, Broan," V-Tor suggested. "Remember it was one of your decrees. Until you can raise your sword to defend your people, he's Warlord." Broan chaffed at being reminded of his own words.

V-Tor shifted uncomfortably in his bed and suddenly realized he had no clothes on under the sheet. "Who undressed me?"

"Eirian," Bronagh and Faber answered in unison.

V-Tor let his head fall back onto his pillow. "And I missed the whole thing?" He shifted again and pulled out a smooth, flat stone from under his lower back. "And who put stones in my bed?"

"Eirian," they said again and began to laugh.

Eirian wandered about, tears blocking her vision. This was too hard. These Mortal feelings were drowning her. More self-doubt and intense irrational feelings clouded her head. She blamed herself for failing to connect with others. All her life was a fight even here with everyone's deeply rooted fears and social bias. Sobbing, she stood in the middle of the inner bailey, attempting to get some bearing on where she was. She wanted to hide. To the right was the tower, her room and prison, the one she hated. "I'll die before I'll return to that forsaken chamber!" She veered to her left.

Taker and Beals came into view and Eirian staggered to the sleeping dogs. Crying, she crawled up against Taker as he lay on his side. She placed her head the side of his chest and raised one arm up and over his back. She was so tired, so hurt, so alone. She closed her eyes letting Taker's heartbeat relax her. Taker lazily raised his head and licked her forehead. Beals, not wanting to be left out, got up and walked over to the other side of Eirian and dropped down, placing his head on her bare feet.

Laeg and BroMac followed RohDin to where he last saw Eirian. "Maybe she went up to the tower?"

BroMac and Laeg shared a look that said 'no.' BroMac then asked the question Laeg didn't want to hear, "Do you think she went over the wall?" They both started running toward the outer bailey.

"Wait!" RohDin called out. "She's over here."

Both Laeg and BroMac stopped, turned, and followed RohDin's pointing finger to where the dogs were kept. Relieved, they walked towards her and came to a sudden stop when both dogs opened their eyes and bared their teeth at them.

"Stop that or I'll take the back of my sword to both of you!" BroMac hissed. They didn't back down. White teeth continued to glisten against black fur. BroMac stared at them with an intensity that would normally have sent them running, and still they stood their ground. Annoyed, BroMac grabbed for Eirian and the dogs instantly growled their warnings.

Eirian's head shot up. Alarmed at seeing the men there, she scooted as far away as she could get from them. "No," she cried. "You'll never get me back in the tower!"

"Eirian! It's okay," Laeg said, trying to assure her.

"No!" she screamed, "leave me alone." She pressed her forearm against her chest again and cried out in pain this time.

"You're ill!'

"No!" she screamed. "I'm…just…I'm just…missing…"

"Being Faery," Laeg finished for her.

Tears burst forth again, this time they seemed unstoppable; she cried and cried, barely able to take a breath.

"Enough of this!" BroMac bellowed, kicking aside Beals. He grabbed her wrist and pulled her upright. Eirian's exhaustion got the better of her and she buckled. In one quick motion, BroMac gathered her into his arms, and headed back towards the Keep. "You need to sleep and not in the tower, Mortal Faery," he whispered.

"Is she ill?" Bronagh asked as she and Faber rushed to BroMac's side. Faber placed a hand on Eirian's cheek. "It doesn't feel like she has a fever."

Feeling very impatient, BroMac stepped past the two women and went up the stairs to one of the guest rooms. Bending down, he went to place Eirian on the bed, but Eirian burrowed deeper into his arms. He stood up again, now embarrassed. "Some help please."

Faber grabbed a blanket off of the bed and directed her husband towards a chair. "She's freezing. Hold her until we warm the bed."

BroMac's eyes narrowed, "Well hurry up. I don't want to hold her all day."

"BroMac! She saved our son," Faber said indignantly. "Just give us a few minutes."

BroMac looked over at Laeg, who seemed to be having a lot of fun with this. "What are you laughing about?" BroMac grumbled.

"You could have left her with the dogs. I'm sure right now she doesn't care where the body heat comes from just as long as it keeps her warm enough to sleep."

A wicked smile found its way to BroMac's face. With Eirian in his arms, he got up and marched out of the room. Into the sick room he went, stopping beside Broan's bed. "Well?" He said, motioning for Broan to move aside. "If you don't want her I'll offer her to V-Tor. It makes no difference to me."

The words cut into Broan, stirring a distant warning. It took a lot of effort but Broan complied, inching over and making room for her on his bed. He looked up at BroMac as he bent to lay Eirian beside him. "You're doing this because?"

"She fought a hard battle and just like any warrior that fights with all they have, at the end they have nothing left...not even enough energy to keep themselves warm. It's the least you can do for her." BroMac smiled after repeating his wife's words. "Besides, Ke-Hern sent her to you. That means it's your job to figure out what to do with her."

"I've been working on that," Broan huffed.

"Alright everyone OUT!" Laeg commanded. "They all need rest." He looked over at Broan and V-Tor and smiled. "I'll see you both later." Laeg motioned to everyone. "Come on, we don't want to undo all the good that Eirian did for us. Let's go."

Eirian slept on her side curled up with her back pressed firmly against Broan's stomach. He knew she didn't realize he was there. So he wrapped his arms around her, sharing more of his body heat. It felt strangely comforting having her near and protected. Smiling, Broan slipped into the dream world after her.

Reality and the dream worlds collided, and Eirian woke. Startled, her head whipped around and she stared at Broan. His eyes were open and his lips were curved into a sweet smile. He looked like a child who had just been caught stealing from the pantry. "Sleep well?" He asked. Her fiery green eyes locked onto his, and without thought, she quickly rolled away from him and fell off the bed, landing hard on the floor.

Broan pulled himself over to the edge of the bed and looked down at her. "Are you alright?"

Eirian glared at him and quickly sat up. "I was until you started taking liberties."

"I must remind you that you were the one sleeping in my bed, not the other way around." Broan quickly dropped his head back on his pillow, arms across his chest. Regret set in and he rose again to look at her. "Sorry," he muttered out loud. Eirian scampered away from the bed, and when she felt she was far enough from his grasp, she got up from the floor, grabbed her things and headed out the door. Broan flopped back on to his pillow with a groan.

"You idiot. I would have kissed her, not pushed her out of bed," V-Tor said

"Oh shut up!"

As V-Tor crossed the entrance of the Keep and into the Main-Hall, he rubbed his arms hoping to get some of the ache out of them. It had been a week since his recovery and still he felt the effects of the illness. He picked up a mug of ale only to have Faber yank it out of his hand and replace it with one of milk. He looked into the mug and turned his nose up at it. "When do I get to do manly things again like drinking sweet wine and ale?" he whined, sitting down next to Broan. He put his mug down on the table and shoved it away.

"When Eirian says you can." Faber answered placing a plate of food in front of him.

"Talking about Eirian, I've not seen her for days now," V-Tor said as he watched Broan from the corner of his eye.

"She's been busy helping Bronagh with the villagers." Faber answered without pause.

"And where does she sleep?" V-Tor asked, already knowing the answer. It was out of defiance more than anything that kept Eirian sleeping out in the open. She had made it clear to them that if they wanted her in the Tower at night they'd have to catch her. And she had no intention of making it easy. After countless evenings of a cat and mouse game, everyone finally gave up. V-Tor reached for a mug of ale again.

"Where ever she wants," BroMac said in his booming voice as he walked into the Main-Hall.

"You've gotten soft," Broan muttered.

BroMac took the mug of ale from V-Tor. "You try and catch her." He sat next to a very dejected V-Tor and nudged him, "I pity her poor husband. I'm afraid the sheets will be very cold for him if she's always sleeping in a different place every night." He laughed, "I can just see it. 'Oh house maid, have you seen my wife?' 'Yes she sleeps on the floor by an open window in the hall...'"

"Or," RohDin cut in, now sitting next to Broan. "She's out sleeping in the henhouse this time; do you wish me to wake her?"

"Of course if he was a talented man, he may be able to give her enough delight in bed to keep her there for an hour or two," V-Tor said trying to join in on all the fun.

"Well if he's anything like you V-Tor, it would keep her in bed for less than two minutes!" BroMac added laughing so hard he almost fell off the bench.

Faber shook her head. "Eirian worked hard helping the likes of you and all you can do is laugh and ponder her imaginary husband's fate. No wonder she sleeps this way. She's trying to keep away from fools like you."

Ignoring his wife, BroMac looked back at V-Tor. "So how's your recovery coming?"

"I ache something terrible. I swear it's from sleeping on rocks!"

BroMac slapped V-Tor on the back and laughed. "It's better to sleep on rocks than to be buried under them."

He then squinted at Broan. "What's cooking in that head of yours? I've seen that look before."

Broan straightened up, replacing the embroidered band into his pocket and sipped his milk. "Where's Eirian now?"

BroMac shrugged his shoulder in response.

"I want her brought here. Call Laeg as well. I think it's time to plan our escape."

Chapter 9

"Out of the shattered, they will come.
Eyes locked forward, minds turned inward."

- The Ancients Prophecy

Eirian casually looked around the Main-Hall. The panic and wonder she first felt coming into this hall a few months ago, was gone. It had all become so familiar. She sighed. Her mind was wandering once again. She had been forced to sit and listen to this wrangling for hours, and she was bored. She laid her head on the table in front of her. "*Idiots,*" she whispered to herself.

Most of the day had been spent in the Main-Hall. The discussion was low, intense and centered on getting Broan and a few selected men to the Wall City. Broan, Laeg, V-Tor, RohDin, Idwal, and BroMac sifted through the dusty known ways to escape, hoping for that one gem of an idea.

"What of the fissure that Laeg used to get to the dam?" Idwal asked. "We could leave through it at night."

"The Ny-dick have already filled it in at the top. I guess if they couldn't use it to get into Solveig, no one uses it." Eirian answered absentmindedly.

"The front gate at night and then down the Blue River of the West?" he asked again.

Eirian didn't even bother to look up. "The front gate, you must be joking! What you may not know is that Shadow Dwellers have perched themselves on the edge of the forest. They're just waiting for you to make a mistake and try to leave that way. Ny-dick are most likely stationed along the road to the Walled City as well as the Blue River of the West."

"How about over the north side of the wall?" Idwal asked in a hushed tone.

"Don't have a rope long enough and it still leaves you on the ground near the Ny-dick…and the Shadow Dwellers."

"SO how would you escape Solveig unseen?" BroMac asked.

It was the tone of his voice more than the question that caused Eirian's head to spring up from its resting place. "Why ask me?"

Broan smiled and sat down next to her. "Why not, it's what Faeries do isn't it? And it isn't that your Faery brain has been languishing. So how would you leave Solveig without anyone knowing?"

"You really want to know?"

"Yes."

She shook her head. "Sorry but it's not something I think Mortals could do."

Broan wrapped his arm firmly around her shoulder and pulled her very near, locking her into position. "But you are Mortal now, which means if you can, we can. Besides…" He put his lips next to her ear, causing a noticeable shiver to rush through Eirian. Smiling he whispered, "I'd be willing to give you your freedom for helping us get to the Walled City. It's up to you."

Shocked, Eirian turned and stared at Broan.

Broan nodded slowly, studying her at the same time.

Eirian broke free with one hard push and studied Broan. "Fine! I will meet you in the last guard tower on the south wall just after the mid-day's hour, and I'll show you. Then you can decide if you have the mettle to do it." With that she stood and turned on her heels, leaving the men a bit surprised.

"Anything else?" Broan called out.

"Yes." She challengingly raised her chin. "If we do go, I will wear only my Faery clothes and dispense with these useless garments. Deal?"

Broan slowly nodded his head again. It wasn't what he would have preferred but he'd figure out how to handle it later.

Eirian turned to go but stopped and looked back at them. "You'll also need someone you can trust … no… better yet, continue the day as you normally would. When you check on the guards on duty, BroMac and I will meet you up in the tower. Everyone will assume

BroMac has caught me doing something wrong again and is bringing it to your attention."

"You worry about us being seen within these walls?" Broan questioned.

"Yes. These days I worry about everything." Her eyes locked on Broan. "And you better keep your promise."

Broan silently acknowledge the implication and nodded his head, "Till mid-day then."

Broan and Laeg worked their way along the parapet just as planned, checking on the various guards and taking time to listen to each soldier's report. It wasn't long after they had reached the south end of the wall that BroMac made his move. With great ceremony and show BroMac pushed Eirian up the stairs in front of him, calling for Broan as he went.

"If I didn't know this was an act, I'd think you were actually enjoying yourself," Eirian told BroMac.

"I am," BroMac answered.

"Now that we're all here, show us the way," Broan said.

Eirian walked over to the narrow window and raised herself up onto her toes. She pointed out to a large tall outcropping of stone that Broan had never given much thought to. It was shaped like a giant stalagmite that grew out of the base of the mountain. Spring rivulets had long ago created this tall, dignified pillar of rock. It stood between Solveig and the now broken dam. Although isolated from the mountainside forest it had a few evergreens gracing its top. "I'd use that outcropping but you'll need the trees on the top of it," she said with a half smile gracing her face.

"You're crazy Faery, don't waste our time," BroMac stated firmly. He stood just behind Broan and Eirian and could see no possible escape that way.

Eirian ignored BroMac and looked to Broan. "I could do it without aid but since you want to come along, we will have to attach one end of a rope..." She looked around the guard's room, "Here," she said pointing to a large metal ring, "and the other to one of the trees. At night, we wouldn't have to worry as much about the Ny-dick or Shadow Dwellers spotting us."

Broan rubbed the stubble on his chin. "And how do we get the rope over there to begin with?"

"I'd climb along the rock face to the trees and secure the rope so you and the others can cross."

He eyed the trees. They were leaning heavily, their exposed roots barely holding on. "That's if the trees remain standing."

"Oh they're strong enough. As misshapen as they are, they've held up against years of winter ice and howling winds."

"So that's the first stop, then what?"

"Once at the top of the stone column I would climb up the rock face to top of the ridge. There are natural indents integrated into the wall of rock. They are hard to see at the best of times and practically invisible at night, at least for Mortals. Once I'm up I'll secure a second rope for you to follow on."

"You're going to climb out there...alone...while we all just...wait here?" BroMac scoffed.

"There's no other way. None of you can make it across without falling. I'm used to climbing such steep walls."

"Yes...Yes you are..." Broan said deep in thought.

"It's the only way left to you."

Broan looked out. He could picture everything, including the steep drop to a certain death if anything went wrong. He watched as the water from the broken dam transformed into flying water droplets. "What about the spray from the waterfall? Are you sure you'll be able to climb up the slippery rock face?"

She looked at him as if he had two heads. "Of course! I've climbed worse."

Broan knew he would be taking a big chance letting her go out on her own... "It looks like you have put a lot of thought into this."

"Wouldn't you?"

Broan stared intently at her.

Eirian remained looking out at the free world as she spoke. "You once told me that you would find me no matter where I went. That's what stopped me from leaving, but it didn't stop me from figuring out how to."

Broan turned back and looked out at the trees. "So what happens when we get to the top of the ridge?"

"We hike away from the waterfall and along that tree-dotted ridge...for about three miles. Then we walk down towards the inner canyon and finally reach your hot springs."

"HOT springs!" BroMac protested. "That's insanity! You're walking right into a trap!" BroMac leaned over her. "There are Ny-dick and Shadow Dwellers waiting down there...YOU said so yourself."

"Not the way we'll be going. Just north of the hot springs is a large forest with dense underbrush. If we continue up from the junction of the springs and lake, we'll be out of sight and well up the next mountain by daylight."

"I agree with BroMac. This is still too close to the Ny-dick, and what of the Shadow Dwellers," Broan said.

"Then don't come with me!"

Broan gave her a stern look. "We all go or no one does."

"Look, we'll be coming at the lake and springs from the far side. It's thick with vegetation and not commonly traveled. I'm sure we can slip past them. As for the Shadow Dwellers, they've been hanging out on the north ridge in the trees above Solveig or near the Ny-dick camp. They're keeping an eye on us, that's why I wanted everything to look normal. If they think we are still here, why would they need to venture out that way?"

"Okay. Go get ready. We'll all meet here just before the changing of the night guard." With that Broan promptly left the tower.

The night was clear and an almost full moon graced the heavens. Eirian talked in a soft hushed tone, "Idwal, did you tell Broan and the others not to show up at the same time and to arrive by different routes?"

"Yes," he answered quickly. "Although, I'm not sure why it's necessary. You know Broan made sure that RohDin has the night watch, so we have nothing to worry about."

"We've a lot to worry about, not only from peering eyes outside Solveig, but the ones that are inside."

"Inside! What do you mean? Does Broan know?"

"I'm sure he'll find out soon enough. Come on, we need to go quickly."

Idwal and Eirian scampered along the base of the outer wall. Once they reached the last set of stairs, they slipped inside and up they went. On the top stair, Eirian paused for few seconds and listened. Just as she stepped into the guard tower, a hand grabbed her and pulled her deeper into its dark recesses.

"Shush," Broan whispered. Then after listening intently, he nudged Eirian towards the window. "We better get going before anyone gets wind of this."

Eirian looked out the window at the dull darkness engulfing this side of the mountain. She felt a sense of eager anticipation about finally testing this escape route. She took a full breath of fresh mountain air and pulled herself up onto the window ledge. Nestled in the vast sheer wall of weathered rock was hope.

After attaching one end of the rope to a large iron ring imbedded in the wall, Broan handed it to Eirian. With a quickness that always surprised him, she leapt out of the window and onto the rock face. Her versatility was never more evident than at that very moment. As promised, once she made it to the trees she fastened the rope, pulling hard on it, testing her full weight against it.

What Eirian was doing was incomprehensible. Broan and the others knew that without her they'd never have been able to leave Solveig. Any trace of doubt about Eirian's intentions evaporated and was quickly replaced with nodding approvals.

Eirian crouched in the small cluster of trees precariously rooted to a thick outcropping. She smiled back at Broan and his warriors who stood crowding the window. That was when she started the hard climb up to the ridge.

The roles of captive and leader had reversed quickly, Broan thought as he grabbed the rope. He laced his hands around the thick cord and then hooked his legs over it. He silently pulled himself along. By the time he reached the clump of trees his limbs were as heavy as lead and any movement in them came from willed conscious thought. Swimming in sweat, he crouched down and rested at the base of the first tree.

As Eirian climbed, the limited light added to her intensity of uncertainty. Indents matched up with the sheer rock face and twice she almost missed her footing. Along with the colorless mist that coated everything, she found that the wild spray made the rock face incredibly cold to touch, enough that it made her fingers burn and hurt.

The pine scented winds and cold feel of hand on stone triggered memories from her life before Solveig, when everything seemed more alive and full of possibility. It became obvious to her that captivity had dulled her senses and had helped to fuel her insecurity. Placed side by side, the two life-styles she had lived stood in stark contrast to each other, Mortal life with all its comforts and Faery life with nature's unpredictability and dangers.

Eirian opened herself to nature and her old ways. With a satisfied smile, raw energy and pure excitement filled her as she continued upward. The climb became tranquil, the stars in the night sky were brilliant and she felt at home for the first time in a long time. Once on top, the view seduced her. The soft texture and scents on the wind sent ripples of pleasure through her and she smiled. After a brief reprieve she sighed and got back to work securing the rope for Broan.

As soon as the rope was lowered, Broan let out his breath. Closing his eyes he thanked the gods. With feet braced against the rock wall, Broan slowly pulled himself up, hand over hand, and inch by inch. It didn't take long before he found that he had arrived at the top. He got up and walked over to where Eirian stood, eyes closed, and a smile on her face.

Idwal decided to be the last to go and no one seemed to care. He thought being last and seeing the others go successfully across would ease his troubled nerves but now that he was sitting up on the window he decided it hadn't helped one bit. He began to second-guess himself, to speculate the odds of success and failure.

BroMac, his brother, came up behind him and patted him on the back. "Are you ready? If we are to keep this a secret you have to go before the change of the guard."

"It's a long way down."

"Then don't look down. Like in archery, keep your eye on the target. It will keep you focused…just trust Eirian."

Puzzled, Idwal turned and looked at his brother. "But I thought…"

"You think too much. That's why you're still sitting here while they're already across and half way up the wall. Now go."

Soon the group was walking along the top of the tree dotted ridge, quietly picking their way through the boulders. After a good long walk in the stillness of the deep night, they finally reached the end of the ridge. They took a very brief rest, and then they began down a rough trail that plunged almost two hundred feet at a steep decline, and wound up on the far side of the lake.

The genius of Eirian's escape plan was almost lost in a heartbeat. They had just crossed a misty haven of trees and ferns when they heard sounds that sent chills up their spines - Ny-dick, and the cries of their latest victims. It was the distinctive cries of a Faery. Ardis swiftly lead them into the thick underbrush. It was so dense that they had to get on their stomachs and crawl through it.

"*I can't leave…I have to try…*" Eirian suddenly swung around.

"DAMN!" Broan whispered as he lunged for her. He pulled Eirian back and covered her with his own body as a Ny-dick stomped near them. They waited in stillness, not moving, not breathing. The Ny-dick sniffed and hissed into the night then turned back to the feast.

"Comfy?" Broan whispered into her ear.

"Get off!" she hissed back as she pushed Broan off.

Her harsh tone made Broan smile. There was that spirit he was counting on. Their goal was the Walled City and nothing was about to keep him from it.

When the early morning sun hit Solveig in a fiery flash, the group found themselves high on the next mountain that overlooked home. Eirian had been right. They had made it by sunrise, and without getting caught.

Broan looked down at Solveig. It shone an incredible array of brilliant white, mauve and pewter gray. "So much has changed among the people; so much has changed in the land, yet Solveig stands, looking untouched by time and chaos."

V-Tor followed his gaze. "She's worthy of her name." He turned and looked up at the mountainside they had to climb. "Are you sure we'll find the old trade route?"

"Yes, I'm sure." He motioned towards Eirian. "I have no doubt she'll find it, she wants her freedom that much."

Shocked, V-Tor looked at Broan. "You promised her freedom for helping us?" Broan nodded his head.

"Why?"

"We need to get to the Walled City and she needed an incentive. It made perfect sense."

"But…"

"Don't worry; I'll come up with something by the time we get to the Walled City."

"Oh…" V-Tor played with the small stone Jelen had insisted on giving him. *"If this really is a good luck stone, I think Eirian will be in more need of it than I will."*

Broan slapped V-Tor on the shoulder as he passed him. "We better get going. Now that morning has come, it won't take long before the Shadow Dwellers and Lija figure out what we've done."

Broan stopped and stood while catching his breath. They were only halfway up and already he was winded. He had calculated in his mind how far they needed to go each day if they were to make it to the Walled City in less than a week. He cast a look over his shoulder at V-Tor and Laeg to see how they were doing. V-Tor was pale and breathing hard, while Idwal and Laeg walked quietly next to him. Perhaps everyone was right and both V-Tor and himself needed more time to recover from the illness. "We just don't have the luxury of time," Broan muttered as he started walking again.

Eirian was glad when the trail eased off and they entered a meadow. This would be a good time for a rest. Under the watchful eye of GarrRod, she sat down on a fallen log in the clearing and waited for her two patients. The fragrant foliage in the humid air reminded her so much of being Faery, being busy with her own work, being free.

She glanced to see the progress of the others who were still a little behind her. She picked at the fresh bandage covering the binding cord. Her wrist was now a mess. The cord cut deeper everyday and a cloudy fluid had dried and crusted over it. It ached both day and night.

"Horse tail clouds," she said pointing at the sky. "There'll be a storm in two sunsets. Let's hope we're on lower ground by then. If we're still in the higher altitudes we'll be faced with snow or sleet."

Broan looked up at the sky and shook his head. "Don't you ever have good news to tell us?"

"That is good news. Until then it'll be clear and warm, good hiking weather."

"Warm!" V-Tor repeated. "You think that is good news?" He dropped down on the log next to her. His mouth was dry and his tongue swollen from all the breathing he had been forced to do by mouth. He wished they could slow the pace, but he also knew this wasn't a summer pleasure trip.

Eirian got up, scooped some fresh creek water into a mug, and handed it to V-Tor. "You'll need to drink a lot today. Your body's having trouble with the extra strain that's been put on it. We'll follow the creek through the forest and have a meal by the lake."

"And you know there's a lake on the other side of the forest because…" Broan asked.

"Because I use to swim in it before you imprisoned me." Angrily Eirian turned her back to him and busied herself checking V-Tor's condition. She didn't know why he bothered her so much. He had promised to give her freedom after all. Eirian just felt…

When the last rays of the sun bid them good night, they had made that day's goal. It had been a tough and somewhat disheartening journey. Legs felt like rubber, backs ached and lungs burned. Broan and the others comfortably huddled around a small fire nestled in-between various large boulders left long ago by moving glaciers.

Eirian was sitting on a medium sized boulder, a ways away from the fire. She pointed into the darkness. "Tomorrow we'll be walking along the barren upper ridges of the next two mountain faces. Even though the grade won't be as steep, the lack of air will slow us down. The day after that we should reach the route you've been talking about."

"Well then, we had better get some rest," Broan said. He looked at Idwal. "You take the first watch. Ardis will take the second." The men shuffled around, looking for smooth patches of ground to sleep on. Eirian got up and started to leave.

"Where do you think you're going?" Broan asked.

"Over there," Eirian said as she pointed to someplace off in the inky night.

"No I don't think so; you'll be sleeping here with us. It'll be easier for the night watch to keep an eye on you."

"I don't need the night guard watching over me. I'll just be over here. I'll be fine."

"No! You'll sleep here with us," Broan answered firmly, hoping he wouldn't have to argue the point.

"But," Eirian stammered, "I can't sleep with you. I…I—"

"You will be sleeping with us for the whole of the trip, so you may as well get use to it," V-Tor said as he brushed away a few little rocks from his back. "Besides it's not like you haven't done so before."

Muttering under her breath Eirian furiously stomped over to Broan. She pointed to the far edge of the fire. "Is over there close enough?"

"No," Broan answered not even looking at where she was pointing. "You'll be sleeping right here." He patted the ground beside him. "GarrRod will be on the other side of you, so don't even think about moving in the middle of the night." He lowered his head to the ground and turned his back to her. GarrRod walked over and without a word, dusted any offending stones from his sleeping area and laid down with his back to her as well.

Eirian just stood there. How could he even think she'd be willing to sleep next to him?

"Lay down Eirian, or I'll tie you down."

Eirian took in a deep breath and sat down on the ground, still refusing to lie next to him.

"Now!"

Sleep has a magic all its own. It doesn't matter if you're on hard ground or a feather bed; if you're tired enough, sleep quickly finds you. Eirian was worn out by the day's climb just like everyone else, and slumber cast its spell on her within minutes. Her sleep filled mind drifted off through old memories and disjointed images, and then to a time with Ke-Hern.

He had often talked to her of her destiny, and although she had only listened with one ear, she had heard him loud and clear. *You can't hide from it. Your moment of truth will come and when it does, you'll be glad you listened to me. So, of all the things I've told you, remember you need to not only trust yourself but those you never thought you would. Like right now!"*

Eirian awoke with a start, Ke-Hern's voice still ringing in her head. "Even from afar you lecture me!" she whispered rolling over onto her side. She now faced Broan as he lay on his back. Her eyes followed the rise and fall of his chest. His breathing was shallow and even, he was in a deep sleep. At least that's what she thought.

"Ke-Hern sometimes haunts my dreams as well," he said turning onto his side and away from her.

Eirian just couldn't sleep after that so she laid back and stared up at the night sky. The stars seemed so much closer up in the mountains. They shone with a brilliance and sparkle that couldn't be seen in the villages. But the beauty in the night sky didn't distract her long. Her thoughts drifted back to Ke-Hern. She missed him and worried about him.

Rolling her body to a sitting position, Eirian stood up which of course got Broan and GarrRod's immediate attention. "I need to relieve myself, and don't tell me one of you must join me, because if you do, let's just say no amount of binding cord will stop me from leaving you all stranded!"

GarrRod grunted and rolled over again. Broan sat up and pointed to a large boulder just past the fire. "Over there, behind the rock and if you're not back in a minute, I'll be coming to check on you," he paused for a second and then continued, his voice filled with a tense harsh threat, "AND I WILL FIND YOU."

Once Eirian returned to the spot between him and GarrRod, Broan settled back down and swiftly fell asleep. Then Ke-Hern entered his dreams.

"There's no half way, no middle ground in this," Ke-Hern warned him.

Broan could see the thick woods and underbrush and realized that they formed a solid wall around him.

"Just take a step," Ke-Hern said.

Broan managed to put one foot down, when suddenly he was pulled back.

"Not that way! You've already been that way, and I doubt you want to repeat that adventure."

"How do you know what I want?" Broan replied as he took a giant step into the wall of greenery.

He regretted it instantly. He was there again, rooted to the ground, shocked and unable to move. He could do nothing but watch as his mother and sister were cut through with a sword. He could not stand to be inside himself. The guilt was too much.

168

Ke-Hern appeared again. "I told you! I told you not to go that way. Until you've let this evil event go and release the guilt, this will always be a trap for you, one that digests a small piece of you each time you remember it. If this is not healed soon, it will come between you and what needs to be done."

Broan was back in the circle of wild growth. He bent over and placed his hands on his knees, taking in deep breaths. "What is this all about?"

"It's the choices you make in the present, not the ones you made in the past that count. You were a different person back then, as you will be a different person in the future. Since you cannot live in the past or the future, think wisely on your choices of today."

"What of being responsible for all your actions? It is not a factor of maturity?"

"Each choice has a consequence. You either learn from it or you repeat it. Choose well today and the consequences will be worth living through in the future."

"Like the death of a loved…"

"You were a boy not a man."

"They still died."

"There are no second chances once you are dead. Only those who live have that privilege. Let it go, or it will haunt you and limit the good you can do today."

"Regret then…"

"is USELESS!"

DeSpon closed his eyes and took in a deep breath of cool crisp mountain air but even the fragrance of the forest could not distract him. He waited restlessly for the Shadow Dwellers, Larden and Falzon, to arrive. Things had been set into motion, and there was a sense that pandemonium was about to erupt. The ground itself crackled with awareness and hope.

He walked further into the clearing and searched the sky for the two Shadow Dwellers he had called. Life had been hard on all of them. Nerves were raw, and self-respect was bloodied. He wondered if he had underestimated their loyalty to Sobus, if you could call it that. It's more likely that fear kept them secure under Sobus' thumb.

Falzon watched DeSpon quietly from behind the steep walls of a towering short corridor of rock. He raised his massive ape arms, gripped the side of one of the stone columns, bent his knees and let himself hang loose. It felt good to stretch his back and take the weight off of his hips and legs.

"So how long are we going to make DeSpon wait?" Larden asked.

Falzon looked over at DeSpon and shrugged his shoulders. "Until I feel he's paid enough penance for attacking Kuiper."

Larden worked his fingers through his feathers. "You know he couldn't help it. I actually thought he held off for quite a long time. If it hadn't been him, it would have been one of us." He stopped talking for a moment to remove one of his loose feathers, and then he continued. "Sobus was very smart to make us both predatory and territorial. It makes it very difficult for more than two of us to gather. You must agree getting together is extremely uncomfortable and hard on all of us."

Falzon grunted and continued to hang from his arms.

Larden walked over to where he could get a better look at DeSpon. "Do you even know what he wants to talk to us about?"

"He either has another great idea to free us, or he wants information on what Lija's been up to."

Larden turned. "You know, you never use to be this cold."

Falzon's large fat fingers let go of the small out-cropping of stone, and he crumbled back down to his deformed size. His knuckles reached the ground and took on some of his weight. "I've always been this cold, but the pain in my misshapen body is worse today, so I'm extra mean, that's all."

Larden shifted his weight from one foot to the other. He'd always been sensitive to Falzon's plight. Their grotesque bodies had both advantages and disadvantages, but for some reason Falzon had gotten the worse of it. His heavy ape upper body had never sat right upon his Manliken hips and legs. Even Bacot, the ox, had better balance.

Falzon growled and pushed at Larden. "Let's go. The sooner we find out what this is about the sooner I can get back and rest my bones under Deleed's nimble fingers."

"Ugliest Ny-dick I've ever seen, and you manage to figure out she has a gift." Larden laughed and then began to shape-shift in preparation for flight.

"Take a good look at yourself Larden you're not that cute either. At least Deleed can relieve some of my pain." Falzon shape-shifted into a raven and quickly rose into the sky. "At least she has talent. You, with all your feathers, can't fly without shape-shifting into a raven."

"Ohhh...now that hurts," he chuckled. "Besides those leather wings of DeSpon wouldn't look good among my caramel color feathers."

Falzon landed not two inches from DeSpon, forcing him to step aside or be run over while Larden eased down at a respectful distance. "You called."

"I'm so glad to see you both. How are the others?"

"Suffering," Falzon answered.

Larden gave Falzon an evil look. "Not bad. What's on your mind?"

"The ones who escaped from Solveig - I think we should keep it quiet."

"And not tell Sobus or Lija!" Larden's eyes got big. "Why? You know we were ordered to report any and all activities!"

"I know what we were ordered to do. I just want to give the escapees a little time, a bit of a head start. It'll help us in the end."

"THE END!" Falzon roared, "There is no end to this punishment?"

"GET OFF MY BACK!!" DeSpon's lion's mane flared and his claws extended out from the pads on his feet. "I'm not proud of what I've done but I know there's hope. I know there's an end."

Falzon straightened his back, making himself large and broad, a mountain of muscle.

"Stop it! The both of you!" Larden yelled. "Just stop it! Calm down! It's hurting us to fight each other. Calm down and think for a just moment. Remember the person inside of you. Falzon, if DeSpon knows of a way to end this curse, I for one am willing to listen and do whatever I can to help."

Falzon finally grunted and lowered his form back down onto his knuckles. He eyed DeSpon with displeasure and distrust. "If Sobus or Lija finds out that we knew, it'll be us who suffer, not you. You're Sobus' golden one," he sneered.

"Not golden one, his most hated one. In the end, it will be I who pays the price. I'm not saying we never tell him. We just need to hold off a little. Eirian needs to be given a chance."

Flazon narrowed his eyes, suspicion darkening his face. "What I find more interesting is why does this Eirian suddenly have your protection? At one time all you wanted to do was hunt her down."

"At one time I was young and foolish and while I'm still maybe young, I'm certainly less foolish."

Falzon shook his head. "Not in my eyes, you're just as foolish as always."

DeSpon noticeably relaxed and let his guard down a bit. At least now they were finally talking. "You always called it like it was and I can always count on you for that. There seems to be a lot of attention focused on Eirian right now. The Seer told me that even the Queen is curious about her."

Falzon threw his arms up in the air. "Well, if the Queen is involved, then of course we should be as well! I mean she's been nothing but kind to us."

DeSpon grabbed of Flazon's arm and looked him in the eye. "You can't argue the fact that if Eirian leads the Faeries into battle with the Mortals, this is probably the war of freedom."

Flazon shook off DeSpon. "For them, not us. We're not as fortunate."

Larden stepped between them and looked at DeSpon, "Wait… wait. If this is the war of freedom, do you think we'll be freed as well?"

"I think if Sobus is defeated, there will be some form of redemption for all of us. That's why…"

"I don't care about Sobus, the Queen, or even Eirian. It is you who is responsible for this nightmare we live in. Perhaps all I have to do is kill you and all of this becomes a sad and frightening memory." Falzon's eyes blazed with hatred.

"Blame me all you want Falzon. Kill me if you like. But it won't change a thing and deep down you do know that. We need the Mortals to have a victory. That means we need to give Eirian some time to escape. I'm willing to fight for us even if you're not. I agree that it was I that took Sobus' offer. I stand guilty before you, admitting it freely. But remember, you decided to join me of your own free will. Do you really want to hold this grudge against me forever? Do you really want to live…like this?" DeSpon said splaying his hands out from his sides. "Won't you join me now and work towards breaking this curse?"

Larden cleared his throat, drawing DeSpon's attention back to him. "What if this whole situation is actually the fulfillment of the Ancient's prophecy and not the war of freedom?"

"Then we talk to the Ancients. And…" DeSpon smiled, "I already know someone who can talk to them."

Falzon stepped back. His anger was still there, but the need to escape this tormented form was stronger. "Okay…okay, all right." He sighed. "We'll tell the others to keep quiet for a while, but if Sobus or Lija start demanding, you know we can't fight them."

"I know and I don't want you to fight them. Tell them what you know if asked, just not right away. Keep busy until you are called." DeSpon's eyes brightened. "Most likely we'll be instructed to stop Eirian, the Faeries, and even the Mortals, but right now, holding back just a little might be enough to turn the tide on Sobus and perhaps even the Queen's power."

"She lied," V-Tor complained. "She said the grade would be more even today. But just look at it. It's steeper."

Broan would have told him to stop complaining, but he wasn't enjoying this either. His body still suffered from yesterday's hike and had protested from the moment he woke up. "Enough," he called out to Eirian. "Let's rest for a minute on the out-crop over there."

Laeg didn't like the looks of Broan or V-Tor. He went and stood with Eirian. "Is there an easier way to the old trade route?" he asked, looking back at his exhausted friends. "I'm worried about them. I don't know how much more they can handle."

Eirian followed his gaze and had to agree with him. They didn't look well at all. "We could go further down through the trees, but we'd have to follow a switchback and that would take at least until tomorrow afternoon."

"Then let's do it. If we take a little easier today, tomorrow may bring them more strength."

"Broan won't like it. He wants to get to the trail as quickly as possible."

"He can't lift his sword to defend his people, so I'm back in charge." Laeg smiled and walked away.

Once they entered the pine forest, Eirian stopped and addressed the group. "We should come to a large meadow in about three hours. I think it would be wise to make camp on the other side of it. Tomorrow will be hard and better tackled after a good night's sleep." No one argued. All heads were bent down. They just kept walking, following her lead. The green canopy high over head didn't give them much protection from the drizzle. The light rain continued for about an hour, just long enough to make everyone cold and damp and miserable.

"She lied again!" V-Tor whined. "She said it wouldn't rain for another day!"

"This isn't rain!" she protested, "and it won't last long. Do you wish to find shelter now, or do you want to carry on?"

"Carry on," they all said in unison.

The meadow was a welcome sight of soft green sage, tall grass, and more importantly, flat terrain. Before they knew it they were on the other side of the clearing among the poplars. After they made camp everyone, except Eirian, huddled around the fire in a desperate attempt to warm themselves.

Eirian was in a difficult spot. Torn between the code she lived by and what was needed, she had to make a choice. Gathering her courage, she quietly walked up to Laeg. "Can you and Ardis come with me for a moment? And bring your bows." This was proving to be one of the hardest things she ever had to do.

Laeg looked over to Broan. He closed his eyes then quickly nodded his head at Ardis. They both stood up and followed her into the forest.

"Each closing of the day shows me how much weaker they are," Eirian whispered. "I had hoped…we wouldn't have to do this, but seeing how we need to get to the Walled City quickly…I don't think we can get away with…out…"

Eirian turned and sang softly into the wind. She watched the sway of the treetops and knew her message had been sent out. She took in a deep sad breath when she heard the answer to her call. She felt sick, her stomach wrenching in a way that would have left even Broan, who was the strongest Mortal around, stressed beyond belief.

With a heavy heart she looked at the two warriors. "There will be a deer coming through the clearing over there." She pointed to her right. "Make it a clean kill please." Both Ardis and Laeg nodded in agreement.

It wasn't long before a young buck walked out just to the right of the dry creek bed. He stood and waited out in the open, as if knowing what was about to happen. Eirian sadly watched as Laeg and Ardis' cedar arrows whisked through the air and quickly found their mark. The deer called Niiel fell to the ground and quickly died.

Eirian didn't know whether Laeg and Ardis were charitable or not but there was no bloodthirsty cry of victory with this hunt, and for that she was grateful. She slowly walked back to camp.

"Laeg and Ardis have downed a deer. They'll be bringing it into camp soon," she said as she walked past Broan, heading beyond the fire and away from the camp.

Broan immediately understood what Eirian had done. He got up and followed her. "We would have been fine without the meat. If it were that necessary, we could have simply hunted on our own, without your knowledge. Why betray your own beliefs when you don't have to?"

"You Mortals are all the same. You just hunt and kill randomly. I asked for permission first. Look, I knew what I was doing. Just leave it be." Eirian suddenly paled and quickly turned away from Broan. She hunched over, grasping her stomach. Forcing her body to relax, the nausea eased and she took a breath in, only to be immediately hit with extreme vomiting. *Child! Whose side are you on?* She cursed silently as she heaved again.

Eirian finally looked up at Broan. "I'll be okay... I just can't ... cutting up of the animal." Eirian gathered some composure. "It's no different than if you knew someone had skinned and quartered one of your friends. Please, I just need a little time."

Suddenly, there was an unmistakable whiff of raw flesh being held over fire, and Eirian backed further away. She looked at Broan with pleading eyes. "I have to..."

The increase of pallor and sweat told him just how much distress she was in. "Let's go for a walk and find some fresher air," Broan said wrapping his arm around her shoulder. It was a simple gesture, one with much meaning.

"Thank you," Eirian whispered.

Ke-Hern's call to the Queen hit her like the crack of a whip. DaNann woke up gasping.

"There's movement outside the gates of Solveig. Where is Sobus?" Ke-Hern asked.

His words felt like hurled rocks cracking through a frozen river, invading the protected stillness of her mind. *"Who walks free of Solveig? I thought it was under siege."*

"Where is Sobus?" Ke-Hern demanded. He worked very hard at controlling his uneasiness, but he failed miserably.

"Just a minute!" the Queen said. She got out of bed and walked over to the window. *"He's out of reach, not within my borders of the land."* She opened her eyes and looked to the west. *"Now will you tell me what's happened?"*

Ke-Hern sat down with a sigh of relief. "Broan and a group of men are trying to make their way to the Walled City. I was worried that Sobus would enter the picture and harm them."

"Is the one called Eirian with them?"

"I don't know for sure. I still can't find her full energy pattern, but there's someone there." Ke-Hern paused for a moment and then continued with what he really needed to say. "I fear things that I started are now very much out of my control."

The Queen closed her eyes. *"Control is an illusion. We're all bumped around in this life by energy and events. Even with all of the deep powers that are wielded here, none of us are in control. We play with it on our own level and pretend we control it...BUT we don't."*

"So you feel even the Ancients have no control over the events of Mortals?"

"Yes, and be glad of it. Nothing good can come from waking the Ancients."

"WHY. Why do you have such fear? I have heard other stories about their awakening that predicts unity and wellness for all."

"That was written long before I arrived," DaNann leaned her arms on the windowsill. *"Everything is wrapped in the cloth of either Alzmer or Venler energy and the two should never mix. They would fight and clash, destroying all that is around them until one extinguishes out the other."*

"Are you sure that the two are never to coexist? Is there no hope of blending the two or…"

"I truly fear that only one power can walk on this planet, this land. It would be a nightmare if I let my guard down." DaNann scowled, totally impatient with her Wizard. *"They sleep for a reason. Now, let them rest."*

Broan sat on a fallen tree, watching the dying embers of the fire. It had been two days since they had arrived at the clearing. He looked around at the sleeping men and assured himself that now that they were rested and well fed, they would make up for lost time. He didn't begrudge the delay, but he was more than ready to get going.

He got up and walked over to where Idwal stood guard. They nodded to each other then Broan went to check on Eirian. Ever since the kill, Broan had allowed Eirian to sleep close by the night guard, away from the fire and the smell of cooked meat. He squatted down next to her. She slept soundly. She was using moss for a pillow and was curled up on the ground between the twisted roots of a tree. Satisfied, he made his way back to his spot near the fire. He lay down and sleep greeted him swiftly, but his sleep was troubled. The woman with eyes of fire was visiting him again.

"Tell me Lord Broan of Solveig, Warlord of Remdor, what will you do for this land and what is truly right?"

Broan stared at her. "Who are you that you come and go in my dreams and appear in delusions caused by illnesses?"

"Avoiding are you?" She smiled at him. *"I'll give an answer for an answer. Fair?"*

He nodded back at her and quite firmly said, "Fair."

"Good. We found that Eirian's energy, although still young and undisciplined, is more worthy of our task. This leaves us with the question. Has she touched the center of your being?"

Broan's forehead furrowed as he thought about the question. "If you want to know if I have feelings for her the answer is No!"

"Don't lie!"

"Well if you think you know the truth, why ask the question?" he tossed brashly back. "Now answer my question. Who are you?"

She smiled at him. *"I am Nerlena. I am a guardian of the Ancients. You built your fortress over the one I guard, just like the Queen's fortress is built over Kurtz's."*

Broan turned his head slightly to one side, motioning to the crest so boldly tattooed on his back. "Then this is your crest?"

"An answer for an answer, remember." She paused briefly, *"Lord Broan of Solveig, Warlord of Remdor, what will you give up for the land and what is right?"*

Broan took time to think about the question. Finally he spoke with a clear voice full of commitment, "My life, my soul, my heart."

Nerlena wasn't smiling. *"I'm not concerned with expected answers, filled with flowery words. I did not ask for a poem or verse, I asked for truth. What are you willing to give up?"*

"You talk too much like Ke-Hern. You ramble on in parables and it's very confusing."

"Then I will make it clearer for you. If words don't work perhaps pictures and feelings will."

An image of Eirian suddenly formed in front of him. The hurt and weariness on her face cut deep into his heart. Like an explosion, the reality of what the question was asking was immediate. He could touch this representation and hold it in his hands and it felt heavy, heavy and sorrowful. Shame and panic swept through him. He looked up at Nerlena. "What does this mean?"

"An answer for an answer."

"My answer is that I don't want to play this silly game of yours any more. Now answer me!" His impatience was evident in each word.

"You are partly right about the symbol on your back. The image is ours but it is not what you call our crest."

Broan didn't want to know about the stupid crest, he wanted to know about the image of Eirian before him and what it meant. "Tell me about Eirian!" he demanded.

"You were the one who agreed to the bargain. Do not get angry with me,"

Broan held her with an ice-cold stare. "Tell me what this means!' he demanded.

"Alright," she said. *"We are concerned about your involvement with her. We do not want you to become an obstacle to Eirian's commitment to us."*

"What do you want of her?"

"Answer for an answer! Will you give her up or do we end what has begun between the two of you?"

"What are you talking about? It was most likely your magic that got Eirian and I physically attracted to each other in the first place."

"We do not control Mortal lust! That was all your own doing…WE just stepped in to save you both of from disaster. Talk to your Wizard sometime and he'll tell you the full depth of the Off-World curse. Just be glad we pulled you both to us when we did." The flame in her eyes burned red and hot. *"NOW will you step aside when it is needed?"*

Broan held his tongue. Not answering at all would be better than giving an answer when he had no idea what the outcome would mean.

Nerlena watched him and waited in silence. Broan still refused to speak, to say those words she wanted to hear. Nerlena shook her head. *"Later then."* And then she disappeared.

Morning light broke through the trees and danced upon the fog. The night temperature had cooled the ground, forcing the air nearest the earth to drop its condensation point. Broan rose and rubbed his arms. The damp cold had seeped into his bones. He would be glad to get out of the high range forest they were in and back into the sun.

He went to check on Eirian only to find her in the process of climbing up a tree to escape from Ardis. He growled causing Ardis to swiftly turn and gesture him to freeze. Ardis then motioned his head towards the other side of the clearing. With a few hand signals, Broan got the message. Quietly, he moved and joined Ardis with his knife drawn.

Ardis' bow was notched and pulled, ready to shoot anything that ventured into the clearing. Leaning into Broan he spoke. "It's my fault," he whispered giving his head an upward toss towards where Eirian had disappeared. "I thought I heard something, so I put my hand over her mouth to make sure she'd be quiet when she woke, and before I could do anything she was up the tree." He turned his attention back to the forest edge.

Broan held his breath and scanned the area.

"There's some movement to the north-east of us, about two hours away. It's what Ardis picked up on," Eirian said softly. "From up here I can't tell if it's a Ny-dick or not but it's defiantly moving this way."

Broan put his knife back in his belt. "Get the others up. We're breaking camp, NOW." Ardis lowered his bow and was off, moving silently through the brush.

Eirian took the lead again and Laeg and GarrRod took up rear guard. It wasn't long before they broke free of the forest and began the steep winding way up the barren swath of mountainside. Pockets of sparse grass and high alpine flowers were crushed under their feet, giving the group some ease as they marched the increasing incline.

Broan constantly looked back and watched for the slightest movement, for any sign of what was following them. He knew that now that they were out in the open they'd be easy to spot. Speed was their only hope, which meant they would have to rush through the patches of loose rocks and clumps of large boulders higher up.

Ardis caught Broan's attention and pointed to the sky. Dark cumulus clouds were developing and rolling towards them. Eirian's storm was well on its way. "Do you think we should find shelter or make a run for it?"

"Move it!" Broan ordered at the top of his voice. Being caught in a downpour on an avalanche conduit would be just like being in a flash flood and they would all be washed down. "Keep moving!" he yelled again, "or I'll feed the lot of you to the Ny-dick myself."

Idwal's muscles screamed as they pushed on. Stones crunched under his feet and the sound echoed out from the large granite boulders that dotted the area. It was so barren, so cold, and so lifeless this high up. He pulled himself up and over the last ledge and rolled himself out of the way of those coming up from behind.

"Keep moving soldier," Broan said as he tapped Idwal's shoulder. "I think the worse is over. We'll look for shelter once we're past this summit. The dense cloud may actually work in our favor. It'll keep our progress hidden from prying eyes."

Idwal forced his body onto his legs and moved in the direction Broan was motioning. "And some people enjoy mountain climbing," he muttered.

The beginning of the old trade route was tucked into a small sliver of rocky land, in an area just below the base of some cliffs. Eirian almost missed it as she walked through the cloudy haze that surrounded them. Breathless, she fell to her knees and sat back on her heels. "We're here," she said, "now what?"

Broan kept walking and as he passed Eirian he hauled her up onto her feet. "We keep walking," he said, not breaking his stride. "We'll rest farther down in the forest."

Eirian pulled her arm free of Broan's grasp and fell in behind him. She glared at his back. "*I tell you child, your father is very bossy!*"

Broan had hoped the thick forest of trees would provide them some safety but something was wrong. Everything was quiet, too quiet, and a low-lying mist added more tension than protection. V-Tor quickly took his place next to Broan as front guard, while GarrRod and Laeg took up the rear guard. Idwal came up and stood by Eirian, his hand on his sword, and Ardis took off to scout the area ahead of them.

They all waited and listened. The atmosphere was thick, intense and had a wraithlike quality to it. Everyone scanned the fog in front of them for any sign - an odd movement, a misplaced shadow, or a noise. But there was nothing, just an eerie silence.

Broan heard Ardis' low whistle and motioned them to move forward. They moved at a steady jog up and down small vales that had been cut by creeks and spring runoffs. Dense damp foliage pulled at their legs as they ran past. Everyone was panting hard by the time they reached the top of the third dale but Broan didn't give anyone time to recover. He continued steadily along the old trail.

They were just inside a natural clearing edged by a craggy rock ledge when without warning, the enemy hit. A Ny-dick charged at Eirian and bowled her over, knocking her to the ground. Within seconds, it turned and was upon her again. With a growl of rage it picked her up with both arms. She drove her small knife into its hands and the Ny-dick dropped her. Eirian quickly sprinted away, and began to climb up a rock face, but she wasn't quite quick enough. The Ny-dick was there in an instant. Grabbing her by the neck, it dragged her roughly down to the ground.

Eirian wasn't about to give up. She kicked out but the Ny-dick easily avoided her legs. With the Ny-dick's fingers wrapped tightly around her neck, Eirian found breathing was difficult. It was obviously toying with her. "Death is not for now," Emm said to her, an evil smile on his face. "Kibria will be so happy to see you again. Once he's done with you, it will be onto the master." The Ny-dick jerked Eirian up by her neck and stood her onto her feet.

Eirian's muffled groans, sent sparks of anger traveling along Broan's nerves. He killed an annoying Ny-dick with his sword and began to rush towards Eirian. Suddenly, a boulder whizzed past him, hitting the Ny-dick squarely in the back. Broan swung quickly around and came face to face with a Giant. Bellowing a litany of curses, he raised his sword and charged it head on. The Giant easily pushed Broan aside. With arms the size of tree trunks, it quickly picked up another boulder and again flung it at the Ny-dick, striking it in the head this time. Shaking its head, the Ny-dick loosened its grip on Eirian and stumbled forward. The Giant quickly pulled Eirian away from the stunned Ny-dick and tucked her up in a tree.

Screaming in rage, the Ny-dick drew a knife and shoved it at the Giant, slashing with fury through clothing and skin. With one brush of the Giant's hand the Ny-dick was pinned against the rock outcropping. With the other hand, the Giant broke off a large tree limb and drove it deep.

Emm was stunned as he looked down at the wooden growth occupying the place where his heart should have been. He looked at the Giant and growled, and then his eyes glazed over and he collapsed.

Meanwhile, Laeg and Ardis were busy firing arrows, aiming for the neck and torso of the Ny-dick trying to suffocate Idwal. Grunts turned into annoyed distress as the Ny-dick tossed Idwal aside and faced Laeg and Ardis. It pulled out an arrow imbedded in its flesh and broke it. The Ny-dick downed its head and began to charge.

Idwal picked up his sword and grasping it tightly with both hands drove it deep into the beast's back. He held it there until the enemy collapsed. The smell of blood, copper and sweet, made Idwal shiver. He withdrew his sword and bravely held on to it, like an anchor in a tempest.

GarrRod jumped onto the back of another passing Ny-dick and repeatedly thrust his knife into its neck until it fell to the ground. With senses explicably on edge, GarrRod rushed towards Eirian but was quickly intercepted by another Ny-dick. It didn't take long for the Giant to break that torturous Ny-dick's neck. The Ny-dick fell to the ground, a quizzical stare on its face.

The Giant laid waste to another two Ny-dick that were making good their attack. In truth, if it hadn't been for the Giant, their quest to get to the Walled City would have ended right then and there. Eirian jumped down from the tree and hobbled towards Stamas. His clothes were soaked with a mixture of both his blood and the Ny-dick's. Stamas turned and looked at her. "I'm trying to be charitable here Eirian, but who concocted such a risky plan to leave Solveig?"

Eirian didn't answer his question. "You're wounded! Here, sit down and I'll see what I can do." She limped back to get her pack and as she passed Broan, she called over her shoulder, "Broan this is Stamas, my friend. Stamas this is…"

"I know who this is," Stamas said as he eyed Broan. "Lord Broan, I've heard much about you."

Broan gave Eirian a quick glance. "And I've heard nothing about you."

Stamas smiled, raised his massive arms and checked for wounds on his arms and lower body. "I'll be fine Eirian, nothing to the bone." He lowered his eyes to look at Broan. "It seems these Ny-dicks snuck by yesterday with hardly a notice. Once I realized they were gone, I tried to get to you before you left your camp, but you little ones travel fast when you want to."

"Had I known you were coming, I'd have waited," Broan said. As a show of gratitude and respect, Broan offered his flask of water to Stamas.

Stamas took the flask and emptied it into his mouth. "No you wouldn't have, and after what we did at Solveig, I don't blame you." He turned his attention to Eirian. "Lija said you'd been taken hostage by those at Solveig. He called on us to help save you from certain death. It never sat right with me, so I decided to wait and watch. When I saw you climb down the fortress wall and then back up again I knew we had been lied to. You weren't here by any other means than your own free will."

Eirian gave him a stiff smile, nodded and hid her wrist behind her back. "I had hoped you'd get that message. Now let me look at those cuts."

Everyone watched as Eirian scrambled over the Giants lap to get to his chest. Stamas was well over twenty feet tall. They marveled at the difference in size between him and Eirian. She began poking at the wounds only to have Stamas reach up to protect them. "Stop that," she yelled at him, pushing his hand away.

"Has she always been that bossy?" V-Tor asked.

Stamas smiled and chuckled, causing Eirian to lose her balance. His hand swiftly came up and gently righted her. "Always," he answered, causing everyone to laugh.

"Thanks!" exclaimed Eirian as she put her hands on her hips. "Here I'm trying to help you and this is how you talk about me?"

Stamas picked her up and tenderly placed her on the ground next to Broan. With much groaning and grunting, he rose to his feet. "Once the Ny-dick are on the hunt they don't give up. They're deadly obsessive. The sooner you move on the better. I'll hold up in the pass and protect your back, but don't let your guard down. Now that they know for sure that you've left Solveig, they'll send more."

He looked at Broan. "If you want to defeat your enemies Lord Broan, you'll need alliances of more than just Manlike and Elftan. Stop blocking the aid Eirian has being offering you."

"I didn't know she was offering me anything." Broan studied Stamas for a moment and decided to keep his thoughts to himself. "Know that I do welcome your aid. Is there anything we can do to help you guard the pass?"

Stamas shrugged. "Just take care of Eirian." He smiled at Eirian and then shape-shifted from Mortal, to rocks and earth. His new form quickly melted into the ground, disappearing from sight.

Idwal was amazed at the magic of the Giants. "They can do that?" he said in awe. Everyone turned and looked at Eirian.

"This is how they usually move around. They shape-shift becoming one with the land, then they travel through it; we walk upon it. What's so strange about that?"

"But they can do both!"

V-Tor shook his head and looked over at Broan. "You're right. There's a lot to learn from this Faery."

Broan pondered his options. "We'll need to move off the trade route." He looked at Eirian. "Can you lead us to Mount Tivdora from here?"

"Yes, but it's not easy. What looks like a direct route to the next mountain isn't."

"We've no choice. Let's move out," Broan said as he pulled his pack back on.

The mountain humbled them all. Its steep inclines swiftly changed to shear rock faces. Their progress was excruciatingly slow as they moved upward. Before entering the vapor clouds, Broan looked back. The forest was a small blur deep in the valley and their trail was nonexistent. He searched for any shadowy figures coming up behind them, but nothing moved.

When they were safe in the mountain mist, Broan pushed the group harder. The sun was low on the horizon and he didn't want them to be climbing in the dark. When they finally cleared the mist Broan wanted to cheer. They had an unimpeded view of Tivdora and the last crest they'd have to climb. Ardis caught Broan's eye, got the nod and quickly moved away from the group.

"If Ardis is lucky we'll have more than dry, smoked meat to eat tonight," Broan announced to the group with a smile.

V-Tor watched Ardis disappear back into the misty cloud. "If I had the strength I'd join him," he mumbled.

"We all would," Laeg said as he passed him. "Come on V-Tor, we're almost done for the day."

A huge harvest moon was just establishing itself on the horizon by the time Ardis joined them in camp. He had a few rock ptarmigan and a few ten-pound hares. Everyone's mouths watered at the thought of the white flesh of the hares and the dark flesh of the birds cooking over the open flames.

Eirian sat just outside of the fire. She absent-mindedly rubbed her bound wrist. The physical demands of this trip had caused the cord to dig even deeper. She was losing the strength and feeling in her fingers and it worried her. Lying down on a flat granite outcropping, she chewed on some herb leaves she had picked up in the forest.

Ardis tossed the game down on the ground and walked over to Eirian. "I've found something for you to eat," he said as he pulled out a few bird's eggs. "You need to eat more than berries and grass to keep up your strength. Do you want them raw or cooked?"

Eirian looked up at him. She couldn't hide her hunger any longer. "Cooked if that's okay?"

Ardis nodded and moved back to the fire.

Sobus had always used others to do his dirty work. That way he was able to avoid a direct confrontation with the Queen. He had planned to slowly destroy her through the very land and people she supported. He would wear her down to submission, and like a dog, she would have to heel, and then he would kill her.

But it wasn't to be. *"Lija,"* Sobus hissed.

Lija sensed more then saw Sobus' form in the smoke of the crackling campfire. Knowing that mind talk was more to Sobus' liking, and the fact that he was willing to waste his power to appear in a tangible form, meant this was trouble. *"Lija,"* Sobus called. *"I'm vexed and confused. My well thought out plan has been ruined by something so unexpected … your weakness and disloyalty!"*

"I don't understand," Lija answered. His whole body began to coil up tight in anticipation of Sobus' assault. "You asked me to lay siege to Solveig, and I have."

"You stupid fool!" Sobus' smoky form circled around Lija like a vulture. *"I've been told that seven people have managed to escape from Solveig and that the Faery leader, Eirian, is one of them! I agree Solveig is a high priority, but Faery leaders and Warlords are HIGHER!"*

With cruel severity, Sobus attacked. Even though he appeared as a misty shroud he had his full strength. Sobus seized Lija and then shot him through the air. Lija bounced off an Ancient monolith and crumpled to the ground. With wispy fingers of smoke, Sobus grab Lija. *"Stand when I talk to you!"* he yelled as he and jerked Lija to attention. *"Why wasn't I informed?"*

"I have had no news of anyone leaving Solveig," Lija wheezed out.

"WELL THEY HAVE. They are making their way to the Walled City by a mountain path as we speak." Sobus tightened his grip on Lija's neck and shook him violently. *"This has forced my hand. Prepare for my coming,"* Sobus hissed as he disappeared.

When Lija felt he was truly alone he sat up and collected himself. Haunting terror was always a residue left in the wake of Sobus' punishment. The terror ate away at Lija's sensibilities like maggots on rotting flesh. But this time Lija knew he had to do what was right. He moved beyond the pain and fear and made his way towards the edge of the forest that overlooked Solveig.

He wished he had the power of the Queen so he'd be able to warn the people of Solveig about the evil that was about to visit them. His only hope was to call on the power within nature to awaken Solveig and save those Mortals within her. He closed his eyes and using all his concentration, he focused on shifting the energy that surrounded Solveig and the land it was built on.

The next day found Broan's group in great spirits. They had made it to the base of Tivdora by the steep valley that ran between the two mountains and into a dense forest. After about an hour walk, Broan led the group down into the shadows of a long coulee.

Swiftly the walls of the canyon seemed to press in on them as the shadows deepened. Branches and fallen trees from the upper surrounding forest made an irregular canvas over the top of the gorge, limiting what light could come through. Half way down the coulee, Broan stopped in front of a dark shadow in the massive rock wall. He ran his hand over a small indent and smiling he looked back at the others. This was the secret entrance to the tunnel that would take them right into the Walled City.

Broan lit the torches they had brought with them. "We're almost there," he said. He was watching Eirian from the corner of his eye. She was very pale and he had been aware for some time that her energy was waning. This journey had proved to be harder on her than he had expected. He approached her and lifted her backpack. "Here let me take that. We'll have to stoop down for a short while and this will get in your way. "

Eirian looked up at him and was going to protest but she realized that she really didn't have the strength to fight him any longer. She gave him the pack and whispered her 'thanks'.

Broan led the way with Ardis taking up the rear point. Everyone had to hunch over as they entered the passageway. They were quickly surrounded in a surreal stillness. Other than the hushed swear words from those who kept bumping their heads on the low ceiling, the silence was all encompassing. It swallowed even the sound of their boots.

The heavy atmosphere pressed in on Eirian. She warily followed the dim light from the torches before her. Her sore wrist bumped against a small outcrop of rock and she had to stop. The pain was so intense. Trying to suppress a cry, she grabbed her wrist and pressed it to her chest.

"It gets quite a bit lower here, but after this we'll be able to stand up," Broan said as he gave her a questioning look. Eirian dropped her wrist. His eyes narrowed slightly and she gave him a brief smile. Broan turned and got down on his stomach. He inched forward, pushing his torch ahead of him.

Eirian lowered herself to the damp floor and followed, keeping her wrist well protected. Once on the other side, Broan quickly took her by the elbow and pulled her clear. "Stand here and keep your back to the wall. There's a drop off to your left." He stood there studying her for a moment then went back to helping the others.

Once they were all through the low passage Broan slowly led the group through the tangled debris of deadfall that had funneled down a narrow gap. At the top of the incline it opened up to a fifty-meter high archway and a cathedral-like cavern.

Eirian was enthralled. This place spoke to her. Never before had she felt the world breathe. Never before had she felt its heart beat. This place mysteriously called to her. She didn't feel crowded and trapped anymore. She felt safe.

She gazed about. On one side of the cavern was an irregular shaped wall. Layers of rocks formed a type of staircase which fresh water cascaded down. Warm waters from a hot spring bubbled up and mixed with the chilly water, creating large pools of aqua blue water at the base of the wall.

Mesmerized, Eirian walked towards this incredible phenomenon of nature. Looking into one of the lower pools she found the water so clear and warm, it was hard not to jump in. She sighed. With all that they'd been through, all the dampness, all the wild winds and bone deep chills, nothing would feel better than diving into the pools and soaking for days.

"V-Tor, stay here with Eirian. I think it best to check things out with my uncle before I show up with a Faery," Broan said. "I'll send Laeg or Idwal back to get you when it's safe." He looked over at Eirian "Don't even think about it."

Eirian tossed him an angry look. "I wasn't thinking anything!"

Broan gave her a challenging look and after one last glance at V-Tor, he went down a corridor and was soon out of sight.

"You or me first?" Eirian asked as soon as she thought they were out of earshot.

"You. I'll set up camp. I think we may be here for a while." He turned towards the gap they had just come from. "I'm going to gather any dry wood I can from that mess back here. I'll whistle before I re-enter the cave. Then I'll…" he paused and looked at her over his shoulder. She'd already taken off her tunic off and was about to raise her undershirt. He quickly looked away and finished, "give you a few minutes to get dressed."

Eirian froze until V-Tor was completely out of sight. After that it only took her seconds to get out of the rest of her clothes, everything except her chemise, which hid her ring. Quickly she lowered herself into the water and unwrapped her bound wrist. She hoped the water would help to ease some of the pain.

"It's about time!" Iarnan said stepping forward to greet Broan. "I've been worried about you ever since Ke-Hern arrived." Iarnan was a tall man with a warrior's body. He had broad shoulders and strong legs, and only the stock of his gray hair and eyes gave away his age.

"You know it would take more than a few Ny-dick to keep me away." Broan said hugging his uncle.

Iarnan looked around. "You came with so few. Was that really wise?"

"You're the one who taught me that when you need speed you travel light and with the best."

Iarnan nodded in agreement and then led the group into the Main-Hall to eat. Once there, he filled a platter with some food and led Broan to a more secluded room. "I've always believed you should never bury history under years of complacency but that's just what we've done here," Iarnan said.

Broan helped himself to the food and sat down on the ledge of the windowsill. "You may be right, uncle. The Ny-dick are back and this time Lija is leading them, which makes them even more deadly. They're better trained and more organized than they were last time. They've laid siege to Solveig, and I fear it won't be long before they head south and isolate the Walled City as well."

Iarnan was silent.

"Why didn't the High Council want me to investigate the attacks along the outer areas of Gearoldin and Anwel?" Broan asked.

"Nothing is easy anymore. Everything has to be debated and argued over. Diplomatic road-blocks are an everyday occurrence now." He looked up to Broan. "Your news is going to ignite a firestorm. Success makes selfish, cranky people, and the elite will want to leave this insurgence to negotiations while grasping at opportunities that may knock on their doors."

"Uncle, there's a whole Ny-dick army out there! Soon the only thing knocking on their doors will be war."

"Pivan," Iarnan yelled. "Call everyone to council. Tell them to meet me there NOW!" He turned back to Broan. "Where's V-Tor? I didn't see him among your group."

"He's coming."

It wasn't long before Broan was standing in the High Council chambers. He stared up at the assembly, and then nodded to his uncle.

Iarnan stood. "Gentlemen, Broan the Warlord of Solveig, is here to give us news of great importance." He stopped and slowly glared at all assembled. "And please remember this, while you debate, hill-sides around villages are now dotted with fresh graves, too many fresh graves. And the question is what will Remdor now do?"

Broan righted his thoughts and stood tall, ready to tell them news they couldn't ignore anymore. Dispensing with the formalities, Broan got right to the point. "The Ny-dick are back! And they are back with the Wizard Lija as their leader! They're at my doorstep and soon they will be at yours. WE ARE AT WAR!"

The whole room exploded into chaos. A cacophony of voices rose to a fevered pitch and the clamor became as steady as a swarm of bees. Some councilmen rushed to floor demanding to be heard, others yelled at Broan, not wanting to believe what he had just said.

Iarnan sat quietly in his chair. He had something to check on and he needed to keep the Committee members busy. Leaning to his right, Iarnan spoke to the young councilman next to him. "Mohr, would you please prolong the debate until I come back. Questions every angle, every suggestion."

Mohr gave a slight nod to Iarnan and stared at Broan. He wasn't sure what Iarnan was up too and didn't rightly care. He would manage Iarnan later, as he always had. He fingered the tassel on his sash and smiled, reflecting on how he had just graduated from the very place that originally rejected him. And now, look at him, a council member and an advisor to Iarnan himself. Life was good and he was going to keep it that way.

V-Tor sighed with deep delight as he got out of the warm pool. He dried himself off and finished dressing. As he walked towards the fire he yelled to Eirian, "You can come in now."

When Eirian approached, he grabbed some bread and cheese from their packs and offered her some. "I've made a bed away from the fire for you, but PLEASE no climbing up the wall to hide." He stared at her, waiting for her promise. She nodded, took the bread and sat down.

Eirian was warm, clean and relaxed. "With your standing as a warrior and a leader, you could be warlord of your own camp. Why are you so loyal to Broan?" she asked.

V-Tor continued to eat and Eirian wondered if he had even heard her. Finally he spoke. "More than once, his blood was spilled for me on the battlefield. That is something one never forgets. I don't need to have my own command to be happy or fulfilled. I'm where I am by choice."

Eirian liked his answer. V-Tor embraced all his passions and choices with a clear mind and an intensity that matched few others. She then pointed to his head. "Why do you shave your head? No one else does."

V-Tor raised his hand and ran it over the stubble and regretted that he hadn't shaved while he was in the pool. "Hair gets in the way when I am fighting."

"I know what you mean. That's why I wear the skullcap. It's hot at times but it does the trick. Nothing is worse than getting your hair caught in a bush when you're trying to hide or get away. I never thought of shaving it though."

V-Tor reached up and captured a strand of hair that had escaped its confinement. He liked its deep amber color. He tested the texture between his fingers and thumb then he slowly let the piece of hair fall from his grasp. "Don't shave," was all he said as he got up to get another piece of wood for the fire.

"You're lax V-Tor! That surprises me."

V-Tor growled and swung around, "Only you Iarnan have ever been able to sneak up on me. Does Broan know you are here?"

"No, I knew something was up when you didn't show up with him. You two are never far apart." Iarnan said glancing at Eirian. "So what is your name?"

Eirian slipped off the ledge and came to stand next the V-Tor. "Eirian. I'm…"

"Faery," Iarnan finished for her. He reached up and gently took hold of Eirian's chin. He studied her face for a moment, and then he smiled, "It's a good thing he has kept you hidden."

"Broan wasn't sure how you'd feel about a…"

"Not Broan." Iarnan smiled, "That old fool, Ke-Hern. He has always been good at keeping secrets but YOU are the biggest secret yet." Iarnan's smile deepened. "I'm fine with you being Faery. In fact, I'm very fine with it, although I'm not sure what the council will think." He glanced down at her Faery clothes. "Do you have a change of clothes?"

"Yes, Bronagh lent me some."

"Good, go get changed, and then we'll go join the others."

"This is going to be good," V-Tor cut in.

Eirian gave V-Tor a dirty look as she grabbed her pack. "I'll be right back." She stopped suddenly and looked around in search of something to change behind.

"Over there," V-Tor said, pointing. "We'll look the other way."

V-Tor and Iarnan waited quietly with their backs turned. The silence was occasionally broken by a curse coming from Eirian's direction. "She's not used to women's clothing. Broan has had nothing but trouble trying to get her to wear them," V-Tor murmured.

"Has he really?" Iarnan seemed shocked. "Well at least she'll have a soft bed to sleep in tonight instead of this hard rock."

"It doesn't matter. She prefers to sleep on the floor or up high on some perch," V-Tor said matter-of-factly. That bit of information surprised Iarnan as well. He went to glance over his shoulder but stopped himself.

"Finished," she announced as stepped into view. There she stood in full dress; a simple white linen gown that went to the floor, with an overlay of a brown shift and a leather belt around her waist. Her hair, thick and rich with color, hung down around her hips. Her smile slowly faded, as Iarnan and V-Tor just stood there gaping at her. She nervously smoothed the front of her shift.

Suddenly Iarnan's brow furrowed and he tossed V-Tor a heated glance. "What happened to your wrist?" he asked stepping forward. "There's blood seeping through the bandage."

Eirian pulled her wrist back and hid it behind her. "Nothing... there's nothing wrong with it."

"Let's see," V-Tor said as he grabbed her arm forcing it out from behind her. "DAMN! The Faery Binding Cord!" In a panic, he started to take the bandage off.

"Careful!" Iarnan cautioned, "You don't want to add to the injury." He pushed V-Tor out of the way and took over.

Eirian closed her eyes. She knew what it looked like and didn't need to be reminded. She tried once again to pull her arm back, but Iarnan held on tight.

Iarnan's fingers hovered over her red, raw, weeping wrist. Anger flashed in his eyes. "How could you have let this happen? I detested these things from the very beginning. I never allowed them into the city." He looked at V-Tor, "and we never had any Faery problems!" V-Tor's shoulders dropped in embarrassment.

"Who put this distasteful thing on?"

"Broan," V-Tor volunteered, "and only he can remove it."

Iarnan looked at Eirian. "Then let's not waste any more time. Come with me. It's time to put an end to this."

"None of us knew how bad it was. Broan wouldn't have let it go on this long if he had known," V-Tor explained but when he got no response, he hushed up and fell in behind them. He was upset with Broan, upset with Eirian, but mostly he was upset with himself for not noticing sooner.

Iarnan pushed against what looked like an old stone wall at the end of a man created tunnel and entered an anteroom. They had emerged through a small portal near the back of a fireplace. Comforting smells of past fires clung to the large stone hearth. Soot darkened the stone and ceramic tile that surrounded the fireplace opening.

"Smart," V-Tor said as he climbed through. "What happens if there's a fire going in the fireplace?"

"The smoke enters the tunnel. You have lots of warning. I once got caught in the tunnel for half a day. It's not that bad. The underground pools are a nice place to swim."

Eirian stood still with her eyes closed. Over the odor of charcoal Eirian picked up a resinous, semi-spicy fragrance. She breathed in the aroma and opened her eyes. "No wonder Ke-Hern likes coming here. It smells of history, power and longevity." She looked at the two of them staring back at her. "Well it does," she insisted.

Iarnan put his arm around Eirian and guided her along, soon exiting the room. "Pivan!" he yelled. A young lad rushed down the wood paneled hallway towards them. "Take these two to my chambers and then go find Ke-Hern."

V-Tor grabbed Iarnan's shoulder in excitement. "Ke-Hern's here? We've been waiting months for him to arrive."

"He couldn't make it through. It became too dangerous so he came here looking for my help. He was very insistent that I allow him an escort to Solveig." Iarnan paused and looked at Eirian. "Now I know why."

Lurking just outside of Solveig in the upper forest, Deeton the Faery watched with special interest. Although he was known to be a warrior, his heart was more moved with history and learning. His interests ranged from learning the language of the Ancients to saving young women from drowning. He knew about Solveig's geological quirk and the magic in the very land it was built on. He had watched from afar as Broan had built his fortress. "Broan still doesn't understand the full impact his fortress is going to make on the Mortals in the coming years," Deeton said to himself. "*In fact,*" he wondered, "*does Ke-Hern even know?*"

He flew low over Solveig's wall. He was glad Eirian had finally left. Now he could get back to keeping an eye on Bronagh. Even though these unknown visits were on the edge of violating the Faery decree, Deeton didn't care. From the first time he saw Bronagh clinging to that upset boat in choppy waters, his heart belonged to her.

Once he was on the roof of the Keep, Deeton changed to his Mortal shape and made himself comfortable. His mop of brown curly hair stood out against the weatherworn wooden beams and gray stone roof of the Keep. His hands rested on his chest and his haunting dark eyes inspected the intense blue sky. Deeton liked days like this, it reminded him of his life before it all was destroyed.

He shifted onto his side, inching closer to the edge of the roof above Bronagh's window. Careful not to be seen, he waited for Bronagh to start her day. He was startled as he watched two millipedes and a few termites crawl out from under the wood beams on the roof. He immediately knew this wasn't normal.

With an uneasy feeling Deeton looked over edge of the roof and studied the ground and buildings around him. Insects where coming out of their hiding places and into the bright sunlight. Moths that were often seen only in the fluttering shadows of the night had taken to the air. Digger wasps were staggering out of their burrows, carrying their larva in tight little white bundles. Spiders stepped out over the edges of leaves and with their silk strings, sailed along wind currents, giving them a speedy escape. Ants, caterpillars and even rodents were coming out into the light of day and forging their way out of Solveig. So the question remained for Deeton, where were they going? Or equally, perhaps as important, why were they packing up and leaving?

Suddenly the wind whipped up and distant thunderclaps were heard. Yet there were no clouds or storms on the horizon. There was no mistaking it. There had been a shift in the energy of the electrical balance in nature, and that had set the lower life forms to motion. Deeton raised himself to his knees, no longer caring if he was discovered. He spied Lija leaving the clearing and wondered what the Wizard had done.

Deeton jumped when he felt a hand on his shoulder. He spun around to find another Faery next to him. "O-Yarr! I should have known it was you."

"Well someone needs to watch your back." O-Yarr looked around them both and raised an eyebrow. "Do you know how close you are to breaking the code?"

Deeton turned his attention back on the activity of the insects. "Not as close as I'm going to be in two seconds," he said changing back into Faery, "Tell me what you see?"

O-Yarr glanced around Solveig. "Insects. So?" He shaped-shifted back to Faery form as well.

"Doesn't their activity remind you of something?"

Suddenly awareness gripped O-Yarr. "The Queen's Revenge!"

"Go and tell Cephas! I'll try and get the people of Solveig to leave before it's too late."

"You can't! Remember…" O-Yarr shouted grabbing tightly onto Deeton, forcing him back from the edge.

Deeton shook him off. "I can and I will. The sooner you tell Cephas the better." He studied the ground again as insects continued to flee.

"But they will not follow you! They didn't believe Eirian."

"They may not follow me but they'll follow Bronagh."

"No, wait!" O-Yarr shouted, but it was too late. Left with no other choice O-Yarr took off to find Cephas.

Deeton landed on Bronagh's windowsill. Luckily her window was open so Deeton stepped in as Faery, and then changed into his once true self— an Elftan from Duronyk. After so many years, Bronagh and Deeton were face-to-face once again. He struggled to submerge his feelings for her, knowing he needed help to save those in Solveig. History only repeats itself for one purpose and that's to give you a second chance to right a wrong and learn a lesson.

Chapter 10

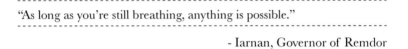

"As long as you're still breathing, anything is possible."

- Iarnan, Governor of Remdor

Iarnan entered the High Council chambers, briefly acknowledged Mohr, and then turned his attention to the Council. "It's good to explore the facts, but I think enough information's been shared," Iarnan said. "It is time to decide. The lives of our people rest in your hands. I, Governor of Remdor, say we join Warlord Broan but understand by law that you, the council, have to decide. Broan, let's leave them to their vote."

Iarnan and Broan left the high council chamber and walked down the hall to the staircase that would take them back up to the living quarters. "Come with me," Iarnan ordered sternly. "There's something you must do before anything can move forward."

Iarnan's tone of voice said a lot and Broan didn't question him. He followed him up the stairs and into Iarnan's quarters.

Broan had always liked Iarnan's quarters. The room was full of nature's colors, hues of green, muted violet and browns, all promoting a tranquil space. As a child he often found himself sitting either on one of the comfortable benches by the large deep fireplace or at the small eating table by the balcony doors. He smiled remembering his long talks with his uncle.

The tranquil essence of fond memories evaporated as soon as Broan entered and saw V-Tor and Eirian. His blue eyes narrowed with anger. "You better have a good reason for disobeying an order V-Tor," he said, then turned his eyes to Eirian, "Or was this your idea?"

Iarnan interrupted. "It was neither of them. I knew when you arrived that you weren't telling me everything. So I went back into the cave and found them. I brought them here because you have to correct a very serious wrong!" He pushed Broan over to Eirian, picked up her arm and exposed her wrist. "Do you understand the damage this thing does? At first it burns the skin, and then it begins to cut! The band gets smaller and tighter over time. Of all the Faeries, whatever made you even think of using it on her?"

Broan was at a loss for words. He had totally forgotten about the damn thing. He stared at Eirian with mixture of concern and anger. He pulled the knife out of his boot and took her arm. "Why did you let it get this bad? You could have asked me to remove it long ago."

"I did, many times. I asked you to remove it after the Sulpets attacked and when I needed to go for supplies. I even offered to fly here to get help!" Eirian yelled back.

"YOU just wanted to fly away and escape! You didn't ask to have the cord removed because it hurt you!" he yelled even louder.

"ENOUGH," bellowed Ke-Hern as he walked into the room, "Just cut the damn thing off!"

"Now you show up!!! Where have you been?" Eirian yelled.

He ignored her and stomped over to Broan. "Well get on with it. Damn! I should've known that this was the reason I couldn't pick up Eirian's energy print. I'm a stupid fool of a Wizard!"

Broan took Eirian's elbow in his hand and guided her over to the small wooden table. After he made her sit at one end of the table, he pulled open the white linen drapes, hoping the light from the floor to ceiling windows would aid him in the task at hand.

Eirian gingerly placed her arm on the table. When Broan took a firm grip of her arm near her injured wrist, her uneasiness skyrocketed "You said you'd never remove it until you trusted me. Do you trust me now?"

"We're in the Walled City, and you helped us get here," Broan said as he took a moment to calm himself and steady his hands.

She pulled at her arm in an attempt to remove her wrist from the table, but Broan just held on tighter.

"This is no time to back down," Broan, said as he firmly held her wrist.

"I'm not backing down!" Eirian pulled harder, trying to free herself. "Do you trust me or not?" she demanded, "I need to know!"

Broan simply ignored her and concentrated on how he was going to release the cord. "HOLD STILL."

"I need to know."

"It's a binding cord Eirian, not a test of valor," he barked back at her.

"Stop this! You're bickering like an old married couple. What the hell happened in Solveig?"

Eirian glared at Ke-Hern. "If you had shown up you would know."

Broan knew he wasn't really mad at her. He knew he was angry with himself for not finding out sooner that the binding cord was hurting her. "I trust you on most things. But I never had any doubt that you'd try and escape the first chance you got…and I didn't want…couldn't let that to happen…" Broan looked Eirian right in the eye and then eased his grip slightly. "Hold still or it'll hurt more than necessary."

Slowly Broan worked the point of his knife under the cord. He stopped and asked for a clean cloth to blot up the fresh blood that was weeping from the wound. "Are you okay?" He asked than waited until she nodded. Slowly he continued carefully working the knife more fully under the cord and forced it upward, away from her skin.

Broan heard the catch in her breathing and paused. "Eirian, don't hold your breath. It'll only make the pain worse." He waited for her to gain control and then continued. He tilted the knife a bit more onto its side only to have the bleeding increase. This time he didn't stop but sliced his knife through the cord. He quickly dropped the knife on the table and raised her arm. Taking one end of the cord he worked it free of her flesh, releasing her from its spell. Without thought, Broan tossed it into the fire.

"No!" screamed Eirian jumping up, trying to grab it. Too late! The cord hit the fire and exploded into iridescent sparks that flew up the chimney and into the sky. She grabbed the stained rag from the table and sat down. Quickly she wrapped her wrist and hid it under the table.

Ke-Hern moved to stand in front of the glass doors of the balcony. He raised his hands to ward off any sudden movements from those in the room. "No matter what you see or hear, do not move a hair," he warned.

Suddenly, two fully dressed Faery warriors appeared in front of Eirian. They wore Faery colored clothing under hardened leather breastplates. Various knives poked out from the leather bands that ran crisscross over their chests. A battle-axe hung off both soldier backs.

"You summoned us," the taller one, called Cephas, asked as he drew his sword.

"Stand down!" Eirian commanded. "I summoned you because I've made my decision. Gather those nearby. I'll address them here."

Cephas calculated the threat of the group in the room. Only after acknowledging Ke-Hern with a brief nod did he step back. "As you wish." He eyed both Broan and V-Tor. "But Hywel stays here with you."

"Fine, but be quick about it before I change my mind," Eirian said as Cephas shape-shifted back into Faery and left.

Hywel may have been the shorter of the two, but he still stood nearly six feet tall. His hair was rich brown in color and hung thickly around his face. He smiled at Ke-Hern and then at Eirian. "Then you've found these Manliken and Elftan worthy to stand with us in this brewing conflict?" he asked, his voice laced with excitement.

"No," Eirian said glaring at Broan, "But their children are."

Eirian buried her wounded wrist deep into the pocket of her shift before she rose from her chair. "Governor Iarnan, Broan, V-Tor, this is Hywel. He and Cephas are my seconds in charge." She walked to the balcony door, avoiding everyone's questioning stares. "It won't take long for Cephas to return. We had better go out on the balcony."

Broan was stunned. He glanced at Ke-Hern hoping for some kind of insight, but all Ke-Hern did was motion Broan to follow her. As they stepped onto the balcony Ke-Hern whispered into Broan's ear, "Don't worry so much. Everything will be revealed to you shortly. Then you can yell at me."

Broan grabbed Ke-Hern's arm. "Wait a minute. Does she really lead a Faery army? Is this the very war you warned me about all those years ago?"

"What do you mean warned you? I've always told you there would be a battle with the Faeries, but as in WITH not against! No wonder Eirian had such a hard time. Next time clean your ears," Ke-Hern huffed, "Against..." He shook his head. "As if!"

Just as they reached the grey stone railing of the balcony, Cephas appeared and stood next to Eirian. Suddenly the city roofs exploded with color. Hundreds of Faeries, all iridescent and glowing, waited for Eirian to speak.

Eirian reached down beneath the neck of her linen dress with her good hand and removed the ring from the secret pocket in her Faery chemise. She lifted it high in the air for all to see. "This is the Ring of

Cian, given to me so that I may lead you all to freedom." She paused, almost too scared to continue. She knew that once declared there was no turning back. "The time has come. The war that will remove the curse is here. We're taking up arms and standing alongside Manliken and Elftan to once again defeat the Ny-dick and this evil that traps us."

Ke-Hern elbowed Broan and whispered, "At least SHE got it right."

Broan ignored Ke-Hern's dig, placing his full attention on Eirian. She spoke with clarity and command but knew that was not enough to lead an army or fight a war. *"What was Ke-Hern thinking?"*

Eirian paused and scanned the faces of her kin. "Go now, before the Ny-dick and Lija find out what we're about. As always, surprise is our most effective weapon." Stepping back from the railing, she looked at Cephas and Hywel. "I want you to go inside and tell everyone what you know. If we are to make this work, we need to start right now." They nodded to her then followed Iarnan back into the room.

Eirian looked into Broan's questioning eyes. "This is my army," she said, pausing slightly before continuing, "I was willing to tell you all of this long ago, but there never was enough trust between us to do so."

Broan could feel the heaviness of her heart. He nodded once and gave her a half smile. Turning he went inside, leaving Eirian to her solitude.

Once alone Eirian slid down the cold rock balustrade and sat on the floor. Tears began to roll down her cheeks. "What've I done?" she moaned to herself.

"What destiny has asked of you," Ke-Hern answered from the doorway.

Eirian turned her face away from him. "I'm not convinced that this is my destiny or that this is the war that will end our imprisonment." She paused, and then worriedly asked, "As you know, if I've chosen wrong, we all go to the void!"

"Eirian, look deep into your heart. You know the truth. It has begun."

"How can you be so sure, when I'm not?"

Ke-Hern walked over to her. "Doubt has always been your problem. Look, destiny is never easy…" He raised an eyebrow, "especially when it has to push you into action."

"IT didn't push me YOU did!"

"Fine," Ke-Hern barely paused, and then continued, "but only towards what needed to be done."

She still held Cian's ring in her palm. It was made of simple silver. No design was craved or added to the wide ring. It weighed heavily now that she had accepted its burden, its power. "Strange to think something so plain holds so much…" She looked up at Ke-Hern. "Why? Why, in so many ways, does this not feel right?"

"Because it's in living your destiny that you find out who you really are and it's always frightening to face one's self."

"That's not helping," she snarled. Regretting the bite in her words, Eirian looked away. "Sorry," she whispered.

Ke-Hern smiled at her. "That's okay. Now put the ring on and let's get things going."

Eirian's hand shook as she placed the ring on her thumb. It was bulky and had been made for a man. "I'll never be able to shape-shift again. I'll never be able to fly," she said with some regret. "This is just as bad as the binding cord."

Ke-Hern helped her up and looked at her with empathy. "This one won't harm you."

"Promise?"

His silence was not comforting. Saddened, Eirian returned her injured limb back into her pocket, entered the room and sat down at the table. She leaned in to listen to what Cephas and Hywel had to say and became drawn in to all the latest news - movements of the enemy, which villages had been wiped out, even their numbers.

"This is all that we know," Cephas said as he stepped back from the table. Fatigue from holding his Mortal form for so long was stamped on his face. "We believe that Lija's magic has hidden a lot more from us," he continued. "As good as Faery eyes and abilities are, we do have limitations."

Broan stepped back, smiling at Eirian. "The intelligence is still better than what we have at the moment and we're very thankful for all you've given us thus far." He looked at Cephas and Hywel and offered his hand. Slowly, each Faery took their turn and placed their hand in Broan's and shook it. Eirian was amazed at the trust that was implied in those handshakes and especially between these particular factions. "*That's what got me into trouble in the first place.*" She wiggled her sore wrist trying to ease the ache.

Eirian didn't get up from her seat when Cephas and Hywel prepared to leave. "You know what to do," she said with a smile. "Once we leave the Walled City, I will need you to meet with me and Broan often to keep us updated. Until then go, and keep safe."

Their leaving had caught everyone's attention except Ke-Hern's. He didn't like Eirian's pale, dazed look and moved towards her.

Eirian couldn't hold on any longer. She started to lower her head to the table in hopes of stopping the mental murkiness from incasing her, but instead she began to fall sideways towards the floor.

"Broan," Ke-Hern yelled, "catch her!"

Broan quickly pulled her into his arms and noticed that the pocket of her shift was stained with blood. "Damn," he cursed.

"This way," Iarnan said as he headed to his bedchamber.

The room was not an overly large room. Along with the standard things one needed, there was a set of leather chairs by the fireplace and a large polished chest that held some of Iarnan's personal things. "Put her there," he said as he pointed to the bed. "V-Tor, get the water jug and some towels from the nightstand," he added as he closed the drapes.

Broan carefully removed her wrist from its wet confines. "Why didn't she say something? I've never known her to be short on words before."

"Broan, where is your head at? She knew that if Cephas or Hywel found out she was injured, they would've wanted to retaliate against all of you," Ke-Hern said adding, "and all of you would have lost." He sat on the bed next to Eirian and began to clean her wound.

"They're that good?"

"Yes, they are. They have had twenty long, full, seasons to prepare."

"Good," Broan said as he watched Ke-Hern work. He moved away from the bed and over to the fireplace. He pondered his options and decided that for the moment, he would follow an old Wizard and a Faery leader. He motioned to V-Tor, "Go find the Laeg and the others. This changes a lot of things."

When Ke-Hern was done, he stood up from Eirian's side and placed his hand on her forehead. He whispered a few words and then turned towards the rest of the group. "She'll sleep for a while now."

"That's good," Iarnan said. "By the look on your face, Broan, I'd say there's a lot that needs explaining. Come and sit. I'll order some food and drink then we can talk."

Broan wasn't hungry. He wanted answers. "So you really sent Eirian to Solveig. Wasn't that a bit of a bold move…seeing as you sent her alone? I could have…"

"She wasn't totally alone, I sent the boys with her."

"So? A note would have been better."

Ke-Hern popped another grape into his mouth, chewed it and looked as if he was contemplating his answer. "Why? You and Eirian did all right. Besides that's the past. Now that the Mortals and

Faeries are willing to fight together, everyone wins...well except for the Ny-dick and..."

"Yes and who?" Broan probed.

"Lija for one. Other than that, know that curses and spells only reveal their secrets slowly."

"You sound like Tellos, which reminds me," Broan said as he rummaged around his pocket. He pulled out the old, embroidered wristband. "Did she make this?"

Ke-Hern took the band and studied it. He shrugged his shoulders. "She was always good with the needle."

"Did you know that the threads hold magic?"

Ke-Hern snapped his head up in shock and looked at Broan. "What do you mean?"

"Well, at least the ones on Eirian's cap do. She used them to heal others."

Ke-Hern studied the band. It did have the same pattern as Eirian's cap but there was no way he had put healing powers in any of the threads. "How did she use them?" he asked cautiously.

"She tied them around some rocks the first time and then wrapped some around some wood another time."

"Ancients?" Ke-Hern pondered out loud and then smiled. "I don't know how she did it, that old flea off a dog, but she did. So how is Tellos?"

"I regret to say that she recently passed."

"Oh, I'm sorry to hear that, but then again it only means ever...y...thing is..."

"Is what?"

Ke-Hern's face flushed as he brushed off Broan's question. "Soon enough, soon enough, now on with the problem. Do you want to get rid of the Ny-dick or not?"

"Of course!"

"Good," Iarnan piped in. "When you leave here you'll need to visit Eamonn and then..."

Broan jumped up. "What are you talking about? I need to go back to Solveig and break the siege. I do not have time to wander about the countryside. Eirian can stay here, out of danger, until we..."

"Broan," Ke-Hern interrupted, "Do you not understand what's needed here yet? There aren't enough soldiers in each region to fight separately and succeed. Gearoldin and Anwel need to unite and bring their joint army back here to fight the Ny-dick."

Iarnan leaned towards Broan. "You have to go and talk to the governors of the two other regions. Help them see the importance of coming here and ending this in Remdor."

"I think not! If someone has to go, I think it should be you, uncle," Broan said crossing his arms over his chest. "They know you and respect you as a leader and a governor. I'll take what troops you give me back to Solveig." The idea was met with a deafening silence.

Iarnan placed his hand on Broan's shoulder and forced him to sit back down. "Sadly, I can't go. Relations between Gearoldin and us are strained. But they know and respect you as a great Warlord. You've seen firsthand what is happening so they will let you speak to the High Committees. We might have a chance with you leading us. It must be you who goes."

Ke-Hern shook his head, "Broan, there's no…other…way. The time for discussion and arguments has long run out. You must trust us. We need to get as much support from the other regions as possible. That means meeting with Tybalt and Eamonn."

Broan sighed, "Fine! But Eirian stays here. War's no place for a woman. I didn't work this hard at protecting her only to put her in harm's way now."

"No," Ke-Hern said. "Eirian has to go with you. The Faeries will only follow her command."

"Although, the Faeries will be the least of your problems," Iarnan added dryly. "I must warn you. You must keep Eirian well hidden from Tybalt. He would use her to discredit you and may actually try and kill her. Now that she's claimed ownership of the ring, she's a threat to many."

"And what of Solveig?"

Iarnan got up and smiled at Broan. "Even though I know how much she means to you, there is more to this land than just Solveig. You have to make the world take notice of what's happening. You have to awaken them to the truth that their peaceful life is an illusion. Their world is about to be destroyed. In the morning we'll review the troops and decide how many should go with you and how many will go back to Solveig."

Broan looked at V-Tor and the others as they entered.

"Did we miss anything?" V-Tor asked as he walked towards the food and drink Iarnan had brought up.

"Only mad plans to end the second invasion of the Ny-dick and free all the Faeries from the curse. Other than that, not much," Broan answered, realizing just how asinine all this sounded.

They hit like a summer squall: O-Yarr, Cephas and Hywel bolted into Iarnan's quarters unannounced, causing Broan and the others to go for their weapons. Ke-Hern, an island in the storm's eye, raised his large black hands and with a flick of his fingers stilled the tension in the room.

"Where's Eirian?" Cephas asked as he removed his hand from his sword.

Eirian stood at the door of the sleeping quarters. "I'm glad Ke-Hern has more sense than the rest of you," she said confidently, as she stepped into the room and went to stand beside Broan. "Otherwise we are all doomed. Cephas, tell us what has happened to bring you here."

With steady coolness, Cephas stepped forward and addressed both Eirian and Broan, "The news I bring involves . . .." Cephas stared at Eirian's stained shift. "You're injured!"

"I'm fine. Ke-Hern took care of it. Now answer my question!"

Cephas glared at Broan and V-Tor. Hywel broke the tense silence, "The Queen's Revenge is heading towards Solveig! The destruction of one region and its Mortals wasn't enough it seems."

Eirian paled. She stood as still as possible hoping to prevent any sign of her shock to show. Old and sad stories filled with terror and horror flooded into her mind. "The Queen's Revenge, are you sure?" she asked.

"It's not the Queen's Revenge," Ke-Hern said. "And I'll be glad the day we stop calling it that. The Queen never destroyed Duronyk."

"If not the Queen then who else would have enough power for such destruction?" Broan asked.

"Who isn't the immediate concern right now; getting everyone out of Solveig is!"

"BroMac won't let anyone leave Solveig especially with the Ny-dick just outside the gate," V-Tor said, "and the only one that he'll listen to is Broan," he paused for a brief second. "Besides, the mountain pass is too hard for most of the villagers to manage."

"If BroMac will listen only to Broan, then Broan needs to go to Solveig," Iarnan said.

"It would take too long," Cephas said.

"Not if he flew," Eirian offered quietly.

Everyone turned and looked at her.

"It can work," she began. "If I could fly with Leif and Jelen on my back, I'm sure O-Yarr and Cephas could take Ke-Hern and Broan back to Solveig."

"Yes …Yes," Ke-Hern said, cackling and clapping his hands. "And I can cast a spell to protect and hide everyone as we make our way back here."

"In the meantime, V-Tor and I will gather the troops and start out by horse. We should be able to meet you more than half way," Laeg quickly chimed in.

Broan blanched. "You really want me to fly to Solveig."

Ke-Hern nodded, his graying hair bouncing about his shoulders. "We could be there within hours."

"In hours!" Iarnan exclaimed. "Life would be so much easier if travel was that quick."

Broan stared at Cephas and O-Yarr. As large as they both were, he still couldn't image straddling either ones back. "When do we leave?" he asked with trepidation.

"Right now," Ke-Hern said as he set his spell in motion. Soon he and Broan were the size of Eirian's hand. She quickly picked them up and placed them in the slings on O-Yarr and Cephas' backs. Broan was curiously silent throughout the whole procedure.

Ke-Hern winked at him. "Have faith Broan, we'll get there fast enough to save them."

Broan looked back at Ke-Hern with an odd smile on his face. "I have faith that we can save them, I just have limited faith that we can fly."

Ke-Hern laughed as they took off from the balcony.

The view was expansive. Broan could see a multitude of things all at once. He was amazed how the landmarks fit together to form a whole new world. They flew past the steep hilly land along the mountains, over rivers and valleys that would've taken them days to cross on foot. They were so high at times that the clouds drifted passed them.

Broan marveled at all he saw, but it was the view of the sunset from up here that was immediately etched upon his heart. The ground was well covered by the long evening shadows of the mountains as the last beams of sunlight colored the sky in hues of gold and cream. Slowly they painted the clouds crimson as the darkening blue sky quieted the land below, inviting it to sleep. He was beginning to understand the full extent of what Eirian had lost. Flying turned out to be a remarkable experience.

Despite the adrenalin-pumping ride, fear rushed in when he flew over the walls of Solveig. The people of Solveig were standing inside the outer bailey screaming to get out, while his guards and his warriors stood high on the walls with arrows drawn, aimed at their own people. As soon as he dropped from O-Yarr's tunic, he was restored to his normal size. "What is this MADNESS?" Broan bellowed. Shocked, the crowd silenced then stepped back from him. They gasped as Ke-Hern magically appeared beside Broan. "It's alright! Ke-Hern's magic is here to save us," Broan said as he smiled reassuringly at the crowd.

He searched the crowd for BroMac and scowled when he saw him charging through the throng of people towards him. "Arrows aimed at the very people you were told to protect?" Broan yelled.

"It's not what you think," BroMac yelled back. He wasn't sure if he should hit Broan for his lack of trust or hug him for coming back in their time of need. "The bugs were…and then your sister…" BroMac suddenly stopped speaking and looked at Cephas and O-Yarr. "MORE Faeries…?"

"Never mind them. What is going on?"

BroMac looked up at the warriors, motioning them to lower their weapons. "I couldn't let them leave with the Ny-dick sitting out there. Bronagh started the whole thing, talking about the curse of the Queen and that it was coming. It put the fear of the gods into everyone. I finally had to confine her to her room." BroMac's jaw came up as if ready to take a blow from Broan's fist for locking up his sister.

"Where did she get that idea from?"

"She said the Faery Deeton told her. The one she said saved her long ago, which of course made it even harder for me to believe her." He eyed the two Faery warriors once again.

Ke-Hern touched Broan's shoulder. "There are at least two sides to every story, and when emotions are running high, rarely does either get heard. He followed your orders and that's all that's important."

"Yes, you're right." Broan said earnestly. "But, unfortunately we do need to get EVERYONE out, including you and the soldiers. With Ke-Hern's magic…"

"Magic! You sound like your sister. Her Faery friend told her that Lija used magic to bring Solveig to life."

Ke-Hern's ears perked up. "Deeton?"

"Whomever that damn Faery is, said Solveig was alive!"

Broan gave Ke-Hern a questioning look, which of course the Wizard ignored.

"Look I don't care, magic or not," BroMac's anger flared again. "We can't leave Solveig naked - with no defenses! The Ny-dick will tear it down and destroy it."

"Solveig can be rebuilt, but you, my friend, cannot. We are all leaving," Broan said as he turned towards the crowd.

It had taken less than an hour to evacuate everyone. Broan looked back at Solveig. She stood silently at the moment, nothing more than a shadow against the mountain. Turning his horse, he followed his people through another tunnel of fog. Faeries sparkled within it, guiding the masses safely along. *"Freely helping us without question, after all that's happened to them. What a narrow view I've held,"* he thought, and it shamed him to realize that about himself.

"It wasn't that narrow," Ke-Hern said

Broan gave Ke-Hern an annoyed look. "You know I hate it when you read my mind."

"I wasn't reading your mind; your face said it all. Besides you were always one to fall prey to guilt. Bad habit."

"So what do you think?" Bronagh asked, as she came up to ride beside them.

Broan looked over at his sister. "So that's the Faery you fell in love with?"

Bronagh shyly nodded her head, "Yes…Twice he has saved my life, and now he is responsible for saving all of us within Solveig."

"So far he's okay. We'll see what comes later."

Bronagh was just about to hit Broan when she noticed the smirk on his face. "MEN!" she grumbled as she rode off.

A full night and most of the next day was spent moving towards the Walled City. When Broan's group finally set up camp it was nothing more than people huddled together around two very small fires. The children were exhausted and if they were not asleep, they were moaning in fear or crying in uncertainty. Some families found a place on the ground to sleep, while others grouped together and talked in hushed tones.

Cephas didn't like what he saw. "Ke-Hern can't last much longer," He said to Hywel. "We should've brought Eirian with us. She could've helped with the cloaking fog,"

Broan's head rose. "I thought only Wizards had power over the weather."

"No," Hywel laughed, "Queens, Wizards and Eirian as well, for some unknown reason." He took a bite from an apple he had picked along the way and then nudged Cephas. "I guess he doesn't know who made it rain on his birthday for the last five years."

"Four years. She made it snow last year, remember?" Cephas said.

"Oh right." Hywel eyed Broan. "I don't know what she saw you doing to make it snow in August, but it must've been really bad."

Broan was stunned. "Eirian has power to control the weather? You're sure."

"Of course, it was one of the reasons she was picked to be our leader."

Broan's face darkened. "So why didn't she tell me? Our travel to the Walled City would've been so much safer."

Ke-Hern's eyes opened and shone with the reflection of the fire. "It's not a power, it's a talent, and she has many. Besides as I remembered she was a little tied up at the time."

"Oh no you don't. You're not putting the blame on me. She's kept far too many secrets. I think if we're going to fight alongside each other, we'll need to have a very long honest talk."

"Talk is cheap. It's listening that is worth its weight in gold," Ke-Hern said.

Broan got up and made his way over to BroMac and Faber's fire. He hated Ke-Hern when he was like this - wise, so darn closed, and talking in circles. As far as he was concerned, if Eirian had anything to offer that would have aided their passage to the Walled City, she should've told him.

Sobus got off his horse and walked to the edge of the forest. Even from this distance Solveig was impressive. He paused for a moment and thought about making it his residence rather than destroying it. "Now that would upset a lot of people, including the Queen." He smiled as he yelled to have Lija dragged forward. With a wicked sneer on his face he glanced back up at Solveig and focused on the energy inside of it. He paled, cursed and stumbled backwards. "HOW?" he screamed.

Lija was tossed to the ground at Sobus' feet. "Why's everything so still in Solveig? Why do I not sense any life within those walls?"

"The Queen's magic," Lija blurted out.

"She came here and you said nothing?" Lija shivered as Sobus' voice rose in pitch.

"No. It was Ke-Hern. He used her power."

"Magic or not, you just let them leave?"

"There was nothing we could do. It wasn't until mid-day that we even figured out what happened."

"And you decided to withhold this information from me."

"No...No! You told me you were coming...I just thought..."

"You thought! That's the problem! FOOL." Angrily, Sobus caught Lija' head under his boot. "How long ago?"

"Less than three days," Lija screamed, "and there's more."

Sobus removed his boot from Lija's head and crouched down beside him. Grabbing him by the shoulders, Sobus locked eyes with Lija. "What more could there possibly be?"

"I believe the Faeries called Solveig to awaken, and it became once again, its own entity."

Sobus struck Lija hard. Blood spurted out of a new wound on his face. He tossed Lija back onto the ground and stood up. "You expect me to believe that those brainless Faeries had enough power to do that?"

"Y..es. Y…ou know what that means. Don't you?"

"I'm not stupid, useless Wizard!" Sobus yelled. He started to pace, disbelief and rage coursed through him, increasing with each angered thought. "That brainless Faery Eirian has claimed the Ring of Cian!"

Lija looked up at Sobus and his whole body shuddered. It was always a nerve-racking wait for Sobus' anger to surface and when it did…

"THAT TWIT OF A WOMAN HAS CALLED THE FAERY ARMY FORTH AND HAS INTRFERRED WITH MY PLANS!" Sobus screamed at the top of his lungs. The truth of his words left him feeling angrier than ever. The energy inside of Sobus boiled and burned.

Kibria, one of the Ny-dick, inched forward a bit, curiosity getting the better of him. He straightened up and sniffed the air. The air was thick with unfocused power. He had never seen Lord Sobus like this - rambling, intense, and out of control. There was a palpable clash of energies fighting inside of Sobus, and Kibria wanted to know more. He marveled at the tension between the energy forces and unflinchingly he step forward again.

The power that flowed from Sobus was extreme. Suddenly the land exploded upward and the air was punched out of Kibria's lungs. Rocks flew through the air and trees burned with a grey-blue flame. The sky lit up with an eye-searing glare and Kibria was transfixed. It was horrifying and yet breathtaking at the same time. The ground was tossed inside out and upside down. The scent of Off-World power lingered in the air. The smell of dust, sulfur and charred wood surrounded them all.

"I want that Faery and I want that damn ring," Sobus hissed through clinched teeth. "YOU," he said, pointing over to one of the Ny-dick that had many killing trophies of male genitalia hanging from his belt. "What's your name?"

The Ny-dick raised himself up to full stature. "Kibria." He said with pride.

"Well Kibria, take a group of Ny-dick and hunt that Faery down. She'll not stay long in the Walled City." He watched Kibria with suspicion, a suspicion that was mirrored back to him behind hooded eyes. "You will bring her and the ring to me. Is that clear?" Kibria nodded in response and headed out.

Sobus glared at Lija with an intense stare and spoke with precise diction. "Take some Ny-dick with you and follow him. And let Mohr in the Walled City know I want prisoners, one's that will talk. The rest of us will go back north." He looked back at Solveig and glared. "It's a waste of time being here and I'll not be tricked into throwing away any more of my precious Off-World power."

Ryu, Captain of the Guard spotted Mohr and followed him up the back staircase and down a hallway near Iarnan's rooms. "You should be more careful Mohr, or your secret way into his chambers will be found out." He walked nearer and handed Mohr a small silk cloth from his pocket. "I don't know how you made it this far in Iarnan's council. You can be read like a book."

Mohr took the hanky and dabbed the sweat off his lip and fore-head. "It's the very reason they trust me. Except that everything on my face is not the whole truth." He went to hand back the hanky, but Ryu lifted his hand in refusal. Mohr sneered and tucked the hanky in his pocket. "I've heard that we're supporting Solveig with soldiers."

Ryu stepped back from Mohr. "Yes, a group of about fifty left not long ago."

"Good, that should give me a few minutes to see what I can find out." he said as he left the hallway. He slipped quietly through the secret door into the Governors rooms. When he turned and saw Eirian at the railing of the balcony, he panicked. He had to think fast. He quietly rushed through the quarters and flung open the door, calling for the Captain of the Guards. "There's an intruder in the Governor's quarters. A SPY!' he yelled.

Rushing in, Ryu suddenly came face-to-face with Eirian when she ran into the main quarters. Her green eyes flashed with a hint of irritation. Her auburn hair softly surrounded her face and continued to cascade in magnificent waves. The cut of her gown and shift seemed to catch her in all the right places, and Ryu smiled.

"Who are you? This is Governor Iarnan's private room!" Mohr yelled next to Ryu.

"I'm a guest of the Governor. I was told to wait here for him."

Ryu simply continued to smile at her. He liked her pout and she had spirit, which was hard to find in women these days. "Pardon us, fair lady. We are only doing our jobs. What is your name?"

Eirian didn't trust either one, especially the captain. She could sense that there was something just below the surface that was hidden from her. His smile was too assured and didn't match the subtle barb in his tone. "Seeing that Governor Iarnan is standing right behind you, perhaps he would be kind enough to introduce us?"

Both men turned and looked at Iarnan standing in the doorway. The look on his face was not a kind one. *"Aha,"* Ryu thought. They had stumbled onto something very important. Important enough that Iarnan had wanted to keep it secret. "Yes Governor Iarnan, would you do us the honor?"

Iarnan narrowed his eyes. "What the hell are you both doing in my quarters!" he yelled. He walked past them and placed his hand protectively on Eirian's shoulder.

"We thought there was an intruder in your rooms..." Mohr muttered.

Iarnan raised an eyebrow. "Hog wash. Now get out of here."

"Of course," Ryu said as he bowed low. "But since this lovely lady isn't an intruder would you introduce us so we may address her properly the next time we meet?"

Iarnan's lip curled. "This is Laeg's cousin from the City of Bridges. He had brought her here to see the sights, but once word came to us that Solveig was under attack he left me in charge of her care." He looked at Eirian and hoped she didn't mind being part of this little lie. "Lady Ree, this is Ryu, Captain of the Guard and Councilor Mohr, my aid and councilor, both of whom are now leaving!"

"Yes indeed but before I go I must ..." Ryu stepped forward and picked up Eirian's free hand and raised it to his lips. "It's a pleasure to meet you, Lady Ree. I am so sorry for disturbing you." He looked over and smiled at Iarnan. "Had I known Laeg had such beautiful women in his family, I would have taken the time to become a closer friend."

Eirian pulled her hand back and resisted wiping it off on her shift. "Laeg did speak of you and he warned me of your sweet words and slippery tongue," she said with a faint smile.

Mohr nudged his way in front. "I must apologize for my rudeness as well. I was just so surprised to find someone here when Governor Iarnan had made no mention of a guest."

"Yes, well, I don't have to tell you everything Mohr. I do have a life beyond the high council. Now leave."

Mohr and Ryu sat across from each other in the back of the soldier's Main-Hall. Mohr looked at Ryu who sat so calm and at ease. He knew that Ryu's façade covered a devious mind. He was ruthless and

Mohr knew first hand just how ruthless. Mohr dropped his eyes to his plate and began to eat. "There's something going on. Something I've been warned about."

"And what's that?"

"I believe…" Mohr paused for a moment, "This coming war is not normal. This one has magic written all over it."

"So…"Ryu shrugged, "I'll play both sides for now until I decide which way the victory will fall."

Mohr looked over his shoulder at the other soldiers in the hall, and then leaned across the table. "Listen Ryu, Governor Tybalt is powerful but this Dark Lord is more so, not one to be played with."

"Big words little man. If this Dark Lord is so great, why does he need my help?" Ryu half smiled at Mohr. "Besides it's my career that'll tumble if anything goes wrong. I already have Iarnan, the old goat, questioning my moves."

"Forget Iarnan. Are you in or not?"

Ryu laughed. "Have no fear Mohr, I'm in, but I want a bigger cut of the spoils."

"Like the Lady Ree?"

Ryu smiled deepened. "That'd be nice for starters."

"Well maybe I can help you out. There's only so much I could find out. How have your visits with the Governor's wife been going?"

"She likes the attention I lavish on her. Men in power are all the same; they neglect their wives thus making them the easiest point of entry to their downfall. Why?"

"Well maybe a visit is in order." Mohr paused for effect and then continued, "Iarnan has sent Lady Ree to stay with Lady Holt."

"Hmmm, things just keep getting better. I'll need time alone with her if I'm to gather information and Lady Holt doesn't like to share me."

"I'll get our friend Tilga to visit at the same time. She can pull Lady Holt away for a while." Mohr stopped, raised his finger and pointed it at Ryu. "BUT we need information; this isn't one of your sexual conquests. Got it?"

Ryu smiled coolly back at Mohr. "And who says I can't do both? I'll visit with Lady Holt this afternoon."

Mohr nodded his head. "Until this evening then."

Eirian was not enjoying the stroll around the city that Lady Holt had insisted on. She looked around her and decided that she really didn't like this city at all. It was a maze of congested streets and alleys. It was too crowded, too big and too dirty. She feared that if anyone were to stay here long enough they would begin to feel insignificant among the masses of building and populace. There was lots of energy and life to this place, but Solveig had more heart. Eirian looked over to her host. "If I had to pick a place to live in, it would be Solveig. It's the most balanced city I've seen so far."

"You judge us TOO harsh. Lady Ree."

"Ryu!" Lady Holt exclaimed as she turned towards the very familiar voice. "You're early. You said tea in the garden at three."

"Well I just so happen to be passing by and spotted you and your guest." He looked around the two ladies and frowned. "I don't see many guards. Your husband will not be pleased."

Lady Holt blushed. "See, Lady Ree, you have nothing to fear. Our Captain of the Guard is always at hand." Then she looked at Ryu. "Please join us."

Ryu smiled and stepped in between the two of them. "It'd be my pleasure." He took Lady Holt's hand briefly. "So what have you shown our new visitor that has caused her such a dismal view of one of the greatest cities in the land?"

"Not much. We were just getting started."

"Good. I have some free time right now, so let's do it right." He looked at Eirian. "What's your fancy, food, drink, panoramic views, or the arts? We have them all."

Eirian should have known this was a set up, but she had to keep up with the "Lady Ree" ruse. "To tell you the truth Captain Ryu, my heart is not really into exploring right now. My thoughts are with the people of Solveig. Have you gotten any word yet?"

Ryu took both ladies arms and tucked them under his. "No word yet, but have no fears, Governor Iarnan sent some of the best to help out. I would expect that we should have news by this evening. Besides, after the Governor, I am the next in line to receive word, so spending time in my company may be well worth it." He smiled at her suggestively. "Let's go. The afternoon is bright and the air is warm."

Eirian was just about to lie about having a headache, when a young woman joined the group. After being introduced to Lady Tilga, Lady Holt invited both her and Ryu back to the villa for tea. Eirian happily agreed, thinking she could make her escape to her room once back at the house. But as soon as they arrived, Tilga pulled Lady Holt away, leaving Eirian alone with Ryu.

Broan shifted the sleeping child on his back and gave a sigh of relief knowing they were near the Walled City.

"Is that it?" asked a young lad next to him.

"Yes...yes." Broan never stopped being amazed at how the Walled City jumped out at you as you rounded that last hill, truly a sight for sore eyes right now. He marched on, leading his horse that was now carrying an old Wizard and three children. Their exile from Solveig was now complete. Broan looked at V-Tor and Laeg and smiled. "Ride ahead. Tell them to open the gates. We've arrived in one piece."

It was a welcoming chaos that greeted them when they entered the city. People cheered and continued to cheer as Broan made his way through the crowded streets up to the main residence. Once there, Broan helped Ke-Hern off his horse. "Let's get you inside. You need a warm bath and a soft bed."

Iarnan rushed down the steps and quickly supported Ke-Hern's other arm. "We were getting worried. Did you have any trouble?"

"A little, but your troops showed up just in time. Ke-Hern is spent from working his magic." Broan looked around surprised he could not see Eirian. "Where's Eirian? She hasn't escaped from you, has she?"

"No. No. People were getting a little too close, so I had her go stay at the villa with Holt." Iarnan looked at Broan, "and her name is Lady Ree." He spoke over his shoulder in a soft whisper, "and she's Laeg's cousin. You'll be wise to remember that for now."

Shouldering more of Ke-Hern's weight as they made it up the stairs, Broan shook his head. *"Oh of course, now she decides to be a lady!"*

Ryu smiled and sat back on the bench as large green eyes repeatedly glanced his way. He liked the indirect attention Lady Ree was giving him. They were 'a perfect match' as far as he was concern. His darkness balanced her fairness, his sophistication to her wit, his confidence and control to her defiance. He chuckled to himself, *"Yes a perfect match, my ambitions to her beauty."*

Eirian got up from the bench and wandered about the garden. Playing a lady was harder than she had expected. She glanced over her shoulder at Ryu once again. She didn't like the look of him. In fact she didn't like much about him at all. He was too self-centered and cocky. *"Broan is a lamb compared to this devil,"* she thought to herself, bringing a shy smile to her face.

That was the wrong thing to do in light of what Ryu wanted. He got up and in two steps was next to her, pulling her into his arms. The fight Eirian gave him made him laugh. Tightening his hold on her, he nuzzled her neck.

There had been a healthy dose of competition between Broan and Ryu over the years, and after seeing Ryu and Eirian in the garden,

Broan decided it had moved to a whole new level. Someone definitely was going to get hurt if Ryu didn't let go of Eirian. Broan rushed in and took Eirian's arm. "We're leaving now!"

Ryu sneered at Broan. "So soon? You just got here."

"And just in time by the look of it, Ei…Lady Ree, Ke-Hern asked me to find you." He looked down at her, a heavy scowl on his face. "And your cousin Laeg has been looking for you. He became very worried when you didn't join Iarnan in greeting us."

Eirian opened and closed her mouth a few times. "My bag," was all she managed to get out as Broan quickly pushed her out of the villa.

"Lady Holt!" Broan bellowed, "Lady Ree needs her things."

Lady Holt ran out the door of her house, her eyes as big as saucers. "Here," she said. Broan grabbed the bag from her, curtly thanked her for watching over Lady Ree, and then turned and walked away without looking back.

Ryu leaned on the doorframe of the villa and smiled to himself. *"Ah, the hunt is on. Lust may get you into the game, but romance always wins. Be warned Broan, I have much more experience with romance than you, and I'll win this game."* He pushed off the door jam and walked over to Lady Holt. He put his arm around her shoulder. "Don't worry yourself. He was never one for social graces."

Ke-Hern rested his head on his pillow and closed his eyes. He was definitely getting too old for these things. A long life was only good if you still had the strength and ability to live it. He had waited for so long for this time to come and didn't regret being alive to see the curse of Duronyk fall away, yet he knew his life was long past it's time. He rubbed his hands absent-mindedly, a habit he picked up from the Queen whenever she needed to remove tension from her body.

"You think of me even in your weary state. That is so sweet Ke-Hern."

"Yes my Queen. You are never far from my conscious thought and never absent from my unconscious ones."

"I worry about you. Your strength has been depleted. I wish I could've gone with you to handle the crisis at Solveig."

"That wasn't possible and you know that. Besides we'll need your power more than mine before this is all over."

"Sobus has been on the move. He has gone to Solveig and back again."

"How did Solveig fair?"

"Solveig is fine but the people of this land aren't. It won't be long until our secret sees the light of day."

"It never was good to make it a secret. Some secrets should never be."

"Like the one about Eirian?"

Ke-Hern paled and remained silent.

"Ke-Hern, there are too many things I don't understand about her. There are reports she was the only child to survive the change and that she is the only one that ages. What do you know of this?"

"I've known Eirian for some time. She's a little different, but that's why they picked her to be their leader. Stories always become larger than life when people are grasping for hope, something to believe in."

"So there's nothing I'd be concerned about?"

"Nothing but her safety. The Faeries need her to fulfill her part of this."

"I know she's claimed the ring. It sent a tremor through the heart of me. I'm surprised that Sobus hasn't made his move on her yet and chose instead to go back across the border."

"Just because he's retreated doesn't mean he's not pursuing her."

"I'm also worried about Aillil. She has started channeling again. She doesn't have the power of Off-World or even Wizards, but she speaks from…"

"The Ancients?"

"Yes. She's been talking in one of their cryptic verses which are always hard to decipher."

"Well I may be able to help with that. There's a young Faery named Deeton who has spent his time studying the Ancient's symbols and verses. He may be able to interpret what Aillil is saying." Ke-Hern paused for a moment to gather his thoughts. "He could tell the difference between the life force of Solveig and the Ancients below it."

"When can you bring him here?"

"Once we regroup, we'll be heading out to Harbor City. Deeton and I will go part way with Broan and then make our way to visit you. I'm hoping to be there within a set of seven sunsets."

"I wait for your visit then. Sleep well Ke-Hern and take care."

Broan's little sister's scream sent a spark flying along his nerves. Harsh rapid breathing followed, echoing in his head. He felt trapped in an invisible… He raised his hands pressing against that which held him fast, but nothing gave… nothing ever did. Broan's nightmares were always dark and bloody. The clarity of his own scream awoke him with a start. Reality chased the nightmare from his mind leaving him to fight the shame and grief once again. He mentally cursed himself. He tried to make sense of his lack of action both at the moment of their attack and in his nightmares but there were no answers for him, only pain.

Deeton surfaced in Bronagh's room in the dim light of the night. He glanced at the door that joined her room and Broan's. The scream was cold and muffled.

"You get use to it," Bronagh said sadly. "His dreams are often troubled and there is nothing you or I can do about it."

"I really shouldn't be here. Eirian will be very angry." Smiling, Deeton pressed her fingers to his lips. "Ke-Hern wants me to go with him to visit the Queen. I just wanted you to know that, if anything should happen to me." He kissed her quickly. "Don't worry I'll find you after this is all over. I promise. Trust me."

Bronagh smiled back at him as she watched him vanish out the window. She quickly grabbed her wrap. She'd been playing with this idea, and now she knew for sure.

Jelen heard his mother and Bronagh whispering, and stirred from his sleep. He sat up, rubbing his eyes. "You know it'll be very dangerous if you leave with the warriors, Lady Bronagh."

Bronagh turned and smiled at Jelen. "I know but it's something I need to do. When you're older and find your true love, you'll understand."

"Deeton is your love?"

"Yes." Bronagh went over to Jelen's bed and pulled the covers up to his chin. "I hope you don't mind but while I'm gone Leif will be staying with you and your mom here in the family quarters." Jelen shrugged his shoulders. Leif and he were like brothers. They were always together anyway.

"I'll need you to watch over Leif for me. Can you do that?"

"Yes...Oh...wait," he said, opening a small pouch. "This is a special stone. Keep it near you, and it'll bring you luck."

"Oh Jelen that's so sweet but I'll be fine. You'll see."

Jelen pressed the stone into her the palm of her hand. "Please. Leif will feel better and worry less when I tell him you have the stone."

"Okay," Bronagh nodded. "Now back to sleep."

Bronagh left Faber's room, walked out of the family quarters, and down the darken street to the main residence. Satisfied by her choice, she looked down at Jelen's stone in her hand and smiled. "I know someone who'll need this more than I."

Mohr pulled Ryu aside as they watched Broan, his soldiers and Eirian leave the Walled City. "While you were mooning over her, look what my little pickpocket found in Lady Ree's bag."

Ryu took the item out of Mohr's hand and fingered the cap's heavy felt and fine workmanship. "Faery." He smiled looking in the distance at the departing group. "She's a bloody Faery!"

Chapter 11

It was a bright, sparkling day filled with crisp air and the smells of nature preparing for the coming winter. Crops had been harvested, and the land clung to the heavy moisture of early autumn days. Broan's seventy-four soldiers, two women, one Wizard, various camp workers and weapons handlers rode away from the Walled City.

Broan turned his horse around for one last look at the place that held so much history for him. The Walled City was where his father had died. It was also where he had become a man, a warrior and now a leader for Remdor. He knew he would always feel humbled and awed by the mystical essence of this place. As he watched, the clouds broke in the distance, revealing the steep faces of the mountains, all dusted with new snow. The contrasting colors were breathtaking. The white snow only added to the impressive ruggedness of deep grays, and the cold black of the rocks and crevices of the mountains.

"It may be an early winter this year," Eirian said.

"Let's hope winter doesn't come too soon. In order to get to Gearoldin quickly we need to make it to through the northern passage in the Celtan range. Once we're in the south and near Harbor City, it can snow all it wants. Maybe it'll keep the Ny-dick at bay until we're ready for them," Broan said with a wishful tone to his voice.

Ignoring him, Eirian struggled with her cloak. "Soon as I'm out of sight I'm changing! The problem with all this female attire is that one can't ride a horse properly!"

"Side saddle is the proper way for a Lady to ride," Broan said, with a small smile.

Eirian glared at Broan, then wishing to change the subject she continued, "Ke-Hern had always warned me to never go south."

"But that didn't stop you right?"

She smiled and then quickly glanced around to make sure Ke-Hern wasn't near. "Only a few times. I wanted to see what all the fuss was about."

"Why doesn't that surprise me?" He nudged his horse, Zantro, against her horse to move them away from the group. "Ke-Hern mentioned you have many hidden talents."

"Other than disobeying you?"

"Now that one I know every well," he answered dryly. "No, Cephas said something of weather control."

Eirian paused, not really wanting to talk about her talents or power. She looked straight ahead as she rode, hoping silence would take them to another topic.

"Both Hywel and Cephas have said that only Queens, Wizards and you have such powers."

"Talent, it's a talent, not a power. There's a difference." Eirian focused on the colors of the leaves on the nearby trees, pumpkin orange, brick red and brilliant yellow. "Besides I can only make weather spells on a small scale, nothing like what people blame me for. You know, short spurts of rain, that sort of thing."

"Or snow in the summer on my birthday."

"Hywel and Cephas talk of things they shouldn't!" Eirian nudged her horse and darted off, away from him.

Broan caught up with her and pulled hard on her reins, stopping her horse. "Eirian. If we're to lead the two armies together, we need to trust one another. This means no secrets, no hidden motives and no lies. So, I really need to know. What are your talents?"

Eirian understood why she had such a hard time talking about these things. Being gifted had led to a life of alienation. She looked away from him not willing to tell him anything.

"We're not moving until you tell me. This is important." Broan said patiently. "I need to know what you and Faeries are capable of. War is not a time for surprises."

"Faeries have one basic talent, shape-shifting and that's all."

"And you?"

The soldiers and wagons began cresting a low hill. She wouldn't be getting help from any of them. She looked up at the sky and knew she wouldn't be getting help from the Faeries either. "I've various talents. Ke-Hern has taught me to use only a few of them."

In the distance, Eirian could see Ke-Hern and the white horse he rode. She had long ago given up the illusion that Ke-Hern was the closest thing to a father she had. He was just a friend, yet his disapproval still stung. She glanced at Broan and shivered. "He stopped teaching me shortly after he started, saying I was already getting into too much trouble and until I learned to control myself he wouldn't go any farther." She shrugged her shoulders trying to hide the hurt. "He never did teach me anymore."

"So what's the difference between talents and powers?"

"Talents are the redirection of the present energy in things, like making it rain. The rain is already in the clouds. I just excite the energy in the clouds to make it fall. Power is adding energy to another form of energy and overtaking it, controlling it for my own purpose, making it do something it couldn't do on its own. Like when Ke-Hern changes the size of things." She shook her head, correcting herself, "No, actually when Ke-Hern changes the size of things, he is removing some energy... No it's more like he's compressing the space between the energy itself." She looked up at him. "If you want to understand more about power, you'll need to talk to him about it. Ke-Hern has always forbidden me to touch mine."

"So you have powers?"

She swiftly turned to face him. "Power...one power and I don't know what to even call it. I think it comes from the land itself but I'm not sure."

"Alright, then what talents do you have?"

Eirian felt sick to her stomach. She pulled at her horse, wanting to leave this inquisition, but Broan wasn't going to let that happen. Once again she looked to the horizon. Her anxiety increased as the soldiers faded into the distance. She finally gave up on the idea of breaking free and began to talk in a clipped, matter of fact tone, as if reading off a list of items needed at the bakery, "Shape-shifting, animal communication, balancing energy both in land and in flesh, weather control, a little ability in moving objects and supposedly image division... and time-shifting, although I never got too far with the last three." Once again she tried to pull the reigns out of Broan's hand.

She really needed to get away from this intense look at herself. This was too much. She felt so exposed.

He didn't let go. "Anything else?"

"NO! So you don't have to worry." She pulled hard on the reigns. "Other than making it snow on your birthday, I've nothing to use against you! LET GO!" she barked.

Broan released the reins and Eirian raced off, her eyes brimming with tears. She didn't know which hurt more, admitting that Ke-Hern thought she was hopeless or having to admit that she was so different from Manliken, Elftan and even other Faeries.

"SHIT! What the hell did you toss my way Ke-Hern?" Broan cursed. He eased his horse forward, slowly following the path of Eirian's flight. He needed to think things over. He thanked the gods that Ke-Hern had held back teaching Eirian how to utilize her full potential, else her little visit to Solveig could have turned out very differently.

Mohr entered the dank pub room, and spotted Ryu in the corner and quickly lost his smile. The barmaid walked by and Ryu forcefully grabbed and swung her around to sit on his lap. Mohr snarled. "Why did I ever think he would be an asset?" He marched over to Ryu and pulled the young lady away. "Captain Ryu I'm afraid duty calls once again. There's no time for dalliances."

"There's always time for such things. You, my friend, are just afraid to take it."

Mohr sat down in a huff. "I just finished talking with a Sha…a messenger." He paused and waited for the young women to leave. Once satisfied he continued, "It didn't seem to surprise him that Lady Ree is a Faery. Yet the Dark Lord wants any and all NEW information we can uncover on her. Apparently, she may be in a position to put the Dark Lord's army at risk."

Ryu, only partly paying attention to Mohr, smiled at the barmaid again. "A Faery…has the Dark Lord scared? Now that is rich."

Mohr grabbed Ryu's sleeve. "There's a ring. Did you see a ring when you were with her? The messenger said it's the Ring of Cian. Apparently it has the power to unite and lead all Faeries into battle. Just tell me, did you see the ring or not? "

Ryu pulled his tunic free of Mohr's grip and stared at him. "The only ring she wears is on her thumb, nothing grand, manly, too big to be a women's. I thought it was simply an archer's ring." He looked at Mohr. "You know, to protect the thumb…but maybe it's the one…" He paused and then a bright smile lit his face. "So if that's the ring and she's wearing it, she controls an army…interesting."

"No, no. The Dark Lord wants facts, not your ruminations or schemes. If she does wear the Ring of Cian he wants her and the ring!"

"Hmm… I wonder…" Ryu tapped the table in quick rhythm while he thought. "So the Dark Lord needs my help…"

"Fool!" Mohr muttered. He didn't like Ryu's train of thought.

Ryu paid Mohr's distress no mind and continued, "Well now… I guess I could pay Broan's little group a visit. It seems a lady forgot her cap and with winter coming, she just may need it." He paused for a moment and then openly declared, "I'm leaving today with a group of soldiers to do a reconnaissance of the region including the northern passage that Broan plans to take." Ryu's smile as he looked around at the various soldiers deep in their ale. He bent in closer to Mohr as he continued, "And I'm going to do one better than just get information, I'll give him…" He rubbed his chin. "Get word to the Dark Lord. I need his Ny-dick to meet me at the village of Dorwell in three days." Ryu stood up and peered down at Mohr, "And tell him I expect to be paid well."

The wind swept across the inland sea tossing the waves to playful heights, tangling the white caps and spraying upper reaches of the cliffs. Aillil was waiting for DeSpon and stood so close to the steep edge that her face and cloak were damp and salty. She licked her cold lips, enjoying the taste.

From hundreds of feet above her, DeSpon dove straight down towards the ground. When he hit the area in front of Aillil, he shifted out of his raven form. In his rush he accidentally missed his footing, and knocked them both over. Luckily they rolled back away from the jagged cliffs.

"I thought you said the Ancients watched over you," DeSpon scolded as he was helping Aillil up. "You were so close to the edge that a slight breeze could've pushed you over!"

Aillil smiled. "The wind was blowing the other way. I was in no danger."

DeSpon breathed heavily to calm his nerves. She played such an important role in the Shadow Dwellers future. He couldn't lose her now. "Don't do that again. I was truly afraid you were going to get hurt."

"I knew you were there and if anything happened, I knew you would save me."

DeSpon shook his head. "Such blind trust," he said dryly. "You're the only one who senses me, and now I have to worry that it may cause you injury."

Aillil stopped dusting off her shift, and kept her face down. "You're wrong. There is another that senses you…the Faery leader, Eirian… I heard the Queen talking to Ke-Hern about her. She, I know, feels you." She reached out searching for him. "Be careful."

DeSpon took her hand into his. "She's nothing. She can sense me all she wants. Her attention is focused elsewhere. That reminds me…" DeSpon dropped her hand and started searching the secret compartment of his leather strap that held his array of knives. "It's my worry for your safety that has brought me here. Eirian may help to win the coming war but you…" He pulled out a piece of paper and then placed it in the palm of her hand. "But you are the one that will save us Shadow Dwellers."

"And how shall I do that?"

DeSpon put his hands on her shoulders and drew her near. "By talking to the Ancients like you have always done."

"With the Queen hovering about me?"

"No. I know of a place where there's no Queen to stop you, no Dark Lord to fear. You'll have the freedom to do as you like. There's another fortress of the Ancients and I want you to go there. I've drawn a map that shows the relationship to Solveig and this island. It will make it easier for anyone to guide you there."

Aillil rubbed the paper between her thumb and fingers. "You really believe I'm the destined one of the Prophecy, the one that is to work with the Ancients?"

"Why not? You already talk with them. Besides, going to the desert fortress will keep you safe, safe from ANY outcome of this war. Please promise me you'll leave soon."

It seemed like a lifetime before Aillil agreed to his plea. "Alright, but I can't leave on my own. Ke-Hern has trapped us here with a spell."

DeSpon dropped his head. "I wish I could just fly you away from here."

"But you can't. I followed Ke-Hern onto the island, and as far as I know I can only leave the same way." She paused for a moment in thought and then her face lit up. "Wait! Ke-Hern is coming to visit. If I make up a convincing story maybe…"

"Maybe Ke-Hern will take you with him when he leaves, which would be perfect! He could protect you while you travel."

Aillil allowed herself to step closer to him. "Will you visit me when I leave here?" she asked.

DeSpon looked at her and smiled. "Yes, I will. Have no fear."

Eirian could actually taste and smell the death and violence that lay around her. Blood pooled on the hard ground and blood-curdling screams were still echoing off the valley walls. Horses and warriors both were gasping hungrily for air. The battle had ended and the damage was great. Saddened, she watched as Broan's warriors wandered through the killing field looking for their wounded and any life in the enemy, which if found was quickly ended.

An anguished scream cut through the air and startled Eirian. She watched as V-Tor swiftly plunged his weapon into an injured Ny-dick. This was her first real experience of battle and all its horror. She kept her chin level. She was a leader now and she needed to be an example for all those who put their trust in her.

Broan looked across the hillside. He had spent much time over the last few days contemplating two very different, yet somber outcomes for this small battle. This was far worse than he had anticipated. Too many fallen, too many injured. He looked over to the Faery warriors, the few who had fought. They stood still as if waiting for something. In unison they nodded at Eirian, dropped their weapons, turned and walked into the woodland forest.

"Follow those fools," Broan barked at Laeg. "See what they are up to."

V-Tor found GarrRod, mortally injured, with an arrow through his neck. His breathing was shallow and blood constantly pooled in his mouth. The only saving grace was that the arrow actually kept GarrRod sitting upright. The arrow had entered from the front, exiting through his spinal column. It had forced his limp body up against a tree pinning him there to experience a slow choking death.

With one violent tug V-Tor freed his friend from the tree and eased him down to the ground. GarrRod mumbled a few words about Eirian, spitting blood over V-Tor's already blood soaked tunic. He shuddered once and with the last wave of pain, fell into death's deep sleep.

V-Tor rose from his place and marched over to Broan. "There's absolutely no reason for this slaughter. The Faeries keep saying that they want to fight with us, so why didn't they join in right away? It would have been over in minutes." V-Tor stood rigid waiting for an answer.

Broan raised his hand and placed it on V-Tor's shoulder. "Good question," he said his fury beginning to rise. He stormed up the embankment towards Eirian, his anger near a boil. "What the hell happened? Why did you delay sending in your men and then send in so few?" Cephas and Hywel quickly stopped his charge. They dug in their feet as they held him back.

Pale and shaken, Eirian looked down at Broan from her horse. "Surprise will play a very critical role in this war." Her horse nervously scraped the ground with its hoof, agitated by the intense emotion that surrounded it. Eirian allowed it to take one step back. "I told you of the Ny-dick's position. You could have easily traveled a different route and avoided all of this, but you chose not to."

Eirian held herself stiff as she turned her horse around, giving Broan her back. He scowled. "You should leave the strategy to those who know. The cost would have been much less if you had lead your army instead of sitting here watching!" Eirian didn't stop or slow her retreat any. It hurt her knowing what was coming.

Cephas stood back from Broan but Hywel refused to let go. "You don't understand how hard this is for her," Hywel said.

Broan shot an angry look at him and shook him off. "No, you don't know how hard it is for us. It's clear we have much more to lose then Faeries"

It was then that Laeg rushed up to Broan, and whispered in his ear.

"Are you sure?" Broan asked and Laeg repeated himself. Solemnly Broan nodded his head. He quickly turned his cold blue eyes to Ke-Hern. "You had better tell me everything or so help me I'll never let you give me counsel again!"

"Walk with me Broan," Ke-Hern said with a deep sigh. "You've always been able to understand how a battle is put together, why it unfolds as it does. I see now that this is incomprehensible to you."

"Everything involving Faeries is incomprehensible to me," Broan yelled. "Like finding out that Faery warriors roll up and die after a fight...a fight that they joined much too late." He didn't even try and hide the disgust on his face. "They watched our slaughter before..."

"So Eirian's right. This fight was nothing more than a test."

"Nothing is right about Eirian! She's no leader! She's not a warrior! She doesn't know the first thing about armed battle!" Broan said looking away from the Wizard. "So it looks like we'll do all the fighting alone from now on."

"There's too much at stake to give up on them so quickly."

"It's not going to work. When you see a hungry Ny-dick barreling down a hill with the sole intent of splattering your blood everywhere... you expect help. And you expect it right then and there."

"But you don't..."

"WE didn't get any support. They profess to want to join in this war and yet they stood and watched until most of the battle was over."

"Broan! Just shut up and listen for a moment. When the Faeries of Duronyk started to rebel and it became quite clear just how effective they could be as killers, a new curse was overlaid on the first one. If any Faery kills, they die soon after. Their life is forfeited. The curse was implemented to make sure that the Faeries could never regroup and fight back. The only ones who can kill are Shadow Dwellers. They're the ones that keep the fear and hatred towards Faeries alive."

"So? We all offer our lives in battle." Broan hissed.

"It's believed that if the Faeries rise up and fight alongside their brethren to overtake this evil that entrapped them, they will find freedom in their death."

"So dying sets them free? So why hold back?"

Ke-Hern shook his head sadly and explained, "Death before the one battle that ends the curse, means their spirits go into the void." Ke-Hern's shoulders slumped. "The void, emptiness unlike anything else you can imagine. You have nothing but your voice to lament." Ke-Hern stole a brief glance at Broan to see if any of this was sinking in. "You know you're lucky Eirian chose this war as the one noble enough to risk it all. To those in Faery form, a few more decades mean nothing."

"It still doesn't account for why I wasn't told," Broan stated firmly.

"I know. But in talking with Eirian…"

"Ke-Hern, it all comes down to trust. She asked for my trust, yet she didn't trust me to tell me the truth. How can I lead an army when this mistrust has bloodied the field already?"

"You will," Ke-Hern said as he walked away.

Evidence of the battle's devastation was evident on the faces of those around her. It made Eirian even more sad. She watched as a tent was constructed just up from the blood-saturated valley, while the injured were quickly gathered. She knew that aiding the injured would be difficult and challenging at best. The victim's minds and hearts were tormented by pain, clouding all sensible reaction. Quickly Eirian decided to help and simply nodded to Bronagh when she entered the tent and rolled up her sleeves.

Bronagh was no longer surprised by Eirian's skill and the ease in which she used it. Her treatments often led to healings, and if recovery was not possible, the fallen moved into the afterlife with as little pain as possible. Bronagh walked up to Eirian, who was tending to a young Elftan. She quietly waited for Eirian to finish a prayer. "With humble hope I wish you life beyond this life, one with joy, love and tranquility. We are not invincible in this life, but surely we are in the next." Eirian raised her hand and closed his eyes, cutting off the distant stare of death.

Eirian's eyes never left the poor young man. She sighed, "Some are too horribly injured to mend. We can only give them bitter tea to ease their pain." She sounded so worn and defeated.

Bronagh placed her hands on Eirian's slumped shoulders, letting her know she understood. "Come take a breath of air with me. There isn't much more we can do for now."

His patience had paid off. Broan rose from his seat as soon as he spotted Bronagh and Eirian passing. He started after them with a strong and steady gait. Once he reached them he stepped between them and took hold of Eirian's arm. Without breaking stride, Broan keep walking, forcing Eirian to either quickly walk with him or be dragged along towards a fire.

"Summon O-Yarr!" he bellowed at her and with a murderous look. "It was he who led the Faeries into battle today, was it not?"

"I will not!" she screamed trying to free herself. "He's done enough for one day."

"Summon him now!"

"NO!" She fought back.

Broan stopped when he reached the wildly burning bonfire. They stood so close that the toe of Broan's boots bumped up against a log and sent sparks flying. He grabbed a fist full of her hair and leaned her over the flames. "Call him now or I'll cut off your hair, toss it in and summon all of them!" He pushed her back a little farther, tipping her off her feet.

Eirian quickly latched on to Broan's arm. She looked up at him with wild eyes. "It'll do no good Broan." She shook her head. "Why are you doing this when you already know the truth?"

Broan shook her hard. "Why didn't you tell me? Their lives would not have been wasted!" He set Eirian firmly on her feet again. He looked at the fire and then at her, his anger barely under control. "The first rule for both a warrior and a leader is trust. You, Eirian, failed on both counts and as a result many lives were wasted." He spotted the movement of the growing crowd around them and he released her with a shove. "WASTED!" he yelled. "Now you have to live with that." Broan turned and walked away.

"I will live with it every day of my life, Broan. Those who die before their time remain with me. I carry them around like a dead weight, a burden I wish on no one." She doubted Broan had even taken the time to listen to her. She felt ashamed for omitting this one vital fact from Broan, but it was too late now. Their collaboration was rapidly decaying, deteriorating before her very eyes, and she felt truly helpless. Eirian started to shake, her confidence crushed under a deep feeling of inadequacy. *"What am I doing?"*

She searched for the ability to shift back into Faery, a bird, anything, but nothing was there. Turning towards a group of trees beyond the camp, Eirian headed towards them. Soon the firelight was gone along with the sound of whispering people. She quickly pulled up the shift that Bronagh had lent her and without hesitation tossed it on the ground. Once she entered the little grove of trees, she got on her hands and knees and felt along the ground until she found the knotted roots of the trees. She may not be in Faery form able to hide within the knots of a tree, but all her life the woods had been her haven. They had kept her safe and sane. Eirian lay down among the roots, placed her head upon the ground, and cried.

"Now that was harsh," Laeg said as he stood back from the gathered group.

Broan didn't slow his pace as he passed him. "No harsher than when we were in training. Ignorance is no excuse when lives are at stake."

Laeg fell in behind Broan; he wasn't going to let this one pass. He was familiar with Broan's anger as well as his sound judgment. This time he felt that Broan had gotten them confused. "She is not in training," he firmly pointed out.

Broan's stopped suddenly and turned so quickly that Laeg almost bumped into him. "Well maybe it's time for some. First rule Laeg, trust. If we don't have that, we have nothing." Without waiting for a reply Broan swung back around and stomped off.

"Now that we understand their actions Broan, placing all the blame on her won't help the situation," Laeg called out, hoping to add some common sense to the situation.

"TRUST," Broan yelled back over his shoulder as he entered his tent.

"How could you?" Bronagh hissed as she ran into Broan's tent. Her face was red with anger.

"Not you too!" Broan groaned. He got up from his chair and started out the door again. Peace, he needed peace. He was tired of people barking at his heels like dogs.

Bronagh rushed out after him, not willing to give up the fight. "You didn't have to humiliate her in front of everyone. She's not you Broan, she not a warrior. She's young and has been thrust into power with only her wits to serve her. She needs your guidance, not your criticism."

Broan threw his hands up into the air as he spun around and looked at both Laeg and his sister. "Is everyone around here crazy?" He gave a questioning look to both of them. "She'll live, believe me. And maybe because of this, more soldiers will as well."

Bronagh opened her mouth to make a comment, but Broan raised his hand and shook his head. "Not another word. Do you hear me? I did what had to be done. Eirian needs to learn the weight of leadership, and fast, if this is to work. Now just leave it be."

When Broan stepped out of his tent in the morning, he was greeted with a crisp wind from the north. It butted up against him as if to push him into leaving. "Soon enough," Broan whispered to himself. Actually, he liked this time of the morning, when life had barely awakened from night's slumber. It was as if time had stopped and was taking a deep breath before beginning the business of the day.

Marching towards the infirmary, Broan suddenly stopped. V-Tor was approaching and in one, brief wordless moment he knew V-Tor carried bad news.

"She's gone," V-Tor said as he handed him Eirian's shift

Nerlena's voice echoed in Broan's head reminding him they could easily pick another to protect her. The thought irritated him more than he wanted to admit. "How long?"

"Don't know. No one can account for her after your little talk. I found her shift just a bit beyond that tent. I think she went into the woods. I'll get a party together to start looking."

Broan scanned the area, hoping to catch some sign of her and handed Eirian's shift back to him. "I'll start now."

It had not been easy for Broan to find Eirian. Her Faery clothes had hid her well, blending her body with the ground between the tree roots. In fact, Broan had passed right by her a few times. Afraid she'd take off again, Broan approached her slowly. "I love watching the world come alive in the morning, the birds singing in the crisp air."

Eirian sat up. She still wouldn't look at him. She nodded in agreement to what he was saying and then she glanced up into a tree as a squirrel started chattering endlessly. "I feel that this yearning to end the curse is a mere trifle when it stands next to the harsh reality of battle." She finally directed her sad eyes to Broan. "How do you separate their pain from yours, their fear, and their worries?"

Broan sat down on one of the knotted roots. "You don't. You acknowledge it. Then you carry on."

Eirian looked away, that was not what she wanted to hear right then. This was only a small battle and she was having trouble coping with it. How was she going to lead them all the way into the final battle? She twisted the ring on her thumb, wishing she had never put it on. Broan reached down and stopped her from playing with it. It was if he knew what she was thinking. "We'll get through this together. Just no more secrets okay?"

Eirian nodded in agreement. She started to get up from among the roots of the tree, stopped, pressed her forehead against its bark and gave thanks for the comfort and protection it allowed her. She straightened and walked back to the camp with Broan.

Broan placed his hand against Eirian's lower back, partly to have a way to grab her quickly if she chose to run off and partly because it felt nice. He liked the feel of her muscles moving under his hand and enjoyed the feel of the Faery cloth that was between his hand and her body. It was thin and soft, not like the heavy woven shifts she had been wearing over her Faery clothing.

Eirian didn't protest Broan's intimacy. His large hand easily spanned her lower back. She liked how it felt, not heavy, but … Suddenly she found her back pressed hard against Broan's chest. One arm was wrapped protectively around her while the other arm held his sword. She opened her senses to the energy around her and smiled.

"It's only Cephas," she whispered as she gently placed her hand on Broan's arm. "I'd be more careful in the future, Cephas," she called out. "Broan doesn't take his responsibility to protect me lightly."

"And he shouldn't," Cephas answered while looking at Broan. "There's small party of soldiers coming up behind you. They wear Iarnan's colors."

Broan lowered his sword and looked down into the valley. "How long?"

"They camped beyond the valley yesterday and started out again only minutes ago. They'll be here in about half an hour."

Broan smiled at Cephas. "Thanks for letting me know. Could you tell Laeg we have company coming and to be ready. They may be from the Walled City, but that doesn't guarantee that they are allies."

Broan's arm still lay across Eirian's stomach. His fingers were wrapped around her hipbone and she was nervous. There were some personal secrets that needed the right time to be told. And this was NOT the time to let anyone know she was pregnant. Eirian tapped Broan's arm twice then she tapped again more forcefully. She was still in his tight grip, even though Cephas had left them to find Laeg.

"Please," she said as she turned her head. Broan unexpectedly leaned over and kissed her. Eirian was shocked and her face showed it. She pushed away from him with all her might, stumbling free and quickly scurried away towards the camp. Broan chuckled.

Hywel suddenly appeared in front of him, hanging from a tree branch by one arm. "You had better keep your mind focused on the war and not on bedding her."

Broan ignored him and walked towards the camp.

"I mean it. I know what I saw. You had that look of 'I'd give up everything just to have a moment alone with you." Hywel dropped down in front of Broan. "Am I right?"

"What I was thinking and what will happen are two different things. The war is not something that anyone will be able to avoid, so you don't need to worry about my thoughts taking me elsewhere."

Hywel studied Broan for a moment and then he hesitantly stepped aside. "She's an innocent," he blurted out. "She's not like any of us, with life experiences to fall back on. In fact that was most likely her first kiss!"

"It wasn't her first," Broan corrected walking away.

"Oh!" Hywel said with astonishment, as he carelessly bumped into Cephas. "He kissed her!" Hywel protested to Cephas. "I don't like this. It'll be hard enough on her without getting those kinds of emotions tangled up in all this."

"If you're so worried about it, why not talk to Eirian? She's a grown woman," Cephas said, pushing Hywel out of the way. War was at hand and he had little time for such things. He reached out and grabbed Broan's arm. "Wait, we have to talk."

Broan gave Cephas a stern look. "Yes, we do need to talk. Let's discuss how it was decided to keep the truth about Faery warriors and the curse away from me."

Cephas looked at Broan with great ignominy in his eyes. "You were right last night. Everything you said to Eirian was correct. We broke the first rule of warrior code and lives were wasted. We can't take any of it back, but what we can do is start making better choices."

Broan looked over Cephas' shoulder at Hywel. "At least someone has brains around here. Why don't you take on the leadership since you know more about running an army than she does?"

"She is our leader, Broan. As inexperienced as she is, she is still the chosen one for reasons most would never guess. Like every other Faery, all I can do is follow her. You may not understand it or like it, but it is the reality." Cephas said firmly.

Broan frowned. "If that's the case and she's the leader we'll have to guide her together. We can't afford any more lies or secrets. If we're going to fight together, let's learn about each other so we can stand together as brothers."

"Agreed, I'll talk to Eirian about calling the Warlords together. It's time you met the troops."

"Let's wait until after our visitors have come and gone. The less they find out about what we're doing the better. Other than Iarnan, I left no one I can trust behind." Broan smiled at Cephas and continued, "Oh, and see if you can get Eirian to change out of her Faery clothes. I don't seem to have much luck in doing that. I don't want whoever's coming to know the truth about her just yet."

Ryu and his soldiers entered the valley and rode through the dark smoke and the smell of burning flesh. As they made their way steadily towards Broan's greeting party, Ryu's eyes searched for Eirian. He patted the embroidered skullcap that dangled from his belt making sure it was still there. "*This is going to be fun,*" he said to himself.

He rode straight up to Broan. "It's obvious this way into Gearoldin has grown more dangerous of late. Can we help in any way?" He smiled down at Broan with a cool, superior twist of his mouth.

"You're a little late, I'd say," BroMac said as he came up behind Broan.

Ryu dismounted and smiled at both of them. "Always on hand aren't you BroMac? I hope you're still happy with your choice to join Broan instead of me."

"Couldn't be happier," BroMac said, crossing his arms over his chest.

Broan was carefully watching Ryu. He knew that Ryu wouldn't have ventured this far from the Walled City unless he had a self-serving interest. Seeing Eirian's cap hanging from his belt made it clear as to why he had come.

Ignoring those around, Ryu chuckled out loud. "Lady Ree. I was hoping to see you. In fact I prayed I wasn't too late to save you. I've risked life and limb to get to you."

"Fine words for someone who doesn't have a mark on him. I think that the warriors lying in that tent over there played more a part in saving me than you have."

"Spirited as always," Ryu looked over at Broan as he fingered the skullcap on his belt. "Look, I came not to judge you Broan, but to help. Although, when I heard you were headed this way with WOMEN, I did think you were crazy."

"What do you want Ryu?"

"I'm hoping you'd agree with me that this is too dangerous a trip for Lady Ree and your sister, and that you would send them back with me to the Walled City and safety."

"I see..." Broan half smiled. "Shall we go to the fire and talk about what needs to be done? It has suddenly gotten unforgivably cold," he said as he walked over to one of the campfires.

Ryu sat down by the fire and warmed his hands. He lazily eyed Eirian. His thoughts quickly went to all the things he wanted and felt he had a right to: a magnificent castle, good wine, good food, a woman or two on his arm... Unfortunately this decadent lifestyle was just beyond his reach...at least for the moment.

He watched Eirian, who sat between Broan and BroMac on the other side of the flames. His thoughts lightened. Yes, having her on his arm would be an added pleasure. She would fit well with his wants, especially if she was as passionate as she was beautiful. "Well Broan, what are you planning to do?"

"Do what has been asked of me. I'll be going on to Gearoldin and then on to Anwel. We need to gather forces before the Ny-dick cut off all the routes."

Ryu waved his hands into the air, pointing to the sky and the falling snow. "In this! Think for a moment. This kind of adventure is for warriors, not young women. They won't last past a few weeks. If the cold doesn't get them, the Ny-dick will. Besides, they'll only slow you down and you already know that time is not on our side. In truth Broan, is it worth taking them with you when they could be safe and secure back at the Walled City awaiting your return?" He smiled at Eirian.

"Good point Ryu," Broan answered looking through hooded eyes.

Eirian glanced at Broan in a panic. "I don't want to go back! I won't go back!"

Ryu smiled at Eirian. "It warms my heart to see you so adventurous, but common sense needs to prevail here. Broan knows I speak the truth. It would be for your own good. Besides I'm sure your cousin Laeg would agree with me on this one."

"Laeg leaves me to decide what's best for me." Eirian firmly stated.

"Then Laeg's not a good cousin. I'm only thinking of your safety."

"And a whole lot more!" V-Tor hissed under his breath.

Broan eyed V-Tor as he addressed Ryu. "As much as your offer is sound and good you can help more by escorting the injured and perhaps Bronagh back to the Walled City. I think she should go and be with Leif. As for Lady Ree, she can make up her own mind. Laeg is here to step in if he wants."

"I see…" Ryu's mind worked fast, "How many wounded do you have?"

"About fifteen."

"Well okay but…" He smiled at Eirian, "Lady Ree, the City of Bridges will always be there and spring is a much better time to travel." Ryu smile deepened, his eyes locked on Eirian. "Think of coming back with me as helping Broan on his quest."

"RYU!" Broan's voice boomed, "Lady Ree has made up her mind."

Ryu shrugged, his smile never slipping, "Well, then..." He turned his attention to Broan. "Can you offer us any extra men, in case we need to defend the wounded?"

"I'll send Hargrave and some men. Be ready to leave in a few hours."

Ryu stood and nodded. "I still think Lady Ree would be safer with me. Your army may have been bred and trained to fight in battle with killer instincts, but faced daily against the armies of Ny-dick, even they'll be hard pressed to protect her."

"Sounds more like a warning than a consideration for Lady Ree's safety," V-Tor said as he glared at Ryu. "Are you perhaps privy to the Ny-dick's plans?"

Ryu's eyes flashed anger. "I am a Captain of Remdor, do not question my loyalty. What I tell you, I know from experience not from any traitorous information." He walked over to Eirian and took her hand. "Lady Ree. Think about what you are planning to do. You can still change your mind."

Eirian's stomach quaked as she felt his thumb firmly rub Cian's Ring. She looked at him with distain as she withdrew her hand from his. "Thank you for the offer but the answer is still no."

Smiling down at her, Ryu played with her cap once more. Slowly turning it this way and that, he walked away to his men.

"Eirian, are you going to ask for your cap back or do I have to?" V-Tor asked glaring at Ryu's back.

"Neither of you are going to do anything. Do I make myself clear?" Broan answered as firmly as he could. Staring first at Eirian and then at V-Tor. "He wants someone to make a mistake. Don't take the bait. Besides, I'm glad that damn hat is gone."

Eirian paced back and forth in her tent. The night pressed in on her. Watching Bronagh and the others leave had been very hard for her. Even Miko had been sent back with the others. Having Broan, a fighting force of forty warriors and Ke-Hern outside her tent didn't help. She felt very alone.

"Can't sleep?" Ke-Hern asked as he stepped into Eirian's tent. He smiled as he handed her the Faery cap.

Eirian's eyes grew big as she took it in her hands. She toyed with the idea of putting it back on her head but knew better. "How did you get it? I doubt Ryu would have just given it to you."

Ke-Hern raised himself to his full height. "Wizards do not need to explain their actions. Besides, I had no other choice seeing it has Ancient power in it," he raised an eyebrow, "You shouldn't leave it laying around for just anyone to pick it up."

She sparked with annoyance. "I didn't leave it lying around. He stole it." She bent down and shoved it into her bag. "So you know about its power."

"Yes, thanks to Broan. You and Tellos have devious minds."

"I didn't even know Tellos before Solveig." She countered.

"Then it is you who has the devious mind. I should have known."

"It is not devious to keep something a secret."

"Ahhh, yes but too many secrets muddy the present. That's why it is time to reveal your army to Broan."

"You want me to call them and introduce them to Broan and his men in the middle of the night? That's not wise. It'll have to wait until morning, when everyone can see everyone. Each can look into the other's eyes."

"It's time Eirian and you know it. The sky is clear and the moon is red on the distant horizon. The growing conflict has filtered the light of the night guardian. There is no doubt now. There is no more hiding in the shadows for the Faeries."

Eirian looked past Ke-Hern at the tent flap. She imagined everyone standing around waiting for her. They were asking her to call on

235

those that were the closest thing to family, her kin. They were asking her to call those she loved, to come and commit to their final battle, their end.

"Come." Ke-Hern gently drew her out of the tent and led her to the fire. With a reassuring nod, he stepped back.

Eirian raised her face to the moon and called out names. In a singsong style, she listed off a long litany of Faeries she wanted to appear beside her. She called Cephas and Hywel, Remy, Mekg, Deter, Kaew, Ong, Thoi, Sebi, Retan, Kiri, and Eloe to start with. She looked at Broan as a growing number of Faeries appeared by her side. "These are only the top warlords that are close at hand. My warriors number in the thousands and we have at least a hundred and fifty Warlords spread across the land."

"Thousands!" V-Tor choked on the word.

Broan stood at stoic attention, not sure what to say. The women warlords surprised him at first, but then he thought about their way of life and it only made sense to give command to whoever was best suited for it. He looked at Eirian and knew this would also apply to her.

Eirian stood beside her warlords and started the introductions.

Idwal's curiosity was plagued by his need to know what talents these Faeries had and cut right into the introductions. "Can they climb like you?" he asked excitedly.

Eirian smiled at him and nodded then she continued her introductions.

"Will they fight as Faery or Mortal?"

"Both, which is one of the advantages we have." Eirian couldn't help but be happy at Idwal's inquisitiveness. His curiosity set the mood to one of excitement and acceptance.

"What of the women. Do they have special powers? Can they fight just as well as the men?"

"IDWAL!" Broan yelled. "Let her finish! There'll be lots of time to figure out who can do what." He looked over to Eirian's warlords. "I'm so sorry for Idwal's impatience. His rudeness is not acceptable."

"Oh I don't know. He sounds a lot like my son Tarir," said the woman who stood next to Eirian. Everyone laughed.

BroMac stood back from the group. This was not what he had thought would happen. Eirian had told him over and over again that women were equal to men and just as able to fight, yet facing them now BroMac had a hard time putting aside his belief that war was not a place for women.

Even the way the female Faeries appeared before them made him wonder if he was dreaming. They had arrived on wings of butterflies. "BUTTERFLYS! And by the firelight, under a red moon," BroMac muttered to himself. It was all too strange. He had never seen such a display of mystical ability and all the females looked like such gentle spirits.

"Are they even real?" BroMac shook his head and griped, "How can something of light and air fight flesh and blood? I know the men can kill. They've proven that many a times. But no one has ever seen or experienced women warriors before. I mean, we'll need much more than tricks from them to overcome the Ny-dick." BroMac looked over to Broan, needing his support. Getting none he continued, "Eirian taught me that they can slip out of your grip quickly, but other than that, I've not seen anything that says they're equal fighters to men."

"Is it that you don't know if they can fight or don't know if you can fight next to them?" Cephas asked back. His tone was not angry, nor did it carry any sign that Cephas had taken offense to BroMac's question.

BroMac crossed his arms over his chest and looked at Cephas. "Both."

Cephas smiled at him. "Honesty! That's a good start. I'll tell you something about the women warlords. If there's any genuine heroism in our realm, they have it. They were dropped into this sea of misery, losing children and parents, yet they continued to believe long after many men gave up. They have faced this brutal curse with honor and faith that one-day they'll help put an end to the suffering. They're our equals and we wouldn't want it any other way. Besides, they're exceptionally more crafty then us men."

"In other words, they can slit your throat in the time it takes you to blink." Eirian reached out and touched BroMac's hand. "It really doesn't matter if you are male or female, we all have to fight. That's the only way out of the curse."

"I see." BroMac said softly. "So there's no other way."

"That's right." Eirian's eyes went to Broan and then to Ke-Hern. "You didn't think the Queen was going to make it easy for us to break the spell, did you?"

Chapter 12

"It takes courage not to abandon your destiny when you are faced with
an easy way out."

- Warrior Laeg

Ryu and the others traveled towards a small stretch of land
tucked high between the drop-off of two valleys. Horses strained
against their harnesses as they worked to move the wagons, full of
injured men, over frozen ruts and clumps of tossed up terrain. Bronagh
worried over her own dilemma. The moaning of those around her
matched the jarring motion of the wagons as they lurched forward.
She had used up what bitter tea Eirian had given her last night and
was now left with nothing to offer them for their discomfort. One
soldier, in a fit of fever, rose screaming from the bottom of the wagon
and threw himself out, almost dragging Bronagh with him. If it hadn't
been for Miko pulling her back just in time, she too would have been
caught under the wheels of the wagon behind them. Quickly Miko
gave up his sit near the front of the wagon and hopped out.

Bronagh smiled at Miko as he fell in behind her wagon. Even
though Miko was older than Leif, he still had that long lanky look of a
boy turning into a man. He was the son of immigrants from Ke-Hern's
home village. His caramel coloring and deep black hair and was the
unique fusion of his mother's dark skin and his father's light skin. She
remembered the first time she saw him and his parents. They had just

arrived with papers from Ke-Hern. He was so young then and though it felt like a lifetime, it really wasn't that long ago.

In less than half a heartbeat, a horrified sound broke the silence and Bronagh found herself tossed forward again. With out-stretched hands she grabbed the wagon's side as she was tossed about. She righted herself and looked back through the dust and beyond the other wagons and saw Miko standing alone in stunned confusion as the wagons rushed away from him. "Miko…" she screamed. She tried to yell at the soldier driving the wagon 'to stop' but the shrieks from the wounded and the drivers yelling at the horses to get them to move faster effectively drowned her voice out.

Above the noisy chaos and high-pitched scream of his horse, Hargrave actually heard the sound of three arrows striking. He bolted off his horse and rolled head over heels to get out of the way of his horse's fall.

Crouching down as he came to his feet, his attention was drawn to the sight of two more horses in their death throes. Within seconds Ny-dick appeared on a far ridge. Their battle cries sent chills down his spine.

Getting up, Hargrave was suddenly yanked to attention by Ryu. "Take the soldiers down to the village. It's our only hope for now," Ryu pushed Hargrave in that direction. "The buildings should give us some cover. We'll be able to hold the Ny-dick off with our arrows."

"But that's foolhardy!" Hargrave shouted.

"I don't have time for this. Now lead them down there." Ryu drew his sword and pointed it at Hargrave. "Move or die. I have wagons of wounded and a group of civilians to protect."

Hargrave considered his options, and then motioned to the others to follow him. He looked back at Ryu only once before charging down the hillside, all the while cursing to himself.

Miko careened down the hill after the others, feeling extremely distraught and horribly nauseated. In a blinding flash it occurred to him that he was not ready to face the Ny-dick. The endless telling of violence, invariably deplorable stories about them had left a deep mark on Miko. He rushed into the large barn and tried to calm his shakes.

Hargrave found Miko crouched near the door. He got down on one knee beside him and took the two long knives out from his leather belt and handed one to him. "Listen to me. Follow my lead and if you can make a break for it, run back the way we came. If the Ny-dick win this fight they'll go after the wagons so you'll have a better chance making it back to Broan's group."

Miko nodded in silence. His eyes suddenly grew large as the reality of what Hargrave said sank in. "Buuttt…but if they go after the wagons… Lady Bronagh could die!"

"Before that can happen we'll do our best to kill the Ny-dick here, and that's why you need to make it back to Broan." Hargrave then stretched up from his position to get a better look at the group assembled in the barn. "Where's Ryu?" he asked. "Now that he has ordered us into this necropolis, what's his next great plan?"

"Look!" one of the soldiers yelled, "Over there." He pointed to where the Ny-dick where gathering. Ryu was racing towards them on his horse.

"What's he doing?" Hargrave asked more to himself than anyone else. He watched Ryu race up the hill towards the enemy. "Is he planning to take them on all by himself?" Then reality suddenly hit him.

"You scum-sucking Rat!" Hargrave yelled with great vehemence. Turning with one swift nod, all of Broan's men quickly surrounded Ryu's foot soldiers with raised swords. Making sure Miko was behind him; Hargrave advanced quickly on one of Ryu's men, pushing his sword against his throat. He stopped just shy of drawing blood. "DROP YOUR ARMS, ALL OF YOU! NOW!"

The soldiers did as they were told. The one facing Hargrave spoke firmly. "I don't know what Ryu is up to but…"

"Shut up fool." Hargrave gave a glance to Ryu's other men. "How do you stand?" he yelled, "with the traitor…or are you with us?"

Ryu's soldier was furious. "We don't have time for this…" He tried to push Hargrave's sword aside but Hargrave glared and held firm.

Hargrave pressed the tip of his sword further into the throat of the opposing warrior. "You're right!" he hissed as he looked briefly at the other fighters, "Are you with us or not? We don't have all day."

"We're with YOU," they yelled, more anxious then annoyed.

"Are you finished Hargrave," Ryu's soldier asked. "He's betrayed all of us, not just you and your men. Now get that sword away from me. We have a battle to fight and a traitor to gut!"

Hargrave nodded his head to his men and everyone lowered their sword. Turning, he looked at the menacing Ny-dick. "When it comes to defenses and Ny-dick, unless it's a fortress, there's not much that stops them," he admitted. "So let's get this over with. Grab whatever you can to use as a shield. We'll wait near the bottom of the hill with the village to our backs. This will give us a better chance to win and… get to Ryu and put his sorry life to an end."

A first thin wave of Ny-dick descended the slope, scrambling and screaming as they charged towards the small band of Mortals. Some of the young soldiers, fearing what they faced, inched back towards the huts. "STAND YOUR GROUND!" Hargrave yelled. "Die if we must, but at least we'll die killing some of them."

Suddenly an arrow lodged deep into the leg of the soldier standing next to Hargrave. The arrowhead was barbed, making it difficult and painful to remove, so Hargrave quickly sliced off the arrow shaft. Gripping the Manliken's shoulder he looked the soldier in the eye. "You still have two good arms, use them. We fight until we die."

Hargrave's small army readied itself. At the moment just before impact, they sidestepped out of the way, dropped low and sliced at the passing enemy, sheering off feet and cutting deep into their legs. Howling like the enraged beasts they were, the Ny-dick twisted around to face these mere Mortals. It didn't take a Wizard's wisdom or a Warlord's knowledge to see the first sign of impending disaster. It looked Hargrave and his group straight in the face.

Metal upon metal, sword and axe pitted against one another, neither side willing to give up. A second wave of Ny-dick hit, surrounding the Mortal soldiers. The battle cries from the Ny-dick, groans from the wounded blended into a surreal symphony. The intense din of combat drowned out Hargrave's orders and encouragement.

The Ny-dick pushed inward and their lethal blows caused serious losses for Hargrave's group. The Elftan warrior next to Miko sliced off the arm of one Ny-dick that was after Miko. For his efforts, his head was cracked open from the downward swing of an axe. The soldier immediately felt numb and confused. Then the pain came, sharp and wrenching. Clutching his head with his hands, the young Elftan dropped to his knees, vomiting. His misery ended quickly with the Ny-dick's next swing that took off his head.

The Ny-dick smiled at Miko as he picked up the severed head of the Elftan and sucked the blood out of it. With its eyes locked on Miko it licked its lips. Grinning, it raised his sword. Miko dove for the fallen warrior's sword. Grabbing it, Miko hurdled himself at the Ny-dick and with great effort drove the sword upward slicing the enemy's chest. Laughing the Ny-dick swung out with its multi-bladed knife. Miko did a shoulder roll and got out of the way.

Hargrave's battle cry was strong and fierce, making the Ny-dick turned his attention to him. Hargrave ducked under the wide swipe of the Ny-dick's arm making contact with the enemy's underbelly. Blood sprayed out and Hargrave sidestepped it, not feeling the sharp sword that had hit low and cut some flesh from his leg. Standing tall,

Hargrave swung wide again but was stunned when his injured leg didn't move on command. The Ny-dick's blade came down hard, gouging chucks of bone from his face. Hargrave stood still, and then stumbled as blood coursed out of him. Another swing of the sword slit his throat and Hargrave crumpled to the ground.

Miko took up the battle cry as he lunged at the Ny-dick. He put all the strength he had into plunging the sword into the enemy's back, over and over again. Panting, Miko stood over the Ny-dick that now lay dead in a heap on top of Hargrave and bellowed his outrage.

The pain caught Miko by surprise. A tight, crushing grip on his shoulders pulled him back off his feet. Suddenly Miko found he was looking up at a different monster. The split-nosed half man, half bull, sneered at him. Stunned by the sight, Miko just lay there. The Shadow Dweller's massive hand came down onto Miko's chest and the weight of it left him breathless. Suddenly coming to his senses, Miko slashed at the Shadow Dweller's hand with the sword still in his hand. Bacot bellowed as he withdrew his hand for a moment. He cursed and pulled the weapon away. Miko scrambled to his feet but Bacot quickly grabbed him, tossed him over his shoulder, and lumbered heavily up the hill towards Lija and Ryu.

Through teary eyes Miko watched as ensuing terror and panic swept through the small remaining band of warriors. Without Hargrave's leadership they soon became unfocused and although they fought savagely, it was unorganized and ineffective. In a sudden wave of Mortal weakness, the remaining warriors scattered, running for their lives. Miko dropped his head, as the Ny-dick instantaneously killed them with arrows.

Bacot dropped Miko to the ground. At least the Shadow Dwellers had no choice in killing innocent Mortals whereas Ryu freely gave up his men for personal gain. *"And they call us monsters,"* he thought to himself.

Ryu looked at Miko. "You should be happy. You're a…gift…"

Miko jumped to his feet and lunged at Ryu. The Shadow Dweller swiftly grabbed him, stilling Miko once again. Lifting his face Miko spat at Ryu. "WHY are you doing this? You're a Captain of Remdor!"

"Because it serves me well. I had preferred Eirian, but you'll do."

"He'll do?" Lija eyed the young man. "What good is he to us?"

Ryu smiled down at Miko. "He was an intimate member of Broan's group. He dined with the men while listening to all their plans. He knows more than you think, perhaps even more than the great Lady Bronagh, who was my second choice."

Miko struggled under Bacot's grip. "It won't take long for the others to figure out what you've done."

"Not if everyone is dead." With an arrogant tilt to his chin, Ryu looked over at Lija. "My business here is done. I'll go join the wagons and keep up my surveillances."

Bacot's knife cut deep into Ryu's his arm, catching him off guard. Ryu screamed and grabbed his arm, trying to stop the flow of blood. "Why did you do that?"

"It felt good." Bacot placed his knife back into his belt. "The lad's right. This makes things look more authentic." Then he slapped the flank of Ryu's horse, sending it on a mad dash through the blood and gore of a lost battle.

Lija looked down at Miko. In a hushed voice he whispered, "Next time keep your mouth shut! Out of bravado, often come words of truth that too often helps your enemy. Keep your tongue and you'll keep others alive."

Even though the sun was low on the horizon, Broan's group continued moving southward towards Harbor City, the capital of Gearoldin. They traveled along a rugged slice of river valley, which chiseled its way through the rolling foothills. It was a steady winding descent into a forest. They traversed over mountain streams and past rocky perches, always moving southward.

Unfortunately, since they were still in close proximity of the mountains, the morning torrents of rain soon turned to blowing snow, quickly slowing down the freezing group. "Eirian can't you do something about the weather?" V-Tor called out. He pulled his cloak tightly around himself, trying to trap more heat around his body.

Ke-Hern glared back at V-Tor. "Eirian's energy shouldn't be wasted on physical comforts. Tie up your tunic and stop complaining."

"But can't she use just a little bit and make the snow stop?"

Ke-Hern rolled his eyes and then stared up at the sky. He whispered a few words and the clouds parted and the snow stopped. "Humph!" Ke-Hern said, as he urged his horse to quicken its pace and move closer to the front of the line.

Eirian slowed her horse down to match V-Tor's pace. "In truth I'm not that good at controlling the weather. I either need more practice or a better teacher."

V-Tor laughed, "But I thought Ke-Hern was the best. So perhaps it's the student, not the teacher."

"You sound too much like Broan!" Eirian turned away and spotted an old abandoned farm in the distance. "Do you think the people of the land will stand up and fight with Broan?"

"Broan once said to never put a man in the position of having nothing left to lose because he will give up everything to change that fact, including his life. I believe that with or without the Governor's blessing, the people will rise up and fight…"

V-Tor's voice faded from Eirian's notice as a quiet murmur of energy caught her attention. The sound soon became the droning cry of warriors in battle, despondent and resentful. Their cry for help was barely a whisper above her consciousness. She stopped her horse and gazed into the distant east.

It wasn't long before the smell of severed flesh and spilt blood filled her senses. It wafted through her consciousness, quickly raising an alarm. An intense necessity burned inside her, an incoherent desire bubbling beneath her placid exterior. Eirian got off her horse, her eyes never leaving the eastern horizon.

"Eirian?" V-Tor called to her. He took her horse's reigns and watched as she walked away. "Eirian!" he yelled sternly, hoping to get her attention.

"Stop her!" Ke-Hern demanded.

Broan immediately spun his horse around, cutting off V-Tor. "Eirian, what are you doing?" he called out to her, but Eirian kept walking towards the east and into the forest, Broan jumped off his horse and bolted after her.

An overwhelming sense of anguish filled Eirian as a cyclone of screams and deaths demanded release. Inconsolable in her altered state, an insistent cry crackled in the air. "CEPHAS!" she screamed, "Call everyone to…"

" NO! No Eirian!" Ke-Hern bellowed. "No! It's a trap! You can't send them."

Broan grabbed Eirian and shook her. "Look at me!" he demanded. He shook her again his grip getting firmer. "LOOK AT ME!" he yelled.

"They'll die without our help!" Eirian chocked out. "I have to help them!"

Cephas appeared, looking weak and fragile. He had been weighed down by the cruel truth, that innocent lives where being wasted. "It'll do no good. Ke-Hern's right. It's too late. It's now nothing more than an evil trick to call us to a battle so we may die before our time."

Ke-Hern looked at Cephas. "Where's Deeton?" His face showed his stark panic. "You've got to stop him! He'll go and try to save Bronagh." He pushed at Cephas. "Go quickly. We'll take care of her."

The magic spell to come save her friends, now turned into a gut wrenching strain for Eirian. She pushed away from Broan and rushed over to a fallen tree as the spell convulsed in her stomach emptying the meager contents. Dropping to her knees, she hunched over, wrapping her arms around her body. The reality of what happened broke her heart, turned her stomach and made her angry all at the same time.

Broan walked over to her, leaned down and offered her his water flask, which she graciously took. He glanced at Ke-Hern, and instantly disliked what he saw on the old Wizard's face. "Are you feeling any better?" Broan asked her. She slowly nodded her head.

"Well then…good." Ke-Hern said, nervously rubbing his hands together. "We need to move from this place quickly. There's too much magic here from too many sources. Let Eirian ride with you. She'll…" Ke-Hern answered gruffly.

"NO!" Eirian said, "I'm fine. I'd rather ride by myself."

Broan was just about to demand that she ride with him, when Laeg's hand landed on his shoulder. "It's okay, I'll ride next to her," Laeg said, helping her off of the cold damp ground.

As Broan watched Laeg and Eirian walk to their horses, he suddenly reached out and grabbed Ke-Hern's cloak. "What happened here?"

Ke-Hern tried to lighten Broan's worry but his face had a hard edge, giving away his own fears. "A harmful spell…poisonous I fear. It built an irrational, excruciating tension in Eirian so she could not think clearly. They had hoped to trick Eirian into calling the Faeries to fight." He shook his head. "When faced with the sad, stark reality that people she knew were dying, the false hope of saving them was easier to believe than the truth…which is that they are already dead."

"How powerful is this new enemy? Who other than the Queen has magic this potent?"

"More importantly, now that the enemy knows about the Faeries and Mortals joining forces, they'll attack full force soon, hoping that we're unprepared. I'd say we have about three weeks…."

"To rally the troops and build an army?" BroMac stated as he approached them. "That's not long."

"Agreed," Broan said, grabbing Ke-Hern's cloak again. "That's why we need to know what we're really fighting. What or who has such powers?"

"Just know this, it can be overtaken, and Eirian is the key to it all. Keep her safe." Ke-Hern tapped Broan's offending hand with one of his fingers making Broan's grip fall away. He straightened his cloak and walked away.

Nerlena's voice echoed in Broan's head, repeating what Ke-Hern just said. "I know...I know keep her safe." Broan muttered to himself as he mounted his horse.

The sun had just settled on the horizon by the time they were on their way again. Only its soft fading light was left to aid them as they rode through the deepening darkness of the valley.

"I found you this herb," V-Tor said. "It'll help with the vomiting." He began to hand it to her, but pulled his hand back at the last second. "Of course there's a price to pay. The next time you want to wander about in the forest, you have to take me with you. I hate being left out."

Eirian smiled briefly, brushing away tears, tears she knew would have to stop on their own. She was just too tired and discouraged to put any effort into controlling them.

Laeg grabbed the reins of her horse and made it stop. He eyed the group around them and made it clear that they were to keep going. He bent down slightly, trying to catch her eye. "Are you alright?"

Eirian finally looked at Laeg. Her face, wet with tears, showed him the pain she felt. "If Ke-Hern hadn't been here, I would've sent the Faeries to fight. I would've sent them all to their death. I would've failed them all."

"It's best not to sit and blame yourself for what could have happened. If you want to do something, think about what you'll do the next time. Ke-Hern said it was a harsh spell. Do you think any one of us could've handled it better?"

"No...oh... I don't know." She looked up the path at the distant warriors. "I... I just wish I wasn't so weepy. It was bad enough having them see me vomit." She shook her head. "I'm not giving them much of an image as a leader am I?"

Laeg laughed. "Well I don't know. Showing us your Mortal side is rather nice. It makes it a little easier to relate to you. Come on. If we get too far behind, Broan will begin to worry."

The night was near when Ryu managed to join the moving wagons. He was hunched over his horse, semi-conscious and his left arm dangled like a limp rag from his side. When she saw him, Bronagh yelled at the driver to stop. She jumped out and ran to him.

Ryu could feel the caring hands that pushed and prodded at him. He could make out voices. It seemed that all were concerned and worried for him. His eyes opened to see if he was dreaming.

"What happened to Miko?" Bronagh asked as she leaned into him. "Please tell me."

Ryu looked at her and shook his head with resignation. He watched as the gravity of what Bronagh thought had happened take hold of her mind.

"I should not have let him get out of the wagon…I should have insisted we stop…"

Ryu watched with delight as her inner anguish grew.

Broan sat on his horse and looked around the small camp he was about to leave Eirian in. He hadn't any doubt that BroMac, RohDin and the others would look after her. Still leaving her in the care of others unsettled him in a way. "We'll be back by tomorrow night," Broan said as he straightened in his saddle.

BroMac scowled. "I don't like just the three of you going into Harbor City. You should take at least two more for safety."

Broan smiled down at BroMac. "With Ke-Hern and Deeton gone to visit the Queen, you'll need all the manpower you can get if the Ny-dick find you. Besides, I like traveling light. It makes for an easy get-away if needed." He turned his horse to the south and led the way. "Tomorrow night," he repeated over his shoulder.

Broan, Laeg and V-Tor followed the Mainiti River. There were at least half a dozen small lighthouses along the river, warning of sudden out-crop of rocks just under the surface water. It appeared that Tybalt, the Ruling Governor of Gearoldin, worked hard to protect trade goods. "*Maybe,*" Broan thought to himself, "*he'll see fighting in this war is the only way to save Gearoldin. It may not be as hard as Iarnan warned.*"

It didn't take long before they passed through rows of houses, inns and boarding houses. Economic prosperity had changed the face of Harbor City, which now stretched north and west along the river that ran through it. Near the city center was a great shipyard with container terminals and crowded docks. Long ago, the city had replaced the simple docks of wood with more sturdy ones of stone and mortar. Spindly forms of cranes dotted the area as they worked to lift goods from the ships. The modern age had made its way to Harbor city. Boardwalks were jammed with a mixture of booths and stalls, all open for business. This was a place that had no shortages, no failed crops, no hunger, and no pain of war. This was a place where faces were painted with cheerfulness and not strained with grief.

Once Broan and the others passed the main port, they entered Commerce Street, a complete variety of banking and investment services. Trade Company buildings were nuzzled in-between these banks creating a feeling of "a vultures nest!" V-Tor said out loud as they rode past.

"It seems that Tybalt took to heart the role of creating a central port for goods in an attempt to stabilize the economy," Laeg commented.

"Too much to heart for my liking. "V-Tor added as he shook his head.

Gearoldin's governor, Tybalt, met Broan on the main stairway. He stood near the top, giving off an air of importance. Due to his modest height, he often used the stairs to command attention. His weathered skin and flyaway hair made him look as if he was always in constant motion, always overseeing, always involved. He also had a thunderous voice that he liked to use in situations like this. "Broan," he began, "the Warlord of Solveig, nephew of Governor Iarnan of Remdor, we welcome you!"

Broan stopped at the base of the stairs. "Governor Tybalt, I've important news that effects all of the regions of this land. I wish to speak to you and the high committee."

Tybalt started down the stairs, opening his arms wide as a sign of welcoming. However, the welcoming never carried through to the rest of his body. It was stiff and his steps were hesitant. "Let's go into my private office and talk. I'll call the high committee if needed afterward."

Broan raised an eyebrow. "This is going to be as hard as Iarnan said it would be," he muttered to himself. Once inside the grand room that served as his office, Tybalt took a seat behind a large desk. He motioned for Broan to sit in a chair on the other side of it.

Broan didn't feel like sitting and he didn't feel like playing these political games. "Governor!"

The Governor quickly cut Broan off. "Please, Broan, call me Tybalt. There's no need for such formality in here." He opened a box of tobacco and started to stuff his pipe. "Would you like some?"

Broan shook his head and leaned on the desk. "How can you be so indifferent to what's happening out there in the world? Mortals everywhere are suffering. The Ny-dick are on the move and since Wizard Lija is leading them, I believe it won't be long before they'll be knocking on your door."

"Ny-dick and the Wizard Lija! Are you sure?" Tybalt's eyes narrowed.

"Yes I'm sure! We've actually been in combat with them and right now they have Solveig under siege. It won't be long before Harbor City will be under attack. We need to gather as many troops from Gearoldin and Anwel to fight them off in Remdor before they even become a threat to you."

"What about the Queen? She was the only one that has been successful in ridding the land of those beasts. Have you ask for a meeting with her? Has Wizard Ke-Hern tried to get in touch with her? I can't believe she's sitting by doing nothing if it truly is the Ny-dick!"

"There'll be no intervention from the Queen this time," Broan said pushing himself off of Tybalt's desk. "We're on our own, even Ke-Hern says so."

Tybalt put down his pipe. "I see. This is bad news." He rose from behind his desk and walked around it. "I'll call a meeting. Come back in two hours." He walked Broan to the door and almost pushed him out. "I have much to do to get everyone together this quickly. I hope you don't mind." And with that he shut the door to the office leaving Broan standing alone in the grand entrance.

"If he thinks he can avoid the problem by removing me from sight, he's so wrong." Broan sat down on a chair near the stairs. He wasn't going to leave until he had his time in front of the high committee.

It took longer than two hours and Broan wondered if Tybalt was taking his sweet time on purpose. Still, he was glad to finally be able to stand before the council. The council room was large and ornate, not at all like the one in the Walled City. He was guided to a chair near the front where he was to wait for a number of dignitaries to address the group first. There were eloquent speeches to introduce Broan. They all talked about how he was widely regarded and how he had developed a reputation as a specialist in warfare techniques, all to reinforce his standing to the group.

Finally after all this unnecessary talk, Broan was able to say his piece. There was a great calm in the wake of Broan's speech. Broan waited as the reality came to life in these councilors' minds.

"For one who has had no direct contact with the Queen, you have lots to say about what she will or will not do," said one of the councilors, who had just been appointed to the committee.

Another asked, "Why send off the military we have? If things are going to get as bad as Lord Broan says we'll need them here to protect Gearoldin."

"Gearoldin or just your wealth?"

The roar of anger was deafening. "We stand for all of Gearoldin. It's an outrage that you even think we don't care for anything beyond our holdings," someone yelled.

"Yes, is this how you ask for help, by insulting us?" another cut in.

Tybalt rose from his elevated chair amidst the various slurs now being directed at Broan. He raised his arms high, "Enough...Enough! This isn't getting us anywhere." Then he faced Broan. "We need to know for sure that the Queen is unwilling to help before we can commit our troops. If they are needed, we'll send them...BUT...not before we hear from the Queen."

"And when do you think the Queen will send you word? Ke-Hern says she is locked on her Island, unable to assist us. Think on this. While you wait, the Ny-dick and Lija move closer to dividing and conquering us all!"

"The committee has spoken!" Tybalt's voice rose to a near voluble shout. "LEAVE! NOW BROAN! And take your ill news to Anwel. Maybe they'll help you."

With a fierce cry Broan yelled, "I'll go, Governor Tybalt, but be warned! For as I go, I'll ask the Warlords along the way if they wish to take up the cause. If you won't save this land, I will."

"You can try and do that but they won't go!" Tybalt said crossing his arms over his chest. He raised his chin slightly and stood a little taller. "I'm their Governor. They'll listen to me...I pay them monthly..."

"Pay them! Do you really think gold can buy the heart of a warrior?" Broan hissed. "But if they're as stupid as all that, you can have them and may the gods be with you."

Council members jumped up from their seats. "Arrest this man!" one screamed. "He's a traitor. He doesn't respect the judgment of the High Committee!"

Broan drew his sword as the council's guards surrounded him.

"Enough! At ease men. Broan, lower your sword." Tybalt slumped down into his chair. "Go...Go now. We've nothing more to say to you on this. We wait to hear from the Queen." Tybalt then raised his hand stopping the cries of disagreement. "We've power and money to keep the soldiers loyal to Gearoldin. I don't believe many will follow him." He looked at Broan again. "Leave."

Broan roared into to camp, violently pulled on the reigns of his horse and came to an abrupt stop. His awful mood had grown to massive proportions since leaving Tybalt and the high council. "Where's Eirian?" he asked as he jumped off his horse.

"Nice to see you too," BroMac answered. "I can tell from your foul mood that things didn't go as well as you had hoped."

"We need to call a meeting with the Faery Warlords. Even though Tybalt and the council didn't want to support us in any way, I've managed to get almost half the soldiers to join us. I'm concerned that Tybalt might have his own plans about this war. With his lack of caution, it wouldn't take the Ny-dick long to slither along the Celtan Mountains and attack us from the south, not the north." He scanned for Eirian again. "We have to make sure that doesn't happen."

"What about the City of Bridges and Anwell's army?"

"Once I've divided the army we have into legions and assigned each a strong Faery and Mortal leader, I'll take Eirian, V-Tor and Laeg." He continued to look around for Eirian. "Where is she?"

"She's down at the lake," BroMac answered as he acknowledged V-Tor and Laeg. "Don't worry she's safe. I've made sure she's always in someone's sight."

Still agitated, Broan turned to V-Tor. "Go get her and keep your eyes open."

V-Tor quickly followed the path down to the lake. It dipped and turned as it made its way through the forest of cottonwood and cedars. Realizing there were many spots along the way that could easily hide the enemy, he increased his pace. He agreed with Broan, now wasn't the time to let down their guard. Now that Tybalt and the Council of Gearoldin had made their position clear, life had gotten a lot more complicated.

He came rushing out of the woods to find Eirian sitting alone by the lake. He scanned the area and wasn't able to find a sign of any soldiers. V-Tor quickly stormed forward, charging towards Eirian. "Where in hell is everyone?" he bellowed at her "I thought BroMac said you were with a guard! I'll have their necks for this!"

"You can have my neck instead. I sent them away. I have my own warriors to protect me."

"You have no idea how dangerous it is right now!" V-Tor shouted in frustration. He grabbed for her hand but she sidestepped and scowled back at him.

V-Tor glared down at her. "I don't care how good they fight. A Faery or two against a group of Ny-dick wouldn't have been able to save you." Catching her hand in his he started pulling her along the path.

There it was again, that feeling of warm energy and anticipation he always sensed when he touched her. It wasn't like anything he had ever experienced before. It pulled at him, growing in intensity each time, drawing him closer towards Eirian. This feeling was in opposition to everything he knew and honored. He looked back at Eirian and wondered what magic she was playing with.

Eirian didn't like the look V-Tor had just shot her, so she quickly dug in her heels. "What?" she asked.

"Don't waste your magic on me," he said as he continued to pull her along.

"I am NOT using magic on you!" She tried to get free of his grip. "I never…"

"Well someone is." V-Tor took in a breath. "Look we'll talk about it later. Right now Broan needs your help."

It was almost dawn before everything was resolved and everyone was ready to take action, ready to fight. Eirian rolled her shoulders to release some tension while she sipped her warm tea. She smiled to herself. Broan had pushed to keep as many Faeries as possible away from fighting until the last battle. The Faeries had agreed and offered their ability to be scouts, messengers and spies, fighting only if necessary. There was no doubting it, Ke-Hern had been right. Broan had been born for this time and this war. He had taken to the job of uniting the armies with strong dedication.

From her seat, Eirian watched Broan in quiet discussion with Cephas. The muscle in Broan's jaw twitched and his stance was off balance, reflecting the ill steadiness of his inner energy. Putting down her tea, she stood. "Broan come here and I'll help take some of your tension away."

One of Broan's eyebrows rose sharply. "And just how were you planning to that?"

"I'll do nothing more than place my hands on your back and untangle some very blocked muscles."

Broan gave her a half smile as he walked towards her. Taking off his tunic and shirt, he sat down on the log near her.

"You didn't need to remove your shirt. I can balance the energy with it still on."

When Broan didn't make any attempt to replace his shirt, Eirian walked around him. She paused briefly when she saw the tattoo on his back. It was circular with an odd shaped triangle in the center of it. Mountains were wrapped around the sides and top, and water sat at the bottom. She bent in for a closer look. "I've been meaning to ask. What is this on your back?"

Broan strained to look over his shoulder, not sure what she was looking at. "Oh, that's the crest of Solveig."

"You mean your crest."

"No Solveig's crest. We found a disk with these markings on it while breaking ground for the fortress and I liked it, so it became the crest of Solveig. BroMac and RohDin have the same tattoo as well. I'm surprised that you never noticed it before."

"I did notice it while you were ill, but so much has happened I forgot to ask you about it."

She rubbed her two hands together to make her touch warmer. Slowly Eirian unknotted his back muscles. Then she placed her palms across the width of his back and pressed into him. Broan could immediately feel the flow of energy rush across his back, from one of her hands to the other. She moved one hand to the top of his neck and the other on the lowest part of his bare back. Once again Broan felt the warm flash of life course up and down his spine. He closed his eyes and took in a deep relaxing breath.

Now finished Eirian placed a hand on his shoulder and leaned towards his ear. "There," she whispered, "Now go to sleep."

"And what of you, I know this evening was hard on you."

"Trust me, BroMac will make sure I rest. He hasn't given up bullying me yet."

The Queen's island sat among the many windswept islets in the inland sea. Deeton had no problem picking it up in the distance. Even from this height, the fortress protected by an old magic, appeared dream-like, an alternative reality. It glowed in various colors of green and copper, colors that came from deep within the land.

Deeton began his decent. Gauging his approach he skimmed by barren fjords at land's end and was just about to head out over the inland sea when Ke-Hern pulled hard on Deeton's tunic, bringing him back to reality.

"Place us down over there." Ke-Hern pointed to an outcropping of land on one of the fjords.

Turning, Deeton did as he was told and once his feet touched the ground, he became his Duronykian form. He placed his hands on his hips as he stared out at the crescent-shaped isle. "Is it really that dangerous to simply fly there?"

"Don't know…never tried it." Ke-Hern answered as he walked away needing to find the secret bridge. He looked at the setting sun and judged where the moon was going to rise. He raised both of his hands and framed the island then scanned the horizon. "Here, we'll need to stand here. Quickly! There are only a few moments when the dew on the bridge catches the moonlight."

Puzzled, Deeton went over and stood next to Ke-Hern. He tried to see what Ke-Hern was looking at, but there was nothing there. "If the only way onto the island is by this bridge, is it also the only way off?"

"Yes," Ke-Hern answered quickly. He was pleased to know that the hardship of being Faery had not doused Deeton's curiosity and that it still burned brightly. What he didn't like was Deeton peppering him with questions since they started out. "Please Deeton, we need to concentrate. No more questions. Just look for the bridge."

Just as the moon rose over the horizon behind them, a bridge of air and light appeared before them. Deeton marveled. It looked like it was made of spun glass as it sparkled in the moonlight. He paused as he stepped onto it. "What's this made of?" he asked as rubbed his fingers along the fragile structure.

"Spider's webs and the stuff of Faery wings. Now hurry. Once the moon goes behind that cloud, this passageway will disappear." Deeton quickly rushed to keep pace with Ke-Hern, making sure they stepped off the bridge at the same time. He didn't trust his life to spider's webs and grand illusions of an old Wizard.

Once on the island, Deeton stood in wonder of the fortress before him. Pillars covered in gold leaf stood guard over the front entrance. Stained glass accents on the windows danced as they allowed the candlelight from inside to pour out into the shadowy darkness of the night. He was surprised that with all its grandeur and size, the fortress managed to give one the feeling of being bottled up and confined. "You built this for the Queen didn't you?" he asked, unable to help himself.

"Yes, now please." Ke-Hern answered, getting annoyed.

"You were able to tap into her Off-World power weren't you?"

Ke-Hern took in a deep breath, "No. Look Deeton…"

"But she hasn't been able to leave since you brought her here?"

"ENOUGH!" Ke-Hern yelled as he stopped short of the steps that lead up to the main doorway. "Deeton, from this point on you must keep your mouth closed and your eyes open. Not another word until we meet with the Queen." He looked up at the doors, still closed and unwelcoming.

Deeton nodded his head and pressed his mouth closed. It lasted for less than a second. "Who are they?"

Looking up, Ke-Hern placed his foot on the first step. "They are the elders, mediators to the Ancients."

Deeton stood immobilized. "Mediators for the Ancients! What magic did you conjure up?"

"Ancient's magic. That's why you are here. There's a girl that lives with the Queen. Her name is Aillil. She's blind, but don't let that fool you. She sees more than you or I combined. The Queen asked me to bring you here because Aillil has begun to channel verses from the Ancients and we hope that with your knowledge of them you'll be able to tell us what she's foretelling."

Deeton stood at the bottom of the stairs, still powerless to move. "And what if I don't understand what she's saying?"

"Then we're in a lot more trouble than I thought."

"Hello Ke-Hern, we've been waiting for you." Aillil smiled as she stared off into space. "And you must be Deeton."

Deeton looked over his shoulder to where she was looking and then back at her. "Yes," he said as he openly studied her.

"It's not nice to stare," she said as she turned to lead the way through the jumble of corridors and rooms.

Deeton's eyes grew large, taking in all he saw. Colors were bright and rich as if they glowed with their own inner source of power. Shimmering, like a mirage, walls appeared out of nowhere, making it hard to understand and trust his vision. He was relieved when they finally reached the Queen's room.

The Queen had not seen a Faery in decades. She took her time studying him until finally she stepped towards Deeton. "Welcome. Ke-Hern has told me much of your ability to understand the Ancients. Let's hope he's right."

"I don't understand. If you live within the Ancients' magic, why not just ask them what you need to know?"

"Because they make nothing easy!" She cursed. "It's a tormenting game dealing with them."

Ke-Hern smiled at Deeton. "Or it could be that we're the ones making things hard."

The Queen tossed Ke-Hern a stern look. "Pay him no mind. He doesn't have to live with them." She turned her attention back to Deeton. "I've written down most of what Aillil said when she was channeling. Here, take a look at this." She handed him a few sheets of rice paper with words neatly written on them.

Walking over to the desk by the window, Deeton began to read the papers in earnest. His head bobbed with the rhythm of the verse. He took time to go over each word as if each one held a story within it. He counted off the beat, flow of the verse, and then smiled when he raised the last sheet of paper. "I know this drawing," he said as he lifted it so they could all see.

"Where did that come from?" the Queen asked a little shocked.

"I drew it," Aillil said. "It's what I saw when they spoke to me."

"How do you know that what you are seeing is what is on drawn on the paper?" Deeton asked puzzled by how a blind girl could have drawn so clearly.

"It's hard to explain, but I just move the pen against the paper as if I was tracing the picture."

"Well it's very good. It's from the Ancients. In fact," Deeton paused and studied it once again, "it is very close to the crest Broan picked for Solveig?"

"Wait a minute." Taking it, Queen DaNann moved over to her padded chair and sat down. "This is like the drawing that was discovered around here. What is this all about?" she pondered out loud.

Ke-Hern stood behind DaNann. His face tensed as he looked at the drawing. "It is very similar but…" He tilted his head this way and that. Suddenly with a chuckle Ke-Hern straightened up. "Close, but actually it isn't a crest or a picture, it's a map!" He quickly took hold of the drawing. "Look at this. If this point is Solveig and this point is the Island, then it only goes with reason that this other point of the triangle is also a place the Ancients once lived." He looked at Queen. "Can you get us a map of the lands? Let's see if this makes sense."

"So you're saying that there's another location where the Ancients once lived?"

"Yes!" Ke-Hern took the map that was given him and measured out the triangle. "Here I'd say." Ke-Hern pointed to a bleak area north of Anwel and just inside of the Duronyk region. "What are they trying to tell us? What needs to be done?" Ke-Hern muttered.

"This is a bad omen," whispered the Queen.

"What do you mean bad? Don't we want their help?" Deeton asked

"NO!" The Queen yelled, "This cannot bring them forward. This had better be to keep them out of our affairs, or all is lost, even if we do win the war."

"It's in a desert you know," Aillil said in a clear and confident voice. "The old Ancients' stronghold… they want me there as soon as possible…or something will…"

The Queen suddenly looked at Ke-Hern and Deeton. "Oh no," she whispered. "If Lija awoke the life force of Solveig then he too may know of this location. We need to get there before he does…he cannot lay claim to it. He would wake them and…" Her breath caught in her throat.

Broan lead his small group away from their camp and onward to Anwel and the City of Bridges. He left behind six divisions, all with Faery Warlords and Mortal leaders to guide them back towards Remdor. Broan planned to have the divisions move out all at the same time hoping that the greater the army appeared in strength, the less likely it would be challenged. Yet he knew most would be feeling the heavy blow of combat soon. Lija would want the Ny-dick to isolate the groups of soldiers, cut them down, and reduce the forces until there were too few to fight in the last battle.

He looked out at the light blue sky. It was dressed with delicate fibers of cirrus clouds that left the sky with a soft silky appearance. Still he didn't find an answer he was looking for up there. He wasn't sure if they should continue following the main road into Anwel. He studied the thick forest ahead of them that seemed to swallow the road. The immense trees with thick trunks were all standing straight as arrows and looking almost impermeable.

There were many auxiliary routes to the City of Bridges. There were networks of paths and trails across the land, passing through woods, plateaus of high ground, and numerous rivers. All were perilous as far as Broan was concerned, which didn't make his decision easy.

He looked over his shoulder at the small group with him. V-Tor had taken up the rear guard, while Laeg and Eirian waited side by side. He watched Eirian briefly. Seeing her exhaustion, he decided which way they needed to go. Broan directed his horse forward down the dusty track of the main road.

The Ny-dick were standing still in irregular rows like shadows among the trees, waiting for the signal to attack. One of the Shadow Dwellers hung about the treetops watching Broan. What he would order all depended on Broan's next move.

Just as Broan and the others entered the forest, a volley of arrows descended on them. An arrow caught Laeg in the leg and two more killed Eirian's horse. V-Tor jumped from his horse and pulled Eirian free of her fallen horse. Backing out of the woods and into a clearing, he pushed Eirian behind a rock. He then partially covered her with his body, protecting her from any further assault. V-Tor was relieved when he saw Broan grab Laeg and pull him clear of the forest and into some thick bushes in a notch of the land.

"Let me get to Laeg," Eirian shouted. "He's hurt."

V-Tor pressed down on her, pinning her to the ground. "You'll stay put. Broan will tend to him for now." He inched his head up and looked over the rock's edge. The Ny-dick let loose bloodcurdling screams as their arrows ejected from the blackness of the forest, ripping up great holes in the earth just in front of V-Tor.

"This doesn't look good." V-Tor hissed. "I think there are two packs of them. We may be out of range for now but it won't last long."

"I can try and call Cephas. We may be able to send in a few Faeries and end this," Eirian said as she tried to squirm out from under V-Tor.

He pressed her down even harder and then looked over at Broan. They were both trapped, pinned down and unable to shift the tides of this battle. Too far apart to talk, V-Tor wasn't about to yell out her plan, so it was up to him. He looked down at Eirian. "I know Broan won't like to waste their lives."

"It's still better than all of us dying." She looked at V-Tor as he continued to shield her. "There is one problem though. I'll need your help. My energy is nearly spent."

His eyes narrowed. The situation was dire, but he wasn't sure if he wanted be involved with her magic. "What do I have to do?"

"You need to open your tunic and shirt."

"WHAT!" His eyes shot over to look at Broan. "Are you sure?" he asked, his voice cracking a little.

"Oh don't be so shocked. I just need to place my hand over your heart. It won't take long, but you will feel the effects for a while, and for that I apologize." Eirian began to work his belt free, so she could raise his tunic.

V-Tor's eyebrows rose, he stopped her hands. "Are you…" he said hoarsely, "sure this will work?"

"Yes!" Frustrated that he wasn't moving fast enough, Eirian pushed his clothing out of the way and swiftly placed her hand on his chest.

The feeling was astonishing. The touch of her hand on his bare chest awoke the same sensation he had been feeling a lot lately. He cursed to himself. Now was not the time or place for this. "Why?" he asked her as he grabbed her hand, breaking the connection.

"Why does our energy recognize each other?"

"So you feel it too!" He eyes studied her face, seeking a deeper answer.

"V-TOR" she yelled, "We don't have time for this. Let me finish calling Cephas, and then I'll try and clarify what it is."

"Do you promise? I'm at wits end about this sensation. Even Tellos questioned it."

"Tellos? What does…" Eirian shook her head. "It doesn't matter for now. You have to be still…and quiet. I'll be using your inner power to call Cephas, and possibly even Stamas."

Broan finished tying a belt around Laeg's wounded leg. "Will you be alright?" he asked Laeg as he got down on the ground next to him.

"I didn't see anything, I didn't even hear anything," Laeg hissed through clenched teeth. He gripped his injured leg and moved to get a better look at the Ny-dick and their positions around them. He looked over at V-Tor and Eirian. "Why is Eirian touching V-Tor?" he asked.

"Well…I don't know, but hopefully it's to aid us," Broan said as he stared at the other two.

At that moment a Ny-dick broke free of its hiding place. With its battle-axe raised, it charged across the field. Eirian looked up at the approaching enemy and changed her mind. She felt there was no time to call Cephas but with V-Tor's energy just enough time to call on her talents. She anchored her free hand on the ground and pushed V-Tor over.

"*Spells are never stagnant. They have more twists and turns than a rodent's hole,*" Eirian recalled Ke-Hern telling her. "*You should feel calm and at peace as you start or the energy will be too scattered.*" With a Ny-dick hastening towards her, she didn't have time to calm herself. "Sorry Ke-Hern no time!" She whipped up the winds like a tempest, tossing dust and debris at the Ny-dick, forcing it to stop.

Eirian wasn't done. She leaned her weight onto both secured hands creating more pull on both V-Tor's and the land's energy. The winds began to spin and churn, dragging up foliage. The storm thundered down, scattering some of the hidden Ny-dick into Broan's waiting arrows.

V-Tor's energy was being drawn from him at an unhealthy rate. He quickly came to understand the painful mystery of magic with its blending of hope and terror. He lay pale and breathless under her touch, unable to even speak. Irregular and restless muscular movements took on a life of their own. The pain was intense, burning, and cold, all at the same time. He became alarmed when he felt his spirit separate from his body.

"STOP!" screamed Cephas as he appeared behind Eirian. He grabbed Eirian and pulled her away, breaking the contact with both the land and V-Tor.

Eirian suddenly realized that V-Tor was near death, all because of her lack of attention. "Let me go!" she demanded as she twisted in Cephas' iron grip. She placed her hand on his chest and an energy blast threw him back. She dropped down by V-Tor and started to replenish his energy. "I'm so sorry," she whispered.

In the excitement, Eirian didn't notice something new taking over, coming from some place deep inside her. Immersed in the control of magic, she fearlessly embraced this stronger, heavier power, never once questioning it.

V-Tor could feel the warm sensation of her touch rapidly spreading through his body. The twitching slowed and then stopped, allowing him to breathe more easily. He looked up at Eirian and was alarmed. Her lips were a cobalt blue and she was panting hard trying to control the force she had unleashed. V-Tor tried to shift his body in an attempt to break the contact between them, but he had no control over his Mortal form. All he could do was watch as fear grew.

Cephas flew over to her again. He quickly took on his Duronyk form and pulled at her. "Stop, Ke-Hern said this was forbidden to you!"

Eirian stood up and shrugged him off as if he were nothing more than a flea. She looked out at the forest that still held the Ny-dick. She closed her eyes as the deeper powers tempted her, inflaming her anger at the Ny-dick. She felt invincible in its grip.

She smiled as rumbling from the land became so ferocious it felt like the earth was going to split apart, but instead it rose up to her command. Where there once was a flat field between them and the Ny-dick, there now stood a raw hill with exposed stone and dirt. The land was ablaze with the simmering of uncontrolled energy.

Cephas raised himself up on his elbows and called other Faeries in to help. Eirian had to be stopped before she destroyed herself. He shifted into his Faery form and attacked her again. Bolts of lightning leaped from her fingers, bowling him over once again.

Worried, Broan rose and started to race towards her. He wasn't prepared for Hywel's tackle that landed him hard on the ground. "Don't move!" Hywel told him. "Cephas has to handle this."

"Get off me," Broan yelled, upset as he watched Eirian charge towards the newly formed hill and the Ny-dick's position.

"NO! Cephas knows what he is doing," Hywel yelled into Broan's ear. Suddenly, the hair on the back of Hywel's neck rose. He looked towards the hill Eirian was running to and his eyes focused on the Shadow Dweller at the top. He stood in his beastly form with his large and hellishly black wings fully extended. Hywel cursed to himself. There stood DeSpon.

Quickening her pace, Eirian charged towards the new hill. She knew who this Shadow Dweller was and it only increased her rage.

She turned her attention to the forest and with a flick of her fingers a loud crack shattered the air as a tree crashed down. One minute it was on the floor of the forest and the next it was flying through the air hurtling towards DeSpon. When it missed him, she screamed her frustration. With face flush from her power, she kept running, even when her body started to protest. Once again the air erupted with the sound of trees being uprooted as she began to hurl them at her enemy.

DeSpon stood defiant as trees and rocks flew past him. He watched Eirian claw her way up the incline of the hill. When she was about twenty feet away from him, she stood up. She looked like an apparition. Her chest heaved with the need for more oxygen. Her hair scattered about her. DeSpon stood transfix at her tenacity as she stood there staring at him, daring him to fight. But when Cephas charged at her again, grabbing her from behind DeSpon backed away.

Just then a formation of earth and rock formed in front of them. "It's okay," Stamas said coming to shape before them. "He's leaving. Unfortunately he got what he came for. Get her out of here while we take care of the Ny-dick."

"But this is not your battle." Cephas said.

"Perhaps not, but her safety is."

Cephas nodded his head. "Thanks," was all he said as he roughly forced Eirian back to the group.

Never before had Cephas felt so totally consumed by his anger. He violently tossed Eirian towards Broan. "Hold her and don't let go!" he yelled as he turned and walked away. He looked at Hywel. "See if DeSpon took flight yet. I don't want him sticking around, especially after Eirian's selfish display of stupidity!" He stomped over to Laeg and checked his wound and then V-Tor. It was clear that Laeg and V-Tor wouldn't be able to ride for a while, which meant that they would have to stay the night. This put them in a very vulnerable position. Now that DeSpon knew of Eirian's power... Cephas cursed to himself and shook his head. His anger rose again to a fever pitch just at the thought. He looked over his shoulder at Eirian and cursed her. "You told him everything! You fool!"

Eirian fought against Broan's grip. "I did what had to be done! I didn't have enough of my natural talent. We were being attacked, and there was no other choice."

Cephas rushed at her, his fists clenched tight, his knuckles white. "You could have called us! But instead you defied Ke-Hern's decree." He pressed his nose against hers, staring into her eyes. "You broke the rules that govern you, and now all of us may have to pay the price for it!"

"STOP IT! I am not a child anymore," she hissed. "I did what I needed to do, and if Ke-Hern had finished teaching me how to use my power," she said, "you wouldn't be mad at me right now. So this is clearly Ke-Hern's fault for not fulfilling his duty!"

"HIS DUTY!" Cephas threw his fists up into the air and stomped away from her. "His duty was to keep you safe. He didn't finish training you because he knew what a reckless, selfish, uncontrollable fool you are! And he knew if Lija found out…"

"My duty is to get everyone safely to the last battle and I'll use whatever I can to do just that."

Cephas swiftly rushed back to her. He pointed at her, his finger only an inch from her face. "You have no idea the danger you put yourself in!"

"And when is that new news?" Broan asked with a smirk on his face.

Cephas looked at Broan and then Hywel. Broan's humor began to clear his head. He could feel the level of his anger begin to drop, his fear dissipate. He looked back at Eirian. "Don't ever do that again."

Eirian wanted to say something but decided not to. She swallowed hard against the dryness in her throat. She didn't like Cephas' emotional outburst, but knew on some level he was right. Once again she had breached boundaries with no concern or knowledge of the damage it could do. She looked over to where V-Tor lay. "*The cost of pride is often shame.*" Ke-Hern voice crept into her head making her feel all that much worse.

With a Faery guard and Stamas nearby, they set up a small camp under a rapidly fading sky. Unwilling to use any talents, Eirian worked the arrow out of Laeg's leg. After cleaning the area, she sewed it closed and dressed the wound. "Thanks," Laeg said to her, as he gently touched her shoulder. Eirian gave Laeg a brief smile as she nodded back at him. Dejected and tired, she walked over to V-Tor.

"I'm so sorry for causing such distress on your body."

V-Tor took Eirian's hand, applying tender pressure to it. "As I recall, you were going to tell me how our energy recognizes each other?"

"Like it does now?" she smiled as she withdrew her hand. "Well, at some point in time our energy connected. That is why it reacts each time we touch."

V-Tor scowled at her. "You have been hanging around with Ke-Hern too much if you think that makes any sense to me. I mean how can our energies, as you call it, have known one another before we met? This has been happening from the first time we touched."

"Energy doesn't live on a time line, it just lives." She looked over at him as he tried to sit up. "Have you ever met someone you didn't like right off the bat?"

V-Tor had no problem with coming up with a long list of characters. "Yes," he said.

"Well, in truth your energy was recognizing their energy."

"So you mean this sensation we have between us is intuition, a 'foretelling' of something that is going to happen?"

"Yes, in a way. It's just that ours is on a grander scale. We are linked for a greater purpose I think."

"So maybe Tellos wasn't wrong." V-Tor smiled. He took her hand again. "So sometime in the future our energies will come together… again?"

Eirian squirmed under his suggestion. "Well, not likely in the way you're thinking at the moment."

DeSpon was stunned by what he had witnessed. Eirian's power was immense. Now he understood why Ke-Hern had chosen her to be the leader of the Faeries. He folded his leathery wings back and out of the way as he sat on a high branch of a tree. Looking out he could see their campfire from where he was and wondered how Eirian was feeling after such a display of her abilities. He paused for a moment, *"but which power does she have, Off-World, Ancient or something newly unleashed."*

DeSpon rested his head back against the trunk of the tree. *"If only I had known then what I know now. I wouldn't have rebelled against Ke-Hern and the other Faeries."* He wouldn't have been cast out with only a few friends and followers still loyal to him and he wouldn't have been such an easy mark for Sobus. He wouldn't have agreed to the bargain that cost him his soul.

"Tomorrow I'll visit Aillil. Maybe she'll have some hope to share with me. Maybe she'll know how we can make Eirian free us."

Chapter 13

Broan and his group had just rounded the corner of 'Raiatua Lake' when Eirian caught sight of the City of Bridges and the sight left her breathless. She had always enjoyed this regal city, this glittering capital of Anwel, where horse-drawn jaunting cars, open restaurants and markets were everywhere. Towers and buildings, straight and tall, glistened in the sun. Whitewashed walls of terraced houses gave the city a surreal feeling of being untouched, spotless and clean.

There were no similarities between the City of Bridges and Harbor city. People in Harbor City busied themselves with trade and commerce, while the people of the City of Bridges were all about taking time to learn the arts. The City was comprised of undergraduates, graduates and experienced teachers and artisans. It had three universities all devoted to the expression of talent in music, painting, writing, and, the most popular, drama. Even the smallest of the universities housed over a thousand students.

Many of who, at this moment, stood in stunned silence. Broan's size and stature made him stand out among the people. A warlord whose calling showed on his body and face, he seemed fearsome to them. Soon groups of youthful people dashed about excitedly, making way for these visiting fighters. V-Tor enjoyed the special treatment, where as Laeg, on the other hand, thought these Mortals were all acting childishly. His wounded leg reminded him that his group was made of flesh and blood like everyone else, and they were not gods.

After making sure the others were secured at Laeg's family home. Broan had no trouble finding the Governor of Anwel. Unlike Tybalt, Eamonn met Broan on the street outside the Government hall. He was a tall, slim, gentle man, a seasoned Elftan of much importance. His principal role in Anwel was to develop a center for the arts, melding the talents of individual Elftans and Manlike. You knew just by looking at him that he was a powerful force of passion. Although Eamonn had taken full advantage of the years of peace, he never took it for granted. He knew Broan would be coming. He knew what Broan would be asking for, and he was ready.

He took Broan's hand in his, shaking it with warmth and confidence. "Come Broan let's go talk about this coming war." Eamonn directed Broan to a small room just off the main lobby. "How is your uncle Iarnan?" He asked as he poured a glass of wine for both of them.

"He's as well as expected. He's working at holding back the Ny-dick from the Walled city."

Eamonn paused what he was doing and let his shoulders slump as he sighed. "This is not a good time for Remdor, and I fear that soon it will be not a good time for the rest of us." Turning, Eamonn handed a glass of wine to Broan. "Tybalt told me you were on the way, not that I didn't already know it. You can feel war in the wind." He paused and then motioned Broan to sit. "So what's to be done?"

"We need to fight the Ny-dick in Remdor, stopping them before they get any further. If they succeed in overtaking Remdor there will be nothing to stop them from marching towards Anwel and Gearoldin."

"Gearoldin…so how did you do?"

"Not bad. Half are coming. They remember what they were trained for, and they are tired of being idle for so long."

"That's good to hear." He sipped his wine as he looked at Broan. "Tybalt and I are like oil and water, always have been. Now don't think I was willing to jump into war right from the start. I wasn't." His embarrassment showed on his face. "I also thought to save the youth of Anwel and let Remdor fight the battle, but I know now that is not to be."

Broan nodded his head in agreement. "Everyone will be affected by this war I fear, some sooner than later."

Eamon sat back in his chair. "You realize we still have to go before the High Council. They are young, but they do have heads on their shoulders. Most have studied the history of written time and have explored the time before that." He stood and took the glass from Broan's hand. "We should get going. I have them waiting."

As they walked up the grand staircase and into the lobby of the council hall Eamonn continued, "You will have to be patient and flexible, unlike your behavior at Harbor City." He smiled. "Yes, Tybalt told me all about it. Did you really raise your sword?" Eamonn started to chuckle. "I would have loved to have seen that. Tybalt's face red with rage…" Eamonn stopped outside the door to the council chamber. "You must hear every word that is said. You are pushing them down a path they are just beginning to understand." He dusted off Broan's tunic like an old father caring for his son. "They will support your cause Broan, so there is no need to fight. Let them come to the only conclusion possible on their own. It will grant you more loyalty than you can imagine."

Eamonn was right. There were energized arguments for and against the cause. Heated debate left no word unsaid. Broan worried that the argument would go on undulating into the night, when out of the blue, one council member spoke up. "Warlord Broan, we have come to the agreement to join you. You and Remdor can count on Anwel. We await your leadership."

"*Finally,*" Broan thought to himself as he rose from his seat. "I thank you for your support."

With such little time, Anwell's army of civilians and warriors got ready within two days. They stood in organized rows ready for the command to head out. Once again Broan had united Faery and Mortal Warlords and gave them their last orders. Only a small group of soldiers would travel with Broan. The others would begin the race back to Remdor by a different route, increasing the odds of a larger contingency of warriors for the last battle.

Meeting for the last time Eamon handed Broan a note. "This is for you," he said, "It arrived last night from Ke-Hern."

"Why not just send a Faery?" Broan asked a little puzzled.

Eamonn just shrugged as he studied Eirian from a distance. Seeing who caught Eamonn's eye made Broan wonder if he should have kept Eirian under wraps longer. After a quick read he handed the message to Laeg and V-Tor. "It seems Ke-Hern wants us to wait for him in the northern hills. It seems urgent."

Paying him no mind Eamonn walked over to Eirian. "So Ke-Hern has kept the best for last." He smiled. "I have no fear that Broan will do his best to keep you safe."

"It's a little harder than you think but I'm managing," Broan answered, placing a protective arm around Eirian's shoulder.

"Good," Eamonn said as he grinned.

The sea dominated the horizon on the far side of the Queen's island. DeSpon hung back in the shadow of the Queen's fortress and took in the view. Bored and a little impatient he watched a cloud scuttle across the sky. There was nothing more he could do but hide out and wait for Aillil to sneak away.

Out in the open, things were moving faster than even he had thought possible. Everyone was abuzz as they got supplies ready for Aillil and Ke-Hern's journey to the desert fortress. Fragrant bread baked in clay ovens were wrapped and placed into saddlebags. Brown linen bags full of fresh rolled oats were attached to the horses. Smoked fish and dried fruit rounded out the food supply the Queen was sending. DeSpon closed his eyes and took in the smells from time long ago and his mouth watered.

He was jarred into the present when Aillil spoke, "It's nice of you to come to see me off, but it's far too dangerous for both of us," she said as she reached out and took his hand into hers.

Aillil was so close that DeSpon could feel her breath on his chest and a shiver escaped from him. He nodded his head even though he knew she could not see his agreement.

"What's wrong?" She stepped back, unsure as to what to expect.

"Nothing...its good news." He looked over his shoulder making sure they were still alone. "I'll be quick. I don't want to endanger you any more than I've already done." He hesitated once again and then blurted it out. "I was able to observe Eirian, the Faery leader, and... she has a great power which leads me to think that she is connected to the Ancients. I even think it's far stronger than yours. That's why Ke-Hern has been grooming her. Maybe it's her link with the Ancients that is needed to free the Faeries...and if them, maybe us." DeSpon felt Aillil's body tense. Pausing he studied her face. He didn't want to hurt her. "Of course we will still need your help, especially since there is no goodwill between her and us."

Disappointment filled Aillil. He was asking her to abandon her dreams of being the one who saves him. It was hard. She had heard his rushed concern and it was ... Aillil quickly forced herself to smile at him. "I thought as much. Both Ke-Hern and the Queen often talk about her and her abilities." Aillil dropped her head and took in a deep breath to calm herself.

"Can you help us in getting her to do our bidding?" DeSpon asked.

"Yes," she whispered, wishing she could see his eyes and know the truth of what he really felt for her. "I know just what needs to be done." Aillil paused as she heard her name being called in the distance then continued. "But you must know that once I set things in motion, there is no turning back. Do you understand this?"

"Yes," he answered holding onto her hands for a few seconds more. "I have you to thank, not only for helping me, but allowing me to be my true self around you. You are my only connection to what I was long ago."

"And you will be that once again, trust me." Aillil pulled her hands away from him and then suddenly hugged him. She knew in her heart that there was only one reason she was alive, that was to be with DeSpon.

DeSpon hugged her back, delighted. "Promise me you will take care of yourself," he said. He kissed her forehead and quickly shape shifted and took flight as a raven.

"Splitting your loyalties is never wise DeSpon. I expected much more from you." Sobus' voice blared in DeSpon's head. He knew what would be coming next, and he readied himself. Suddenly he felt his body being pulled rapidly through time and space, away from Aillil and back towards Sobus' fortress, back towards his doom.

"Did you think you could hide your betrayal... from ME? Stupid fool! And you risk all for a blind girl? And not just any blind girl, but one that works for the Queen."

DeSpon could feel Sobus' rage. He could feel it tear into his flesh. "How?"

"How? The right question is WHO?" Sobus began to laugh, a deep evil sound. "One of your own," he gloated.

DeSpon chuckled "So I almost made it."

Sobus roared with disapproval. "When, oh when, will you ever learn? No one gets away with anything unless I want them to."

Time was lost to DeSpon. "*How long?*" he asked himself as he hung suspended in the air like a rag doll. Sobus poked at him again with his sword, drawing blood from yet another wound and laughed. Suddenly DeSpon was released from the magical hold on him and he landed hard on the ground, unable to move, bloodied and beaten down.

"See Lija, even my mighty DeSpon can't betray me." Sobus glared at Lija. "So be warned." Laughing he turned his attention back to DeSpon. "I have such a special place in mind for my mutinous Shadow Dwellers. Shall we?"

The balcony doors sprang open and Sobus pushed Lija into action. The Wizard pulled the half conscious body of DeSpon through the doors and into a mysterious mist. One minute they were at the fortress and the next they were in a horrifying place. They stood on what looked like the toe of a lava trail, all barren and desolate. The intense heat came more from below than from the day's sun.

"Come out of your water prison; come and collect your fearless leader." Sobus ordered. Smiling, he looked at Lija. "I made a different kind of hell for these fools. You see if any of them step outside of the rain, they die. That's the good news." Sobus' eyes glowed with malice. "Soon the rain will close in on them, making it harder and harder for them all to stay within its safety. They'll have one choice, forfeit their own life to save the others, or kill the others to save themselves." Sobus looked at Bacot as he lifted DeSpon up onto his shoulder and made his way back into the rain prison, "It'll be interesting to see what each will choose."

A full moon rose magnificently over the flat valley that stretched out beyond their campfire. Sparks from the fire danced in the upward draft, escaping into the night sky. The crackle and pop of wood burning kept the silence at bay. V-Tor sat on a fallen log away from the fire as he watched Eirian.

"Wishful thinking?" Hywel asked as he came up behind V-Tor.

V-Tor's knife was up in a second and just as quickly as it was raised, it was dropped. "You've got to give some warning before you do that. I fear our friendship will end before its time."

Hywel sat down on the log next to V-Tor and pointed towards Eirian. "She is pretty isn't she?"

"It's not like that," V-Tor said as he shrugged his shoulders. "She explained."

"Not well enough by the look of you."

"Oh forget it." V-Tor glared at Hywel.

"You know V-Tor there are other youthful female Faeries." Hywel looked over at V-Tor and smiled. "You need to meet Cephas' sister."

"Which one?" Cephas asked from behind them. "I have five."

Hywel laughed. "I think Tusa would be nice."

"She's too bossy."

"Well what about Sora? She has hair like Eirian."

"None have hair like Eirian. Sora's is more yellow red, not copper like Eirian's."

"Well then who do you think would suit V-Tor?" Hywel asked as he crossed his arms over his chest.

"Your sister."

"What! I only have one and you want me to hand her over to a Manliken?"

Cephas nudged V-Tor. "He has one sister and eight brothers." He shook his head. "I think with nine brothers to fight off, she can handle a Manliken. She is a very good with the battle axe."

"Battle axe! How big is she?"

Cephas laughed and slapped V-Tor on the back. "She is a little bigger than Eirian. You don't have to be big to use a battle axe, just fast."

Eirian's head shot up. She sensed riders approaching from the valley. She stood and stared into the distance soon spotting two riders and a lot of Faeries. This surprised her somewhat. Broan had said that they were waiting for Ke-Hern, which meant only one rider. "Cephas, who's with Ke-Hern?"

"Someone from the Queen's island."

"Great!" Eirian said as she stared at the approaching riders. She wasn't sure what this was all about, but just knowing it was someone from the Queen's island didn't sit well with her. Anything to do with the Queen left a bad taste in her mouth.

Hywel got up from his seat and walked over to Eirian. "It'll be okay. You need to trust Ke-Hern."

"Trust him. The last time I trusted him, I landed in Solveig."

As soon as the Faeries were near the camp they scattered among the bushes and trees of the area. Like fireflies, they lit up the night, creating a wondrous atmosphere of light and excitement.

Broan and the others got up and went to meet the riders. He took the bridle of Ke-Hern's horse as it stopped. "Any trouble?"

Ke-Hern laughed at Broan as he dismounted. "Not with a Faery guard! Where is Eirian?"

"Here," she said stepping in next to Broan. Suddenly a feeling of imminent danger overcame her. "Why did you bring this witch to our fire?" she hissed as she pushed past Ke-hern.

Ke-Hern grabbed Eirian and turned her around to face him. "Aillil is here to help us end the curse and you'd be wise to keep your tongue!"

Eirian glared at Aillil, yelling at her loudest. "You have what is MINE! And you have no RIGHT to it."

Shaken, Aillil pulled hard on the reigns of the horse, causing it to rear up. "What you sense is a good thing, not an evil thing. In time you will understand. Please Eirian, I'm here to help, not hinder."

"Let me go!" Eirian screamed as she fought to free herself from Ke-Hern's grip.

Ke-Hern began whispering quiet magical words while Eirian kicked and thrashed. "Don't you dare put me under a hex," she yelled, but Ke-Hern persisted until Eirian went limp.

Ke-Hern quickly rubbed his thin hands together and then placed them on her head. Whatever had taken life in Eirian's head, whatever awoke upon seeing Aillil, Ke-Hern buried it away from present thought in hopes of calming Eirian so they could move forward and do what needed to be done.

Eirian woke her head spinning. "You used a mind fastening spell on me!" She rubbed her head. "How dare you!"

"You left me no choice. Your own fear," Ke-Hern said as he walked away from her, "is clouding your thinking. Now come we have much to talk about." She took her time. How could she ignore the slight quake she felt under her feet?

Once at the fire, Ke-Hern looked at everyone and smiled. "This is Aillil, the Queen's right hand maiden. A very loyal subject and…"

"I wouldn't speak so well of her, you have no idea what she will do soon enough," Eirian said, her voice brittle and cold. She stared at Aillil, "The land's energy says our meeting is evil and destructive. I will trust the land. You Aillil, I will not. You may see the beyond, but remember I felt it and I am warned."

"Eirian please!" Ke-Hern shook his head. He should have known the spell wouldn't work long on her. "We are in the present, not some possible future, so we have to handle what is here and now. Not, your fearful illusions."

Glaring at Ke-Hern and then Aillil, Eirian turned away from the group and stomped into the darkness. She neared an old oak tree and with one jump she was secured upon a branch.

"There is such an inner hostility about her," Aillil said as she listened to Eirian leaving. She was going to call out again, but stopped. It didn't matter if Eirian sensed her plan. Now that it had taken flight nothing could change its course. She reached out and grabbed Laeg's arm.

Suddenly, lightning bolts crashed in his head. He was locked in a moment in time, and was shamed by what he saw. He quickly released his arm from Aillil's grip, letting it drop away. Struggling to contain his emotions he slowly backed away from the group.

Ke-Hern's eyes narrowed as he watched Laeg's reaction. He put his hand on Laeg's shoulder and spoke softly, "Seeing the future is often harsh because it comes without preparation, without understanding and without the full story. That's why I never liked using it. There are no guarantees in visions only slight chances." He smiled at Laeg. "Will you be alright?"

Laeg nodded slowly. Satisfied, Ke-Hern pulled his attention back to the matter at hand. "Everyone, let's sit and talk. There is much to do before we can go back to Remdor."

Deeton did most of the talking, although he often looked to Ke-Hern to make sure he was exact. "There is a place that Aillil must go and claim before Lija finds it. The Queen is sure he would use it for evil, which would lead to the destruction of everything we know and love. The place is located in the southern regions of Duronyk, not far from the border of Anwel."

"WHAT!" Cephas yelled as he jumped to his feet. "You can't possibly think of taking Eirian there!"

Ke-Hern raised his hands and asked Cephas to sit down. "We are not asking Eirian to go there; we are asking Broan to go."

Eirian shouted as she jumped from her branch and onto her feet. She quickly ran to the group by the fire. "No good will come of this. Once in Duronyk there will be no way of saving him and he will be caught." She pointed her finger at Aillil. "Is this your idea? Hand Broan over to Lija on cursed land?"

"No!" Aillil cried, raising her hands into the air. "Eirian's right, Broan cannot be allowed to go either. This is not a job for him. His path is not in Duronyk, at least as far as I can tell. I need someone else to take me. Ke-Hern cannot go because he is a Wizard and Lija could figure out what we are up to. We must find this place and occupy it. I do not know what the Ancients have in mind but I do know if Lija controls it and captures Ancient power, we are all doomed."

"I'll go with you," Laeg said from the edge of the group. "We will leave tomorrow at dawn."

Surprised, Eirian studied Laeg and then V-Tor when he volunteered as well.

"Eirian can we not aid them by giving them an escort up to the border? This is more important than you realize." Ke-Hern asked.

Eirian nodded her head slowly, still watching Laeg intently. "Cephas, who best knows that area?"

"Pera, Hywel's sister for starters."

Eirian raised an eyebrow as she turned to look at Cephas. "Pera?"

The next morning Broan helped Aillil onto her horse. He handed her the reigns and waited for Ke-Hern to join them. "Are you sure you only need guides and not someone to stay with you?"

"Yes. Once I'm there I will be fine."

"The desert is a hard place for sighted people to live let alone a blind person. I'm beginning to have some reservations. This whole thing doesn't ring true for me."

Aillil dropped her hand towards Broan's shoulder and barely touched it. "It will be fine. The Ancients will care for me just like they care for the Queen, so have no fears. When all is over, we will meet again, and you will see I was right."

Broan looked up at her. "I don't want to know the future if that's what you are offering me. I've seen what kind of information you tend to pass on and it is not one of happiness."

Aillil pulled back. "Laeg saw so little of it, he never saw the end. I feel it in my heart, we will meet again and it will be with great joy." She paused for a second. "Broan will you do me a favor? Tell Ke-Hern that Eirian needs to learn how to use the Image Division talent. She will need it to escape."

Deep furrows developed on Broan's forehead as he turned and looked over at Eirian. "She already knows too much about escaping. I'd like it more if he would teach her to stay in one place long enough to enjoy it."

"Just tell him."

Broan rode next to Ke-Hern as they made their way down from the hills of Anwel and towards the open fields and plains. He looked over to the tall black Wizard riding next to him. "Aillil asked me to tell you that Eirian needs to learn Image Division Spell, to help her to escape..."

"Escape! Why would I want her to escape?" He looked at Broan. "Image Division is very powerful... I think it's best to leave that learning until after the war. We have enough to handle right now." He shook his head. "What was Aillil thinking...Image Division ...who's side is she on?"

Broan smiled. "Good. I was worried that you might agree with her."

The Faeries that guided Laeg, Aillil, and V-Tor had come as close as possible to the border as they could. Now they hung back, hiding in the trees and the underbrush of the forest. The border was not hard to see. It was as if everything had stopped living just on the other side of Anwel. Animal bones lay among the dry landscape of this environmental illness. V-Tor loathed the thought of going into such a barren land. In the distance he could see a gloomy, dry riverbed with bleached white tree trunks still standing guard over it. Soon they'd be riding on sand trails that traversed the relatively flat, unbroken land of Duronyk. "Do we really have to go there?" V-Tor questioned. "I mean she has no idea how bleak it really is. If she did, do you think she'd want to do this?"

"There must be something liberating about being the questioning soul you are," Laeg said. "Always asking questions that will not change anything."

V-Tor took offense to Laeg's comment and pulled back on his horse. "My questions come from living in reality, not in that dream world that still haunts you. The place she wants us to go is barren and cursed! I only ask to see if there is another way!"

"There is no other way!" Laeg barked in anger. "If you wish, you can stay here and wait for me, or go back and I'll catch up with you and Broan later."

V-Tor gave Aillil a heated look and then took in a deep breath letting it out slowly through clenched teeth. "I'll go with you. Someone has to watch your back. Maybe Eirian's right. Maybe this is evil at work."

"The only evil is the doubt in your head," Laeg roared at V-Tor.

"Stop it!" screamed Aillil. "Stop this bickering. Can you not see that the wickedness that holds this region captive is doing this to you? Is there no common sense to your actions? The sooner we move on and get this over with the better." She closed her eyes. "I don't have to see it to know just how bad it is, V-Tor. I feel its illness in my heart."

V-Tor's clenched jaw twitched in anger and frustration. He had no more words for either Aillil or Laeg. He nudged his horse forward from the green haven of Anwel and into the desert of brown and lifeless yellows. Aillil and Laeg followed him. Barren ridgelines were pale white as if even color was not allowed to live here. Shimmering heat from sun-baked rocks caused the land to dance in dire warning that something deeply evil lived there.

They had hoped to find a secluded grotto to rest at, but found nothing but openness and endless misery. Drifting sand and strong winds robbed their skin of any moisture. They wrapped scarves around their heads, making sure to completely cover their mouths and noses. Narrow strips of flesh and eyes looked through the coverings as gritty blasts of wind rushed at them and their horses.

Night came quickly to the region. The sun set as quickly as it rose, taking with it the paralyzing heat and soon leaving a bitter cold. It was as if there was no in-between in this northern land. They cooked a small meal over a fire as they huddled together for warmth. Laeg and V-Tor had hoped for at least some semi-desert steppe with shallow bogs so the horses could drink. There were none, so they shared what they had with their horses, rationing off the limited amount of water they carried.

"I wouldn't worry about the water, it is not far now. If we leave at sunrise, we should come across it by mid-afternoon," Aillil said as she tightened the blanket around her shoulders. "There will be plenty of water once we get there."

"What are we looking for? A lost city or castle?" V-Tor asked as he worked at getting sand out of his ears.

"It is not something to be seen from the desert, but to be felt. It is below the horizon."

V-Tor shook his head as he looked at Laeg. "If we cannot see it, how will we know we are there?"

"I will tell you. I will feel the crackle of Ancient life as we near and sense the liberating moisture of their fortress."

"Great," V-Tor rolled his eyes, "I'm going to check on the horses. I've swallowed enough useless stuff today."

Aillil stared into the darkness. "V-Tor, you will have more than enough demons to fight in your future, don't needlessly make Laeg or myself one. Your love for Eirian will serve you well, but watch that you are not trapped in its grip. "

V-Tor kicked at the sand as he stomped off, muttering under his breath about some things needing to be kept secret.

"Why did you tell him that?" Laeg hissed. "He is doing the best he can right now and without him, I doubt we would have made it this far. Your words cut and torment people."

Aillil eyes began to water. "I only told him because soon he will be faced with many choices. Hopefully V-Tor will remember and make the right choices for Eirian… for all of us."

Laeg stood up and looked away from Aillil. He disliked what he heard and he did not like the feeling of dread that still lived in him. "Stop it. Stop this offensive channeling and leave us to our own lives and choices. If we make mistakes, we live with them. If we don't make mistakes, we celebrate. Stop trying to guide us down a path we have no knowledge of."

Aillil dropped her face into her hands and cried, deep soul cleansing sobs. "I can't help it. As we get closer I find I can't help but

275

reveal what I know. I don't mean to predict your doom; I only can tell you what I see."

"Then don't tell us anything!" Laeg said as he walked away.

The morning light was liberating. As much as it foretold of another unforgiving day of hot misery, at least they could start out again. It wasn't long before the ground beneath the horses' hooves began to crackle and snap under the weight of the animals. They were now on an old lakebed and that excited Aillil. "There will be a deep gorge nearby. Deep in it is the fortress."

Laeg and V-Tor rode abreast scanning the horizon and ground before them. They slowly made their way across the parched lake, ghastly crunching sounds ringing in their ears. As the sun raised higher overhead, the glare off the flat stones and packed clay bounced back into their eyes and blinded them. Laeg got off his horse as he shielded his eyes. "I don't know how much more these horses can take."

"Horses! What about us?" V-Tor hissed as he got off his horse. The heat of the ground clung to him like a heavy weight. It pulled at his very soul. "You stay up there," he said as he took hold of Aillil's horse. "It will be easier for us to find something we can use for refuge."

"Wait!" Aillil raised her hand and pointed to an area just to the left of them. "It's over there! I can feel it."

Laeg and V-Tor walked in the direction Aillil had pointed. Suddenly, the ground dropped off. It was so well blended with the surrounding area that if they still rode their horses they would have swiftly gone over its edge. "Glad you got us off the horses," said V-Tor as he peered into the canyon. "It's a long, long way down."

Laeg nodded then went to get Aillil off her horse. "Now what?" he asked her.

"There is a path in the vicinity. Scan for an indent. That is where the path starts." Laeg did as he was told, and sure enough he found the trailhead. Nodding to V-Tor, Laeg took Aillil's arm and lead the way while V-Tor took the horses.

V-Tor looked up at the dreadful route they had just taken and gave thanks for having sight. The dramatic difference between what was up on the land and what was down here in the canyon was extraordinary. "I thought all of Duronyk was destroyed. Why wasn't this place?"

"The Ancients lay claim to this area, just like they lay claim to the island in the Inland Sea and the mountain Solveig is built on. Each area will defend itself and tend to itself. It is a life force of its own." Aillil smiled and raised her hands high in the air and slowly spun around. "There is an underground fortress over there." She pointed to the left. "That is where you'll find me."

"Find you?"

"Yes. Laeg, you will come here once again. Broan will have to face many challenges and Eirian will need to look into the very center of her soul."

"Her what?" V-Tor's eyes narrowed as he stared at Aillil. "You talk in riddles, very evil ones. I'm ready to go, Laeg." He moved his horse away from the pond and nearer the path they had just come down.

Aillil shook her head. "It is alright V-Tor, you will soon forget all of this. The words will not haunt you, nor distress you once you are out of the region of Duronyk."

"I doubt it." He growled.

Piloc, the cook, stomped over to Broan. "Here," he said, as he handed Broan a large bowl of oatmeal. "She refuses to eat again! See if you have any better luck." Broan looked down at the hot oatmeal. "Damn!" he muttered as he set off.

He came upon Eirian as she was standing on the edge of the lake. Hushed and still, she stood gazing at the mist, which was so thick not even the jagged outlines of trees on the distance shore were visible. He put the bowl of oatmeal down on a flat stone. Not wanting the crunch of his footsteps to assault her place of silent retreat, he came up behind her as softly as possible.

Eirian knew he was there. She quietly leaned back against him. "There once was an inescapable, buoyant logic to what Ke-Hern told me of my destiny. But I've lost those words of wisdom and now only hear the cries of the injured. I feel only the terror and pain of the families who have lost everything. I fear that I never should have started this."

Broan was undone by those words. He wrapped his arms around her, hoping that it might give her a bit of strength. "Eirian, we all have fears and doubts. It's not easy taking on the responsibility of so many. Even I, after years of training and practice, have moments of questioning things. You are doing fine for one tossed in war so quickly." He gently squeezed her.

She stood quietly nestled against his body and waited for the morning to greet them. The sun suddenly edged over the distant mountains and quickly began to heat the air and lake before them. The fog began to lift and its grayish white color quickly changed to a buttery yellow, pale and soft. There was a calm beauty about the feeling of Broan's arms wrapped around her. Eirian wished that they could stand in such silent peace forever.

Miko's head hit the floor. Blood from his nose and mouth sprayed the wall nearest him while tapered streams of red ran down another. He lay motionless. His face was hideously distorted; dirt and old blood matted his hair.

Falzon stood over the limp body waiting for the next order.

"Well! Pick him up and take him to the huts." Sobus yelled his brow furrowed in concentration. "I may still need him." He waved his hand in quick jerks, dismissing Falzon. He slumped into a chair and turned his back to the group of guards. "Get me Lija," he bellowed. "He has a lot to answer for."

Sobus picked up an apple from the table next to him. There was a snap as his teeth cut through the taut skin of the red fruit. Tart juices ran down his chin as his bite went further into the apple. Sobus didn't look up when Lija stumbled into the room and continued to ignore him for some time. When Sobus felt that Lija was uncomfortable enough he broke the silence. "I need to get that damn Faery. What do you suggest?" Sobus took another bite of apple.

"I don't have much to say about it."

"Yet you had lots to say about my plans to destroy Solveig. In fact Miko told me that it was you that used the magic to bring Solveig to life. What do you have to say about that?"

Lija gazed out the window and thought about all the carnage and savagery that would have happened if he had not stepped in and saved those in Solveig. He didn't hold any ill feelings towards Miko. He knew how young the lad was and how ill prepared he was for Sobus and his ways of persuasion. "I did what I thought was right."

"Right...wrong...it won't matter. You will come with me to Solveig, you will remove the spell, and you will watch the destruction of it. Then you will follow me to the Walled City and watch the fall of your Mortals." He threw his half eaten apple at the wall and watched it smear blood as it slid to the floor. "Oh and remember, YOU cannot escape me...because I AM IN YOU."

Deeton sat at the fire with Laeg and V-Tor. They had caught up with Broan's army five days earlier and they still weren't saying much. Deeton had tried everything, but nothing seemed to free the information that had been locked away in a far corner of their brains. They professed to not really know where the damn place was other than a day's ride into the desert under terrible conditions. Deeton tried talking to each of them alone and also together, but he had learned nothing, not even the tiniest morsel that would soothe his undying need to learn more about the Ancients.

"You know what I believe…the Ancients are alive. They are just not seen. They are in the air we breathe, the water we drink, and the heat of the flames we sit by."

"You sound like Aillil," V-Tor said with a huff, "insane."

Laeg studied Deeton for a moment. "You won't stop will you? You'll haunt us to our graves."

Deeton stood up in a huff. "And what is wrong with wanting to know. History is where we came from and it is where we will end up. If we learn from the present we can make a better future."

Laeg smiled at V-Tor. "He does sound like Aillil. He uses flowery words that make your head spin." He sipped his warm ale and looked at Deeton, "Aillil got worse as she got closer to the home of the Ancients, and yet for the life of me I can't clearly recall anything she said."

"Either can I and I don't want to. All I remember is the feeling of doom she placed in my heart and that I will not forget." V-Tor growled as he stood up. "And don't ask again. I respect you because of Bronagh but next time my fist will speak for me."

Deeton watched as V-Tor faded into the darkness of the night. "I didn't mean to upset him."

"That's all good and fine but…" Laeg lowered his head. "There is a reason we do not remember. I trust that it is a good reason."

Kuiper arrived on the heels of his brother Falzon. Sobus had finally sent the Shadow Dwellers all to hell. Angry eyes glared at him from dark places within the rain area. They all knew of his indiscretion, his betrayal. It was now out in the open and there were no more disguises and delusions to provide protection. Kuiper knew his fate. His end was near. He removed the ragged cape from his shoulders and tossed it aside. Then he knelt, hunched over, and exposed the back of his lizard neck for DeSpon's sword. He did not cower in some corner, trying to hide from his doom. He waited in silence.

"Revenge is Sobus' blood sport not mine!" DeSpon said from his ledge under a narrow out cropping of stone.

"WHAT are you talking about?" screamed Larden, as his feathers ruffled outward, making him appear bigger than he was. He extended his talons as he approached Kuiper. "Wounds and bruises heal, but what he has done will not heal and it will never be forgotten! Make an end to his black heart. It is your right! So do it!"

DeSpon rose from his lair and limped through the heavy rain towards Larden and Kuiper. "He will suffer his due, but it will not be wasted here and now. Remember, as the walls of rain coming crashing in, someone will need to be forfeited. Besides we all know Sobus' evil mind. He would have trapped us, with or without Kuiper's help."

DeSpon hunched over Kuiper and grabbed him by the back of his head. He slowly started to squeeze. "Of course this doesn't mean you are forgiven, Kuiper. Just be glad that right now I'm in a good mood."

Chapter 14

"Greed always offers easy schemes and tempting alternatives but no truth."

- Governor Eamonn

Lija made his way through the ramshackle and filthy collection of buildings that lay at the base of the main tower. Quickly he entered a small hut. Without pause Lija slowly bent down over Miko and brushed his old hands over the young man's body. Energy, from a healing place the Queen had taught him to use, flowed through his hands.

"You need to find Broan and let him know that Sobus is going to attack the Walled City very soon. He must be ready." Lija pulled Miko to his feet, "All the rivers flowed south to the sea. Follow the riverbed and get out of Duronyk." He watched Miko to make sure that he understood and accepted what was being said. Miko nodded. Lija guided Miko into the night's darkness and the cold winds of Duronyk. He placed his cloak over Miko's shoulders and pushed him on. "Go and find Broan."

Miko started down the dry riverbed. It was composed of stones and boulders. He stumbled along from one boulder to another, inching his way south. Morning came all too soon. Sore, tired and overwhelmed with guilt Miko fought with the icy blasts that ran over the land. He pulled Lija's cloak closer to his skin, hoping to keep the cold out and the heat in. Flat, gray clouds echoed the flat, gray land. Remdor seemed so far away. Then Lija's words echoed in his ear, *"Find Broan,"* and he started moving again.

Aillil knew where she would use the small amount of Off-World power the Queen bestowed on her, and she knew the reason why she helped DeSpon. She knew it all, save this. She had no idea why she was to draw a young man of mixed heritage to the desert fortress of the Ancients.

Aillil needed clarity for this new request. She made a small altar and covered it with bowls of water, salt, sand, and stones. She placed a burning candle in the middle of it. She sprinkled the salt over the water and then poured the water into the bowl of sand. She sat back and hesitated, for a moment uneasy. Calming her nerves she quickly continued her spell, burying the stone in the sandy, salty mud.

"Always in the depth of the land, I serve only you, who saved my life and gave me purpose," she quietly whispered. "Tell me who is to come my way, so I may better serve you now and forever."

"Why do you call to us when you already know our request?"

"I do not understand it."

"You never questioned us before. Why do you question us now?"

"I just wish to understand who is coming and why. I just wish to keep things clear."

"Clear? We know of what you've started and disagree with your actions. You are forcing the elements of time and fate."

Aillil sat back on her heels. "So that is why you are sending this Mortal...as punishment."

"There is a bigger purpose then your foolishness."

"Foolishness! I know you seek Eirian for your prophecy. My plan will serve two purposes. One will be the freedom of the Shadow Dwellers and the other will be to deliver her to you. Is that not what you have wanted from the beginning?"

The Ancients where quiet for a long moment. *"Do not think that you know our mind Aillil, that has been the downfall of many. You have created a great imbalance. The future holds nothing but struggles and attacks of wills for those you have tampered with."*

Irritation picked at her. "Look, if you are that worried about the outcome, then help do not hinder. In the end we'll both get what we want."

"Things are not as simple as you believe."

"It doesn't matter now does it? My idea has life and will be followed through. Now tell me who you are sending me?" Suddenly a new understanding of this young man was caught in a whirlwind vision of the past, not the future. Even though she questioned the wisdom of the Ancients in this matter, it brought her delight.

Quickly, Aillil got up from her altar and hastily found her way up the steep path to the desert where she called to this man, her brother.

"Be warned Aillil, there are no shortcuts for ending this curse on the Shadow Dwellers," the Ancients whispered. "Be warned."

Broan recognized Cephas' birdcall and it drew his attention to the side of a distant hill. He could see movement in the forest and knew it was Ny-dick on the hunt. They had caught their scent and were rapidly rushing towards Broan's group. "It looks like not all the Ny-dick are ahead of us. Prepare for battle," he yelled as he drew out his sword. He quickly sent V-Tor and his division up and around the hill. Hopefully they would be able to advance on the Ny-dick from the rear, while Broan's group provided a diversion, drawing the enemy's attention. Once surrounded, the fight would be on. The Ny-dick would most likely be out-numbered and the battle should be quick and victorious for Broan's warriors. He hoped.

Some battles are won in hours and some in minutes. This one was not won that quickly. It took the full afternoon, and was well into the evening before the killing field had been cleared of the injured and the dead set ablaze. It was impossible for Broan not to think about their situation. They were but four days away from the hills of the Walled City and unfortunately they had been forced to fight on their way there, losing time, and losing warriors, losing Faery fighters.

Although Broan's losses in this skirmish were singularly small thanks to the Faeries that came to help, his mood was heavy and black. To him it was still an enormous setback. He looked at Eirian who stood by the fire of the night's camp. "The Faeries will be vindicated," he said as he dropped down on a fallen log. His clothes were still wet with blood and his hand still held his sword.

Eirian walked over to him and took the sword. She raised her hands and placed them on his slumped shoulders as she briefly looked into his eyes. Her concern and compassion showed.

Slowly she shifted the energy in Broan's tense, worn out muscles, making it easier for him to relax. Her hands gradually moved down his arms, working their magic, finally coming to rest on his hands. She took one of his hands into hers and started to massage the palms, her fingers working to release the cramps in them. Eirian didn't look up at him as she continued to warm his hands and stretch out his long fingers.

Broan gently stopped her. He cupped her chin and raised it up so she would look at him. Then he bent down and kissed her. It wasn't like the kisses before, all stolen and brief, but a lingering kiss that held her to him. Eirian didn't refuse. She closed her eyes and allowed the exchange of feelings between them. Satisfied, Broan slowly pulled away from Eirian and stood up. He smiled down at her as he walked away from the fire and stepped back into being a warlord.

"Hell," said V-Tor from his spot near the fire.

"Hell," Aillil said as she stood in the middle of the desert fortress.

"*Hell*," said Nerlena

Sobus sat high on the back of his gray stallion and he looked down at Lija. "All your planning, plotting and interference may have saved one young lad but not Solveig." He sneered at Lija, "You really are the fool in all of this."

Lija didn't bother to look up at Sobus, but simply waited for the excruciating pain in his head to start. When nothing happened he chanced a peek at Sobus only to find him smiling down at him.

"I will deal with you after you've freed Solveig and I get my due," Sobus said as he got off his horse. He walked to the river and stood there, staring at Broan's fortress. "The walls should be splattered with the flesh and blood. The dead burned bodies should be lying on the ground as a testament of my power and vengeance," he hissed to the Lija. "Where there are pools of water, there should be pools of blood. The gates of Solveig should be torn from their hinges, and she should be left open and ravaged." He cursed out loud as he turned and looked at Lija. "But now, thanks to you, I have a much better idea. Release Solveig NOW!" he growled.

Lija stumbled to his feet and looked out at Solveig. "I'm so sorry," he whispered as he began his chant to call her to him. He waited patiently for her reply. It wasn't long before he felt a bombardment of sensory impressions.

It was widely audible. Solveig grumbled in response to the request to give up her stewardship of the fortress. She picked up Lija's frustration as he channeled his limited and dwindling strength. She protested her return to stillness, not wanting to give up her awakening.

Lija was able to ease her worry some. He helped her to understand that she served all best by returning to the stones and land of Solveig. It was a sad battle of wills and emotions, but Solveig finally rested in the ground again, hushed and still, waiting for another time.

Sobus walked into Solveig alone. He took his time to plant his evil spell. He ushered it in slowly not missing one square inch. He laughed.

Eirian rolled her neck and stretched her back as she got ready to move on to the next injured soldier. She was sluggish from lack of sleep, lack of food, and most importantly, lack of any good news. Now that she was Mortal she tried to eat better and sleep more, but this war was not making it possible.

Eirian pressed her hand against her stomach. She wasn't sure if it was really upset because she hadn't eaten much that day or if she was pregnant. Being Mortal was harder than she had imagined. Not only did she have to watch out for hunger, thirst, and fatigue. She also had to deal with her complicated emotions. If she wasn't depressed by the fall-out of war, she was excited from being around Broan, "*Damn!*" Everything was so different and much more complex now. She closed her eyes, wishing for the past.

Ke-Hern came and stood in front of her, his face barely an inch away from hers. "Leave!" he scowled. "You are no good to us like this! By the large shadows under your eyes, I'd say you are on the brink of collapse." He took her hands into his and firmly massaged them. "You are nothing more than a collection of bones! Cold ones at that! Out with you, go to the fire and eat…and grab what sleep you can. It won't be long before we will be at the Walled City, and you will be needed even more."

Eirian knew she had overdone it, but there were people who needed help, and that was the one thing that she could lose herself in. "NO," she protested.

"OUT!" Ke-Hern's voice rang in her ears as she was being pushed out of the tent. Eirian soon found herself standing in the cold night air. She turned around and was about to re-enter the tent.

"Don't even think about it!" Ke-Hern barked. "I have spells I really don't wish to use on you but I will!"

She screamed in frustration, turned in a huff and started towards a nearby fire. As she began to walk away she was surprised by the heaviness in her legs. Her left leg was about to collapse so she quickly adjusted her gait. She only managed to limp a few steps before she fell to her knees. The thought of getting up left her breathless. She continued to kneel there mystified by what could be wrong with her. Lights quickly formed before her eyes and in the next breath she felt like she was flying unrestricted, empowered and weightless, the feeling of bottomless air under her.

It was well into the night before Broan decided to take a break and finally found a spot near a fire. He ate what little bread and meat there was. Regardless of how tired he was there was one thing that always got his immediate attention, and that was when "its Eirian" quickly followed the roar of his name! Broan shot up from his seat and pushed his way through the gauntlet of soldiers. Shaking his head he knelt next to Eirian. "Get me some milk!" he demanded. "And a blanket." He picked her up in his arms and carried her over to the fire he had just been sitting at.

"Will she be all right?" V-Tor asked as he wrapped the woolen blanket around her.

Broan brushed away a few strands of hair from her face. He touched the back of his hand to her forehead. "She doesn't have a fever. I think she is just overtired."

"And under nourished!" V-Tor added as he stood up with his hands on his hips. "I'll get the cook to make up something for her… WITHOUT meat or drippings."

Broan nodded as he worked at tucking the blanket more securely around her. She was so cold, and he wondered just how deep inside this coldness lay. "Where's the milk? I want hot milk!"

Piloc stood still in front of Broan with a cup in his hand. "It's not hot! No one said anything about hot milk, just that you needed milk!" He turned to run back and get more.

"Stop!" Broan held out his hand to Piloc. "It'll be fine. She just needs something in her stomach. You can bring some warm milk later."

The sensory-based awareness was Eirian's first clue that she was somewhere in the real world. She could hear voices; she could feel a hand rubbing her back and once in a while a hand touched her face. She could just make out the roughness of the blanket around her as it brushed against her skin. She didn't mind where she was. She enjoyed the warmth she was feeling and the security of being held close. She understood all of these things, but she couldn't figure out exactly where she was. She cracked open her eyes and found Broan looking down at her.

"Here drink this," he said to her as he pressed the cup to her mouth. "And no protesting. I can see you need more taking care of than I first thought. You will be eating three times a day with V-Tor, Laeg or myself, and you will sleep under guard if necessary." He frowned as he looked down at her. "You scared us to death. Whose side are you on?"

Suddenly, Eirian knew she didn't want to be here at this particular moment. She tried to wiggle off Broan's lap, but he was having none of it.

"You will get your freedom once you have drank this milk and eaten what Piloc has prepared for you." One of his eyebrows rose as he tilted his head down towards her. "And it will be without meat or drippings, so you'll have no excuse. Now drink!"

Broan and his army finally arrived at the Walled City and set up camp in the nearby hills. Tents and fires were built. They no longer worried about hiding from the Ny-dick, they were finished running. They had arrived at the fields of hell and the battle that would decide everyone's future existence.

He entered his tent only to find Eirian glaring at him. She paused slightly then turned on her heels and stormed out, not speaking a word to him. Broan looked over to Ke-Hern, "Can you tell me what that was all about?"

"War is hard...a lot harder on her than on you. She alone will suffer the consequences of her action if this is not truly the last battle for the Faeries."

Broan frowned at Ke-Hern. "But you've said...you've always believed...Shit!" He started towards the tent flap when Ke-Hern called to him.

"No, best if I go," Ke-Hern offered Broan as he got up to find Eirian.

"Why stand in the sleet when you can divert it?" Ke-Hern asked as he came up beside her.

"I like it. It makes me feel more like a part of nature." Eirian raised her head and let the cold freezing rain cleanse her face, wishing it could cleanse her heart and soul. She ached with a vague sadness.

Ke-Hern shrugged his shoulders, "This isn't a good time to catch a cold," he muttered as he raised his hand and stopped the rain from falling on her. "I can read you like one of my enchantment books and right now you are worried and doubtful."

Eirian looked up at him, deep sadness filling her eyes. "What will happen to me after the battle?"

"I don't know. No one's future is written in stone. If we succeed, you will live to do the blessing. If we fail, I do not know. Is this about facing death and defeat, or..." He studied her intently, "or do your suspicions around Aillil still plague you?"

Eirian quickly turned away from Ke-Hern. "Everything about Aillil is worthy of my trepidation."

Ke-Hern reached for her arm and turned her to face him. "Why do you say that?"

"There is more than myself to worry about."

"So you are worried that Broan may die?"

Eirian pushed free of Ke-Hern's hold and shook her head briefly. "No…Yes!"

Ke-Hern's laugh was soft and kind. "You are no longer Faery. It is okay to have feelings for Broan. To tell you the truth, it has not been hard to pick up that you both have feelings for each other."

"Ke-Hern, it is much bigger than that."

"Bigger then love? You've lost me."

"It's Aillil. It's so much bigger than you can imagine."

Ke-Hern went back to studying her intently. "I never enjoyed being able to see the future. It taints the present, creating an opening that allows it to come to life." He gently put his hand under Eirian's chin making her look up at him. "In other words we create what we are told. We become the self in self-fulfilling prophecy.

"Not if it already has truth as its anchor."

Ke-Hern stopped smiling at her and brushed a strand of hair from her face. "What?"

"I reacted to Aillil so strongly upon seeing her because I am already carrying the offspring she means to take from me."

Ke-Hern paled. "BUT..But…I know I felt something but when I saw you in the flesh I didn't think…there was no way… you couldn't have had…with Broan. Normally, unions of such kind would shatter a Faery's body and soul. It's quite a mess."

"Well I did. Not that either of us can remember anything about it." She looked sternly at Ke-Hern, "We just know it happened, and now this."

"So what I felt was right?" A little stunned he gazed around them. "Does Broan know?"

"No. I couldn't tell him. He has so much to think about."

"I see…well…trust me, I wouldn't waste much time after the battle. The longer you wait, the harder it will be. Broan is not the enemy. Remember that."

"Then you think we will survive and win this war."

He pulled her near. "If not, it will not matter, will it? Death is an end that no one can avoid. It comes for all of us, even the Queen." He hugged her one more time then he turned to leave. "Trust your heart Eirian. It will always help you find your way."

Eirian watched Ke-Hern walk away. She looked back up at the dark sky, moved her hand and let the freezing rain come down on her once again. However, this time there was a sound with each drop. Each different, yet each linked. They entangled her in ghostly sounds:

inexplicable, demanding, and mournful like the calls of those deep in the void. She suppressed a shiver. "Cephas," she called.

Cephas quickly appeared mere inches from her. He threw his cloak over her shoulders. "You shouldn't be out in this. Tomorrow will be taxing enough without having you ill."

Eirian smiled at Cephas. "I've known you all my life and Ke-Hern has known you even longer." She paused for a moment and then pulled the ring of Cian off her thumb. "This is for you. Lead all of us into battle and out of this painful curse."

Cephas looked down at the ring. Shaking his head he backed away from her. "No, this is not the way it is to be."

"Yes it is. I freely give the power of leadership to you. I did my part and brought the armies together but I am no warrior and it is time for you to take over."

Closing his eyes, Cephas clenched his fists. He shook his head again. "No…this is madness."

"It's not mad. It's what needs to happen." She then took hold of his hand and placed the ring in it. "Trust me."

You could see them if you knew what to look for - small bits of light that floated in the air or sat on some tree branch. It had been a hard day for the Faeries. Dark thoughts played on their minds. Everyone was tense, everyone was fearful, everyone's faith was being tested, and it was now worse for Hywel and Cephas.

"So now what do we do?" Hywel asked as he drifted into the air in front of Cephas.

"There is no denying that we've been taught to follow Eirian's lead, and this is her choice." Cephas answered. His eyes still on the ring he now wore.

"I know, but it just doesn't seem right. How can she fulfill her destiny and ours if she backs away from it so willingly? Why come all this way? Why go through all she has to only give up her leadership now?" Hywel's unsettled thoughts made his hovering more erratic.

Cephas' eyes narrowed as he grabbed for Hywel. "Be still! You know how much I hate it when you flit about with nervous energy."

"Of course I'm nervous! Ke-Hern told us to leave everything to the hands of fate. Well I don't believe her." Hywel said as he sat on the branch next to Cephas.

"Maybe this is fate, Hywel. Maybe this is the way things are supposed to play out."

Hywel suddenly pushed Cephas off the branch. "You just like it that she gave the ring to you."

289

"And you hate it because she didn't pick you."

Hywel glared at Cephas. "I just don't know why Ke-Hern would leave out such an important point."

"For crying out loud Hywel, let it go and save your energy for the battle tomorrow."

"Fine," Hywel said as he nodded. He looked down at Jelen's strange stone that Deeton had given him and played with the leather rope it hung on. He suddenly tossed it away. "She won't need this after all Deeton. You should have kept it for yourself."

"Hywel please," Cephas whispered.

Hywel looked at his friend. "Save your worry. I'll be there tomorrow."

For the first time in her life, Eirian gave in to her needs. She slipped quietly into Broan's tent. She stood so still and so close to the tent wall that she could feel it against her fingertips as her hands hung pensively by her side. Eirian watched him as he slept. Even in the dim light of the tent she could see him clearly. She found herself holding her breath, unsure as to what to do next.

Broan senses were alerted to her presence before she had even stepped into his tent. He lay there on his stomach, smelling her scent, hearing her anxious breathing and smiled. He slowly rolled over onto his side and looked at her. He raised the edge of the blanket, welcoming her. She quickly accepted his invitation and crawled in next to him.

Broan placed his hand firmly behind her neck and allowed his fingers to spread into her hair, supporting her head. He kissed her forehead with such gentleness that Eirian shivered. She placed her hands on either side of his face and made him look at her. "I do not know what will happen tomorrow. But this I do know. If it is the void that finds me, knowing I shared this time with you will make it bearable."

She began to run her hands over his body and at each place they stopped it was as if her touch awakened some new sensation in him. He captured her hand with his, stopping her from touching him. "This time I want to remember." He smiled down at her. Taking her hands he raised them over her head. "And I'm not taking any chances." Broan suddenly stopped. "Your ring. Where is your ring?" He got up onto his elbow and looked down at her. "You can't lose it now."

"It's okay Broan. I gave it to Cephas. He's the one to lead the charge."

"What? But you're the leader they picked." He studied her for a moment. "What are you not telling me?"

"What is that suppose to mean?" Eirian tensed and started to scoot out of the bed.

"You're holding something back. It's not like you to back away at the last minute."

"Back away! You think I'm backing away. Running scared like an animal?"

"I didn't mean it like that and you know it. What's happening Eirian?" He reached for her but she slipped out of bed and out of his reach.

"I should have known you, of all Mortals, wouldn't understand."

"Understand! That's what I want to do, understand why you would give up…"

"Give up! Now I'm giving up."

"Well aren't you?"

"For your information the Faeries follow the ring no matter who wears it. Cephas is a good leader. Even you said so. They will gather in his strength and follow his lead."

"Then…you don't need to be…"

"What? There to fight?"

"Well if you don't need to be…you could…"

"Hide away. You are more of an idiot than I first thought and I thought you were a very BIG idiot back then." Eirian flipped back the canvas door and stormed out of Broan's tent.

"I'm not as big a fool as you think." He got out of bed and dressed. "Where's the cook?" he bellowed. "I think Eirian could use a good cup of hot milk with a lot of Eeban in it."

Deeton had just been summoned. It wasn't hard to figure out the reason Ke-Hern picked him to go to the Walled City. He was just grateful that Ke-Hern had a romantic heart. As Deeton rounded the last tent, he caught the flash of a familiar stone. Bending down he picked it up. "Jelen's stone." He looked about wondering how it got there. Catching sight of Eirian, he quickly ran after her. "Eirian!" he called. "Wait for a moment. Here, Jelen wanted me to give this to you."

Eirian looked down at the stone. "That's so sweet but I really think he would have wanted you to keep it."

Deeton draped it around her neck. "No! I…I want you to have it." He hugged her and was off before she could say anything more. Overhearing Broan's demands for hot milk and the herb, he froze. There was only one use for Eeban.

"Deeton!" Ke-Hern called, "Don't just stand there. We can't wait all evening. We must leave now. Iarnan needs an update. Besides…"A little saddened, Ke-Hern looked around at the gathered solders. "I can't be in this battle of flesh and blood. My stand will be later if all goes well."

"Yes...but" Deeton started to walk towards Ke-Hern. "Something is wrong. Why would Broan..."

"Deeton! Stop messing with things you have no business in. Leave Broan to his duties. Now let's go."

"But..."

Ke-Hern grabbed Deeton by the ear and pulled. "This way. Like I said, leave things be." As they marched away Ke-hern glanced over his shoulder and smiled. *"Leave lovers their time...it is always far too short."*

Broan walked into Eirian's tent with two mugs. "I'm sorry," he said. "Here's a peace offering." He handed the mug to her as he sipped his.

Eirian narrowed her eyes and handed the mug back to him. "I'm not interested."

"Listen Eirian, we are all very tense right now and...I may not have said things clearly. I never meant to imply that you are anything but honorable. And you are right. I don't know anything about this curse and what needs to happen. I'm sorry. Truly sorry."

Eirian kept her back to him.

"Here take the mug. We'll sit down and you can tell me everything."

Eirian held back.

"Please. Take the hot milk. You don't have to say anything if you don't want to...I just want us to spend some time together before tomorrow. Please join me." Broan pleaded.

Eirian finally complied. She took the mug, glared at him and walked over to her cot.

Broan sat next to her. "Don't let it get too cool...its warm milk. Best thing before a battle."

Eirian looked at his cup with curiosity. "Hot milk?"

Broan took a gulp of his ale. "Yours, not mine."

"Broan...I..."

"Drink. Come on. After all, I did to go to all the trouble to get this for you."

Eirian shook her head and obeyed. It had a funny after-taste but it did warm her on the inside. "Broan..."

"Drink, then I'm all yours."

Eirian sipped again. She felt odd and took a deep breath in. "I need...to..."

"Finish your milk. Here." He helped her raise the mug to her mouth.

"I feel…" Her eyes closed and Broan smiled. He laid her down on her cot and took out the rope he hidden in his shirt. "Just in case you wake up too soon, this will make sure you stay put, safe and sound in your tent."

Sobus' tent was set up on the steep stone cliffs, which gave way to a clear view of the Walled City and the high wall of granite that surrounded it. Knowing that Broan's army was coming down from the north and BroMac and the others were set up east and south of the Walled City, Sobus picked the high moorland for his army's camp.

Row upon row of threadbare tents lay just below Sobus' campsite. The sea of dirty brown canvas and moldy green makeshift shelters had invaded the area, hiding the brilliance of the late fall colors. The camp itself was crammed together with often only standing room between the tents. Just by the sheer numbers, Sobus' army of Ny-dicks had inflicted significant damage to the region. They had cut a wide swath of destruction on their way to the Walled City, and now in camp, they robbed the area of anything good.

Crossing the area between the Walled City and Sobus' camp was fraught with danger. It was almost as dangerous as trying to slip out of the city. But Mohr felt it was worth the risk. He had information that if acted upon, might swing the battle in Sobus' favor. Therefore Sobus should pay for this little piece of news and he should get what he wants. It only made sense.

Mohr joined up with Lija about half way. As they came closer to the edge of the Ny-Dick camp, Mohr could see the many heads of Mortals atop spears, their enlarged purple tongues hanging out of their mouths and eye sockets blackened and burned. The sight left Mohr shivering, yet Lija seemed unmoved by the brutal images around them.

Once inside the encampment, rank odor assaulted Mohr's senses making him gag. To his left Ny-dick fought over half-cooked flesh still attached to the leg bone of some person. A chill ran through him as paused for a second, scanning the area. "*Calm yourself!*" he chided. "*The greater the risk the greater the reward!*" Smiling deviously he continued to follow Lija through the filth and bedlam.

"Pessimists and nay-Sayers all said I would not have the ability to fight for control of the land, and yet here I am, knocking on Iarnan's door," Sobus said as Lija and Mohr came near.

Lija lowered his head and stepped back from Sobus while Mohr advanced purposefully. "I have news that will make all those "nay-Sayers" eat their words. With this information your victory will be at hand."

"So tell me and make my night a little more comforting."

Standing only inches from him, Mohr smiled at Sobus. "I will, but I do have one request of you. It is small, but only you with your great power will be able to grant it for me."

Sobus cocked his head to one side and looked over Mohr's shoulder to Lija. "It is clear you didn't warn him." He looked back at Mohr. "I already have a sense as to what you wish to ask for. My only question is why would you want such a demon as a Shadow Dweller for a personal servant?"

"After you win this Great War and Tybalt and Ryu are given their regions to rule, I would like to travel and explore the land for it riches instead of ruling a portion of it. A Shadow Dweller would come in handy to protect me and aid me in my quest. And…since I have already become accustom to the one called DeSpon I was hoping… "

Sobus watched Mohr with discerning eyes.

Mohr tensed. "Of…Of course…whatever I find…I…I'll…share with you…"

"Yes. Well that was a given I'd say." Sobus studied Mohr a moment more. "This news you bring me must be very significant, if you feel you can barter with me…so Mohr, what news do you have that is worth the price of a Shadow Dweller?"

"Then…then we agree?" Mohr questioned as he leveled his chin.

Sobus leaned into him "Agree? I guess so, but it better be worth it little Manliken."

Sobus' breath on his cheek sent a shiver down Mohr's spine. He quickly blurted out, "I…I overheard the Faery Deeton tell Broan's sister that Eirian will be staying in camp and will not be fighting tomorrow."

"Why? If she is their leader she needs to be there."

"I overheard them saying that Broan's planning to drug her." Mohr snorted. "Love…Fools. Guess he wants to keep her safe and all to himself." He chanced a look at Sobus. "I'm telling you this is your chance to defeat Broan and his hacks. Just think you can take the ring. Hell, you can take Faery Eirian…and …"

"…rule the Faeries, now that would be interesting." Sobus smiled and patted Mohr on the shoulder. "Did you know that all living Faeries have to be on the field? I wonder if Broan knows that. He may have just prevented the curse from breaking all on his own." Sobus' eyes sparkled with evil intent, "Hmm…it just may work."

Mohr stood and humbly looked at Sobus. "So do I get DeSpon?"

Sobus smiled wickedly at him. "You'll get all that you'll need to capture and control a Shadow Dweller. Lija will give it to you once you are beyond the encampment." Sobus suddenly pulled Mohr near and whispered, "Although I do have one favor to ask of you first."

Lija shuffled next to Mohr. His head hung low, his body hunched over. "I'm only to take you to the edge of the camp. From there you are on your own."

Mohr grunted his reply, still angry about his deal with Sobus. He held out his hand. "So...then give it to me," he demanded.

Lija stopped and looked at Mohr. "Are you sure? You bargained with an evil lifeforce. It'll only get worse."

Mohr glared at Lija. "It's still better than being a servant to one and a man to none. Now hand it over."

"Fine." A small box formed in Lija's hands. "I hope it brings you the happiness you think it will...although I doubt it."

Mohr grabbed the box. He quickly drew it in and held it tightly to his chest. "Anything is better than..." He swiftly drove his knife into Lija's chest and twisted the blade to the left then back over to the right. Satisfied, he let the knife slip out of the wound as Lija's dead body fell to the ground. Mohr wiped the bloody knife on Lija's clothes and then he looked once over his shoulder at Sobus' distant tent. "I held up my part of the agreement, now hold up yours." Mohr peered into the box. There was a note and a six-armed compass, one for each Shadow Dweller. "The magic compass will help you find your prize, but you still have to be smart enough to solve the riddle. Then you will have power over the last one standing in the safety of the rain," Mohr read out loud. He tossed the magic compass into his pocket and marched on cursing under his breath about making deals with demons and insane fools.

When Broan woke he could see his breath in the early morning air. As he dressed, the murmurs of soldiers awakening crept into his tent. Metal workers were busy with their hammers, making last minute repairs. Upon hearing the grinding of steel on stone, Broan raised his sword and tested its sharpness. He wouldn't need the metal workers this morning.

He wandered from sentinel to sentinel, sharing whispered reports. He welcomed the changing of the guard and helped to calm any fear, while trying to build the spirits of those getting ready to fight.

These were his warriors and he was their leader. After making his rounds Broan returned to his tent and finished getting ready.

Dressed for battle and sitting on his horse, Zantro, Broan paused outside of Eirian's tent. He was beginning to question what he had done, when Laeg and V-Tor approached.

"Can you feel the movement of history?" V-Tor yelled as he came up next to Broan. The ground shook, as thousands of horses, riders and foot soldiers started moving out.

Broan nodded to him, "Let's head into battle and may the gods be on our side."

The field was quiet in the dusky haze of early dawn. Broan's group of warriors gathered on the edge of the fields near the Walled City. They were vulnerable standing where they were, out in the open with the high stone palisade of the Walled City behind them. With anticipation burning in their blood, the men stood in quiet strength, their fears and worry put behind them. They were focused on what they needed to do even though they all knew they could die on these harvested plains this very day.

Broan sat on his horse, listening, waiting. He watched as the sky turned a glorious pink, soon followed by a golden sunrise. It was unfortunate that there wasn't an autumn fog this morning. He would have liked a little more coverage for the Faeries.

He wondered how they were doing, having to wait in silence, unsure as to when the call to charge would come. Broan had noticed a growing unease and impatience among many of the Faery warriors. They were tired of waiting for their freedom. His thoughts went to Eirian. He was glad that she was safely tucked away from all of this.

Broan glanced over to his left flank where V-Tor, BroMac, Ardis, and Captain Cage of Gearoldin waited. They hid among the low rolling hills and in the forest that skirted the battlefield. They were as ready as they would ever be. Now all they needed was the enemy and this battle could start.

He didn't have to wait long. Trumpets from the high turrets of the Walled City crackled through the air announcing that the Ny-dick were approaching and everyone's eyes were drawn to the high plains just beyond the fields.

With a flurry of battle cries, thousands of the Ny-dick rushed down from their encampment to the long wide flat plains. Then the Ny-dick did something Broan never would have thought possible, they formed a wall of warriors and waited for the command to charge. He watched as the Ny-dick pounded their swords against their shields and their spears on the ground, building themselves up into adrenalin frenzy while they waited.

From self-serving brute force to a structured attack meant the Ny-dick now had both size and planning on their side. Broan realized this shift could become a problem. Broan thought of his army of both Faery and Mortal. He held to his belief that they would all do their best and adjust to the many changing tides in this unholy combat.

Broan didn't know what triggered the Ny-dick to finally advance. As frightening as it was, his warriors held back knowing they were the bait. "Just a little closer," Broan whispered, "Just a little closer."

The Faeries were hiding carefully among the rock and rubble, listening for the chaos of the charging Ny-dick. They too were surprised by the tight formation the enemy presented. They watched and waited. Soon the faintest of chants rang out from Cephas followed by a primitive magical sound radiating from the ground. The many clumps and heaps of stone tumbled loose as the Faeries started to reveal themselves. It seemed as if the ground was giving up its dead as the Faeries launched their attack on the Ny-dick.

Broan raised himself up in his stirrups to gain better view of what was happening. The bile rose quickly in his stomach. He wasn't sure what magic had been used, but it was obvious the Faeries were trapped in Mortal form and were stuck in hand-to-hand combat against the Ny-dick. Fury flashed in Broan's blue eyes as he watched another Faery get cut down. As angry as he was, he had to give Lija credit.

The Ny-dick continually reformed themselves, moving together and constantly tightening their phalanx. The tightness of their charge increased their odds of killing the Faeries while remaining safe themselves. Broan was frustrated and angry. He knew there was no support they could give the Faeries right then. The slingers and archers had to hold back until the fighting spread out. It was beginning to look as if the Ny-dick somehow knew their strategy.

At that moment another group of Ny-dick came out of nowhere and formed a second wall. Marching behind shields held high, they charged towards the fray, hoping to sandwich the Faeries between the two groups.

The intensifying moans and screams of the dying Faeries filled the air. This was not what anyone had planned. The Faeries were dying on their own and NOT in battle with Mortals. Why was nothing being done? If this continued, Idwal feared the Faeries would not have a chance to break the curse. Seething inside, Idwal began his charge. He drove down from the right bank of the valley and his friends, who were just a band of youths that could barely be considered warriors, quickly charged after him. It didn't take long for the rest of the division to follow. Armed with their short swords, they steadily advanced, and soon joined the Faeries in hand-to-hand combat.

"What's he doing?" BroMac screamed. He looked to Broan for leadership, fear and concern etched on his face.

War is filled with surprises for even the brightest leader and Broan had to quickly change his strategy. Determined to prevent the two groups of Ny-dick from meeting in the middle, he signal and let his warriors on both flanks loose.

That was all BroMac needed. Armed with long spears and swords, he led his group of cavalry into battle, well ahead of the other divisions, hoping to aid his foolish younger brother Idwal.

A wave of real dread rushed through Idwal as he was pulled from his horse and slammed down on the ground. It went from bad to worse in two short breaths. A Ny-dick quickly trapped him with its foot. Its sword was already on the downward swing when Tarir, a young Faery, propelled himself off of a dead warrior and caught the Ny-dick in the side of the neck with his knife. He swiftly drew it through its throat. Idwal saw the arch of blood shoot from the falling enemy.

Idwal pushed the Ny-dick's dead body away and rolled into a crouched position, ready for the next attack when he saw an axe swiftly hit Tarir. The agonizing look on Tarir's face said it all. In moments the young Faery with pale green eyes dropped dead.

Enraged, Idwal charged, only to get knocked flat to the ground once again. Rolling between the Ny-dick's legs he quickly came up behind his enemy. He was not going to let the beast of his nightmares get away with killing Tarir. Just as he was about to swing his short blade, the Ny-dick backhanded him and he went flying. Landing hard, Idwal lay unmoving in a crumpled heap near Tarir.

Thoi saw what happened and started towards them. She slashed her sword, cutting open a Ny-dick's torso from top to bottom. It growled at her as it swung its lethal axe. She rolled to the side, easily slipping out of the way. Coming up on her feet, she quickly pushed her sword through the ribs of the Ny-dick. Thoi didn't look back to see if her strike was fatal, she just ran to her fallen son, Tarir. Speed and determination was a wonderful combination but this time it was not good enough. With her head almost taken from her body, she quickly died next to her son.

Deeton watched as if in slow motion, as the Ny-dick advanced on Idwal. His lips parted in a chilling scream, as he charged in with his sword. As the Ny-dick reached for Idwal's still body, Deeton's blade came down hard on the enemy's arm, taking most of it off. The wounded Ny-dick growled and swung up with what remained of its arm. Jumping back and out of the way, Deeton suddenly felt strange. He looked down to see the bloody end of a Ny-dick's blade protruding from his midsection. Stunned, he stood still, clutching his stomach. Deeton felt the Ny-dick pull its blade out of his back. With a Ny-dick victory scream it pressed its foot against Deeton's back and pushed. Deeton fell, never to get up again.

Broan was getting use to using what fate decided to give him. He charged head on into battle aware of the position they all were in. Arrows and projectiles from Ardis' soldiers suddenly and swiftly flew over Broan's group with a deafening whistle, momentarily drowning out the thunder of their horse's hooves as they raced forward. Hopefully the steel pellets and arrows bombarding the outer line of Ny-dick would keep them away from Broan and his men.

Broan's group split and raced up the sides of the central Ny-dick group. His warriors leaned out of their saddles and swiftly cut the hamstrings of many of the Ny-dick marching on the outer edges, leaving them powerless to march on. Broan watched in stunned silence as the Ny-dick next in line stepped on or over the fallen to re-establish their formation. It would take more than a simple slice and a cut hamstring to stop these beasts from their organized attack. The Ny-dick kept moving, either unaware or not caring of its injury. Broan couldn't leave well enough alone. His faction quickly cut to the left and then swiftly swung around and rolled into the side of the tightly formed Ny-dick, trying to shatter the formation.

Now deeper into the battle, Broan swung his sword low catching a Ny-dick, who had just decapitated a young Elftan soldier. It never got to taste the Elftan warrior's fresh blood and that pleased Broan. He sliced another Ny-dick on the small of the back, leaving it bleeding and paralyzed. Broan' horse followed his commands, quickly rushing forward. A shrill scream cut through the air as the wounded Ny-dick got trampled. From the corner of Broan's eye he saw a Ny-dick's spear swing wide. Its blood coated, razor sharp end barely missed him. He disabled his opponent with a boot to the mouth and a slice through the head. He smashed his sword into another Ny-dick's shoulder, sending it tumbling over, just as a broad fist caught Broan in the side, denting his armor. He shook off a blow that came from behind and whipped his horse around. Swinging his sword sideways, he sent half a head skyward.

With ribs still throbbing, he raced towards another heavily armed Ny-dick. Ducking quickly, Broan caught the enemy by surprise and cut its stomach open allowing entrails to slip out. It roared at Broan as it charged, intestines dragging between its legs. Three arrows from Ardis finally stopped the Ny-dick, but did nothing to remove the hatred in its eyes.

From Ardis' vantage point it seemed impossible to believe, but since early in the fight the Ny-dick were organized and determined, attacking with vicious intensity. A few now broke formation and went about executing the wounded while scavenging among the dead, eating while they went. It was obvious that they were becoming over confident. That's when Ardis saw his opening. He subjected the wandering Ny-dick to a murderous volley of arrows.

Taking his archers into closer combat on their mounts, Ardis led the way down the left embankment and along the edge of the forest. They were able to fire while pivoting on their mounts, and with a continual volley of arrows, proved masterful in decimating the Ny-dick on the edge of the battle. Each attack was frenzied, quick and deadly.

Ardis spotted Broan, still on his horse, slashing away at a growing number of Ny-dick surrounding him. Riding hard, Ardis quickly led his group towards his warlord. He threaded quickly in and out of the Ny-dick. All of a sudden, a curved blade sliced across his shoulder, leaving a deep gash. He laid his bow down and took up his sword in his good hand, slashing as he went on splitting chest bones open and slicing heads off.

Bodies littered the area like stones on a mountain pass. V-Tor was definitely feeling the effects of a hard fought battle against the intimidating Ny-dick. He was glad to see some relief coming his way in the form of a division of Geardolin's army.

The captain of the Gearoldin army, Captain Cage, saw what needed to be done and divided his forces in two. They quickly made their way to the outskirts of the fighting and smashed through the Ny-dick's lighter-armed soldiers. But the attack seemed to infuriate the Ny-dick more than anything else. One Ny-dick grabbed a mounted warrior by the back of the head and threw him a few dozen feet then grabbed the Faery off its back and flicked it away.

V-Tor screamed when he saw Pera, somersault through the air. Never taking his eyes of the Ny-dick who tossed her, he charged. Coming up from behind, V-Tor yanked the Ny-dick's head back and slit its throat. He whipped his horse around and raced towards Pera. She was groping around aimlessly, unaware that her back was broken. V-Tor leveled another enemy with a cross-body slice, opening its chest and stomach. For every Ny-dick he maimed there were more to take its place. He watched helplessly as a Ny-dick grabbed Pera's hair and smashed her face down against some rocks over and over again.

With extraordinary determination V-Tor finally reached the Ny-dick attacking Pera. He rammed his horse into the ugly beast, causing it to drop Pera as it turned. A boot to the jaw and a slice to throat and V-Tor dispatched it to hell. Whipping off his horse, he crouched down and turned Pera over. The shine in her eyes faded quickly as her blood spilled from her wounds and soaked ground. Shaking with anger, V-Tor mounted his horse and charged back into the frey.

In the past the Ny-dick had characteristically turned any mêlée into a slaughterhouse, taking the time to eat its victims as they fell. They always pressed hard as a group, making any battle one of annihilation and feasting, but this time it was different.

BroMac didn't like the new Ny-dick tactics and he quickly regrouped his men. He knew what he had to do. Knowing that warriors from Anwel, mostly bowmen and slingers, would continue their assault from the right creating some coverage, BroMac rushed his division on and into a tight group of Ny-dick.

The abrupt stopping of his horse caught BroMac off guard and he came down hard, tearing his lip open. Winded he rolled to his side, only to be faced with his dead horse with a spear through its chest. BroMac quickly staggered up from the ground.

A hard punch and kick from an advancing Ny-dick, forced air out of protesting lungs and brought BroMac down once again. He dragged himself up to one knee. A searing pain in his left arm made him curse. Once he made sure it was still attached, he smiled and readied for the attack with his sword in the other hand.

Seeing BroMac's situation, Hywel did the unthinkable and sprang onto BroMac's back as if he was going to attack him. Stunned, the Ny-dick paused. That was all the opening Hywel needed. Springboarding off BroMac's shoulders, he drove his knife deep into the Ny-dick's eye socket and twisted. Withdrawing it quickly, he then drove his knife into the beast's temple making sure it went deep.

It wasn't enough to stop the enemy. The Ny-dick quickly seized Hywel around the waist. Grabbing his forearm, it then quickly ripped Hywel's arm out of its socket. Blood shot everywhere. Dazed, Hywel dangled from the Ny-dick's grip as it chewed on the flesh of his arm.

Enraged, BroMac announced himself back in the battle with a flurry of screams. He lowered his head and charged. The Ny-dick was about to have its lunch taken from it so it waited until the right moment and back-handed BroMac, sending him flying. It kicked away BroMac's sword and roared its displeasure.

Facing BroMac, it dragged Hywel's body up to its mouth. With a deafening crunch, it bit into Hywel's chest. Spitting out the bones it glared at BroMac and than dove back in to eat the heart. Finally satisfied the enemy threw Hywel's lifeless body away.

BroMac unburied a sword from a heap of dead bodies. Swiftly, he began to hack away at the Ny-dick starting with the legs and moving upward. Blood seeped and sprayed. He didn't stop until he was sure the monster was dead

Cephas could feel his facial skin tear under the wide sweep of the mace the Ny-dick was using. The impact sent a shock wave through him and he fell back. A metallic tang filled his mouth and he used his sleeve to wipe the blood away. Wincing in pain he readied himself for another attack.

The mace came low this time, crashing into his legs and flipping him to the ground. Jagged ends of his collarbone protruded out of his uniform, his arm limp. He stood up and felt dizzy and sick. Pain was more about shock than panic and he needed to get himself past it. He let the weight of the sword pull it from his hand. Reaching for his long knife with his good hand, he crouched, ready to lunge at the Ny-dick after the next sweep.

Broan's sword sliced the Ny-dick's head from its shoulders, cutting short the dance between Ny-dick and Cephas. The satisfaction on Broan's face soon changed to alarm as he watched Cephas stumble and fall.

While Laeg covered his back Broan removed his helmet. He dropped to his knees. "It should have been different," he said.

Cephas smiled up at him from his badly damaged body, sweat pouring off his face. "It was an honor to have fought with you." He thrust the ring into Broan's hand, "Give this back to her." His eyes faded and so did his smile. Cephas was gone.

Eirian woke with a pounding headache and her eyes refused to open. The taste of Eeban filled her mouth. She gagged and spitted repeatedly. "Broan! I'm going to kill you!" she yelled. She pulled against her bindings. Her hands were tied behind her and they were attached to a...tree? "No, I'm going to skin him alive. Slowly, painfully and..."

"She's awake."

The words cut through her anger as she struggled to open her eyes. "*Ny-dick!*" This was a first for her. Usually she was just beyond the clutches of these beasts and most times she was distracting them from their victims. She tried to touch her power.

"It won't work this time. There will be no enchantments." Laughing, the heavier Ny-dick approached her. "The Dark Lord told us that once the battle started all Faeries would revert back to Mortal...to die as Mortals...to suffer as Mortals. All your special tricks and powers are gone." He widened his mouth unhooking the double-hinged lower jaw and exposed razor-sharp interlocking teeth. It appeared as if he was going to eat her whole.

"You don't scare me!" she lied as she tried to kick him. He threw his weight against her, quickly knocking the wind out of her. Then he simply grabbed her leg and twisted it with his massive hand. "It's useless to fight against your inevitable future." He gave her a toothy leer.

Eirian spat at him, hitting him square on his broad snout. "The future is to those that adapt, which leaves your kind out. All you've done is slither through the ages, scavenging like..."

Smiling, he leaned into her face. "Death is not adaptation but a dead end." He belched and then laughed. He dug his filthy nails into her arms as he pulled down on them, knowing all too well that the pressure on her limbs would be great.

The pain was incomprehensible. Why were they keeping her alive when killing and eating was usually the first thing on any Ny-dick's mind?

"Careful Kibria, you don't want to make her pass out again. There's no fun in that," a second Ny-dick said.

Kibria stepped back and swung at her, hitting her hard on cheek. "Yes, I do like hearing them scream and plead for mercy. Besides I've waited a long time for this." Eirian forced her mouth shut, clamping her lips together. She wasn't going to give them the pleasure of succeeding on any front.

"The orders were to keep her alive. He didn't say anything about untouched, now did he?" Zamal, the other Ny-dick, came charging at her with a knife in his hand. For a man of such large girth, Eirian was surprised how light he was on his feet as he jumped up in the air before her. It quickly drove the knife into her right shoulder. Eirian kept her mouth locked, allowing only whimpers out.

"Come now, you know you'll be screaming sooner than later. Make Kibria happy. You owe it to him. You tricked him and made him the laughing stock of the Ny-dick. " He smiled, giving Kibria a knowing look. "I don't think she remembers you."

"It's okay because I remember her. Now out of my way!" Kibria yelled as he punched the other Ny-dick. Sneering, Kibria poked at her new wound and then rubbed his fingers through the blood running from it. He licked them, his eyes locked on Eirian. "Once the Dark Lord is finished with you Faery," Kibria leaned in and whispered, "you're all mine." He pressed his filthy face next to hers and then in a barely, audible voice whispered. "And I'm going to make sure you scream and scream and scream. We have some unfinished business you and I."

Suppressing her fear, she dragged up her courage. "So you're the Dark Lord's dog... what a good boy." She found it hard to complete her sentence when Kibria's fist found its mark. Weak and winded she fought to keep her head.

Kibria grinned. "Your feeble attempt to enrage me won't work. The Dark Lord's plans benefit me as much as it does him." He turned and walked away from her. "I've been patient this far. I can wait a little longer for my revenge and the taste of Faery meat."

"Not much of a... Ny-dick if you... have patience. What happened... to the savage taking... you... are famous for?"

Kibria swiftly turned "YOU. You happened to me."

Eirian had to change her tactics if she was going to find a way out of this mess. "What would benefit both you and the Dark Lord?"

"Your ring....your army...your death." Zamal laughed hard. He walked over and grabbed her hair, wrapped it around his fist and yanked, snapping her head down. He hit her once with his fist and watched more blood trickle from her mouth and nose.

"What..." Eirian shut her mouth, keeping the truth from them. She thanked the gods for the foresight. Now it made sense as to why she felt she needed to give the ring to Cephas. "It won't work. I'll never give you my ring even if you disembowel me," she yelled. She shook her head in an attempt to stay conscious.

"We'll see," Zamal hissed as he licked some the blood off her face.

"She's mine, remember?" Kibria sneered as he slammed into Zamal, knocking him to the ground. Zamal bared his lip and growled but then backed down, giving Kibria his right.

Satisfied, Kibria leaned heavily against her, trapping her legs between his and pinning her to the tree. "You got away from me once, Faery, but not this time." He raised his knife and brushed the sharp edge of it against her cheek and then continued lower along her neck. He switched hands and ran the knife down her chest, smearing blood from the wound in her shoulder along the way. Eirian twisted, desperate to get free. Kibria laughed, enjoying her struggle. Slowly he inched his knife under her breast and watched as terror overcame her. He smiled. "Your skin is responding to my touch, it quivers with anticipation and skin never lies. You're not much of a Faery…not even much of a Mortal, but we both know that."

"My skin is not quivering, it's crawling!" she hissed and then suddenly smashed her forehead against his.

Stunned, Kibria's head snapped back. "Stupid bitch! You'll pay for that," he growled. Eirian kicked out at him, hitting Kibria high in the gut. With an enraged scream, he swiftly connected his two fists with her face, causing blood to spray everywhere.

Spitting out blood, Eirian lowered her head and tried to concentrate. She continued to hope that if she got them mad enough, they would just kill her and put an end to her problem.

Suddenly all went still. A shadow passed by, and Eirian looked up through her lashes. Her swollen eyes and the blood flowing down her face made it difficult to see yet she caught a glimmer of someone with pale and fine skin. The two Ny-dicks backed away, with heads bowed. "*The Dark Lord!*" Eirian cursed, feeling doomed.

Anger and instant awareness filled Sobus. "What have you done?" he hissed as he reached for the Ny-dick's knife. "Get out of my sight!"

"Yes my lord…but all you said was to keep her alive," Kibria pleaded.

Sobus glared at the both of them. Then he turned to face the young Faery. His breath caught in his throat as he sensed something. "IS this possible?" Sobus croaked out. "How can this be?" He stepped in closer and raised Eirian's chin. His eyes narrowed as he removed the strands of her hair caught in the clotting blood and tucked them behind her ear. He examined her face more closely, looking beyond the bruises and blood. He turned it side to side as if he were doing nothing more than pondering the freshness of some fruit or vegetable. Dropping his hand, he quickly stood back. "Haidee…'s?" he asked, with astonishment in his voice.

"Haidee was the wife of Governor Cian."

"And your mother," Sobus said his face filling with anger. "I will never forgive Ke-Hern for…"

"For what? Helping…?"

"Helping the Faeries? He only helps the Queen, even you must know that." He paused briefly. "I can't believe that all these years he selfishly kept us apart. You are Haidee's child. No wonder the Queen worked so hard to keep me off her land. Stupid evil bitch. If it wasn't for her we'd be a family, the three of us- you, me… and Haidee"

"I am not Haidee's daughter," Eirian said as she shook her head.

"You have more of Haidee in you than you think." He smiled softly and continued, "I know this is hard to believe but I can feel your Off-World power. It is deep within you..." He pause then placed his hands on her head. "It didn't come from Ke-Hern and I doubt the Queen could or would part with what she has. So there is only one other way you could have it."

"I don't have Off-World power!" Eirian argued.

"You mean to tell me that in all your training, Ke-hern never talked to you about this inner power you have?" He ran the back of his hand over her cheek.

Eirian shook off Sobus' hand. "He told me of my power, but it's not Off-World. That won't make sense."

"It would if he was serving the Queen. He won't want you to use it against her...now would he?" He leaned in, "Here let me show you." Gently he brought her head up. "Feel the truth within you as our energy speaks to one another. You are...Off-World."

Nerlena gasped and twitched. She could feel Sobus' energy joining with Eirian's and it filled her with fear. She began to hum and sing on levels that one barely heard. "Water beings rise, rise and help release this Off-World's hold." She raised her arms. "Beings of rock and land, rise and tear the bond apart." Nerlena concentrated harder. "Beings from energy of this land and once from this land join in the tempest."

The ground water from deep within the land's belly drew upward. Singular moist drops floated up out of the soil. Dew and frost on the leaves grouped, gelled and joined with the newly surfaced ground water. They pulled together. Faces and arms formed as whispering sounds united and chanted. The water beings swirled around Sobus, reaching out they began to wrap their misty arms around him. While Nerlena set the tempest around them, she whispered words into Eirian's ear, words that would free her.

Kibria and Zamal grabbed their weapons, ready for the enemy they felt but could not see. They stood back to back and started swinging. The ground beneath them shook and trembled, knocking Zamal to the ground.

"Show yourself," Kibria yelled. "Come face your death."

"It's not out there you fool it's him!" Zamal pulled himself up to his feet and rushed at Sobus. "Whatever you are doing, stop it. Your magic is..." Zamal swiftly turned at the thunderous sound of boulders smashing into trees. "Stop now," he screamed as he yanked Sobus free of Eirian.

Under the canopy of the trees, between the storm and unbending energies of Off-World, land, and Ancient - words tumbled out of Eirian's mouth in hushed low whispers. She felt the connection to the spell. She could feel the separation happening. She savored the power to escape, the clarity beyond the pain.

Sobus stood in stunned silence. He stared at Eirian who was limp and motionless. "Your power is definitely intact...way beyond your comprehension...and soon to be mine." He laughed hysterically, weak with the burning energy, crazy from its brief union. Looking around him then finally came to his senses. "Grab her! Quick!"

Kibria turned and attempted to grab Eirian but his hand went right through her. Stupefied, he looked up at Sobus. "What kind of magic did you use on her?"

Sobus' eyes grew big. "She used the image spell! Smarter than I thought." He caught the two Ny-dick staring at him. "Well don't just stand there! Even if she's invisible she is too weak to go far. Fan out and look for her."

Sobus started to inspect the ground. *"Invisible or not I will find you."* Without lifting his head he called out. "Listen Eirian, I know this is all too much for you. Please, please come out and let me help you. I only want the best for you. Just give me a chance to prove to you I speak the truth." He paused and listened.

Eirian knew she didn't have enough strength to go far or to fight them off. So...she went back to her limp body at the tree. *"Look all you want out there. I'll stay right here under your nose."* Re-entering her body was far more difficult than she expected. The pain was intense. As hard as she tried to fight it, the blackness soon swallowed her.

The brutal side of the curse could not be missed. In the end it was written in the blood-soaked field and numerous bodies that lay upon the battleground. All of the Faeries were gone and countless Mortal warriors as well. Some of Broan's men had started combing the killing field for the injured, having to wade through grotesque broken bodies with fatal deep wounds. The copper smell of blood drenched the cool evening air making the victory a somber moment.

Broan stood with V-Tor and Laeg, happy to know they had survived.

"On to a victory celebration," V-Tor laughed as he got on his horse. Broan just ignored him and mounted his steed.

"To the Wall City," Laeg added as he mounted his horse as well. Broan turned away from the city and cantered towards the camp they left behind.

"Where is he going?" V-Tor asked as he kicked his stallion into action.

Within seconds both were beside Broan. "You know your uncle will be waiting for you and you know he doesn't like to be kept waiting?" V-Tor said.

"He'll understand duty before pleasure."

"What is this about, Broan?" Laeg asked.

Broan smiled to himself. "I drugged and tied up Eirian before the clash. She had given the ring to Cephas and I felt she didn't need to be in danger. I promised myself I'd go and set her free as soon as it was safe."

"YOU did what? Boy, I'm glad you're the one setting her free. Now there is going to be one very angry woman," V-Tor commented as he dropped his horse back behind Broan's.

Broan knew how to pick himself up immediately after a battle, when the reality of it hit hard, but he didn't know how to handle what he felt now. The few men left behind to attend the camp were dead. Their throats had been cut, bodies half eaten. Kicking his horse on, he rushed to Eirian's quarters.

Jumping off his mount, he ran towards her partly collapsed tent. In his anger, Broan ripped at her tent as he screamed. How could he have failed her? He hadn't kept her safe, he had practically handed her over to the enemy. "Search for her and pray she's still alive," Broan demanded.

The three of them surveyed the ground for any sign of a trail, for anything that would give evidence as to where they had taken her. They divided up. Broan went to the east of her tent; Laeg went west and V-Tor north.

Once over a large rise, Laeg found the enemy's tracks. Leaves torn from branches and roots ripped out of the ground left a wide path that was easy to follow. Laeg's spirits lightened. How arrogant? What a lack of discipline. Did they really think they would win this war, and that no one would follow them?

Laeg suddenly paused. He could hear chaos and the howls of wolves. Quietly he retrieved his sword. Moving slowly towards the sound, he soon came upon a diminutive clearing. Off to the side he saw a small group of wolves eating its prey. Concerned Laeg inched his way nearer to the edge of the clearing and then he saw her. Eirian was tied to the tree. The hair on the back of his neck rose, she was so motionless.

Quickly, Laeg scanned the area making sure all was clear. Satisfied, he swiftly ventured to Eirian's still form. Her body hung from her secured wrists, her legs gapped in an unnatural position having given away. The brutality of what he saw caught his breath.

Bending near, he was greatly relieved to find Eirian still breathing. Worried he'd cause her more pain, his hands trembled, hovering just inches from her. He closed his eyes for a second, and then tenderly placed his arm around her ribcage to support her. With one swift movement he cut the ropes that held her. She dropped against his arm and he eased her to the ground. Laeg removed his tunic and tightly wrapped it around her. Then he picked her up in his arms and started back towards camp.

Laeg rushed into camp with Eirian in his arms. Her face attested to the fact that she had been repeatedly beaten. The amount of dried blood on her clothing gave testimony to worse injuries. He walked into the tent they directed him to and with much care placed her on the cot. He looked up at he shocked faces of Broan, V-Tor and Ke-Hern. "It gets worse," he announced. "She has a stab wound on her right shoulder and," he paused and looked away. He did not want to look into Broan's eyes when he told them the rest of it.

Broan shuddered at the thought that Eirian could have been beaten with such force. He wondered if she would ever look at him again. Could he ever forgive himself? He walked over to her. The glint of Jelen's silly rock caught his eye. He pulled hard on it, breaking the leather cord it hung from. "Stupid thing is good for nothing but bad luck and pain." He angrily tossed it aside.

Puzzled, Ke-Hern walked over to the stone and stared at it intently. "Who...who gave her this stone?" he tried to pick it up but the energy coming from it was very strong. Turning, he looked up at Broan and the others and demanded, "WHO gave her this stone to wear?"

"She was wearing it last night so most likely Cephas or Hywel. How they got it from Jelen, I don't know," Broan answered.

"Jelen?"

"Why? What does it matter?"

"This is an Ancient's conduit stone." He looked over to V-Tor. "Come here and pick it up. You need to make sure it gets back to Jelen. IT found him and should remain with him until IT chooses to leave. It will only bind to one."

Bronagh had entered the tent looking for Broan. Her uncle was not happy that Broan had chosen to go back to the camp rather than attend the victory welcome he deserved. The gasp that escaped from her as she stood in the doorway caused them all to turn and look at her. V-Tor tried to grab Bronagh, but she skimmed off his arm and rushed forward.

Bronagh fell to her knees beside Eirian and slapped away Laeg's hands. "Leave her alone. I'll do it." With much care she opened the tattered edges of the bloodstained shift, exposing the wound on the shoulder. She slowly continued to remove the garment and with a ragged breath she yelled. "Get Out! All of you get out!"

Laeg got up and moved to stand by the others. Sadness and help-lessness surrounded them. "Get out!" Bronagh demanded again.

Ke-Hern herded the men towards the doorway. "V-Tor, go and get some warm water and find some clean bandages. Laeg, send word to Iarnan about Eirian and that he can start the celebration without us. Broan...Broan." He had a hard time getting his attention. "Go sit by the fire. There is nothing more you can do here." But Broan didn't move, he just stood there and watched, frozen with guilt and worry.

Bronagh knew he was still there, even though she had her back to him. "Get out Broan and you too Ke-Hern." She sat back on her heels, unwilling to go any farther until they both left.

Ke-Hern turned and grabbed Broan's arm as he headed out of the tent door. "I need you to tell me everything. Why was she not on the field?"

By the fire, Broan straightened his shoulders and looked Ke-Hern in the eye. "In truth there was no reason for her to be in such danger, I made sure she stayed in her tent...I drugged her."

"WHAT? HOW...HOW? No...No. WHY? Why would you do such a thing? YOU fool."

"It made sense at the time. She had given the ring to Cephas and I wasn't about to stand around and let her ride into danger for nothing! I found a way to protect her, and I took it"

"The ring!" Ke-Hern paled as he grabbed Broan's shoulders. "We have to find Cephas' body and retrieve the ring."

"It's alright, I have it." Broan fished the ring out from under his belt and handed it over. "Cephas gave it to me before he died. He said as long as it was on the field, all would go as planned. He made me promise to give it back to Eirian. I think he knew."

Ke-Hern looked at the ring now coated with blood. "Nothing has gone as it should, yet...yet..." He thought of Jelen's stone. "Perhaps greater things are at play here."

Chapter 15

"Hope is for those that have no power."

- Sobus

Eirian could just make out voices. They were not loud and demanding or even threatening, yet something in Eirian knew she needed to wake up or she would regret it. These voices were talking about her in hushed tones, making plans for her future. She struggled against the heavy weight of pain and weakness. No one was ever again going to decide what was going to happen to her BUT her! She shook off her physical bonds and forced herself towards the conscious world of the voices. A blood-curdling scream crashed from her tormented center and was followed by barely civil words.

"Damn you all. I've had enough of your secretive plans." She still couldn't open her eyes. No matter how hard she fought to open them, she couldn't. Eirian decided she was wasting energy on that little problem. She grabbed the edge of her cot and pulled herself upright. That was, of course, short lived.

"Keep still or you'll open your wound," Bronagh said as she eased Eirian back down on her cot. Bronagh then turned and looked at the group of men that were standing around the tent. "Go take your talk outside. She has been through enough already and she doesn't need you to upset her needlessly."

Eirian was still working on opening her eyes. Why would they not just open. "Damn!" she swore again.

"I'm sorry Eirian, I'm trying to be gentle," Bronagh said as she checked Eirian's bandages for fresh bleeding.

"It's not that," Eirian answered in total frustration. "My eyes will not open. I need to see. I need to find…" She started to pull herself up again.

"Eirian stop! You can't open your eyes because your face is swollen. If you want to talk to Broan, he's here." She looked angrily at her brother. "Right or wrong he has been near you constantly since you were found."

"NO! Not him!" Eirian hissed through her teeth. She brushed fingers over her face. "What a mess," she said out loud. "How could he? I have to talk with Ke-Hern. ALONE!" She tried to get up again.

Her words cut deep adding to Broan's guilt. This was his fault, his failure, and this would haunt him for the rest of his life. Bronagh looked over her shoulder at Broan. "Well don't just stand there, go get Ke-Hern, before she rips out all her stitches."

Ke-Hern walked in a sat down next to Eirian. "Calm down Eirian, you'll do yourself more damage than even the Ny-dick did. I've already replaced the ring on your thumb, WHICH should not have been given away in the first place!"

She growled at him, "It's not the ring that worries me."

"Then what?"

"Are we alone," she hissed.

Ke-Hern turned and watched Bronagh and Broan leave the tent. "Yes we are alone. What is so important that you needed to wake from your body's healing sleep?"

"Who were my parents?" Eirian's question was answered by silence. Moaning she asked again. "Please tell me the truth. I have a right to know."

"There is nothing to tell Eirian. You are in no condition to make sense of the truth."

"I'll be the judge of that. For once tell me the TRUTH! All of it."

Ke-Hern didn't say a word but took hold of her hand. He stumbled to start and then gave up.

Eirian began to cry. "So it is true. You directed my life as if I was nothing more than a puppet. WHY? OH…please… I need to hear it from your own lips."

Ke-Hern sat hunched over as he took in her anger and fear. He had known this day would come but had hoped it would be under better circumstances. "What do you think you know?"

"THINK I know!" she hissed. "Sobus told me WHO my parents are, told me what happened, told me everything!" She turned her head away from him. "How could you?"

Ke-Hern paled as he straightened up. "If Sobus told you any-thing worth knowing, I can guarantee it was only a half truth."

"Which is still better than NO truth?"

"Is it?" he asked with a heavy sigh. "If I had told you, or anyone for that matter, Sobus could have found out and would have destroyed the only hope we had and I could not, would not let that happen. Do you understand? We had to…"

"What part of we was I, the sacrificial lamb?" She spat vindictively.

"That is not true. You are too hurt and confused to make any sense of this. Heal yourself first then we will talk." He reached over to place his hand on her abdomen. "Heal for the both of you."

Eirian grabbed his hand stopping his progress. "You have failed me. You lied to me and still do, so don't give us your pity." Her grip was strong and unwavering.

Ke-Hern shook off her hand, got up and began to walk out of the tent. "Pray Sobus doesn't know that you're pregnant. He is the one who has lied to you, not me."

"Don't walk away from me! I'm not finished. You COWARD!"

"I would hold your judgment if I were you." Ke-Hern stood at the open door of the tent and looked out at the group of men who were standing around waiting, worrying. His back stiffened with resolve. If Eirian was mad at him now, just wait. He turned and let the door flap fall back in its place and returned to her side. He placed his hand on her forehead and began his spell.

She fought him hard. "NO!" she screamed. "Don't do this. I don't want to sleep! Don't you put that spell on me… KE-HE..rn…"

It was silent as Ke-Hern exited the tent. "When I want you to sleep, you will go to sleep." He brushed his hands off, very proud of what he had just done. He walked over to the fire where Broan and the others waited. "Things are worse than I thought. We have to move Eirian to a safe place as soon as possible. Everything depends on her now."

"You can't move her," Bronagh protested, "she'd bleed to death."

"What about the Walled City?" Laeg asked, ignoring Bronagh's outburst.

"Too many people. It would be too easy for someone to slip in and kill her."

"Kill her!" Broan yelled. "Are you going to tell us what this is all about?"

"Not...."

"Not yet? By now I'd think you would come up with a better answer," Broan said, his words holding the strain of everything that had gone wrong.

"I need to go to the Queen's Island, and while I'm gone, Eirian will need protection."

Broan looked at Ke-Hern with narrowed eyes. He hated not knowing what was going on. "I'll take her to Solveig then. I know everyone who will be returning there. It would be hard for someone to sneak in."

"Good. Can you leave tonight?"

"She cannot travel! Does no one understand that?" Bronagh yelled.

Ke-Hern smiled at Bronagh. "It is okay, I've placed her in a deep sleep. She will be fine."

"I'll get my horse while you wrap her up in a heavy blanket. It will be a long and hard ride back to Solveig," Broan said.

Laeg spoke up. "I'm coming with you. You may need help along the way."

"I'm coming as well," V-Tor said as he stood next to Laeg.

Broan smiled at them. He turned to BroMac. "Gather anyone who wants to return to Solveig and have them follow us tomorrow. Iarnan will take care of the injured. Get Idwal..."

"Idwal didn't make it," BroMac cut in, sadness filling his words.

Broan placed his hand on BroMac's shoulder and shook his head. "Do you wish to stay behind then?"

"No. I'll gather the men and we will leave tomorrow."

Broan nodded slowly. "Okay then have Ardis follow in two weeks with anyone left behind. It's time to bring Solveig back to life." He looked deep into BroMac's eyes. "Bring Idwal's body. He would have wanted to be buried at home."

Broan then turned to Bronagh. "I need you to trust me more than you ever have. I will take good care of Eirian until you return to Solveig. For now, I need you speak to Iarnan and let him know what is happening." Broan suddenly took out his knife and grabbed the bottom of Ke-Hern's cloak. He sliced a long narrow piece of material free.

"What are you doing?" Ke-Hern asked as he examined his cloak's now tattered hem.

"I'm making a binding cord for Eirian."

314

"What?" He grabbed for the piece of cloth, creating a bit of a tug of war. "It won't work."

"I know, but Eirian may not figure that out for a while." He pulled the rag free from Ke-Hern's grip. "It was hard enough keeping Eirian out of trouble with a real binding cord on, at least this way it may keep her quiet enough to give herself time to heal."

"She'll be mad as a hornet. Trust me, it is not wise to deceive her again."

"Maybe, but she will be safe."

In the dim early morning light, while safely cocooned in a quilt, Eirian slightly opened her eyes and quietly watch Broan. He was a sight for sore eyes. She watched him brooding in a chair that was positioned close to her bed. His face was covered with day's growth, which added to his weary appearance. Eirian smiled. "You look so tired." She gently patted the bed beside her. "Come lay down, there is room enough for the two of us."

Broan's head was resting back on the top of the chair. His eyes were locked on the ceiling, deep in worry so when Eirian spoke to him he thought he was dreaming. She was far too pleasant. He slowly sat up, and then little by little he leaned forward in his chair, watching her intently, looking for any sign this was not just an illusion. He rose from his chair and hesitantly moved towards her. His hand wavered as it pulled the quilt up more around her chin. "Go back to sleep," he said as he turned and started towards the door of her room.

Eirian pushed down on the covers. "What's wrong?" and then frowned when she noticed something tied to her wrist. Glaring at the twisted material that was wrapped around her good wrist, she looked back at Broan. "What is this?"

Broan didn't even turn around. "It's for your own good. Ke-Hern promised it would not hurt you like the other binding cord, but it is just as limiting."

"He put this on me?" she whispered

"No. I did," he answered, as he paused, waiting for her reaction.

She wanted to cry from the depth of her soul. "Why? What have I done?"

"It's to keep you safe and still until you are healed. I'll take it off then."

"Don't do this to me! Not again, please!" Various sensations grew as her real world came to life. Puzzled she gazed at Broan's broad back. "What...is..." Suddenly vague images and memories rose from their hiding place. Eirian fought them. Pain rode on their backs. They scared her, but it was a losing battle, and the pain of a beaten body and a wounded shoulder came crashing in on her. Her world was once again teetering and unsteady. She turned to look at Broan, and her heart lurched as she watched him leave, unsure as to why he was abandoning her. She looked passed the empty doorway wishing he would return. She wanted him to stabilize her in the midst of pain, anger and betrayal.

Broan's steps were lighter. Feeling that she would truly be all right, his tightly curled hands finally gave way and relaxed. Broan agreed with himself that he would give her some time to fully understand what had happen and then handle the anger before he would ever get into bed with her again. She was still far too ill to know that what she just offered him was forgiveness. He sighed to himself. She didn't fight the cloth strip on her wrist, which meant he had time— time to make things right. It had been so hard to hold on to reason these last few days, but now he had hope.

Eirian awoke in a cold sweat during the night. She knew there was no one in her room, yet she could have sworn a voice woke her up. She listened to the quiet air and reached out to feel the energy of Solveig. There was silence, but there was no peace here. There was a gathering of Mortals and … something else was also here in Solveig.

As Eirian searched for clarity, a multitude of whispering voices slowly competed for her attention. The voices of those lost on the battlefield were carried on the mountain winds. They grew more and more and more intense until all she could do was rise to answer them.

Eirian struggled to get up.

"I know what you are thinking. You are still too weak," Sobus' voice entered her mind. *"I'm sorry but I'm only thinking of your health and safety."*

Eirian looked around the room. She knew that voice. "Where are you?"

"You really are too ill if you have to ask that question. Now lie down before you fall down," Sobus commanded.

Eirian paled knowing he was in her mind and could read her thoughts.

"Relax, Don't be so fearful of me. I know our first meeting didn't go that well, but believe me it was such a shock to find you. I'm sorry for everything. I really didn't know who you were. If I had, I wouldn't have let the Ny-dick touch you. I was just trying to stop a possible bad, unchangeable ending for the Faeries."

Eirian shook as she took in a shallow breath. "Just leave me be. I know what I have to do. Leave me to it."

"But all I want is to help you finish what you've always wanted to do- restore the Duronykians back to their rightful place. AND you cannot succeed without me."

"Why should I believe you?" Eirian asked. She tried to focus but she was so weak. The heaviness from Solveig was creeping under her skin.

"You are so right. Why should you believe me? I'm sure Ke-Hern told you many things about me. Some, I regret, are true."

"Like what?"

"For one, I am Off-World and just like the Queen I have unbalanced the land and caused a string of events to unfold that needs to be righted before I can ever be at peace."

Working hard to concentrate, Eirian stayed quiet.

"I'm sure you heard much worse." Sobus' voice rushed in, filling the void.

"No. No…In fact I heard nothing about you until the war began."

"Ke-Hern didn't…Oh my! Then…then all of this, this war and trouble that tried to lay low the land would seem so horrible to you… and for that I am …"

"Save it. Now if you don't mind I have someplace I need to go." She tried to step away from the bed.

"What are you doing?"

"I'm going to stop the noise in my head…all the voices, music, thoughts…they are all crowding in on my sanity!"

"Then please tell me that Broan will be going with you, to protect you. It is not a safe place for a Mortal female out there in the wilds."

"You don't know much about me, do you? I've lived most of my life out there and did quite fine on my own." She paused and chided herself for speaking so freely. She changed the subject. "Tell me something. Why…why did you lead the Ny-dick in this battle?"

"Everyone has a part to play in history. Good people sometimes have to play the bad parts. I have had to play the hardest part in ending this curse on the Faeries, but I still did what needed to be done. Just like you… It wasn't easy for you, was it? You are the bravest of us all."

Eirian said nothing. She felt emotions coming to life that she wished wouldn't.

"Yes. Well I'm sure that Broan has told you that many times lately. He of all Mortals knows what you've gone through."

Eirian's eyes began to fill with tears. Broan's abandonment and betrayal battled within her. It was all too much to handle. She was filled with anger. "Go back to where you came and leave me alone!" She fell back onto the bed.

"Yes of course. We can talk later when you are stronger." Sobus paused then added in a soft whisper. *"Just so you know I AM trying to go back to where I came from."*

Queen DaNann sat at her stylish desk of handcrafted cherry wood. The open upper section revealed six compartments filled with paper, inkwells and quills. The desktop was cluttered with used sheets of rice paper and maps. She rested her head against the sloping lid, hesitating to close it. "No amount of numbers or graphs will make things any clearer." She wished Ke-Hern were with her right then. "Perhaps if I too had created my own Faery guard like the Shadow Dwellers, this would have been over quicker."

"I'm certain the battle for power would have just gone on longer. There would have been much more suffering," Ke-Hern said as he stood in a doorway.

"Ke-Hern!" DaNann said as she closed the lid to her desk and rose to greet him. "Come sit. Please." She pointed to the hand woven rattan bench.

Ke-Hern liked the bench. It smelled of her and lavender. "Come sit with me. There is much we have to talk about." He patted the space beside him.

DaNann eyed him closely. "Why do I get the feeling things are going to go from bad to worse?"

"Because you are wise."

"If I am so wise, why do I not know what you are about to tell me?" DaNann questioned.

"Because this is something I worked hard to keep from you."

DaNann hesitantly sat beside her long time friend and waited.

"There was a time in my life that I thought this news would be joyous to you, but now I fear it will only bring you more pain." He paused for a moment as he took her hands into his. "You thought that your family ended when Haidee died, but it didn't. Haidee had a child with Cian." Ke-Hern paused again to give the Queen a little time to absorb this information.

DaNann nodded her head as she slowly started to draw her hands out of Ke-Hern's.

"Haidee had a daughter not long before Sobus appeared. Her nursemaid hid the baby away, saving her." He waited again. "Her name is Eirian, our Eirian."

DaNann shot up from her seat and backed away from Ke-Hern's hunched figure.

Ke-Hern's soft eyes implored her to listen as he continued, "That is why Eirian as an infant never went into the void. That is why she aged while others didn't. That is why she has more talents than others," he whispered.

She stared at him. "But why not tell me. Why keep this from me? You knew how hard it was on me to lose Haidee."

"I was keeping it more from Sobus than you. I was even able to keep it from most of the Faeries." He looked back at her, sadness in his eyes. "There is more that you need to know. Sobus has found out about her, and I worry about what he will do."

"You must bring her here!" she yelled back at him, "You can't protect her out there." DaNann hurried to the window and closed her eyes, searching for Eirian's energy print.

Ke-Hern rushed to her, grabbed her by the shoulders and spun her around. "You can't do that. You have to hold back. We don't want to give Sobus any more help."

"But she will be left open to his powers."

"She has her own power and talents. Broan is taking care of her in Solveig. He'll keep guard over her until she is healed."

"HEALED! What happened?"

"Calm down." Ke-Hern pulled DaNann back to the bench and forced her to sit. "Broan meant to keep Eirian safe and unfortunately landed up giving her to the Ny-dick."

"WHAT THE HELL!"

"Calm down DaNann. It's not how it sounds. Somehow Sobus discovered her, but left her...I know he realized who she was...yet he left her." Ke-Hern patted the Queen's hands. "So she is safe in Solveig and knowing Broan, recovering well. Our biggest problem is figuring out the next step to take against Sobus while keeping Eirian safe."

"If Sobus has entered her mind, we will be hard pressed to..." A shiver ran through DaNann's body. "Bring her to me now!"

Ke-Hern put his arms around DaNann and hugged her. "No. We need to wait this one out, no matter how hard it is for you."

"Alright then..." She raised her head and looked at Ke-Hern. "I'm going to the Walled City. NOW!"

"NO!"

"We have to. If Sobus wants me, then so be it. I'll draw him away from her and I will face him, as he wanted. That way you'll have time to save Eirian. Now get ready to leave. I know you are the one who holds me prisoner here, not the Ancients as you led me to believe." She raised one eyebrow as she stared at him.

Even though walking was still exhausting for Eirian, she often wandered about Solveig, pushing to build strength in her muscles. One day she was so wrapped up in a self-dialogue that she found that she had walked near a group of people. She stood still for a moment and watched. The mood was sunny and everyone was animated. When the topic shifted to her, everyone became darker and more emotional, causing a palatable stir of apprehension.

Uncomfortable and holding back tears, Eirian walked away. It was becoming more and more apparent that this was not a place to call home for her and her unborn child. "It really doesn't matter. It won't be long now and I'll be leaving," she muttered to herself, knowing damn well it did matter…a lot.

"Are you sure you can break the last of the curse?" Sobus' voice cut in.

"I'll do whatever I have to."

"Then know that you have to be ready to use your Off-World powers. There will be no avoiding it." Sobus paused and then continued slowly, *"You do know how to use it, don't you?"*

"Sure…" Eirian stumbled with the lie.

"Tell me the truth now. Ke-Hern did teach you, didn't he?" He waited for a reply which he knew would not be coming. *"I see. Then, that just means I will have to, once you are fully recovered. How does that sound?"*

She smiled. "It sounds very nice. Thank you."

"Until then I'd advise you not to play with your power. You'll need all of it. Fighting off an evil Queen is not simple."

Eirian shifted her thoughts and focused on her leaving. There were things she was going to need and gathering them slowly, before anyone got wise to her plan, was the best way. With effort, she entered the Keep.

Eirian peeked in the Main-Hall. There was no one there, yet a soft resonance could be heard. It was alive and real and drew her in. She started to cross the hall, wondering if the composition was coming from the side entrance they used to bring in food from the kitchen hut. Startled, Eirian suddenly stopped. There in the middle of the floor, its trap door left open, was the entrance to the dungeon. Dizzy by the sight of it, she reached back and guided herself down on a bench.

The dungeon was no more than a deep hole in the middle of the Main-Hall. Over time, whenever the hall was washed down and cleaned, the degraded food and dirty wash water was simply thrown down it, never giving it a second thought. After a while the smells from the sewer pit crept out in the hall and a rug was place over it to block out both the smells and the sounds of rats feeding.

"There you are," V-Tor said as he entered the Main-Hall. "Ready for an adventure?"

Startled, Eirian jumped up and turned to face him. "What did you say?" she asked nervously.

"You heard me." V-Tor looked a little offended. "I asked you if you're up to an adventure…among the trees." He stopped in front of her and crossed his arms over his chest. "Unless you're too scared…I mean…with Broan and…"

She smiled, "Forget Broan!"

"Good." His smile deepened as he took her arm and linked it to his.

Eirian glanced back at the dungeon only to find it closed and safely tucked under a rug once again. Unnerved, she realized the music was gone as well.

Eirian and V-Tor sat comfortably tucked among the trees inside the wall. He had set up everything before he had gone to find her. There were blankets to keep away the season's chill and simple foods to lengthen the stay. This was as close as he could get them to actually being outside the fortress.

Eirian smiled, not missing a thing in V-Tor's behavior. There was some unintentional humor in this situation. "Adventure among the trees. . . . right?"

"Broan is the very epitome of a committed, intense Warlord. He may be busy, but he does have his eyes on you."

"He keeps his eyes on all the prisoners."

V-Tor scowled a little, "You are not a prisoner!"

"Well the wrist band says otherwise. Besides, if this is how the great Broan treats guests, I'll be glad upon leaving."

V-Tor's scowl turned rapidly into a pained look. "You shouldn't talk about leaving. You know you have a place here in Solveig." He paused briefly and then smiled. "Now do you want to play the dice game or not?"

"I get first roll." Eirian took the bag that held the dice and removed them. The dice were identical in weight and size. Both had six corresponding pictures, one for each of their sides. Matching them up at the end of a roll was the purpose of the game. It took some skill and a whole lot of luck. Eirian cupped the dice in her hands and whispered to them.

"Hey! Hey! No magic here. This is to be a good and honest game."

Eirian smiled and then laughed out loud. Moments with V-Tor had lately become playful, full of teasing, laughter and jokes. He seemed to be able to sooth the worry in her mind.

Raising her hands, Eirian shook the dice and then let them roll. Fragments of music came to life as the dice toppled over each other. Eirian looked at V-Tor, wondering if he had heard it to. She watched as he bent over to read the dice. He laughed, but his laughter was dulled and subdued by the resonance still coming from the dice. She watched intently as V-Tor blew on the dice in his hand and tossed them her way. The dice generated a wild variety of tones both harmonic and clashing, randomly playing the multitude of combinations the dice rolled through. Eirian closed her eyes feeling the reverberations enter her. She was mysteriously taken away by sounds both lofty and mundane.

The word 'sorry' woke her, as did the touch of a hand on her shoulder.

"What?" she asked a little confused.

"Sorry. I've not been taking care of you. I guess I was feeling so good about this precious bit of fun we were having that I over-taxed you. I'll get you back to your room so you can rest."

Eirian's hand reached up to cover his. "No. No. I'm fine. Let's at least finish the game."

"You were dozing off," V-Tor said as he rose and pulled back his hand. "Are you too tired to walk?"

"NO!"

"Good. It is that or over my shoulder, and I'm not sure what Broan would think of that." He reached out his hand, offering to help her up. "Come. Next time we'll stay longer."

BroMac pulled himself out of bed early with a deep need for the comfort of the wilderness. He was not prone to suffering from exhaustion and depression, yet he felt a sense of wariness since returning to Solveig. After rolling and stretching out his injured shoulder, he quietly dressed, not wanting to disturb Faber or Jelen. He silently made his way out of the hut. On the surface, Solveig looked bright and clean with a dusting from the first snowfall, but deep down it was sad, and he knew it.

Glad to have the morning to him, BroMac walked to the stable. He needed to get away. Within minutes, he was riding over the scuff of snow and along the fringe of a thick forest.

Delighted to be out of Solveig, BroMac stopped his horse. He closed his eyes and lifted his face to the sky. There was a small sunbeam that slipped past the thick branches of the trees. It felt good to feel the warmth on his face. But he was puzzled. "It is the same sun. Why do I feel that it reaches me out here and not in Solveig?"

"Because you are NOT in Solveig, which I fear is under a spell."

BroMac twisted around. There were large rocks in a jumbled pile that looked as if they had been dropped in a heap from the very hands of the gods. As he studied them, one somehow bounced off the pile and rolled to the bottom. Soon the illusion of a mound of rocks vanished. In its place stood a creature of flesh and blood.

BroMac immediately went for his sword, but all Stamas did was smile, and then sensing the need to break the ice, he spoke. "I mean you no harm. I just need an answer to a question that only one from inside of Solveig can answer."

BroMac's eyes narrowed. "Who are you?" he asked boldly.

"I am Stamas. I am a friend of Eirian's. Lord Broan has met me and will recognize my name."

BroMac kept his sword raised and pointed at the Giant. "So what is your question?"

"Is Eirian alright? Ke-Hern said…"

"All Wizards are an absurd lot!"

"Yes…But is Eirian alright?"

"She is alive and healing." BroMac lowered his sword a little.

"Solveig has become dim and dreary. There is a feeling of sadness and agitation that coats everything there. Tell Eirian to beware. Magic is involved and it's highly possible that it involves Off-World magic."

BroMac glanced in the direction of Solveig. "Off-World magic! We just fought a war for the Queen. Why would she put a spell on us now?"

"I do not sense that the Queen is involved, but I fear someone blacker has put his hands on Solveig."

All the disheartening moments in Solveig suddenly came back to BroMac. Since returning home things had never been quite the same as they had been before the war. The poignant reality of what this Giant was saying hit him hard. A deep chill crept out of his heart and into his veins. "So what can we do?"

"Keep Eirian safe."

"No, I mean the curse. What can we do about the curse?"

"Nothing." Stamas closed his eyes. "I would join her if I could, but I cannot. Giants may travel through the land, but only through the land of nature, not Mortal made."

"But there has to be something we can do," BroMac insisted.

323

Stamas shrugged. "I have no power over magic but Eirian on the other hand...may hold the key...so she needs to be kept safe. Tell Broan, he'll understand."

"Great!" BroMac muttered as he threw up his arms.

Stamas cocked his head to one side and studied BroMac. "There is something else though, one more thing about Eirian that is important..."

As soon as BroMac returned to Solveig he pulled Laeg and V-Tor aside. "Come with me," he grumbled as he led them to his hut. "Take a seat," he suggested as he went to the fire and began warming his hands. The talk with Stamas had left him with a chill that went deep into his bones.

Laeg sat in a chair, and V-Tor perched himself on the arm of it. "Okay, we're sitting. What's on your mind?" V-Tor asked.

"You know a Giant name Stamas don't you?"

"Yes..." Laeg answered as he looked up at V-Tor. "What's this about?"

"I bumped into him in the woods. He told me that there is a dark spell that hangs over Solveig. He's right because even I can feel it." BroMac turned and looked at Laeg and V-Tor. Both of them were nodding their heads.

"I think everyone feels it," Laeg said. "So why not go straight to Broan? Why tell us first."

"Because Stamas also told me something else that is not as easy to confirm, something that Broan is not aware of ..." BroMac paused, "He said Eirian is carrying."

"Pregnant!" Laeg and V-Tor shouted together.

"Quiet!" BroMac hushed as he stepped nearer. "So what do I do? Tell Broan without knowing if it's true or not? Adding more problems to the mess when it could be all for nothing."

"Well you could always just ask her." V-Tor suggested.

"HOW? Do I just march to her and demand to know?"

V-Tor shrugged his shoulders. "Well you've done it in the past... although it didn't get you anywhere."

"This isn't funny." BroMac hissed. "The spell is big enough of a problem but if she's pregnant then what?"

"Ask Faber to ask her," Laeg interjected. "She's been helping Eirian a lot. It would make more sense coming from her."

"You're right..." BroMac paused and thought about it. "I'll talk to her later...first I need to tell Broan about the curse."

"Well let's go," V-Tor suggested as he headed for the door. "By the way did Stamas tell you how to get rid of this spell?"

It was the middle of the night and Eirian was still in a deep dream state, as she entered the shadowy Main-Hall. She had followed murmured words and unusual sounds from her room to here. Her eyes were closed as she lingered in the reverberation of exotic patterns and pitches around her. It was as if the sound itself had massive roots, which snaked around her, embracing her, dancing her nearer and nearer to the opened dungeon door.

Suddenly, she was overcome with intense deafening sound. Every aspect of Solveig, each item and element that made up the world around her became alive with its own tone. She bent forward, covering her ears, trying to block out the overwhelming noise.

Eirian landed with a thud. Pieces of half-rotten food and the heavy smell of spilt ale and mead, and other things she tried hard not to think of, greeted her as she landed in the middle of it. She scraped away the mess from her face and began to gag. Shocked, she stood up, now aware of where she was. To help keep her balance in the watery muck, she stretched her hand out to the earthen wall. A twinkle of gold was just peaking out of the dirt wall right in front of her. She slowly released it from its prison only to find it was a small ring. Confused by her find, she began studying it. Suddenly Eirian raised her head just in time to catch a brief glimpse of a hand lowering the trap door. "NO!" she screamed, but darkness engulfed her, and her childhood fear manifested itself into cold reality.

With unwavering determination, Broan and a group of riders passed the huts and the fields that overlooked the river. He didn't want to relive the bloody images of what could have happened to Eirian, but with each passing minute he was finding it harder and harder not to. He hadn't heard from Nerlena for some time now, but she suddenly crossed his mind. She had quietly latched onto his thoughts, and with humming reverberation, she amplified the need to go back to Solveig. Broan swiftly turned Zantro around and picking up the pace, he rushed back towards his fortress.

Pulled by an unseen source and following the weak song, Broan rode his horse all the way up to the front steps of the Keep. He jumped from his saddle and ran into the building. At least he now knew she was within the walls of the Keep, now he just had to figure out where. He re-entered the Main-Hall and paused. He closed his eyes and listened with everything he had. He could barely hear a faint, well-muffled sound. "Where is that coming from?" he asked out loud.

"From the dungeon I think. I noticed it this morning when I came for the morning meal."

Broan looked back at Leif. "And you told no one of it?"

Leif shrugged his shoulders. "Everyone seemed so busy. Besides it's probably some animal that got trapped down there. You know rats feed down there at times. Jelen and I have both seen them, with their beady eyes and slick bodies."

Broan pushed Leif aside and cursed again at the innocence of a young mind. He cleared the area around the dungeon trap door and then with a great heave, opened it. The trap door landed on the tile and stone floor with a resounding crash. His mood quickly slid from dread to a relief. Unable to move his eyes from Eirian, Broan called over his shoulder to Leif. "Get the ladder. It is over by the side wall."

Drenched with filth and filled with fear, Eirian slowly climbed the wooden ladder until she reached the last rung. Broan grabbed her and pulled her up the rest of the way causing the sudden light to sting her eyes.

Broan picked Eirian up into his arms. With surprising tenderness, he looked down at her. "You need rest and… a good bath. You stink!"

"So kind, as always." Eirian said as she peered over Broan's shoulder. She could still hear the complex hidden sounds that spoke to her and her alone.

"So how did you get down there?" Broan asked as he mounted the stairs.

"It is too illogical to explain, but I will say someone closed the door on me even though I screamed for them to stop."

"Someone wanted to trap you down there?" Broan scowled. "It looks like I have no other choice than to keep you close at hand. After your tub, you'll be locked in my room."

"What?" she gasped.

"Until Ke-Hern tells me it is okay to let you go free, you'll stay where I can watch over you."

All her hopes of being able to go to the battlefield outside of the Walled City came crashing down around her. "You can't do this to me."

"I can and will."

Her eyes narrowed as she stared at him. "You sir, are… "

"Your guardian." Broan dropped her into the deep tub, turned on the water. "Someone will be in with clean clothes. I've got things to do." Very smugly he left the bathing room.

"We don't have much time," Sobus yelled into Eirian's head as she was just pulling the last of her clean clothes over her head *"Ke-Hern has let the Queen out of her cage and she's on her way to the Walled City!"*

"What?"

"You have to go to the Walled City and say the blessing. Hopefully it will not be too late."

"Too late?"

"If you get there quickly you may have time to release your kin before she changes things. If not, you know what needs doing. I'll be there to help as soon as I can. Now that she's freed she can't sense me like before. Hurry!"

Eirian looked around the hallway, unsure as to what to do next. "How will I get past Broan?"

"You'll have to use some of your weather talent," he whispered.

"But I have a binding cord on."

"Eirian have you not realized that the binding cord is not real? It is nothing more than a trick?"

"What!"

"I'm sure Broan meant well."

"Yeah right!" Eirian glared at stairs as she turned and rushed down them, taking two at a time. Angrily, she pushed open the door to Broan's bedroom.

"What are you doing?" Sobus asked a little panicked.

"Getting my Faery clothes. Broan hid them from me, and I want them back!"

"But you are wearing clothes good enough for the trip. Listen, you need to get to the Walled City now. There is no time for this silliness."

"Wrong! There is no way I will be coming back, and I am not about to leave them behind. If I have to face the Queen, I want her to know who I am. So, help me, or shut up!"

"Good point, very good point." Sobus paused for a moment before continuing, *"It would be powerful to remind her just who you are and what she has done. Fine…but hurry!"*

Once Eirian found her clothes, she ran back into the bathing room and changed. As she passed Broan's room again, she angrily tossed her borrowed Mortal clothes and the useless binding cord in the doorway.

Quickly she made her way to the stable. She needed a fast horse, one that would find its way back home once she was finished making her escape. Squaring her shoulders, she walked down the row of stalls and straight up to Broan's horse. She touched his flanks as she whispered to him, "Are you up to a little adventure?" His head came up from the feed bin and snorted dust at her. "Hmm. Well if you don't want to go for a run, just say so and I'll take V-Tor's horse."

Zantro snorted at her as he began to back up out of its stall, which delighted Eirian. She stroked his side, happy he had decided to help her. "You know it is only for a short time. You can go back to him as soon as I'm done." The horse shook his head, making Eirian laugh. "Now don't tell me you're mad at him too." She jumped on, grabbed Zantro's mane. "Now for a little distraction," she said. "What would slow Broan down the most?" Rain was her best bet. The clouds where already there so she just warmed them and then stripped what moisture she could get from the mountains and lakes. The clouds grew heavy rapidly, and with a snap of her fingers it started to rain in sheets.

The storm caught everyone by surprise. The heavy rain blocked their vision and mystified them all. Broan was just leaving his den when BroMac walked in soaking wet. Stunned Broan looked at him, "Snow in summer and rain in winter!" He paled. "Eirian is up to something…"

"Like escaping, are you coming?" BroMac said as he turned swiftly and exited the Keep.

Broan ran out of the Keep and followed BroMac to the stable. He rushed down the row of stalls only to come to a sudden stop. "SHE took Zantro! She stole my horse!" He slammed his fist into the railing and started to curse again. He grabbed another horse and mounted it bareback. "If Zantro doesn't kill her, I think I will!" he yelled as he charged out the gate after her.

"She really did it this time. It's bad enough to run away, but to steal his horse. That's just mean!" BroMac stated to the others as they charged out after Broan.

With thick clouds overhead, and an infrequent break in the rain, Broan was finding it hard to pinpoint Eirian's trail. "*Where is she going,*" he wondered. "*Stamas?*" He quickly stopped his horse and turned. "BroMac! Where did you say you came across the Giant?"

BroMac raised himself up as best as he could and looked around. "It's not far from here." Taking the lead, BroMac rode away towards west.

Nearly an hour had passed and there still wasn't any sign of Stamas. "You think he would be on our side and leave us some sign," Broan muttered out loud, still angry that Eirian slipped away. "Keep her safe…keep her safe… How the hell do you keep a crazy Faery safe?" He looked at the mountains ahead of them and closed his eyes briefly. The first real winter snow was near. You could feel it in the air. It created urgency within him. "She won't last a day out there if the snow comes."

"Not true," Stamas said. "She has lived all her life out here."

"As a Faery, not a Mortal."

"True." Stamas studied Broan for a moment and then said. "Lord Broan. You must take her to the Walled City, and she needs to go now."

"Not you too!"

"There is no way around this. Either you do it or I do. Which is it?"

"Okay, okay. We'll leave in two days, with a proper guard and camp."

Stamas crossed his arms across his chest. "No, now. The others can catch up to you quickly enough."

Broan glared at Stamas. "FINE! Now where the hell is she?"

"Go due south. When you reach the second creek, follow it east until you reach a sharp bend. Just beyond it is the cave I've set her up in."

Eirian could hear the thunder of horse hoofs crashing down on the stones along the creek. She swung herself onto Zantro's back and whispered a few words into his ears. The horse took off in a flash. Now it was a race to get away from whoever was after her.

Zantro did not slow at all as he galloped down the slope of the hill, causing Eirian to grab on tighter. She chanced a glance over her shoulder. In the dim light she caught the sight of riders coming full speed after her. She tapped on the horse's side with her hand. "If you don't want to feel the wrath of Broan, you better make good our escape." That was all it took. Zantro charged forward. Every second took them farther and farther away from Broan, and closer and closer to the Walled City.

A sharp and clear whistle cut through the air. Zantro stopped with a skid, loose rocks and frozen chunks of ground spraying out before them. Eirian dug her fingers deep into Zantro's flesh, to stop her from flying over his head and onto the ground. The whistle came again. Zantro tossed his head about and turned towards Broan and the group.

"Traitor!" Eirian muttered, knowing this was the end of her escape. She waited for the verbal storm that was coming. Instead Broan calmly said, "You can stop this damn rain, I'll take you to the Walled City. BUT you move one inch away from us and you'll be VERY sorry. Understood?" Broan then looked at his group of men. "BroMac, you take charge of Solveig. Send the others tomorrow. The rest of you are with me."

Eirian wasn't sure if she liked this cool Broan. Usually his temper was visible, not seething just below his skin. Yet for the last three days he had been…she didn't know what. He didn't even argue about letting her have her own mount, although he reminded her to stick with the group or pay the price.

Late that afternoon they could just spot the white shimmer of the city's walls on the horizon. Even though they still had some distance to go, Eirian could clearly hear the Faeries frantic voices which evoked uneasiness within her. It was getting harder to seal away her heart from the cold reality of those in the void. Eirian risked a quick glance towards Broan and regretted it. Immediately his cold blue eyes met and held hers, warning her to keep her promise. Eirian dropped her gaze, still uncertain if she should tell him what she needed to do. Her retreating strength, to keep the voices at bay, worried her. With shaky optimism, Eirian nudged her horse nearer to Broan.

Broan watched her approach and gave her a controlled, pinched smile. She backed off a little. "Tired of eating dust?" he asked.

"Just wanted to know if we were going straight into the Walled City or camping tonight?"

"I feel it is safer to go directly in to the city." He studied her. "Was there a point to your question?"

"Could we stop on the field first?"

"No."

"Please. You have to let me…"

"NO! The sooner we are inside the walls, the better," Broan snapped.

Eirian looked towards the Walled City. With each step her horse took, the bombardment of emotions from the battle field grew. Eirian was finding it hard to breathe and harder to think. Eirian strained to stay focused over the raging demands of the fallen Faery warriors. She closed her eyes and hummed a tune hoping to block out their cries but they seeped in anyway. She reined in her horse and fell back to ride with Laeg and V-Tor.

"Are you alright?" Laeg asked noticing how pale she was.

Eirian didn't answer him. She shivered visibly. Like a magnet, the need of her kin pulled hard at her. She kept looking towards the field that came and went into view as they rode past clumps of forest. She urged her horse forward, leaving Laeg and V-Tor wondering what was wrong.

Once beside Broan, Eirian opened her mouth to ask if they could stop again, but nothing came out. The clash between her promise to Broan and her kin produced an emotional storm. The cries of the fallen filled her head and drowned out any sense or words that she needed to say.

Suddenly Eirian bolted away from Broan, crashing through the forest that separated her from the battlefield.

Broan's stallion was used to tight places and battle. It charged at Eirian's mare, trying to pin it against a tree to stop it from escaping. Just as Broan managed to grab on to Eirian's tunic, a branch whipped Broan in the face. He wiped the blood from the cut with the back of his hands and with one swift pull, he had her off her horse and across his lap. "Move one inch and I'll..." he barked.

"Please Broan. They were calling to me!" she cried. Tears of frustration choked her. "I'm, sorry."

"Not another word," Broan cursed as he yelled at RohDin to take her horse. He then quickly rode on to the Walled City.

"You!" Broan growled, startling Eirian. "YOU..." He stopped himself once again for he knew he would lose his temper. "What do I have to do to get through to you? I've tried everything - threats, patience, everything short of putting you in the dungeon myself. I can't continue like this, Eirian. You make me so angry," he paused, and then quietly said, "This is hopeless!"

Eirian tried to sit up.

"Keep still. I warned you about moving. I'm not about to let you slip off my horse and have you run away."

"Could I please sit upright?" she asked as she raised her head a little to look at him.

Broan pushed her head back down. "No and I also warned you about saying anything. Do you NOT know how to listen?"

Eirian let her head drop. She was so exhausted from her internal battle. "Please," she begged. "I need to sit upright."

"No." Broan replied heatedly as he pushed his horse to a gallop. "You don't listen, you pay the price." At full speed Broan quickly covered the space between the convoy and the Walled City. He charged through the gate. Not slowing down one bit, he kept going until he was outside the main residence of Iarnan.

People had gathered around to welcome the hero but froze at the sight of Eirian. Still in her Faery clothes, her position exposed a very nice butt. This only made things worse for her as the crowd started to laugh. Eirian started to kick and squirm. She wanted nothing more than to get away from him, and away from the laughter.

"What is going on?" Iarnan yelled at the sight of Eirian. "BROAN, let her down. This is no way to treat someone who has helped us so much." He turned and looked at the crowd. His stare made them all stop laughing. Then he walked up to Broan's side and gave him a heated glare. "What on this land is going on?"

"Eirian is learning a lesson."

"And what would that lesson be?"

Broan eased Eirian off his lap. "Obedience."

As soon as her feet touched the ground Eirian backed away, bumping into Iarnan. "He treats me like an animal," she hissed.

"Well you act and dress like one," Broan responded harshly.

Eirian's eyes narrowed as she squared her shoulders. "I am not like you or anyone else here, LORD Broan. I do not have land. I do not have home or even kin anymore. I don't have rooms with trunks full of clothes and valuables. I only have what's on my back. You may not think it is much or worthy, but it is mine, and I wear it with pride."

"Enough of this! Come Eirian I'll show you to your room," Iarnan said as he took her arm. He gave Broan a quick glance of disapproval.

"Oh no you don't," Broan glared at her. "You can't trust this one, once a Faery always a Faery. You're best to just put her in my room."

His words were needlessly cruel. It was too much. Eirian froze and looked at the stunned faces in the crowd. She had no come back for it, no witty phrase, no redirection to make light of it, or even anger to attack it.

"She will be placed in a room near me and away from you," Iarnan announced firmly as he guided Eirian away.

The Queen watched from her window. She held back from using Off-World power on Broan. She would have loved to see him shaped like the jackass he was. Her fingers twitched with desire. Why Ke-Hern thought Eirian was safe around Broan was beyond her understanding.

Broan cursed himself. What had come over him? He deserved her hate. Easing on the reins, he nudged his horse to move away from the emotional battlefield that had just been bloodied and went on towards the stable.

The stable was dim and quiet. Broan needed time to think. He refused the stable boy's help, deciding to take care of his horse himself. One moment he was standing there, placing his saddle on the rail, and the next he was on the floor with V-Tor on top of him. Broan tried to move, but V-Tor was not going to allow it. Annoyed, Broan used all his might to force him off his back. "What is this all about?"

V-Tor rose to his feet but pressed Broan back down. "If you ever come within a mile of hurting her, I'll…"

"Oh save it," Broan said annoyed. "It was only heated words."

V-Tor angrily shook his head. "You have come a lot closer to physically hurting her than you may think."

Broan raised an eyebrow and looked at V-Tor. "Words may sting but they do not kill."

Calmly, Laeg walked his horse into its stall. "Eirian is carrying your child. At least we still hope she is."

"That was not for you to say!" V-Tor yelled as he stormed towards Laeg.

"Sometime secrets cause more damage than they are worth." Laeg then took up a brush and tossed it to V-Tor. "Start putting all that anger to good use."

"Are you sure?" Broan asked as he rose to his feet and dusted himself off.

"When has Faber ever been wrong?" Laeg removed his saddle and looked at Broan. He glared at him as he continued, "And don't say it's not yours, or I'll be the next to knock you over, and it will not be as easy getting me off of you." He shook his head as he went back to work on his horse. "So if you come within a mile of hurting her, it will be ME not V-Tor who raises a sword against you. Trust me."

"For two souls who know a lot, why didn't you tell me sooner?"

"Faber said it was up to Eirian to tell you. But," Laeg continued, "since the way you treat her has put THEM in danger, I thought now was better than later."

Mid-day light seeped away as the evening darkness leached in to its place. Eirian woke with a start. It felt like she had just closed her eyes, yet the room was dark and quiet. She didn't know how long she had slept. Was it evening now or early morning? She turned to check the window she slept under and almost screamed when she caught Laeg looking down at her.

He was sitting above her on the windowsill. "Have a good nap?" he asked, jumping off the sill and landing gracefully on the floor beside her. "Are you hungry?" He stretched out his hand to her, waiting to help her up off the floor.

Eirian stared as she studied him. "I can manage on my own," she said as she pushed herself up. "How did you get in?"

"Iarnan." He shrugged, "There is a lot happening this evening and he wanted to make sure you were fed and not overwhelmed by all the celebrations."

She started to shake her head. "I have a blessing to do and the sooner the better."

"Not tonight. Besides you don't have a choice." Laeg pulled her along as he walked towards the door. "AND, you don't need to worry.

V-Tor and I are going to make sure Broan doesn't come within a mile of you."

"Some comfort that is now."

He smiled at her. "Look, I'd really love to take you to your first celebration. It will be lots of fun." Laeg checked Eirian's eyes to see how much resistance she was going to give him. "Come on. You know, if I don't show up with you soon, Iarnan and Lady Holt will come to drag you about the city…with Ryu in tow. At least with me and V-Tor you'll have lots of muscle to protect you from the two beasts called Broan and Ryu."

Eirian half smiled and then nodded. "But…I still…"

"No buts… let's just have some fun for now." Laeg stepped back and gave her the once over, "Here," he said as he picked up a coarse woolen shift. "I think this over your Faery clothes will make things more comfortable for you."

The evening with Laeg and V-Tor was enjoyable. It was lovely chaos as people danced and sang in the streets of the Walled City. The carnival atmosphere prevailed all around her as she wandered in and out of shops and courtyards, yet she still couldn't fully release herself from the pull of the battlefield. It weighed heavily on her mind and her spirit. To make matters worse in the midst of all this, Ke-Hern spotted her. One minute she was next to Leag and V-Tor, and the next she was hurrying through the arched gateway.

V-Tor responded quickly. Catching up to Eirian, he pulled hard on her arm, making her stop. "Do you care to tell me what that was all about? I thought you and Ke-Hern were friends?"

"Were says it all."

"It's okay. If you want us to keep him away we will," Laeg said catching up to them.

V-Tor playfully started to make a list on the palm of his hand. "I don't know the list is getting very long: first Broan, then Ryu and now Ke-Hern. Anyone else?"

"If you're not quiet you'll be next," Eirian laughed, taking hold of both men's arm.

The pub was nestled back from the main street. Its warm wood interior and large hearth had welcomed many over the years. Soldiers especially liked coming to this pub because the ale was cold and the women were pretty.

Achurst, Ryu's lieutenant, watched as RohDin and Ardis walked into the pub. "Now it starts," he said. "Here come some of Broan's men."

Dolny, another lieutenant, took a gulp of his ale and wiped his mouth on the back of his sleeve. "What starts? We are all on the same side."

"You drink too much Dolny," Achurst said as he pushed at his friend. Turning back to his drink he watched RohDin from over his mug.

Dolny followed his friend's gaze, and then whispered, "The truth is, our timing couldn't have been worse when it came to the last battle. While we sat safely inside these walls, Broan's blended army fought victoriously."

"What are you talking about? We were there when needed. We were there to end the mess Broan created," Achurst hissed.

"Slow out of the gate I'd say, and I'm sure RohDin would agree."

Achurst pushed Dolny almost off his stool. "We followed Ryu's command and who better to follow? Ryu has got all the makings of being one of the best captains around, even better than Broan. In fact rumors are that someday Ryu will be given the position of Warlord of Solveig."

Dolny glared at his friend. "Lord Broan won't let that happen, and you know it. He is smarter than Ryu. Just when you think you've seen all his army can do, he gets them to do even more. No, I doubt the Queen will take Solveig away from Broan."

"You are wrong about Ryu. Some could call his tactics devious, but his stunts have always worked out in the end. He has great value and integrity, and that is why he will become warlord."

Dolny's eyes scanned the tavern for RohDin again. "Obviously, only time will tell, as Ryu hasn't made payment for his misdirection in this war yet."

Achurst disliked his friend's tone and thought to leave when he was finished his ale. "A toast to Captain Ryu, one of the greatest warriors around," He yelled. He downed the drink, slammed his mug down onto the tabletop and stood up. Achurst looked at the other soldiers from his unit. "In all his battles, Captain Ryu has impressively lead us warriors to succeed, and that is worthy of my praise and loyalty."

"Hear! Hear!" screamed the soldiers from the Walled City.

"If you are so against our Captain, then maybe you should drink with Broan's men," Achurst hissed at Dolny as he started for the door of the hostelry.

RohDin rose from his seat and opened his mouth, much to Ardis' concern. "I'd say you all missed a glorious opportunity to show us that your bragging is more than hot air," RohDin called out to Ryu's men.

"We delivered when it mattered most. We came to your aid and saved your sorry asses from the Ny-dick," a drunken soldier said, as he burped loudly, "In fact, as I recall, even your Faery friends couldn't help you in the end. They all just laid down and gave up."

"What do you know?" RohDin yelled. "There is a lot of difference between fighting for your life and fighting for honor. It was the most difficult thing they did, fighting for us all the while knowing that they ALL would die, victory or not."

Another soldier, bearing the colors of Ryu's division, started to laugh. "Broan's great army needed help from us and FAERIES. They didn't have a chance at victory alone, yet they dare to take all the glory."

"At least we fought," RohDin hissed back. Ardis came up beside him. "Enough," he said as he began to pull him to towards the door. RohDin smiled at the group of men. "It must have been a daunting task for Ryu to bring together an amazing group of fools who can't pull themselves together long enough to do the right thing."

Ardis pulled his blade out of his boot and pulled hard on RohDin's tunic just in time to avoid a mug of ale from hitting him. Out the door they ran together, out the door and into the cool night.

"You'll regret that someday," Ardis said as they walked away.

"Someday but not today," RohDin laughed.

Chapter 16

"It would not be destiny if it was easy."

- Wizard Ke-Hern

Eirian peeked out from the shadowy doorway and listened with great intensity. Satisfied, she made her move and glided down the cobblestone streets, moving from one shadow to another. Everyone had long ago sung themselves to sleep, but that still didn't make Eirian feel any safer. She paused near an archway that separated the core of the city from the more humble homes of the workers. She looked around still unable to shake the feeling she was being followed... *"no watched,"* she said to herself, as she looked over her shoulder one more time.

Eirian quickly moved down the narrow street towards the gate that led outside to the ramp and the battlefield. "I hope you're happy, Laeg and V-Tor. I wouldn't be doing this if you two had only been willing to help," she said out loud, still a little upset at the two of them. She chided herself for once again needing to rationalize why she was darting away in the middle of the night, and then promptly reminded herself of Broan's anger, the reason for much of what she did these days.

Eirian looked up at the guard's watchtower and prayed. She hesitated briefly, wishing she could use some of her talent or power. *"Oh, it would make this so easy."* But she feared she would need all of her power and talent to face the future. She stood there quietly watching and after not seeing any movement up in the guardhouse, Eirian made her move. She rushed forward, under the torch light, under watchful eyes. She almost began to laugh. *"This is amazingly uncomplicated!"*

"Escaping from the Walled City is better done if you first get help from one who knows the way, Eirian," Ardis stated as he step in front of her. "She's over here, Laeg. I told you she was on the move."

Eirian froze! She couldn't believe it. She had just left them all sleeping with their heads down on the table and their hands still holding their empty mugs of ale. She quickly sidestepped away from Ardis but Laeg's arm easily reached out and caught her. "Do you know just how foolish and dangerous this is?" Laeg said more than annoyed. Eirian struggled against his hold. "Eirian stop it! I'll take you in the morning."

Eirian continued to resist but to no avail. He could have been a giant for the strength he used to hold her still. "Fine," she yelled, giving up her struggle. "Fine! Now let go." Laeg didn't let go but began the long walk back up the cobbled street away from the outer gate and freedom.

Eirian's resolve strengthened. She didn't want to go back towards the inner workings of the city and the crowds of sleeping people. She tried to dig in her heels but Laeg easily pushed them on at a steady pace. Laeg let out a deep sigh. "Eirian I'm trying to help. Now either we have an agreement about tomorrow, or we march straight up to Broan and let him know what you're up to."

Eirian gasped, "You wouldn't!" She twisted around and looked up at Laeg. "You told me you would keep him away from me, not feed me to him!"

Laeg didn't smile. "Well maybe you deserve Broan's treatment."

"I can't believe you just said that. No one deserves Broan's wrath." Eirian studied Laeg for a moment, amazed that he just sided with Broan. She lowered her eyes and turned away.

"Answer me now, Eirian. Tomorrow morning or do we go to Broan?"

"Tomorrow morning is fine," she answered.

"Good." Laeg started dragging her past where her room was.

"Where…where are we going? I said tomorrow is alright." Eirian sputtered.

"To the barracks so we can all keep an eye on you."

Early morning couldn't come soon enough for Eirian. She didn't sleep at all. With all the snoring and belching that happened in the barracks, along with all the lamenting cries of those stuck in the void waiting for her, how could she? The never-ending rush of need and obsession filled her constantly and yet she could do nothing about it but wait for Laeg to escort her to the battlefield.

When dawn came, Laeg was the last to wake. "You are worse than an old woman! Everyone else has long gone, even V-Tor. I never knew a warrior could be so slow at fulfilling his promises," she huffed.

"And I have never seen one so impatient in my life," he teased her. "Come on. Let's get this over with before Broan finds out."

"Yes please," she answered as she pulled him out the door and down the street.

Laeg allowed himself to be led. The Faeries had done their job, and his world was safer for it. Change had an opening now. Besides, if Eirian said she needed to bless the dead then as far as Laeg was concerned she should be able to do just that, with or without Broan's permission. Finally Laeg waved to the guards up in the watchtower, and together they eased their way through the smaller side door.

Once Eirian stepped off the ramp and on to the ground, she turned and with a silent prayer in her eyes asked Laeg to step back and allow her room to do her blessing. Laeg nodded and waited to watch the mystery of the Faeries unravel before him.

Even though Broan was with Iarnan and Ke-Hern, it didn't take long for him to find out that Eirian was outside the gates. His lack of sleep and growing frustration at his limited ability to keep Eirian safe made Broan roar with anger. "That is it! I'll have her tied to my waist from now on. That woman does not know how to stay put!"

"Maybe you haven't given her a reason to stay put, Broan. Have you thought of that?" Ke-Hern stated calmly as they rushed to the east gate.

"Would marrying her be reason enough?"

Iarnan looked at his nephew. "After entering the city with her across your lap, I don't think anyone would marry you. I mean if that's how you treat your love…"

Broan brushed off his uncle's comments and cursed under his breath. Suddenly the word 'trouble' rumbled through his head and an ill feeling soured his stomach. He moved at a brisk pace towards the gate. He rounded the wall of the last archway and rushed through the gate and stopped. "Stupid," he said out loud as he slapped the wall with the palm of his hand. There was Eirian and Laeg out on the battlefield alone. "Laeg, of all my friends," he groaned, feeling even more defeated, "He should know better than to take her out there without any guards."

Broan pointed to one soldier standing nearby. "Tell V-Tor to gather eight warriors and have them meet me here."

"But," the guard stammered.

"NO buts. Go!"

"But V-Tor and others are all ready out there."

Ke-Hern smiled at the young solider while waving him away. "Give her some space, Broan."

"SPACE?" Broan began yelling again. "There is no protection out there."

"But everyone needs space now and then. Even you do. And for Eirian there is no life without it."

"When I don't have to worry about her safety or about her running away I'll give her all the space she wants. BUT not now, not when anyone could be planning to kill her." Broan quickly started down the ramp.

Ke-Hern hooked Broan's cloak with his staff. "She's only doing what has been asked of her, a duty which most would have backed away from. She needs protection and she needs your strength now, not your condemnation."

A growl was all Ke-Hern got as Broan stormed away.

Eirian stood tall with her arms by her side. Slowly, her palms raised parallel to the ground as if searching for something. Her voice became powerful and clear and seemed to emanate from her very soul. Rising over the land, it sounded like a lament, ancient and lost in time. Ke-Hern watched with great inner pride and then sadness clouded his vision in the form of tears.

The Faeries' souls, weeks dead, rose over the battlefield like a creeping early morning mist. Thick and heavy, those that fought clung to the ground as they faced her. They were free of the void, that limbo in death. She had released them from the immortal blackness, but it wasn't over yet. The wind carried their woeful sighs as they moved on. Their home far to the north called to them now. That is where they would wait for her to finish what she started.

For so long Eirian had lived captive to the idea that freedom from the curse would come at the end of the battle or after the blessing. And now to find out still more was being asked of her, she felt despair rise within. She had hoped it would not come to this. Her body shivered at the stark reality of what her next step was. Sadly, Eirian watched her kin leave.

Broan gave Laeg a brief cold look as he came up beside him. "Are you finished Eirian?" He asked stepping closer to her.

She quickly became thoroughly annoyed. She didn't want him here and she didn't have time to put up with his ill humor. "Go away." She shouted. "Just leave me alone." Tears threatened to spill.

Broan felt horrible. Under her anger, Eirian sounded so lost. "Not until you are inside the gates," he said quietly.

Eirian stood with her back to Broan. She refused to look at him. She knew he couldn't help her, no one could. It was up to her and her alone and if she was wrong... Suddenly fear overwhelmed her, fanning the flames of her anger and revulsion. "Why must there be more to do?" She spat her words out with rage.

"I don't know," Broan murmured humbly. "But you are stronger than you think."

Blinking hard to restrain the tears, Eirian turned and looked at him. "I...I.." She closed her eyes. Her dismay was boundless.

Broan didn't hesitate to take her into his arms. His kindness shook Eirian to the bone and broke down her walls. She gave into him and began to cry. Raw pain and distress rushed out of her. "I failed them," she moaned. "They did not return to the flesh. They have been waiting since the battle for freedom, and I could not give it to them."

Broan looked up at the large group of Mortals high up on the parapet and noticed more peering out the crenellations. Word had spread and now a crowd was gathering. Nightmarish consequences flooded his mind. *"This unknown menace could be anywhere, even up there."* Gauging the danger they were in, he looked down at Eirian. "Come on let's go back inside the city. We can go find Ke-Hern. I'm sure he'll know what to do."

"No," she screamed as she fought to free herself from his grip. "Just leave me be!"

"Let her go," Laeg barked. Jaw squared and shoulders back, he stared at Broan. Broan's brow flinched as he raised his empty hands in front of himself, respecting Laeg's challenge. Laeg reached for Eirian, sword in hand and ready.

Eirian took Laeg's hand as she stepped angrily away from Broan. "Just stay away from me!" Eirian demanded her voice cracking. "Don't... ever..." She looked over her shoulder at Broan. He stood quietly saying nothing, nodding only slightly. He looked so dejected it startled her. A bright flush crept across her face. She turned not finishing her sentence and walked silently towards the harsh glory of her true destiny.

Queen DaNann leaned out the window of her quarters with little concern about her safety. "She has spoken the words!" She rushed away from the window and opened the door to her room and nearly bumped into Ryu.

"My Queen! Is everything alright?"

DaNann quickly stepped back. "Yes, yes, everything is fine. I was just going to go look for Ke-Hern. Have you seen him?"

Ryu gave the Queen a dazzling smile and then called over his shoulder to one of the appointed guards. "Go find the Wizard Ke-Hern and tell him the Queen requests his presence in her quarters." He turned slightly away from the Queen. "Now!" he ordered.

DaNann smiled back at Ryu. Somehow he breathed air into her life whenever she saw him. It was tantalizing for her to get his attention. He had come forward the night she and Ke-Hern had arrived and declared his life's purpose was to protect her at all costs. He brought with him unprecedented notoriety as well as a mountain of criticism.

Ryu liked the Queen for what she was, the ruler of the land. "May I come in and keep you company until Wizard Ke-Hern comes? It must be so lonely sitting all day in your room, but your safety is most important," he said sweetly.

DaNann stepped aside for Ryu and nodded her acceptance of his offer. Together they walked to the chairs on the other side of the sitting room.

"Wizard Ke-Hern is truly one of the most loved and respected men on this land," Ryu said as he leaned towards her and smiled. "But to say his first love is being a Wizard would certainly be wrong. He may have tried to fool everyone, but I know that you are his first love."

DaNann sat up straight. "You speak very boldly."

"I only speak the truth. His constant concern for your health and safety tells all." Ryu leaned a little closer to the Queen. "And I can tell by your blush that you have similar feelings for him. It is too bad those feelings are not for me."

DaNann raised one of her eyebrows. "Now you are just speaking badly."

Ryu smiled at her. "But I do speak the truth, at least about wishing."

Ke-Hern's knock on the door came sooner than Ryu had hoped for. He stood up and smiled down at the Queen. "That would be your Wizard. I leave you in good hands." He calmly walked to the door, and just before opening it, he turned and smiled at her. "Until later then."

"You requested my presence? Did you really say that?" Ke-Hern asked as he watched the door close behind Ryu. "You know Broan does not trust Ryu, and rightly so."

DaNann brushed off Ke-Hern's concern. "He is rather engaging once you get him talking. He is very thoughtful and knowledgeable about security and takes his position very seriously."

Ke-Hern looked at DaNann. "His actions are more calculated than you think. He hasn't changed any of his security strategies, which leaves openings for Sobus and makes us all the more vulnerable."

"He has had his men crisscrossing the land for days, securing the area. I've been told he saved Bronagh and some of Broan's wounded warriors against the Ny-dick...while he was injured himself."

"I'm just telling you not to let that calm demeanor fool you. Ryu is fiercely competitive and expects to be given Broan's position as Warlord. To him, being nice to you is just a way to get what he wants. I would still feel better if you would allow Broan to become your guard."

"Broan!" She narrowed her eyes. "Did you see the way he treated Eirian? No, Ryu will do fine. Besides, we both know being protected physically won't be much use as Sobus will attack mentally."

"Yes, I know, but at least allow a silly old Wizard some sense of security."

"No." DaNann got up from her chair and walked over to Ke-Hern. She took his hand into hers and smiled at him. "I know Eirian spoke the words."

Ke-Hern smiled down at his Queen. "Not much gets past you does it?"

Sobus didn't like having to act like a Mortal, but now that he was in the Walled City itself and with Ke-Hern and the Queen so close by, he had no other choice. He stood just inside the archway to the lower south area of the city. He watched as the whores sold their wares in bold fashion. The open fronts of their dress exposed a lot of flesh, and they often revealed their white legs by hiking up their shifts.

Sobus looked away, scanning the street for Mohr. He hated waiting for others at the best of times and this was definitely not the best of times. He needed a little inside help and that's all that kept him from leaving his spot.

Mohr rounded the corner of the street and looked over his shoulder, making sure his passage was unobserved. He worried that meeting Sobus in the daylight was too bold a move. Wearing a cloak, its hood pulled up over his head, he shivered slightly as nervous sweat trickled down his back. He looked along the wall of the crowded street and his step quickened when he saw Sobus. "In here," he said as he walked past and slid into one of the whorehouses.

Sobus looked around the small room Mohr had led him into. "So what news do you have?"

"Ryu is still in charge of security. Ke-Hern's pleading to the Queen to have Broan installed, has fallen on deaf ears. That doesn't mean Broan isn't doing something on his own. Between him and Iarnan, they plan to have Broan's men waiting for you."

Sobus rubbed his hands together and smiled. "The news just keeps getting better and better. It will be nice having Broan around to see the total defeat of his efforts. Nothing can save the Queen." He looked at Mohr through hooded eyes. "Tell me, which of Broan's men will be there?"

Mohr looked at his fingers, as if each finger was branded with a name. He started to name off the warriors, pushing a finger down for each, "There is V-Tor, one of Broan's best fighters."

"Yes I know. He is crafty. He darts in and out of holes created by his sword. Who else?"

"Laeg. His speed alone is enough to win battles, but then there are also his arrows, which always find their mark."

"Yes, well we'll see soon enough."

"And then there is Ardis. He's just as good as Laeg. He is the problem. He hides and takes note of everything with his sharp eyes and ears. He misses nothing."

Sobus raised an eyebrow and sneered at Mohr. "Much like you, I'd say." He looked Mohr up and down and then continued, "well except the warrior bit."

Mohr glared back at Sobus. "RohDin is about as well, getting into trouble from what I hear."

"Broan didn't bring that battering ram, BroMac with him did he?"

"No. I heard that BroMac is back at Solveig. Why?"

With a flick of his hand Sobus brushed off Mohr's question. "Tell me of Ryu. Tybalt has much faith in him."

Mohr took in a shallow breath. He had firsthand experience of the power Sobus could use if he wished information. "Ryu is loyal."

"Aww, but to who?"

Mohr looked down to the ground. "To Tybalt and himself. He does have a large part of Iarnan's army following him. Believe me, nobody can rally the troops quicker than he can." He paused briefly. "Especially when he is all fired up and determined."

"Well after the Queen's death, you'll have to have him visit me. I want to make sure he is loyal to me and only me."

"You know Ryu wants to be Warlord of Solveig. He's always wanted what Broan has and will do anything for it."

Sobus studied Mohr for a second. "Broan's soldiers are a different breed. They hold a loyalty out of respect, not duty. Once Broan is removed, they would be as good as gone. Ryu may move into Solveig, but it will not be to lead Broan's men." Sobus turned away from Mohr. "That is why Broan and his group will need to be the first to fall. They would only cause more problems than they are worth. Anything else?"

"Yes. I have prepared for your passage into the grand hall tonight. There will be a young girl outside waiting in the alley. She will walk you into the building through a side door. You may have to carry baskets of food, but no one will question you or be the wiser."

Sobus almost laughed at the thought of doing manual labor. "The things I do to get what I want. So be it. Until tonight then."

"But first…" Mohr reached out to grab Sobus' shirt then suddenly pulled back, unsure what kind of a response he would get. "I want more than a riddle. Tell me what I need to know to control DeSpon."

The Main Council Building was a brick and mortar-structured gem atop the only raised area in all of the Walled City. It stood five stories high with the guard station, kitchen, storage, and staff quarters on the main floor. A large staircase took you past all of that and up to the second floor, where the committee chamber was. Above it, were the living quarters for Iarnan and his wife, plus rooms for their guests. On the top floor was a grand hall for special occasions.

Up the doublewide staircase and through large walnut doors, you entered into a massive hall. Mosaic tile floors were surrounded by raw stone walls. It was an overwhelming room that stood at least two stories high. Half way up, against the sidewall, was a long balcony that overlooked the floor. It was used for musical players, singers or those giving speeches. Out of sight and behind it, was a staircase and walkway that the servants used, allowing them to move around without interrupting the proceedings. Along one of the exterior walls was a row of large glass doors that led out onto a terrace. From there the view of the streets of the Walled City was amazing. You could see the main water fountain and at least three of the seven arches that separated the different areas of the city.

The grand room was set for the evening's event. The atmosphere was quite jovial. Musicians played. A large blend of Mortals, from areas far and wide, mingled as they stood waiting for the Queen's arrival. Ryu and his men had stationed themselves at key points: the entrance of the hall, the door the Queen would be walking through and other strategic places along the walls and windows. Broan's men were a little more creative; they hid among the guests, various places along the food and wine tables, and most importantly, up in the rafters of the ceiling.

Still uncomfortable wearing the dress Governor Iranan sent her, Eirian started to smooth out the front of it. "Stop fusing," Laeg said as he stood next to her waiting to be announced. "You look normal for once."

"*Normal?*" Eirian chuckled to herself as she looked down at her bare feet and wiggled her toes. The small ring she found in the dungeon sparkled back at her. She shook her head. "Bronagh hid my boots. She said they were too worn out to be seen with this dress."

"Good," Laeg said as he stepped forward. "You won't be able to run away as fast."

In an effort to keep Eirian safe, Laeg was always looking over her shoulder, scanning the room and checking the positions of the other warriors in his group. His grip on her arm often tightened when uncertainty made him even more cautious.

For added protection Laeg had them stand well back in the crowd. Eirian was fine with that but Laeg's constant hold of her was a problem. There was still one thing more she would have to do for her kin.

Broan scanned the assembled group. He looked up at the roof beams at Ardis. It had taken a lot of effort to get the archers up there, but he was now glad they did. Most people don't look up, so the men were well hidden, and yet had full view of everyone in the room. He moved into the crowd and closer to V-Tor.

"Do you know where Eirian and Laeg are?" Broan asked as he stretched up on his toes to see if he could find them on his own. Suddenly Broan's heart stopped, his breath catching in his throat. The face of someone from his past, which still sported a malicious grin, stood not five feet from him. At that moment the horn blared and the crowd surged forward, all wanting a glance of the Queen. He watched as the evil face that still haunted him, faded back into the mass of Mortals.

Nerves raw with alarm, Broan scanned the assembly of cheering people. He found Laeg and Eirian near the edge of a group standing by the windows. He hurriedly started towards them, only to be cut off by Ryu's men. Broan turned in quick haste, seeking out another way to Eirian. Ryu's men were there as well. "Damn it! Get out of my way!" yelled Broan

"It's you who will have to move. Captain Ryu's orders are to keep you as far away from the Queen as possible." The solder smiled, enjoying his power over Warlord Broan. "The Queen is passing this way, so get lost."

"Fool!" Broan cursed moving back. There was no way he could get to Eirian from here. The room had been cut in two and they were on opposite sides. Spotting the balcony and servant's stairway, Broan quickly saw another opportunity and sprang into action.

Eirian finally spotted Sobus and started to walk that way, but was jolted to a stop by Laeg's grip on her arm. "No, this way," he said as he dragged her back to the edge of the crowd. Satisfied they were once again close to an escape route he let go of her for a moment only to have Eirian swiftly slip into the mass of bobbing heads.

It only took a second for Laeg to feel both failure and just plain anger. He jumped on top of a bench, trying to catch a glimpse of Eirian and motioned V-Tor to search for her as well. Looking up to the overhanging beams he caught Ardis' eye.

Ardis spied Eirian dipping in and out of a group of council members, inching her way closer to…not the Queen, so he wasn't sure where she was going. Feeling uneasy, he drew his arrow and waited. Seeing that, Laeg also pulled back on his bowstrings and lined himself up, ready to swiftly take aim.

"Eirian, look out," yelled Sobus. "They're going to kill you!" At the same time that he yelled at her, he raised his arm and sent a cold blue light towards the offending arrows, causing them to shatter as if made of ice.

Laeg was the quicker one. He managed to grab another arrow but fumbled with it, his heart and mind were lost to his mission. Thunder then echoed around him, pushing him into a strange black silence. He collapsed to the floor.

Ardis was able to let his second arrow go. It landed just a few inches in front of Eirian, stopping her. He quickly rolled back behind the support beam just avoiding the blast of light that shot up at him. He motioned to the other archers to find the source of the power and fire on it.

Wild winds came out of nowhere and tore at the soldiers. Their arrows scattered and broke and they quickly found themselves tilted on the edges of their perches. Just as quickly as the wind started to punish them, it stopped. The Queen smiled, pleased that her reflexes were quick enough to counter Sobus' spell.

With his sword and knife drawn, V-Tor charged through the confused assembly towards Eirian, ready to protect her at all costs.

347

Suddenly he was hit with an energy bolt and felt himself going down, deeper and deeper. It was as if the bolt wanted to bury him within the land itself. It kept pounding against his physical body, trying to do the impossible. It continued until he was unconscious.

Not wanting to be part of the Off-World fight, the rest of the gathering scattered to the edges of the room. Blackness suddenly filled the room, quickly settling on them. Doors slammed shut and locked, fireplaces closed up. People were crying and calling out names of friends and family, fearing the worst.

"Are you planning to waste all your energy on silly tricks that don't do more than put fear into these Mortals?" the Queen growled from across the room.

Sobus' laughter echoed into the darkness and then in a flash, light was bathing the room once again. He began his desperate search for Eirian and was pleased she was standing in the vacant area in the center of the hall. His smile deepened. Calmly, Sobus made eye contact with Eirian and spoke in a most soothing voice, "Come, my sweet child. It is not your fault that the blessing didn't work. Together we can fix that." Stretching his hand out to her he continued, "Come to me. I will protect you from those controlled by the Queen."

"Run Eirian," Ke-Hern yelled as he swiftly placed himself in front of Eirian, shielding her from Sobus, "He is a relentless, malevolent enemy - not one you can trifle with."

Eirian freed herself from his protection. She shook her head at Ke-Hern. "I will not listen to you ever again. You betrayed me from the moment of my birth. You have told me nothing but lies. So just leave me be."

"Going to him is not the answer Eirian. He's the cause of all the suffering, not the Queen."

Sobus didn't mind having Ke-Hern spew out his words. He was expecting that it would come to this anyway. He looked at Eirian, happy to see she was unaffected by his words. "For a Wizard you are not too smart are you?" And with that he blasted Ke-Hern with an energy bolt of lightning that tore through his flesh and tossed him across the room.

The servant's passageway was filled with chaos. Everyone was pushing and shoving their way, desperately trying to find a way out. Broan managed to get to the balcony and once there found things weren't any better. He needed to get to Eirian. He tried to push through those amassed on the balcony, but made no headway. Frustrated by his unsuccessful attempt, he finally jumped over the banister and onto the floor of the hall. Broan called to Eirian, but she did not turn or acknowledge him. All his frustration and worry amassed in that moment.

With a knife in one hand and his sword in the other, Broan started towards Sobus. "Leave her alone!" Broan warned, bringing the attention to himself. He succeded and the Queen was able to attack Sobus. Broan quickly veered, grabbed Eirian's hand, and started pulling her back towards the servant's staircase.

Eirian quickly pulled back. "No!" she yelled but Broan just pulled harder, not stopping for a second. They didn't make it very far before she was ripped from Broan's hand and he was tossed hard against the wall of stone.

"Sorry Warlord Broan, but I don't think the lovely Eirian wants to go with you. I'm not the enemy here, and she knows it," Sobus said smugly.

"Wrong. You are definitely the enemy," Broan growled back, his body shrieking with pain. "You are the one who killed my mother and sister, and you are not going to get the chance to do the same to Eirian and the Queen."

Sobus laughed out loud. "I have no intentions of harming the sweet child, so you can stop all your bluster."

Turning and looking at Sobus, Eirian quietly asked, "Did you kill them?"

"Who?"

"His family?"

"NO," Sobus clearly answered, "You know he has lied to you from the beginning. Do you think he'd stop now? He'll say anything he can to save his Queen and you know it. Think Eirian, think."

"It was you. I was right there," Broan said as struggled to get near Eirian again.

Sobus hit Broan with another energy bolt. "If you were right there, then why didn't you do something to help them?"

"It is a mistake I will not make again," he stated matter of factly.

"Eirian," Sobus called softly. "Come to me now. You know in your heart what needs to be done and only I can help. End this now. It's time to set the Faeries free."

She looked back and forth from him to the Queen again, a frown forming on her face. Could she trust herself to make the right choice? She briefly closed her eyes.

Sobus reached out, his palms open to her. "Eirian. Come, please." He stepped closer to Eirian. "Remember what she's done to all those you loved. Thanks to the Queen, you have no family and no home."

"She does have family. She has me," DaNann said. Her head was held high; her eyes clear and focused on Eirian.

"She has a home too. Solveig is her home," Broan called out, as he rose to his knees.

Sobus stretched out his hand again. His fingertips were a hair's breath away from hers. "Come join me. I cannot force you, but together our powers will be more than the Queen can fight off. We can make her pay for all the pain she has inflected on you and together we will finally free the Duronykians."

"Eirian, please," Broan pleaded. "We'll go home and leave these two demi-gods to fight it out. Please Eirian…please,"

Suddenly the unthinkable happened. Eirian reached out and took Sobus' hand. She slowly turned and looked at Broan. "Your family is not mine, and Solveig is not my home. I will do what I must for MY kin." She smiled oddly at him and then turned her back on him.

Eirian slowly moved with Sobus to one of the far walls. She stopped and looked over her shoulder at the Queen. There was a strange and piteous smile on her face as she said, "You betrayed my kin and now you will pay."

"Eirian STOP!" Broan yelled. He then cursed out loud.

"She has a mind of her own, Lord Broan. There is nothing you can say or do." Sobus grinned and concentrated his energy on Broan's physical form. He wanted to pull the great warlord to his knees in front of everyone and have him beg like he did once before. With a simple spell said under his breath he encased Broan, locking him in an invisible prison.

This was not the first time Sobus had made him watch pure brutality. This time he would not helplessly listen to screams of agony caused by the sadistic fury of Sobus. Broan staggered to his feet, his body sweating with the effort. He stared at Sobus. "I am not the boy you froze last time."

Broan placed both of his hands against the wall of the energy field that trapped him. He calmed his feelings and controlled his thoughts. Centering himself he willed it to be gone, and it disappeared. "It's easy to trick a young boy, but it is not as easy to trick a man."

Sobus looked down at Eirian with great concern in his eyes. "Don't worry I'll protect you." It was hard for Sobus to not show the delight he took in blasting Broan one more time.

"Stop this," Eirian said. "My Lord Sobus." Eirian spoke his name so softly that it shifted his attention from Broan and back to her.

"Yes, my sweet."

Eirian rose up and kissed Sobus on the cheek. "Thank you for finding me and telling me the truth. Now let's get this over with."

Broan dropped his head in wide-eyed horror, refusing to believe what she was doing. "Don't do it," he called out.

"Can I just end him?" Sobus asked.

"NO! I want him to watch," Eirian chirped.

Sobus' smile deepened as he stared at the Queen. He took Eirian into his arms and hugged her. "Now for your first lesson on using that power of yours." Slowly he turned her around to face DaNann. Taking each of her arms into his hands, he ran his fingers down them until they reached her wrists and then turned them over. He pulled her back against his chest, leaned into the side of her face and spoke smoothly. "Let your hands fall naturally at the wrists, and then focus on where you want your power to go."

Sobus paused for a moment as he scanned the room. "Like that roasted pig over on the table, Focus…Focus… and then when you are ready…" The pig began to sizzle and was instantly propelled through the glass window.

Eirian's eyes widened with excitement. She looked over her shoulder at Sobus and smiled. "May I try it on my own?"

Sobus shrugged and laughed. "Yes of course."

"How about I use her for a little practice." Eirian giggled. The Queen didn't move.

"Yes! Yes! How fitting."

"Okay," Eirian said as she rolled her shoulders. She looked back at Sobus once more. "Step back a little. I want do this all by myself." Sobus complied and stepped back but remained still squarely behind her, using her as a shield.

Eirian fidgeted, making a grand show of this new ability and just as the energy within her began to peak, she swung around. There was no pause or hesitation in Eirian's release of her powers. The blast was full and painful.

"What?" Sobus screamed as he hunched over. "How? You said Ke-Hern never taught you."

"I'm a fast learner."

The Queen quickly released Broan and the others from Sobus' spell. She yelled at them to get Eirian out of the way. But Sobus was faster. He grabbed Eirian, raised his fist and hit her hard, stunning her. "Bitch! I'll soon beat that defiant streak out of you," he screamed. "To think your mother sacrificed herself to protect you and it was all for nothing. You'll die just like she did, slowly and painfully."

He grabbed the hand that she wore her father's ring on and squeezed, crushing her fingers and then he suddenly kicked her feet out from under her. "But first I want the ring." Sobus glared at the DaNann. "It's the ring that has the power to defeat me, isn't it?" He laughed coldly. "You didn't think I knew, but I have my spies and they left nothing out." He hit Eirian again as he raised her hand with the ring. "Now give me the ring!"

To Eirian, it was as if Sobus was suddenly talking a foreign language. She stared at him in confusion. Both her father's ring and the old ring that she had found in the dungeon started to tingle. The energy of sky and land, light and dark, of past and future collided within her. Surging up from the very ground she sat on and rushing in from the very sky she loved, it filled her heart and her soul.

She stood up and looked Sobus in the eye. Eirian had become a conduit for a new type of energy, a blended energy. She raised her free hand and placed it on Sobus' chest. "BE GONE!" she commanded.

The energy tore through Sobus, pushing Eirian away with the blast. His body twisted as it began changing. No longer was he a slim young man. His body became its true self, deformed and mangled from years of hatred. Life's bitter experiences had left no room in him to be anything other than pure evil.

Without hesitation, the Queen used what energy she had to blast Sobus, which quickly set his body on fire.

Stunned and confused, Eirian stood up. Blinking back tears she looked down at her dress. "I ruined it." Her hands were shaking like leaves as she held the gown out in front of herself. "Just look at it! My only dress and…"

Broan limped across the room towards Eirian. "Are you alright?" he asked.

She stared at him for a second, then continued her ramble, "It's ruined…it's…"

"It's all right, I'll buy you another," Broan said as he paused for a moment to study her. She had a strange look in her eyes. It was as if it came from a faraway place. "Are you alright?" he asked again with worry.

It happened at an alarming rate. Eirian's words got caught in her throat and she started to have difficulty swallowing. She could feel tingling and numbness rushing up her body. Suddenly her legs went cold and heavy, and she dropped to the floor.

The rain stopped, the clouds parted and their prison disappeared. The Shadow Dwellers knew Sobus had lost his last battle.

"I had hoped the end of you would be the end of your curse!" Larden shrieked as he thrust his clinched fist into the air. "Look at us. Nothing has changed!"

"I had hoped as well but knew it may not be possible," DeSpon said as he placed his hand on Larden's shoulder. "But regardless of our physical reality, this freedom is welcomed. Now we are free to make our way to Aillil, find Eirian and talk to the Ancients. They are the only ones who have the power to change us now."

Marcoff shook his head as he eyed DeSpon. "That sounds good but how do we leave this island? The mainland is barely on the horizon, and there is a deep, churning sea between it and us," Marcoff said pointing to the distant shore.

DeSpon smiled. "I have an idea."

The warriors crowded around Eirian as she lay on the floor. "Let me through," the Queen demanded as she made her way through them. "I just met my granddaughter. I'm not about to lose her, all in the same day." As she knelt beside Eirian, she used her hands to scan her limp body. The Queen's hands suddenly stopped over Eirian lower abdomen. "She's with child," she said glaring up at Broan. "Your child...no children, she bears twins." She watched Broan's reaction closely, the intake of his breath and the pallor of his skin. She still had mixed feelings about this Mortal being connected to her granddaughter. First impressions were hard to negate.

V-Tor nudged Broan. "Guess you can't hide from the truth any longer."

"I never wished to hide from it. I was waiting for Eirian to trust me enough to tell me."

As the Queen continued to examine Eirian she spoke up. "There is no way Eirian was going to tell you, until all was safe. She is too much like her mother." She turned and looked at the pile of smoldering flesh that was once Sobus and suppressed a shudder. In most cultures cremation signified the release of the spirit. For the Queen, it signified the end of Sobus and the freedom of this land.

DaNann sat back on her heels. "Get her to a room where things are a little quieter. She'll need rest. I doubt she understands the cost on her body from using such powers."

"This way," Iarnan answered as he crossed the floor to a hidden staircase. Broan scooped up Eirian and as he moved past the Queen she noticed the ring on Eirian's toe. Tiny and unusual, the Ancient markings and fragile symbols came to life as it passed the lantern light. The ring awoke an old warning in the Queen, and she cursed. This was something she would need to talk to Ke-Hern about and it wasn't going to be nice.

DaNann walked over to Ke-Hern's body. "I didn't extend your mortality just for you to waste it away." She placed one of her hands over Ke-Hern's chest and the other over his head. She spoke a few strange words and Ke-Hern suddenly gasped for air as his lungs filled.

Eirian opened her eyes and looked at Broan. The muscle in his square jaw still twitched, showing his stress. She shifted her weight in his arms and put her hands around his neck.

"Good to see you awake," Broan said, smiling down at her. "Let's hope once we're back at Solveig, you will stop this crazy death wish of yours. I can't keep running after you and saving you."

Eirian stiffened a little in his arms and gave him a puzzled look.

"You are the most reckless woman I've ever met, and if you think for one moment that I'm going to continue just letting you get yourself in trouble, you are so wrong!" he said continuing his rant.

Eirian let her hands fall away from Broan's neck.

"Oh don't give me your pout! I'm telling you now. Once we are back in Solveig, you'll be lucky if you see the outside of my bedroom after this." He paused and smiled as he continued, "Of course you'll be my dutiful wife, so no one will be able to object."

"WHAT!" Eirian squirmed and pushed away from him, trying to loosen his hold on her.

Broan just tightened his hold a bit more. "Oh no you don't. If you think I'm about to set you free, forget it."

"PUT me down!" she screamed.

"Ahhh. I see things are back to normal," Ke-Hern said loudly from behind the two of them.

Eirian quickly peeked over Broan's shoulder. "Ke-Hern!" she yelled with relief. "I was so worried." She tried again to push herself off Broan, and when that didn't work, she hit him hard on the shoulder. "Put me DOWN!"

Broan finally agreed and reluctantly placed her on her feet. She quickly slipped past him, rushed to Ke-Hern, and hugged him.

"I wish you had told me what you were going to do," Ke-Hern muttered. "You had me very worried! I'm beginning to agree with Broan. You are a handful, although I have always known that."

"Permission to tie her up as soon as we get home?" Broan jokingly asked.

"Eirian has much to learn about being Off-World. She needs to come with me," said the Queen in a serious tone.

"No. I think she actually should come back with me to Duronyk. The land will need her help to come back from the hell it has been caught in. Besides she needs to take her place as Lady of Duronyk," Ke-Hern argued.

Broan grabbed Eirian's arm and pulled her next to him. "You are both wrong. She is going back to Solveig with me! Eirian has done enough for the two of you. I'll be taking care of her and until I say so, you two are to leave her alone. This is my family you are all talking about."

"*What the hell?*" Eirian fumed within. It appeared that nothing had changed in regards to her personal life. Everyone still wanted to tell her what to do. She looked at the Queen. It was still so strange and foreign to think of her as a grandmother or friend. Broan was being a bully as far as she was concerned, and even Ke-Hern appeared to have his own agenda. It seemed everyone wanted a piece of her and her future. Fatigue latched onto Eirian and was not about to let go. The weariness seemed to have seeped into each and every cell and clouded her thinking. "I...I," she was about to tell them that they were all wrong and that she would not be going with any of them, but she lost focus again. She bit her lower lip, unsure what to do next.

Broan quietly picked her up into his arms. He turned and looked at everyone. He held the Queen's gaze, challenging her. "She needs her rest and I plan to give it to her. So until tomorrow you'll have to excuse us." And with that he walked away from the group and into his room.

He kicked open the adjoining door between his and Bronagh's room and walked over to his sister's bed and gently placed Eirian on it. "I'll get someone to find Bronagh. She can help you undress."

Eirian nodded her head slowly. She was tired, annoyed, and even a little frightened. Her mind was caught in a battle between thinking and wanting to sleep. Looking up at Broan, Eirian wondered if he would ever understand that she was not truly Mortal, not fully Off-World, not even Duronykian. "I don't fit in anywhere. So..."

"That's not true. Solveig is your home now."

"No." She yawned. "I mean...I need to figure this out myself."

"Yourself! Eirian we belong together. You, me and the twins."

"Twins?"

Broan nodded his head as he gave her a reassuring smile. "The Queen exposed your little secret so there is no getting away from me now."

"No," she muttered as she pushed against him again, "you don't understand…" She was so tired. Too tired to fight or even think anymore.

Broan reached out and gently held her shoulders. "It's okay." He gave her a reassuring squeeze. "Rest for now. We can talk later." He smiled back at her as he left the room.

Once she was alone, Eirian's shoulder slumped. *I need to go. I need to breathe, to think for myself…for my children.* Her body shuddered again from the unnatural fatigue. She drew in a deep breath in an attempt to steel her nerves and then concentrated hard on her talents. The intense stilling of the mind and body needed was difficult. Her temper and confusion kept getting in the way. She took in a deep breath again and slowly, ever so slowly commanded her image to separate from her being. Once finished, she touched her arms and stomach feeling the density of her body even though it was invisible. She turned and looked at this creature that now dutifully sat on the bed waiting for Bronagh. She was so tiny, so pale, and so alone. *"So this is what others see. Oh hell."* She quickly found her old boots Bronagh had hidden and tugged them on and grabbed a cloak nearby.

Suddenly, screaming from the street below startled her. "BRONAGH! WHERE ARE YOU?" She knew that voice! Eirian rushed to the window and looked out. There stood Deeton in all his Mortal glory. *"It's done… I can truly leave now…"* Cautiously she entered Broan's room, took one last look at him and the others, and then invisible to them all, silently walked out of the room.

The candle lanterns from the streets only made Deeton appear more mystical and handsome. He paid no mind to the people that crowded around him as he looked up at Bronagh. "Well are you coming down or do I come up?"

Bronagh was frozen in place. She was so scared right now. She was worried that if she moved, this miracle would evaporate before her very eyes.

"You better come up. I think she's in shock," Broan called down to Deeton.

It didn't take any more encouragement than that. Deeton immediately started the climb up the wall and quickly entered through the room's window.

"Is that really you?" Bronagh whispered. She took step forward and touched his cheek, still afraid that he wasn't real. Deeton smiled at her and then began to seriously kiss her.

"It worked!" Ke-Hern exclaimed as he rushed into the room. He looked over at Broan and shrugged his shoulders. "The breaking of curses and spells are hard to predict at the best of times. I am so relieved that this one worked out." He stepped towards the happy couple with his attention focused on Deeton. Ke-Hern pinched Deeton's arm wanting to make sure he was flesh and blood. "Have the others turned to normal yet?"

Deeton removed his lips from Bronagh's and began rubbing his arm. "I don't know. I never wandered back to Duronyk. I wanted to be near Bronagh, even if only in spirit form."

Broan left the growing crowd in his room and went in to check on Eirian. She sat in a trance-like stillness. He quietly walked over to her, bent down and went to place his arms around her, but they past right through her. He was left holding air. Stunned he stood there looking down at this perfect image of Eirian. He scanned to room quickly. "Shit!" he growled. Turning quickly, Broan re-entered his room. "Eirian is gone!"

Shocked, Ke-Hern pushed past him, needing to see for himself. "How…" He started then stopped. He could feel the warmth of the talent she used on what sat before them all and he smiled wryly. "Image splitting spell. She is a fast learner but also not a very wise one."

"We have to find her," Broan insisted.

"Forget it. There's nothing we can do. We would walk right past her and never even know it," Ke-Hern answered matter-of-factly.

"I'll not give up that easy. Remember she's tired. Hopefully she doesn't have the strength to hold the spell for long." Broan pushed by the old Wizard and went out the door. Deeton gave Bronagh a quick kiss and started after Broan.

"Deeton?" Bronagh questioned.

Deeton smiled at Bronagh. "Someone has to save the Eirian from him." And with that he was gone.

The wind off of the sea was damp, bone chilling, and monotonous. Far below the edge of the cliff, the surf foamed against the rocks. Their prison of rain was gone, and now the Shadow Dwellers found themselves on an island that had lost its ability to support life beyond yellow stub grass. The land was barren and flat with only a few rock clusters. Even the birds refused to venture here.

Falzon looked over at Bacot. "What do you think of DeSpon's plan? Of all of us, you are the heaviest and have the least chance of surviving."

Bacot sighed and looked over the edge of the cliff at the massive waves below. Forty-foot waves were moving in at speeds that made him dizzy. They tossed and curled onto themselves. "Well if I'm to die that way, at least it will be quick." He looked around at the barren plateau now called home. "Starving to death would be worse."

Marcoff curled his lip and bared his fangs. He did not like the thought of starving either. They all had forgotten the demands life placed on the Mortal body. Hunger seemed to quickly narrow down the choices they had.

"I'm with Bacot," Marcoff said. "Although I think DeSpon is crazy, I don't think there is much hope for us if we stay on this island."

Falzon rose up and leaned on his massive ape arms. The unnatural form wore even more heavily on his Mortal leg joints now. He looked out towards the land. "I never thought I'd miss shape-shifting into a bird. It would have been so easy to just shift and fly away on my own wings."

Bacot nodded his significantly sized head. "But here we are, and with DeSpon, the only one given leather wings. We have little choice but to trust him." He planted a bulky hand on Falzon's back. "If it will help to give you courage, I will ask DeSpon to take me first."

"Oh I have courage. It's my common sense that is getting in the way."

Kuiper slipped up to the group. "No brother, it's not your common sense. You are just a bloody pessimist."

Falzon playfully swung at Kuiper, knocking him over easily. "Whatever it is, it has served me well. I am still alive and I am still your older brother."

Kuiper laughed and rolled on the ground. The thought of getting off the island excited him. "DeSpon wants to start soon. He is planning to take both Larden and me at the same time."

Falzon shifted his weight off both arms and onto just one again. He pinned his brother to the ground. "Well DeSpon can't."

"Do you have something to say to me?" DeSpon asked standing just behind him.

Quickly, Falzon spun around. "Yes! I think your plan is mad at best, and taking two at once is even more so. Gamble with your own life not ours."

DeSpon remained silent for some minutes. "Like everything else in our lives, this is all about choices. I know this is beyond both your understanding and even your imagination, but I truly believe I can do this."

Kuiper shook out the dust and gravel now imbedded in-between his scales. "I believe he can too and so does Larden. We are both light and if he can make it across with both of us, we will know that he will most likely make it across with you." He poked at his brother, "with your heavy thoughts, which are about as heavy as your body."

Falzon, Bacot and Marcoff hung back and watched as DeSpon latched Larden and Kuiper to his torso with a rope. He tested the weight of the two travelers and bounced on his muscled lion legs, making sure the bindings would hold. Taking a firm grip of both passengers, he opened his leather wings and jumped out over a two hundred foot vertical drop, into the open space called air.

Falzon's face echoed his alarm as he watched DeSpon get dragged down towards the hammering waves and large boulders at the base of their island. He closed his eyes, not wanting to see the watery death of his brother.

"It's okay," shouted Bacot as he pointed at the flying group of Shadow Dwellers. "Look Falzon! They're flying!"

Falzon opened his eyes. The three airborne travelers had to dodge mountainous waves as they barreled past them. He held his breath as he watched, fearful that any movement would turn the tides on the fragile trio. Finally as the group neared the next island, Falzon was able to let out his breath. He watched as DeSpon glided down, landing on his feet.

From the far distant shore they could hear DeSpon's resounding roar. Falzon smiled as he watched Kuiper and Larden rolled in the dirt as they laughed uproariously. They made it, which meant the others would too.

DaNann dowsed the candles then moved through the darkened room of her quarters. She needed time to think with no distractions. She had two pressing issues to handle and Broan was the lesser one. "Damn Ke-Hern! He started the wheel turning by sending Eirian to Solveig to begin with! He must have known."

She paced for a minute or two and then stood still in the middle of the dimly lit room, her anger building within. "I hadn't thought the Ancients would hide their direction in the midst of these events… clever and very treacherous - just as I feared." She squeezed her eyes shut. Her head was crowded with dozens of questions, all of which needed quick answers.

When DaNann heard the tap on the door, she quickly sat down then loudly told Ke-Hern to enter. He barely got his foot through the door when she started. "Why didn't you tell me about the Ancients' ring that Eirian wears on her toe? Why keep that a secret? Or is that your specialty, keeping secrets from me?"

"What are you talking about?"

DaNann rose from her chair. "I'm talking about you never telling me that the Ancients where linked to Eirian! How could you betray HER and me like that? Where is the honesty we once shared? There was a time I could trust you." DaNann threw her hands up into the air. Frustration boiled. "How long has Eirian been wearing the ring on her toe?"

"I know nothing of that ring. I never saw her wear the blasted thing, and she has never talked about it."

"You knew that the Ancients were utilizing this event to further their cause, and still you supported it." DaNann shook her head. "You are helping them to come back. You knew they were slipping through stonewalls of Solveig and still you sent Eirian."

"I worried about the possibility, but in no way did I willingly help them."

They stood facing each other, both expressing their frustrations. Their words and stares hid nothing from one another. Then Ke-Hern's face softened. "I'm sorry, but I really had no knowledge of them using this situation to their benefit." He checked DaNann's reaction. Satisfied he continued. "I came to tell you that Eirian has escaped using an image splitting enchantment. Can you help to find her?"

DaNann paused, closed her eyes and concentrated. Nothing, nothing but cold stillness echoed back to her. Her search found nothing. "Just as I feared, with that damn ring on her, they are able to hide her from me. They work on a different level than the one I work from. I am helpless in saving my grandchild." DaNann bowed her head in defeat as she began to cry.

Ke-Hern quickly wrapped his arms around her. "Don't worry we'll find her, Ancients or not."

Broan stood in the middle of the street and looked towards the great wall that enclosed the city. "She is invisible so she could escape any way she wants to." His voice was low and urgent. "She's far too weak to climb over the wall...the gates are closed so she'd have to wait for the guards to allow someone in or out, which won't happen till morning...so where does that leave us?"

"I can help find her," Deeton stated boldly. "I was often assigned the job when she was young and roamed free in the woods." Now that quickly got Broan's attention. "We may not be able to see her, but I can sense...or tell where she has passed."

"Good enough for me."

Deeton smiled at Broan as he eyed a few of Ryu's guards hanging out across the lane. Feeling a little uneasy he turned his back to them and then closed his eyes and touched the steps leading to the entrance. "I'll tell you this much. She didn't come this way." He looked up at Broan "She's still…"

Broan's eyes sparkled. "Of course!"

Eirian changed back to visible form, causing the image she had left behind to fade away. She didn't care. She was safe now in Broan's secret passage. She scanned the cathedral like cavern. Small cracks higher up allowed some moonlight in, making her passage a little easier but Eirian knew she still had to be careful. On the other side of the large cave, hidden in the darkness, was the steep passageway that was full of the tangled debris of deadfall. It was slick and dangerous but it was her only way out.

"Eirian why are you here?" Stamas called out. "You need to go back."

"Stamas! Thank the gods you're here." Relief washed over her as she walked towards him. She stopped suddenly and leaned against a bolder. She cursed at how much this Off-World power took out of her. "I need…"

"To go back."

"NO. What I need is to get away." She raised her chin a little and squared her shoulders. "Whose side are you on anyway?"

Stamas rose to his feet and towered over her. "I am on the side of common sense. Which side are you on?"

Eirian took in a deep breath. "I'm on MY SIDE! Please Stamas, help me. I need time to think. I need…"

"You need to return to Broan!"

Eirian picked up a stone near her and threw it at him. "NO. That is the last thing I need right now. NO! NO! NO!" Too tired to stand any longer, she dropped to her knees. Holding back tears, she hugged herself. "Please Stamas, please. I just need some time to think."

Alarmed, Stamas picked Eirian up off the ground and slowly started to climb the inner wall of the cave.

"Up there," Deeton pointed.

"Where? I don't see anything." Broan narrowed his eyes, scanning the rough rock face of the cave for Eirian. "She's not going to try and climb is she? She's too weak. She'll fall!"

"No. It's Stamas. Just watch."

Broan studied the area that Deeton had pointed to. Sure enough there was movement among the rocks high up on the left side. He watched in amazement as a Stamas slowly vaulted up onto a high indent in the wall and then paused.

Stamas turned then and stared straight at Broan. "Move out of the way," he called down. He motioned them all to back up a bit then descended much faster than his climb up. He was half way down when he jumped and with a single bound he stood in front of Broan.

"Stamas, where is Eirian?" Broan asked.

"She is with me now. Have no fear, I will keep her safe."

"No! Damn it Stamas, don't do this. Please."

"Go back, Broan. Being near you is not what Eirian wants right now." Stamas quickly turned to leave.

"Please Stamas let me talk to her at least."

Stamas shook his head while giving Broan a stern look. He then quickly glided up the steep embankment and the wall itself. Once back on the upper ledge Stamas turned and looked down at Broan. "Turn around and go back, Broan. You will not win this one."

Lady Tilga sat pouting on the chair as she watched Tybalt pace the floor. "Why didn't you get to her before this evening, like I asked you to?" Tybalt screeched. Tilga didn't answer the question this time, because no matter how many times Tybalt asked it, the answer would be the same. She had tried, but the witch Bronagh was always there. *Damn! What am I doing here?* she asked herself. *I could be dining with young men and having fun instead listening to this old fool.* She shifted in her seat and turned away from Tybalt only to spot Mohr hanging out against the far wall. She didn't like the 'know-it-all' look on his face. She smiled to herself. She wondered if Mohr had a secret hideout in the women's quarters and if he went there more to watch than to listen.

Tybalt's tirade was interrupted by a quick knock on the door. He swiftly glanced at Mohr, who seemed happy enough to stay at the back and hold up the wall. Tybalt gave him a heated stare, then rushed over to the door and placed his ear against the wooden slab and listened. "Who's there?" he asked weakly, trying to sound as if he had been resting.

"It's me Ryu. Let me in quickly!"

Tybalt opened the door and scanned the hallway, making sure no one was watching. He hurriedly stepped aside for Ryu. "What news do you have?"

"Eirian's fled the city!"

"That little minx has run off with Cian's ring," Tybalt yelled. "Shit!" He stepped away from Ryu, rubbing his lower face with his short stubby fingers, contemplating his next move. "Any ideas as to where she went?"

"No. Broan and a few of his men are in hot pursuit, but…" Ryu walked over to Tilga, giving her a very inviting look. "But don't worry. He'll not get far…" He sat down on the arm of her chair and rested his arm on her shoulder. Seductively he started playing with her golden hair. "I saw to that."

Tybalt walked over to Ryu and grabbed his arm. "You make too light of this."

Ryu jerked himself free. "Relax! I've already talked to the Queen."

"You did WHAT?"

"I spoke to the Queen. On bended knee I offered my services to help find Eirian. I stressed that even though Broan is a good warrior he has obviously lacking in the ability to protect Eirian." Ryu started to laugh. "The Queen even muttered under her breath that it was probably him that Eirian was running from!"

"You can't mean that the Queen wants you to take over finding Eirian."

"Yes. And I have her permission to do whatever it takes…like keeping Broan stuck here in the city while I capture her granddaughter," Ryu quietly said as he calmly inspected his fingernails. "I knew as soon as I met the Queen that she and Eirian were related. SO I worked at getting close and earn the Queen's trust. Now that her guard is down, she's open to just about anything I suggest." He looked up at Tybalt and Mohr. "I even know she is as Mortal as we are. She told me that death comes to all, even Off-World Queens. She placed her hand over her heart and lamented about how little time she'll have with Eirian once she is back."

"So."

Ryu smiled oddly at Tybalt. "I have a plan."

DeSpon and his group finally reached the mainland and for that they were grateful. They made camp on the gradual slope of a shore, between the boulders and natural debris of wind and sea erosion.

Not long after as the moonlight glistened off the sea four Shadow Dwellers headed out to find food and horses. There were a few small settlements just beyond the fjords that they could scout out.

Concerned about DeSpon's exhaustion Bacot stayed back with him. All the non-stop flying had taken its toll. Bacot poked at the fire which DeSpon slept by, making sure it didn't die out. He stood up and stretched his large frame. "I'm truly amazed that you were able to carry me across the sea. Although dipping me in and out of the waves was not what I had expected. To say that angry waves rose up to swallow me is a bit tame. It felt more like monstrous sea demons with ice-cold hands were clutching and tugging at me constantly." he muttered to himself.

"You're welcome," DeSpon said as he sat up.

"It's a good thing they are going for horses as well," Bacot said. "You picked the longest route possible to get to the desert. My feet just ache thinking about it."

Sore and cranky, DeSpon shifted his body as he looked over to Bacot. "I picked the safest way. Most of the route is along the untamed frontier with only a few pockets of settlements along the way."

"It's the Mortals you fear isn't it? Otherwise you would have chosen to head straight north along the borders of Gearlodin and Remdor."

"For an OX, you are smarter than I thought." DeSpon smiled at him. "We may have made good our escape, but I doubt that the very people we once terrorized would be that welcoming." DeSpon looked down at his muscled legs that were all covered with golden fur. He stretched out the toe pads on his feet, unsheathing his claws. "Because of our hideous forms, we have no other choice."

Bacot tossed another log on the fire. "Then it is the long way. We go east along the coastal hills just north of us. From there we'll go into the low Aktis Mountains on the far eastern boarder of Anwel. Once we make our way around the City of Bridges, we can follow the stars until we find the desert fortress and Aillil," Bacot said as he looked at DeSpon. Then he added, "Bet you didn't think I'd remember."

Chapter 17

"The problem is that no prophecy is exact."

- Deeton

After all the excitement at the Queen's presentation yesterday, the streets and alleys in the Walled City were now cloaked in a more quiet tone. People were confused and scared and they remained indoors, only going out if needed. As if to reflect the mood of the people, dark and pensive gray skies hung heavy over the city.

It was just after the midday meal and Tilga slowly walked up the stairs of the main residence. She knew that Leif would be itching to get away from Bronagh and find a new adventure. Especially since his mother was keeping him on a short leash. She positioned herself and waited for the plan to unfold.

Tilga got her wish. It wasn't long before Leif raced out of the room and right into her. She tumbled against the wall and cried out in pain. This of course got the attention of the one person she needed. Tilga had to work hard not to smile as she watched Bronagh discipline Leif.

"I'm fine Lady Bronagh," Tilga said. She took a small step making a big show of weak ankle. "Oh my, I guess I twisted my ankle a bit." She leaned nearer to Bronagh. "I had just come up to see if anyone had heard if Lady Eirian was all right. She was so nice to me every time we met. I'm just heartsick with worry after all that happened yesterday."

"Yes…we all are…She's. She's not here right now." Bronagh looked at Tilga. She was uncertain what to say or do with the unwanted guest.

"Well. I don't want to impose on you. What you could do for me is tell Lady Eirian I asked about her."

"Of course," Bronagh answered quickly.

Tilga limped again and looked at Leif with big eyes. "Oh my! It really hurts. Do you think you could help a damsel back to her room?"

"Sure," he said jumping at the chance of freedom. He turned and smiled at his mother. "I'll pick up the fruit you want on the way back. Okay?"

"Well…yes…of course," Bronagh sputtered. "as long as you come right back."

"Sure," Leif agreed as he got under Tilga's arm. Together they hobbled down the hall. Not once did either look back at Bronagh.

"Come right back." Bronagh weakly called out again. Slowly she went back into her quarters.

Out on the street Tilga limped even more. "I have a big favor to ask of you." She looked down at her sore ankle playing on Leif's guilt. "I was supposed to deliver the Queen a gift from our town, but now I won't be able to. Could you help me out?"

"Well…I," he said as he hung his head.

Tilga stopped and looked at him. "Not up for an adventure? I thought you would be excited to see the Queen up close. I heard she has a scar on her chin from a fight long ago. Not many boys can say they actually saw it. BUT if you'd rather sit indoors with your mother, I can find another to help me out."

Tilga decided to up ante. "Look, how about I take you to the combat-room after…Just to thank you for delivering the flowers?"

"The COMBAT-ROOM!" Leif exclaimed out loud. He always wanted to get an inside look at the famous war-room, where hand-to hand combat was taught only to a few special warriors. "Well…maybe if I'm real quick in delivering the flowers."

"I won't tell anyone if you don't." Tilga smiled at him. "Come on. I'll make sure Iarnan's Captain of the Guards gives us a quick tour. Maybe I'll even show you a rope trick I know."

Leif looked up at his mother's window and smiled. "Okay. I'll just tell mom I went as fast as I could."

When they were finally in her room, Tilga pointed to a great cluster of purple blossoms that peeked out from a paper wrapper. "The flowers are over there."

Leif had never seen such brightly colored flowers before. The sight of them dazzled him. "They are very beautiful. What are they called?"

"Gorsets. They are native to the area east of my town. They are pretty aren't they? I do hope the Queen will like them."

Leif picked up the flowers and rushed to the door. "I'll be right back."

Aillil emerged silently from the fortress. The golden hues of morning light had finally found their way to the bottom of the canyon. It slowly washed away the chilly night. Wind sculpted rock formations and canyon walls vibrant with red, orange and honey-colored rock were not lost to her blindness. Aillil took in a deep breath and placed her hand on the rock face near her and saw it all in her mind's eye. Now that she knew DeSpon and the others had made their escape, she felt her stay here was a gift, a blessing. She sighed. "Strange how one single event can touch so many, even those far from it."

"What?" questioned Miko, who was two steps behind her.

Aillil's smile faded as she turned towards his voice. "I told you to leave me alone!"

"I can't, I'm your brother."

Aillil groaned as she turned around again and started to walk away from him and his meddling ways.

"You can't get away from me, Aillil. I have eyes, ears and more sense than you."

"Well let's hope your senses will make you accommodating."

Miko reached out and grabbed Aillil's arm. "What do you mean?"

"DeSpon's ingenuity has liberated the Shadow Dwellers from their prison. They will soon be here."

"You never said that DeSpon was a Shadow Dweller! What the hell have you done?"

"What has been asked of me, I'm to help free them from their curse...just like Eirian did for the Faeries."

"So you called them here, like you did me." The thought unnerved him. Miko started to pull Aillil back towards the fortress as he scanned the sky. "Back inside, I'll have to make preparations."

When the call to join the Queen in her quarters came, Broan was unsure what to expect. "What's this about?" Broan asked Ke-Hern who was standing outside the Queen's room. "I hope it's not another limitation to my freedom."

"You have only yourself to blame. You have been…let just say, not your wonderful self lately." Ke-Hern smiled back at him as he opened the door.

Together they entered the dimly lit room. A heavy odor of flowers assailed them immediately. Puzzled, Ke-Hern started to make his way to the window but dizziness quickly overtook him and he fell to the floor.

"What…?" Broan questioned as he reached for the knife in his boot. He crouched down as he raised his dagger before him. "Ke-Hern!" he yelled his eyes darting around the room. He stepped back towards the door only to find it shut. He shook his head trying to clear the clouds that were forming. "Ke-her…" was all he got out before he lost consciousness.

"Overkill Tilga. It stinks in here!" Wrinkling his nose, Ryu entered the room while holding a wet cloth over his nose. He calmly stepped over Broan's body and picked up the vase of flowers. He went to the window and tossed the deep purple flowers out onto the cobbled stone alley below. "There," he said aloud, "Done with those." He took in a deep breath of fresh air and then looked back at Broan's prone body. "Too bad you didn't notice the type of flowers. Gorsets will absorb anything, even a sleeping drug, and then once put in water they exude it into the air."

"It's a clever little trick," Ryu boasted as he walked over to Broan. He picked up Broan's knife. "Too bad you're not that clever." Without pause Ryu walked over to the Queen as she lay on her bed, and stabbed her in the chest. After removing his knife, he approached Ke-Hern and stabbed him in the back.

"There, done with those as well." Satisfied, Ryu walked over to Broan and placed the bloodied knife back in his hand. Pausing briefly to make sure everything looked just right, he quietly exited the room. He didn't have to wait long to hear Broan stirring. With great show Ryu broke down the door. He sounded the alarm and waited for things to unfold as he had planned.

"Take him!' Ryu screamed to the guards as they rushed in. "He's killed the Queen and Ke-Hern." Ryu grabbed Broan's hand that held the bloody knife. "Look…he still holds the weapon."

Broan was dragged to his feet, his mind still dull and confused. His eyes widened when he saw Ke-Hern lying on the floor with blood surrounding him. Broan looked down at his knife and let it slip from his hand.

"Not so great now are you?" With a sneer Ryu punched Broan in the gut. He grabbed Broan by the hair and forced him to face him. He leaned in close. "And don't worry. I'll take good care of Eirian and your sister."

Broan went wild, fighting to get free. Ryu laughed and then nodded to his warriors. "Take him to the dungeon and round up his fighters. I don't want them to try and help him escape before the trial."

Smiling, Ryu looked over his handy work and then yelled over his shoulder. "Achurst! Have you caught the other Governors yet?"

"Yes Sir."

Ryu took one last look around the room, "Good, now to catch a Faery."

Achurst had a hard time to stop the shiver that climbed up his spine. "Are they really dead?"

"Yes."

"It just seemed so easy." Achurst looked back at Ryu and paled. "I mean…they have special powers…and…"

Ryu snickered as he turned to walk away. "Special powers or not we are all Mortal, and can be killed."

Laeg hung back in the crowd as he watched Broan being dragged out by the guards. He slid back into the alley and waited. Looking up at the open window above him, he wished that Eirian had taken the time to show him how to climb unaided. After scanning the alley, he tossed his rope up to the beam that was just above the window. He gripped the rope with both hands and began to climb. *"Elftan style. Not as quick as Eirian but still effective."* He hung outside the window and listened, making sure that no one was in the room. Satisfied, he pulled himself in.

Laeg stood in shock. Both Ke-Hern and the Queen lay in so much blood.

"Don't just stand there. Help me," Ke-Hern whispered to Laeg as he tried to get up. Laeg rushed over to him. "What happened?" he asked as he aided Ke-Hern to sit up.

"It was a fool's attempt at removing those in power." Ke-Hern pushed off Laeg and stood up weakly. Quickly he made his way over to the Queen. "We have to get her out of here."

"Is she alive?" Laeg asked coming up next to Ke-Hern.

"Yes. Thankfully the fools don't know where her heart is located." Ke-Hern hastily placed his hands over her wound and whispered a few words. Suddenly the Queen took in a breath. "Good. Now quickly Laeg, we don't have much time. I think I can hide us in a cloak of shadows until we get to the gate."

"No. The gate's too far. Let's go to the tunnel." Laeg used the cloth from the side table to bind up both KeHern and the Queen's wounds and then picked her up. He followed Ke-Hern to the door. Together they paused and listened. Then ever so slowly they slipped out into the hallway.

Ke-Hern's magic worked. It was as if they were nothing more than shadows as they walked past everyone. Relief over came both of them once inside the tunnel and away from all the chaos.

The combat-room was larger than the first room Leif and Tilga walked through. Other than a few support posts in various places, the room was empty. The simple wood and stone walls gave the room a cold feeling. Leif stomped his feet on the ground amazed that the dirt floor was hard from overuse, polished to almost a rock hard surface. He smiled to be in the one place where a man's mantel was not tested by his use of a sword. Here a combat of a different type was taught to Ryu's top men.

"Are you ready?" Tilga asked as she headed over to one of the posts.

Leif was so excited that he was going to learn how to escape binding ropes that he quickly joined her. "It won't take long will it?" he asked as he sat down.

Tilga shook her head, "No." She continued to wrap the rope around Leif. She pulled tight on the rope and knotted it. "There," she said as she stood up. "Are they tight?"

Leif twisted and wiggled, testing the ropes and knots and nodded back to her. "So now what?" he asked.

"You keep still and quiet," Tilga said as she sat back on her heels.

"No. I mean how do I break free?"

"You don't." She smiled at him.

"What!" Leif began struggling in earnest. In a panic he kicked out at her only to get a slap for all his efforts.

"That is no way to pay me back for bringing you in here." She stood up and chuckled. "Guess you'll be a little later then you promised."

Leif tried to kick her again, but she simply sidestepped his feet and laughed. "Temper, temper," Tilga said as she turned away. Without pause she walked out the door, slamming it shut behind her. The slick sound of the big bolt sliding across the coarse wood made Leif sick to his stomach. He was quickly engulfed in darkness and worries.

Even in warmer Gearlodin, the weather had a mind of its own. Cold rain fell off and on for days and the sun hid behind thick flat clouds that ran from horizon to horizon. It was bone chilling. This of course had no effect on the Shadow Dwellers. Driven, they moved as swiftly as possible through southern Gearlodin.

DeSpon looked over at his determined band of friends. They had spent most of the daytime hidden, analyzing their location and next leg of their journey. At night they pushed hard, using their animal like eyes and ears. At the speed they were managing, DeSpon felt they would make it to Aillil within two weeks, which made him happy.

"Is it still a crime to steal another's horse?" Larden asked as he mounted a speckled gray mare. Everyone looked at him with stunned looks on their faces.

"Look at us Larden," Falzon said as he came up next to him. "I doubt anyone is going to care about their horses if they set eyes on us. Besides, we are only using them. They can all come and collect them when we are finished."

Everyone chuckled except Bacot. His workhorse was big enough to handle his weight but it wasn't very smart. "I'd gladly give back mine. He is useless."

"He carries you, so be happy," DeSpon said. "With winter's tumultuous storms and the rocky crags of the mountains, you'll be glad you have such a steady horse beneath you."

"Steady! I think the damn thing is dead."

Marcoff started to ride past Bacot and DeSpon. "Well if he is, we can eat him tonight. Especially since Kuiper scared off today's meal."

"Scared it off! How was I to know you were after the goat and not the woman?" Kuiper bellowed.

"Woman?" DeSpon's ears perked up.

"Thanks, loud mouth," Marcoff growled back at Kuiper. "It was nothing. I was well hidden, crouching near a waterfall when Lord Lizard jumps down from a tree, scaring off the woman, the goat and my good humor."

"It was a twenty foot drop to the ground. And I thought I was saving her and her child."

"Child?" DeSpon eyes grew with alarm.

"Yeah," Kuiper clarified. "The woman clutched a child, a young boy I think, as she dashed off screaming."

"Screaming!"

"DeSpon there is nothing we can do about it now. No one got hurt, not even the goat," Marcoff huffed.

"No one! How long do you think it will be before the men folk decide to hunt the beast that tried to eat a child?"

"A long time," Bacot answered as his horse finally started to move. "First, they will be too scared to do anything but talk about it, then news will travel, turning us into fireside stories. After that we will become the basis of myths told to children to keep them in line. And finally, in time we'll have our place in legends, along with other beasts."

Everyone just looked at Bacot as he rode past them. "Surprisingly profound," DeSpon said as he kicked his horse into action, leaving the others still stunned by Bacot's summation.

Bronagh was going crazy. It was now past the evening meal and she still couldn't find Leif. She wrapped her cape tightly around her, trying to keep out autumn's crisp air. She didn't find anyone in Tilga's room, so she walked up to the guards and asked if anyone had seen a boy leave the city alone. None had.

"It would be just like him to run away in hopes of finding Eirian," she said to herself. Old fears rose within her and they brought back memories of the time the boys were lost in the woods outside of Solveig.

Bronagh wanted to scream out of fear, out of frustration, out of knowing she would have to go to Broan and tell him. She knew that Broan had enough on his mind with everything else that was happening. "Oh why can't you just keep out of trouble for at least one day?" she yelled out loud as she walked back to the main residence.

"Who's in trouble?" a voice behind her asked.

Startled, Bronagh swung quickly around. "My son has gone missing, which only means he's up to mischief." She eyed Ryu. There was something about him that pricked at Bronagh's nerves.

"I know where he is. Come," he coaxed as he stretched his hand out to her, "I'll show you."

Bronagh didn't accept his hand but did nod her head as sign she would go with him. "Thank you," was all she said.

RohDin didn't like being chased! Especially when those who were after him made it clear they wanted him dead! "I guess I should have held my tongue the other night." He took a sharp turn into a side street, grabbed onto a low hanging merchant's sign and pulled himself up and onto a windowsill. Within seconds Ryu's soldiers ran underneath him, up the side street and out of sight. Giving a sigh of relief, he took a moment to think things through. His orders had seemed to be simple at first. He was to find Bronagh and Leif and get them out of the city, but nothing that day had turned out to be simple.

He took a quick look down to the street below. Satisfied, he swung his feet over the edge. He jumped down and quickly pulled back into the doorway and listened with all he had. Satisfied that no one was around, RohDin raised his hood and started out, keeping to the shadowed side of the street.

Just as RohDin entered the training field, he spotted Bronagh and Ryu walking together. The hairs on the back of his neck instantly rose, giving him an immediate warning. He slipped back into the shadows and watched. Suddenly he noticed that Achurst was forcing Deeton to the field as well. "What are they up to?" He inched closer, careful not to lose sight of them. He suddenly stopped as he watched both Bronagh and Deeton getting pushed into the combat-room. "Great, only one way in and out."

RohDin was just ready to rush towards the combat-room and rescue them, when a strong hand grabbed his shoulder. RohDin grabbed his knife from his belt and swung around, almost cutting V-Tor's neck.

"What is this?" V-Tor cursed as he grabbed RohDin's arm, forcing it back.

RohDin lowered his knife. "Sorry, but after having Iarnan's army chase me around the city with murder in their eyes, I'm a little jumpy." He looked back over the field at the door to the combat-room. "Any plans on getting Broan out of the dungeon?"

"Ardis and Laeg are working on it right now. I was supposed to gather who I could find and bring them back to the tunnel."

"Not until we get Bronagh and Deeton out of that building. They were forced there by Ryu and Achurst."

"Ryu," V-Tor hissed. "I never liked the guy."

At that moment Cephas and Hywel came swiftly around the wall. "There are about a dozen soldiers coming this way. I think it's time to leave," Cephas advised matter of factly.

"What are you two doing here? I thought Deeton said you all went north."

Hywel shock his head, "And leave Eirian here alone?"

"Right, well, we still are NOT going anywhere until Bronagh and Deeton are released," RohDin hissed through clenched teeth.

Ryu roughly tossed Bronagh through the door. "Let's get this over with so you can join your brother in the dungeon."

"What!" she yelled. "Why are you doing this?"

"Power, wealth, the usual," Tilga answered from behind her. Bronagh spun around, stopping inches from Tilga.

"Oh don't look so surprised," Tilga said wickedly. "Do you really think Tybalt was going to sit around and let the Queen give everything to your brother?"

"Enough!" Ryu yelled as he took Bronagh's arm and pushed her up against the far wall. "Do you know what is behind this door?" he teased, pointing to the door next to them.

Terror gripped her. "Leif!" she screamed as she made a grab for the slide lock.

Her nails dung into the wood as Ryu pulled her away and tossed her to the floor. "That's right. He's in there, and if we get what we want, you can see him."

"What do you want?" Bronagh asked as she started to cry.

"Leave her alone," yelled Deeton as he tried to get to her.

Ryu pulled Bronagh off the floor and hit her hard across the face. "You are in no position to ask favors of me. Tell us where Eirian is!"

"Eirian? What does she have to do with this?"

Ryu hit Bronagh again. "No questions. I only want answers." He raised his fist again. "DO I make myself clear?"

Deeton struggled against Achurst and then lowered his head and nodded.

"Good. I'm glad you came to your senses." Ryu let go of Bronagh. "Now where is Eirian?"

"The truth is I don't know," Deeton answered. He never saw the swift punch to his midsection. He fell to the ground, clutching his ribs.

"Stop it!' Bronagh screamed. "Deeton wouldn't lie. Think about it, if Deeton knew where she was, don't you think Broan would be with her right now?"

"She has a point. Even I couldn't get Broan to look away from the witch," Tilga said sadly.

"Too easy an answer," yelled Ryu as he began to pace. "Broan became less worried about Eirian, so I know you helped." He glared down at Deeton, "NO. You know she is safe somewhere." He kicked Deeton in the face causing him to crash into the wall behind him. Ryu bent down and grabbed Deeton by the hair and pulled his face up to look at him. "Now tell me where she is."

"She's safe with the Giants."

"GIANTS! You expect me to believe that. They are the stuff of old wives tales." Ryu backhanded Deeton hard, making his nose bleed. "Where is she?" he hissed savoring absolutely every moment of Deeton's torture.

"I told you, with a Giant. I'm telling the truth."

Tilga cocked her head to one side. "Maybe he is telling the truth. I remember that oaf of a warrior, RohDin, telling me just the other night how the Giants laid siege to Solveig to rescue Eirian. I thought it was just boasting from a silly young man but others have told the same story."

"It's true," Bronagh yelled. "Giants have long lived with the Faeries. They did come to Solveig. They are real."

"Faeries and Giants…so what… Do you know where Eirian is?" Ryu asked as he studied Deeton. The silence that followed was not to his liking, so he slammed Deeton's face into the floor. "Time to up the stakes." He looked over to Tilga. "Open the door."

Ryu grabbed Bronagh's hair and pulled her through the door and into the combat-room. She tried to stifle her terrified whimpers as she was forced to look at Leif, who was tied up. "Let him go. He's only a child."

Ryu pulled on Bronagh's hair, making her head bend so her ear was near his mouth. "Take a good look, because if Deeton does not help us find Eirian, this will be the last time you see him."

"NO!" screamed Bronagh as she desperately clawed at Ryu's hand.

In one easy move Ryu had Bronagh on her knees, head lowered ready for his sword to come down on her neck. "Bring in Deeton," he barked.

Tilga got out of the way as Achurst dragged Deeton into the room. "No! No! Wait! I'll take you to her! Just let them go!"

"How? I want to know how you'll do that."

"By placing my ear to the land, I can feel their energy through the stones. I can lead you to her."

Ryu let Bronagh up. "Is that so…" He tossed Bronagh over to Tilga as he walked over to Deeton. He studied Deeton for a long moment. "Okay, then this is what will happen. Bronagh will stay here with LanVi while Leif joins us on the hunt… and if you take us on a wild goose chase he dies." He looked back at Bronagh and smiled. "And Lady Bronagh dies as well but very, very slowly." Ryu grabbed Deeton's jaw, forcing him to look at him. "So you better be right and you better find the quickest path to Eirian because I'm NOT a patient man."

Bronagh was enraged. There was no way she was going to be parted from Leif. She swung out at Tilga and broke free. As she started to run towards the Leif, Ryu's sword came up and caught her in the stomach.

RohDin had to be held back when they heard the blood curdling screams. "Wait. Look!" Hywel pointed to the door of the building as it opened. Everyone fell back into the shadows and watched. Ryu came out followed by Achurst carrying Leif, bound up and tosses over his shoulder. RohDin wanted to move in once again but that's when Tilga exited the combat-room leading Deeton behind her.

"Cephas and I will follow Ryu and the others," V-Tor said to RohDin as he glared at Ryu's back, "as soon as you can get Bronagh out of there." With that he and Cephas quickly left.

Once all was clear, RohDin and Hywel quickly crossed the field and leaned against the outside the door, listening for any sound coming from inside. RohDin raised his sword and nodded to Hywel. They slowly pushed the door open and stepped into the room. There was no one there. Puzzled, Hywel lowered his sword as RohDin walked over to the next room.

RohDin froze at the sight of Bronagh on the floor. Her blood soaked hands were stretched out in front of her as if she had been trying to reach for something. He dropped to his knees. "Bronagh, can you hear me?" he asked as he rolled her over onto her back. Blood spilled out of her wound. "Get something to stop the bleeding," he yelled as he pressed hard against her wound. Hywel rushed over, ripping at his shirt. He quickly handed over the strips of cloth. RohDin pack her wound as best as he could and picked her up. "Come on we've got to get her to the tunnel," he said as he started towards the door.

Stamas paused at the top of a crest and looked at the sleeping Eirian in his arms. Torn, he looked out at the valley and then to the northeast where Solveig was. "That is where you belong, little one, not in here the Giant's Valley."

There was a network of trails leading into the valley. The vast crisscrossing of the paths confused most people who happened upon the valley, giving it the legend of being cursed. If you didn't know where you were going, you could easily get lost and wander the valley for weeks on end. Stamas shrugged his shoulders as he thought of it. "It keeps Mortals away, making it one of the safest places for Eirian at the moment."

Wanting to keep the early winter chill away, Stamas tucked Eirian's cape around her more securely. He took a narrow trail to his left and rumbled down it, soon coming to a creek with trees bare of foliage. Stark branches reached skyward as if praying for guidance. He noted that the view reflected his mood. He crossed the creek and continued down the trail as it whipped around a group of large boulders and then went onward in a series of switchbacks that took them through a mixture of forest, bush and marshes. There were ghastly chutes on this trail caused by water and ice cutting deep into rock and soil. These drop-offs were covered in mud so if anyone lost their footing, they would easily fall into a bottomless canyon.

Stamas marched on, unaffected by the natural hazards of the valley. Finally he made it to the top of a ridge and stopped. Wanting to wake Eirian but not startle her Stamas called her name softly.

"Where are we?" Eirian asked as she opened her eyes.

"Your new home for now. Look." Stamas put her on the ground and pointed to a small hill in the distance. There was a cluster of majestic evergreens just beyond it, while smaller bushes and groups of winter thin trees had worked their way onto the hill itself.

"A hill?"

"Not just any hill, but an Ancient's lodge. Can you see the cluster of rocks to the right? That is one of two entrances."

Eirian studied the area Stamas pointed to. It took her a few moments to see the door in the soil.

"Ancients actually lived here?" she asked.

Stamas placed his hand on her back and began to gently push her towards the lodge. "Yes. It was one of their earlier fortresses. You can see the rows of fortifications here and another one over there, past the ditch."

Eirian's eyes widened. This looked vaguely familiar to her. She stopped and looked up at Stamas. "This has the same defenses as Solveig! Although the fortifications are worn down by years of weather and the ditch is half filled with debris, you can still see Broan's plan."

Stamas chuckled and shook his head. "You mean you can see the Ancients' plan in Solveig."

Eirian followed Stamas as she thought of what he had just said. "You know something, don't you?"

"In time I will tell you. Right now I need to get you settled." Stamas stopped outside the door he had pointed out to her. "Once you are inside you will find an oil lamp. There is a living area in the center and two chambers to either side of it. It may be smaller than Solveig but..."

"Good," Eirian cut in. "I've had enough of Mortals and their fortresses."

Stamas cleared his throat, stopping himself from telling her just what he thought of her unwillingness to get along with others. "As I was saying, it may be small but you will find it comfortable. There is also a well in the back of one of the side rooms." He pushed her towards the opening. "You'll find everything you need for now. I'll be back soon with food for you."

Eirian pushed back. "Wait! How do you know what it's like inside? The lodge is much too small for Giants to enter."

Stamas nudged her towards the door again. "You forget that all Giants were children once. I played here often. Now go inside. I'll be back soon."

Eirian walked into the lodge and marveled at its simple beauty. There was a slab of marble that lay across two long narrow stones making a table, and stone stools around it to sit on. She walked over to the stone shelf and ran her hand along its edge. It was smooth and straight. Smiling she ventured into the other rooms, which were bare, only holding a stone ledge to use for a bed. The straw for the bed had long ago gone missing, but Eirian didn't mind. She was used to the hard floors of Solveig.

Eirian stopped for a moment and thought of Solveig. What was she going to do? She sat down on the stone bed and placed her hands on her growing stomach.

Stamas knew Eirian's energy print on the land. He knew every place she had gone and where she was, except when she was on the ground of the Ancients. They hid her from even him it seemed. It may be just their way but right now he didn't like it. He paused and listened for her. "I caught a fish and gathered some wild rice for you."

Eirian appeared at the doorway with her head hung low. It didn't take much for Stamas to figure out she had been crying. "What ails you? You were the one who wanted to run away."

"I know Stamas. I'm just so unsure right now." She looked up at him. "I've never been so unsure of myself."

"You've also never been carrying a child."

Eirian almost fell over. "How did you know?"

Stamas continued to put a stick through the fish so he could cook it over the fire. "You forget Eirian, I've known you a long time. There is not much you can hide from me."

"Oh Stamas. What am I going to do?"

"The question is what are you going to do for your child?"

"Children, I'm carrying twins. At least that is what the Queen says." Eirian looked up at him, her chin trembling. "And you know I would do anything for them."

Stamas placed the fish over the fire and dusted off his hands. "Well then I want to know why you keep insisting on giving your children the same childhood you had." Eirian was stunned and just looked at him.

Stamas came and stood next to her. "You lived your life out here with no family and almost no friends. You called no place home. Is that what you want for your children? Ask yourself, were you happy?"

Eirian dropped her gaze and shook her head. "No I wasn't happy."

"Then give your children what you always wanted, a family and a home. That's what Broan is offering you."

Eirian's eyes started to tear up again. "But he's always trying to control me. We fight all the time, and he's either trapping me with binding cords or locking me up. There is no freedom being around Broan."

"If you show Broan that you have no plans of running away, he'll stop trying to keep you from leaving."

Caught in Stamas' wisdom Eirian sat in deep thought. Raising her chin to him she asked, "So what do I do now?"

"You eat and grow big with child for now."

Broan knew it was Ardis that had died so near his dungeon. His scream was low and quiet just like he had lived his life. All the commotion from the guards outside Broan's cell had made him wonder if his whole army had come to rescue him but it was only brave Ardis, the quiet one, the one with the eyes of a hawk and the ears of deer that had come.

Broan let his head fall and rest on his chest. His hands, chained to a stone wall behind him, were of no use. He knew it wouldn't be long before Ryu's men would be back to beat him again. It seemed like the new favorite pastime for them.

"Broan?" a weak cry from the next cell called out, "Are you alright?"

Broan raised his head and answered Iarnan, "Yes. I am a little bruised and beaten but I'm still breathing."

"Was it Ardis that died?"

"Yes," Broan answered sadly.

"There has to be help on the way. Maybe the others have gone to Solveig for help."

"Hopefully."

Silence filled the two cells, leaving each man reviewing his thoughts about their family and friends that were now out there and helpless. It was a sad night for the two of them.

Out past the confines of the Walled City, Ryu and his party rode towards higher ground at the base the Remdor's mountains. Normally one could easily see the mountains just west from these hills, but low hanging clouds obstructed the view. Thick clouds that blotted out all but the shape of the sun, pressed down on them, agitating the horses and making Ryu's mood even blacker.

Ryu stopped the horses at noon. He walked over to Deeton and pulled him onto the snow-covered ground. "So Faery do your stuff, find Eirian and that Giant." He slammed Deeton's head against the frozen ground and placed his foot on it. "You were the one who said you could hear them moving. Get to it, because every second brings Leif closer to his death."

Deeton didn't hear anything, yet he knew better than to say so. He twisted his head back up against Ryu's foot trying to knock it off from its perch. "I can only pick up old steps." He pointed to the northeast. "They went that way."

"You better be right, or I may have to start cutting off fingers for each lie." Ryu pulled Deeton to his feet. "I heard Faeries like to run." Ryu looked up at Tilga on her horse. "What do you think? A little exercise might help him hear better?"

Tilga laughed and nodded her head. She looked over at Leif, tied up and riding in front of a guard. "You don't have to worry, Deeton will be fine. We need him too much." She nudged her horse to where Ryu was standing. "Here, give me the rope. He can run after my horse until evening camp." With a quick pull, Deeton was jarred forward as Tilga's horse started off down the trail.

Half the time he had to run after her horse and other times he was dragged across rutted paths, hard and sharp-edged from the winter's freeze. Soon snow turned to slush, and the dampness and freezing cold mud clung to him. When night came Deeton was happy to be still for a while. He shivered and huddled by the fire and then exhausted, he drifted off. It was not a restful sleep. He tossed and turned continuously, while dreaming of Bronagh.

The pain in Falzon's hips and knees was almost overwhelming, but he wasn't about to complain. The heavy slushy snow was making walking difficult for all of the Shadow Dwellers as they lead their horses up the steep switchback of the west face of the mountain. Each night the temperature dropped, and then the morning sun would warm the frozen layer of snow, adding to their troubles. "Traveling by day was suppose to be easier," Falzon muttered out loud as he followed hardy evergreen shrubs that barely showed through the snow. Their consistent size and shape poked out in a uniform pattern, helping him keep on the trail. Falzon suddenly stopped and leaned against his horse.

Marcoff came up next to him, laboriously breathing through his mouth. This climb was hard on all of them. He smiled at Falzon, exposing his jagged teeth and fangs. "Here I'll help you get up on your horse. You can't walk much more and we need to get to the other side before nightfall." He grabbed Falzon's arm and pushed him up on to the saddle.

"Hold!" DeSpon yelled. "Let's rest for a while. We all could use a break." He slumped down onto the ground, not caring if it was wet and cold. He tossed some snow into his mouth and let it melt before swallowing it. "Look," he said as he pointed to the stunning view before them.

The Aktis mountain range spanned out on both sides of the Shadow Dwellers, leaving them a splendid view of the territory of Anwel before them. At this elevation they could see Lake Raiatua that nestled the City of Bridges. They could see rivers and forests and a bevy of fields, now barren, waiting for spring to come. Snow had yet to come to the lower ground, but one knew it was not far away.

"If you don't want your ass frozen to the ground, you better get up," Kuiper said as he passed DeSpon on his way to be with his brother. He had worried about his brother's state of health for days now. The hill climbing and steep embankments were difficult enough for those who had strong lower bodies, but for his brother it was murder. He wrapped his cloak around himself a little more tightly, feeling the chill against his scales once again. "How about I take the lead for a while? I can see the top ridge from here."

As Kiuper passed his brother Falzon, he took up the reigns of the horse and started to lead it. "It's nice to be in charge for once," he said as he kept on walking. Everyone got up and started to follow. Just as Kuiper had promised, it wasn't long and they were starting a gentle descent around the north side of the mountain.

It was about noon when the shadows of the mountains began to lay across the landscape. Cold wet haze crowded in around them as they worked at each step they made. The descent was steeper now, and gravity pushed heavy on their shoulders, wanting nothing more than to topple them down into the vast forest below. Their footing was uneasy, as crushed gravel and snow blended into mud beneath their feet.

Kuiper soon came to a crevice that had been formed over the years from the washout of each melting spring. He waited for DeSpon to catch up with him as he scanned the area for some way across.

"Doesn't look any better from on top of a horse," Falzon said as he leaned forward.

No one knew for sure if that simple shift of weight that caused the ground beneath Kuiper's feet to give way, but within a blink of an eye, Kuiper was gone from Falzon's sight and was sliding down the mountain chute.

After the initial shock, Kuiper tried to grab at the sliding ground around him. He watched as rocks and ledges flew past him. The jagged edges of the canyon chute were rapidly narrowing. He braced for impact knowing what was coming. He bounced off one side of the gap and was just about ready to smash into the other when he felt the weight of DeSpon's body.

Barreling down the side of the crevice at top speed, DeSpon had taken off after Kuiper. Once he got to the narrow rift in the mountainside he leaped off its edge and reached for Kuiper. Coiling his arms around him, DeSpon tried to slow the pace of their descent. He extended his legs out and with great force and dug his claws into the ground. He pushed back at gravity and soon the speed slackened.

They slowly came to a stop near the end of the run, body parts intertwined and bruised. A sharp end of a fallen tree trunk poked at Kuiper as he tried to crawl out from under DeSpon. "If you don't get up, I fear I'll be trapped here forever," he said as he started to push DeSpon away.

DeSpon slowly rolled over on to his back. He lay there in a daze, his breathing very labored. The impact of hitting the ground had bruised several ribs, and they now robbed him of his breath. He was totally winded and spent. He wheezed again, as he stared up at a clear blue sky.

"Well that's one way to get down," Marcoff said as he jumped off the rocks near the bottom of the chute. "How's DeSpon?" he asked as he helped Kuiper up.

"Still cursing I think."

Marcoff walked over to DeSpon and checked him out. "Winded are you? Good. Now we can all rest for a while." He pointed back up the mountain. "I'm going back up to help the others with the horses. We may take a little longer coming down than the two of you, but I think it's wiser." Marcoff slapped DeSpon on the shoulder and left him to the misery of sore ribs and bruised muscles.

Eirian entered the lodge feeling full and sleepy. She had much to think about after talking with Stamas. She lit the oil lamp and walked into the living area, untied the laces on her cloak and pulled it off. She leaned on the stone table and started to remove her worn out boots. She tugged and pulled at them, glad to get them off.

There was no sound to ease her into the scene that opened up before her. There was no increase in light to prepare the way. When Eirian looked up, she stood in shock. The room before her was alive with people from the past. There were four women dressed in long shifts of coarse wool and three men dressed in battered jackets and animal skin pants. They seemed to be going about their normal lives right there in the lodge. Someone had just pulled berries out of a clay pot and woman of good height walked right past Eirian as she brought in freshly baked bread.

Eirian stepped back from this family life, a little scared and a little embarrassed. She felt she had intruded or was imposing on this family gathering. She stepped back even more, inching her way to the exit.

Eirian suddenly noticed one of the men working on a tablet of stone. He appeared to be carving symbols into it. Eirian looked down at the ring on her toe. The symbols carved on it were very similar, and it made her wonder.

Her attention was finally drawn to an old man who sat on the floor near the back wall. His slim body and ragged clothes told of a long hard life. His weathered skin was dark, but not as black as Ke-Hern's, and it hung from arms that looked too thin to be of any use. His age was hard for Eirian to even imagine.

The elderly man's slanted dark brown eyes peeked out from under folds of wrinkled skin, and they seemed to be looking right at her. She stepped closer as if drawn to him somehow, and when he smiled right at her and started to point, she quickly shot back.

She pressed herself against the wall and looked around nervously. Surely now that he had started chanting and singing in his foreign tongue, everyone would become aware of her. But the people of the lodge never acknowledged her. They started to talk to the old man, reassuring him and calming him down. They gave him something hot to drink, but his dark eyes never left Eirian.

Again he raised his hand towards her, but this time it was as if he was motioning her to come closer to take his hand. Eirian shook her head and started to inch towards the door again. Grabbing her boots, she bent down and slipped them on. When she raised her head, everyone and everything had disappeared. The happy family life of the Ancients and the frightening old man were gone.

"Eirian!" Stamas called. "You better come out here. There is trouble coming."

Eirian rushed out of the lodge and ran right into Stamas who stood near the entrance. She looked up at him. "Have you ever seen strange things in the lodge as a child?"

Stamas straightened up and looked down at her. "You're not getting scared of your own shadow now are you?"

Eirian peered back at the doorway to the lodge and shook her head "No," she said and chided herself for thinking it was real.

Stamas squatted down next to her. "There is talk of a group of about ten warriors looking for you. One is of Faery ways and uses the ground to listen. There is also a boy bound to horse and soldier. They are camped a day away and it looks like they are coming towards the valley."

Eirian turned and looked into the dimness of the night and thought for a moment. "Has anyone spoken their names?"

"It is said that the boy is called Leif. The land heard the woman call his name."

Eirian paled. "If it is Leif, then is Bronagh the woman?" She turned back to Stamas. "If so, that would make the one to use Faery ways, Deeton." She paused for a moment in deep thought. "This doesn't feel right." A puzzled look formed on her face. "And why tie up Leif?" She turned and entered the lodge again. "I'm getting my cloak."

Eirian made a mad dash for the side room to get her cloak. She nearly jumped out of her skin when she saw the same old man sitting alone on the floor by the bed. He looked very annoyed with her and raised his hand to her again. He screeched as if he was trying to tell her something. Eirian snatched her cloak and rushed out of the room. She stumbled out of the doorway, tripping over the cloak she held in her arms. She quickly spun it around her shoulders. She looked back to make sure the elderly man stayed in the lodge and didn't follow her out. "Any more news?" she asked.

Stamas listened to the wind and watched the sway of the trees. He placed his hand on the ground and closed his eyes. Stillness was like magic to Giants. Within it they could hear everything. Slowly his eyes opened and he focused on Eirian. "There is a second party coming up behind them. Two men. One Manliken with no hair and one in Faery ways."

Eirian wished she could shape-shift and fly overhead to see for herself what was happening. "The one with no hair is most likely V-Tor which now poses the question, has Deeton run off with Leif and is V-Tor is trying to save them, or is Deeton and Leif captive to the others in the party?" She looked back at Stamas. "It doesn't matter which is correct, we will need to go and find out for ourselves. Feel like going for a walk?"

Stamas picked up Eirian and placed her on his shoulder. "If there is any trouble, stay by me no matter how tempted you are to check things out."

Eirian patted Stamas' large cheek and agreed. "I just want to look for now. Do you know if the two men following the first group have bedded down yet?"

Stamas stopped walking and listened. "NO, they are still on the move."

"We need to get to them first. They are the ones driven by a greater need."

Deeton was kicked awake. Frozen clumps of dirt and pine needles shot at his face. "Wake up! There is work to do," Ryu growled at him.

Deeton sat up and saw Leif sitting by the fire. He tried to catch his eye, but Leif looked away disheartened.

"Come on!" Ryu screamed at Deeton as he pulled him up. "I want you to listen again." He grabbed Deeton, bringing him up close, and hissed in his face, "If we do not get a sure sign that we are on the right track, one of Leif's fingers will be gone by noon. So you better make sure we are headed in the right direction." He pushed Deeton away, causing him to stumble over backwards.

Deeton got up and move to an outcropping of rocks. He quickly dusted away the snow that remained in the shadows of the trees. He placed his head down on the frozen rock and hummed low against it. The answer he got back was a surprise. Stamas was no more than a mile away. He stood up and looked back at Ryu. "I've heard where the Giant is. If Eirian is not with him, I'm sure it will tell us where she is." He turned and pointed northeast again. "The Giant is that way. It's best we get going."

"You better be right." Ryu tossed the remains of his mug onto the fire. "Mount up. The sooner we get this over, the better."

The cold damp air and gray sky mirrored the bleakness in V-Tor's heart. He would have preferred to attack Ryu and his party

385

last night but was talked out of it. Three against Ryu's men were not good odds even with a Giant on their side. Now minutes seemed like hours. Too much could happen in a minute, too many things could go seriously wrong and he really didn't like the thought of Eirian being the bait. "This just feels wrong," he muttered to himself. He checked his bow and arrow and laid his sword within easy reach.

He hid behind a rock with Cephas, waiting for Ryu and his group to arrive. "I wish we had a few more warriors at hand." He looked up into the trees. With a few archers up top there, it would be over before Ryu could reach for his sword.

"I agree, but we don't so it's up to us." Cephas half smiled at V-Tor, "You fight pretty good for a Mortal so this should be over quickly."

"For a Mortal! Thanks…" V-Tor jokingly protested as he once again checked their weapons.

Waiting by the fire Stamas looked down at Eirian, "You will make a fair mother I think."

Eirian head shot up. "Just fair! I think I'll make a great mother! I'll teach my children to live with nature, balance the energy and…"

"And fight with everyone around them?"

"No! To stand up for their freedom."

Stamas smiled at her. "You are already like a bear with her cubs. What is Broan going to do with you?"

Eirian crossed her arms over her chest. "Hopefully, nothing."

"That I doubt."

Stamas stood up and looked over at V-Tor and Cephas who were crouching behind a rock outcropping. He needed to know if they were ready. Once the trap was sprung, there was no going back.

Just north of the River Helm, Ryu and his group rode out on to a ridge. They were high enough to see Eirian and the Giant in a clearing that seemed to interrupt the forest around it. The rock-strewn glen was on the edge of a canyon where the River Helm foamed and rushed between steep cleft rocks. The crash and roar of the hastening river was loud to Ryu's ears even at this distance. He shook his head. "If the Giant had plans to protect her, he is not that smart. The sound of the river will cover any noise we make. Our coming will be a total surprise."

Ryu leaned over to Achurst and pointed to the other side of the canyon. "Go upstream and cross the river. Once I have Deeton secured, I'll return here and wait until you are ready. You better be deadly accurate with your arrows. I don't want the Giant to have any chance to save her." Achurst nodded his head and rode off.

Tilga watched Eirian and the Giant. "You're not scared of a small little Giant are you?" She smiled as she teased him.

Ryu barely acknowledged her, his eyes totally focused on Eirian.

Tilga nudged him when he didn't take part in her fun. "So what is my part of this plan now that we have found them?"

Ryu smiled at her. "You have the best part of all. I want you to ride into camp holding a knife to young Leif's neck. I doubt Eirian will try and use any of her magic if it means you'll kill him."

Tilga laughed out loud. "Can I make her beg?"

"Just make sure she doesn't try anything while we take care of the Giant," he said frowning at her. "Once we are in possession of the ring, I don't care what you do." With that Ryu turned his horse around and rode off the ridge.

"That I doubt," Tilga whispered.

Stamas stood as soon as Tilga broke from the trees. He was scanning the area for the other soldiers when he suddenly felt Eirian's hand grab onto his leg.

"Either of you move one inch or even bat an eyelash, and I'll kill him." She smiled as she pressed the knife further into Leif's neck, drawing blood. Slowly she made her way towards them.

Eirian locked her eyes on Tilga and Leif. This was definitely not part of her plan. Suddenly the whistling sound of arrows cutting through the air pulled Eirian's attention to Stamas. Time seemed to slow down for Eirian. She stumbled back when she saw another two arrows drive into Stamas. She covered her ears trying to silence the awful screaming she heard. It wasn't until she saw Stamas' twisted smile that she realized it was her own voice she was hearing. She was the one who was screaming.

V-Tor jumped over the stone outcropping as soon as Eirian started to scream. He was attacked from the side before he could even clear the trees. Ryu's soldier swung heavily and quickly with his sword, only to have it thwarted by the quicker V-Tor. Grabbing the tunic of the soldier, V-Tor drove his sword upward into the enemy's gut. He simply deposited the mortally wounded soldier on the ground and stepped over him with little regard.

A second soldier charged forward but was stopped by Cephas' arrow in the back. V-Tor started forward again but quickly found himself under siege by two more guards. He raised his elbow and struck one of the attackers in the jaw and landed a deep slice to the other's throat.

Trying to get to Eirian, Cephas was attacked from behind when a large rock smashed into his shoulder toppling him over. One of Ryu's soldiers rushed in and rammed Cephas' head against the rock. Cephas shook off the blow, grabbed the soldier by his tunic and tossed him on to his back. He then dropped his forearm heavily onto the soldier's neck, crushing his windpipe.

From out of the trees to the right of Eirian, Ryu charged at Stamas, his sword unsheathed. From on top of his horse, it was easy for Ryu to drive his sword into Stamas' mid-section. He withdrew the sword and in a great heaving effort, plunged it home once again, firmly lodging it into the backbone. As Stamas started shifting of flesh to stone Ryu raised his foot up against Stamas' hip and pulled hard, freeing his sword. The blank look on the Giant's face told Ryu it was over and he smiled deeply.

Ryu jumped from his horse and grabbed Eirian. Holding her hard against his chest, he cinched one arm her under her breasts crushing her arms against her sides. With his free hand he grabbed her hair and pulled back firmly, forcing her head to rest against his shoulder. "We meet again but this time Broan won't be interrupting us."

Cephas was usually able to maintain his composure, but lost it at the sight of Eirian being held captive. He drove his knife and sword into the two other soldiers. He began to move towards Ryu. Without warning, one of the soldiers stood up and caught Cephas in the leg with his knife. He felt the strike enter and cursed.

V-Tor watched as Cephas staggered back from the blow, blood running down his thigh. Turning swiftly V-Tor cut the soldier down, almost removing his head from his shoulders. Quickly, V-Tor ripped the shirt of one of the guards and tied it around Cephas' wound. "Will you be all right?" he asked. Cephas nodded his head. That was all V-Tor needed to see and he nodded back. With their swords ready for battle, they closed in on Ryu.

"STOP or they both die!" screamed Ryu. "Tilga will start with the boy and I'll finish with her. DO YOU HEAR ME?" He backed away from the two men and inched towards his horse, dragging Eirian with him.

Ryu suddenly saw a flash of movement out of the corner of his eye. Quickly turning his head he came face to face with another Giant. With ease it grabbed both of them. With a sneer on the Giant's face,

A SHARD OF HISTORY

he separated Eirian from Ryu's grip and then tossed him through the air and into the canyon.

Tilga quickly dropped her knife and pushed Leif off her lap and started to race away from the glen. V-Tor dashed madly towards her, throwing his knife at her. He watched with some satisfaction as her body went limp and slumped off the racing horse and onto the ground.

The Giant, Braz, walked over to Stamas's body, now nothing more than a grouping of rocks in the clearing. Back to the land, and back to the soil, where they had all come from. Braz said a few verses of an old prayer and asked forgiveness for being late. A gentle breeze rushed over the wild grass of the glen and brushed up against Braz as he said his last good-bye.

The stillness was deafening as Eirian rushed towards Leif. "Are you alright?" she asked as she went to reach for him. With an easy movement, Leif repelled her arms. Stunned, Eirian knelt beside him. "It's okay. It's me, Eirian." She reached for him again, but Leif only inched further away from her. "It's over Leif, you're safe." He turned away from her again and curled up into a ball.

Braz announced himself to Eirian by clearing his throat. "There is another mortal tied to a tree back over there. Do you wish me to free him?"

Eirian just nodded her head, her focus entirely on Leif. She reached out to touch him again. "Leave me be!" Leif screamed. He curled up into an even tighter ball as he was pulled even farther into the gray haze of regret and sorrow. His tears finally came in a rush. "It's my fault! If only I had listened to her, if only ..." He looked back at Eirian. "She's dead...my...my...mother's dead."

Cephas hobbled up to the two of them. "Don't be so sure of yourself." The bandage on his leg was soaked with blood. He leaned down and pressed his hand against his wound. "As soon as you and Deeton were taken from the combat-room, RohDin and Hywel went in to get your mother. Knowing them, they got to her in time."

It took a lot of persuasion but DeSpon was glad he finally was allowed to fly ahead and check in with Aillil. He didn't want to cause her any alarm so he landed on the edge of the canyon. DeSpon got the surprise of his life when he found out Aillil was not alone.

After watching Miko for over an hour, DeSpon decided the young man was going to be a challenge. Needing to handle this now, he walked down the path to the base of the canyon. *"Better than just dropping in from the sky,"* he thought. *"The less scared the better…I hope."*

"It takes more than a snare to catch a shrew," DeSpon said as he approached Miko.

DeSpon's voice paralyzed Miko. Filled with apprehension and insecurity, Miko slowly shifted his eyes and scanned the area where he last noticed Aillil then stood up and glared at DeSpon. "You're not welcome here, so just leave!" He slowly began to inch away from DeSpon and closer to the way his sister went.

DeSpon didn't move to stop him. He knew Miko wouldn't wilt under the weight of the responsibility to protect his sister. "Cassava is more poisonous if prepared right," he said. He waited for Miko's next move.

The statement only made Miko more self-conscious about being so young and so ill equipped to fight off this enemy. He lunged at DeSpon with his makeshift knife and then exploded into a high jump, an action that reflected his fear and hatred. DeSpon sidestepped him as he pushed him away. "It's good to know you'd take care of Aillil, even with so many dangers nearby."

Miko hunched over, ready to attack again. "And you are the one thing that Aillil needs the most protection from." He lunged forward, knife ready.

DeSpon sidestepped him again, driving Miko's head into the wall of the canyon. "This could go on forever, but it serves no purpose. Please stop and listen. I discovered this fortress some time back knowing we would need a place to weather the storm of change. I sent Aillil here to protect her. Just like you, all I want is her safety."

"Then stay away from her!"

"I can't do that." DeSpon raised his hands to all that was around them. "This is an isolated outpost, and it is our only home for now. We will share it with you and Aillil, or we will share it with just Aillil. It is up to you."

Miko shook his head. "You'll have to fight for it."

"Look, I don't want the fortress. In fact I can promise you that none of us will ever enter the fortress. You can keep it. We will set up camp further down the canyon."

Miko's eyes narrowed. "If you think that I'm stupid enough to believe that you would keep your word, forget it," he hissed. "I know just how much you can trust a Shadow Dweller, and it is not very far."

"That was then but this is now." DeSpon looked at Miko. "Let's not make this more complicated than it is. We will be moving into the canyon. You can waste your energy trying to stop us, or you can work at protecting Aillil, even with us around." He turned his head slightly. "Your sister is coming Miko. You don't have much time to make up your mind. Is it a truce for now, or do we move in with the intention of fighting you?"

Unable to fully realize the magnitude to which his answer would bear on him, Miko opened his mouth and let DeSpon know his choice. "We will never welcome you in any part of this canyon, so go and find another soul to torment."

"MIKO!" screamed Aillil. "Unless you want to suffer the wrath of the Ancients and me, you better change your tune. The Shadow Dwellers are welcome here, and if you have a problem with that, leave!"

"Stay out of this!" both men yelled back at her.

DeSpon kept his eyes on Miko, ready for another of his attacks. "I'll ask one more time. If we stay near the caves and promise not to venture this way, can we have an agreement?"

"NO!"

DeSpon shook his head and started to turn away. "It is nice to see such youthful dedication but it is also very distressing to see that it is not tempered with common sense. We will be coming here and we will be staying. Like it or not."

"I'll be waiting."

DeSpon sat and told the group about Miko and the challenges ahead. Still, they all felt they had no other choice. Kiuper knew his brother Falzon was losing his battle with his misshaped body. His bones now creaked and ground together under his ape shape. Larden was finding that sand, which found its way deep under his feathers, was causing weeping sores and raw skin. The pain grew more intense every second. So onwards they moved through the night, half asleep, guiding their horses.

By morning all six Shadow Dwellers arrived at mouth of the canyon. You could see the signs of a river that once rushed out of the canyon and into a lake that now was nothing more than a desert. Both sides of this old delta grew rapidly into towering cliffs, creating the canyon that soon would be their new home.

"So this is it?" Larden said as he studied the sight before him. "Where's the fortress?"

"Near the other end. About half ways up the canyon are caves that will be our camp."

"Until we get this damn curse lifted," Bacot said as he stood next to Larden. He looked back at Falzon. "And I hope it's soon. Falzon's not looking good."

"Speak for yourself." Falzon said as he started to get off his horse. "I'm more than strong enough to swing along those rock outcroppings." He limped over to the low ledge of the canyon and then reached up, taking a firm grip of the rock face. "I'll race you there," he said as he swung himself from one rock to another disappearing into the inky blackness of the growing gorge.

Smiling, DeSpon mounted his horse and together with the others charged after Falzon.

Together in the dull morning grayness, in the belly of the coulee, the Shadow Dwellers walked up to the clearing in front of the fortress. They were a fearsome sight. Their faces were layered with sand and dirt, their hair and feathers matted and hanging about their faces.

With a raucous yell, Marcoff summoned Miko to come out and meet them.

This was met with the opening of the stronghold doors and crude arrows being shot at them. Bacot was fast at catching the ill aimed missiles with his hands, and he had no problem breaking them in two.

"Come out Miko. We need to talk," DeSpon encouraged. "No harm will come to you or Aillil. We just want to talk."

This of course was answered with the toss of two spears, one landing a little too close to Larden for his liking. He wasn't sure about this idea of DeSpon's.

"There is nothing you can do about this, so let's figure out how we can make it work."

That was answered with more arrows and a few stones propelled from a slingshot. DeSpon was beginning to worry when Aillil suddenly rushed through the doors and towards him and the others, Miko quickly running after her. It only took seconds for Falzon to grab him. In one large swoop, he lifted the young lad off the ground. "Listen, we mean you no harm!"

"I'd find that a little more convincing if your hand wasn't trying to crumple my throat!" Miko wheezed out.

Falzon loosened his grip and looked at the lanky young man who at that moment was giving him a fierce glare. "You certainly have courage lad, and that is something rare. You would do well to put it to good use and not waste it on things you cannot change."

DeSpon walked up to the two of them as they dangled from the rock face. "Come down Falzon. You are scaring him even more."

DeSpon patiently waited as he watched Miko. "You have a choice. You either agree with our terms, or we'll have to imprison you in one of the high caves. Which will it be?"

"We agree!" Aillil yelled. Calming herself and in a quieter voice said, "now let him go."

"Stay out of this, Aillil," Miko shot back.

"No I won't. DeSpon and the others have every right to be here. If it hadn't been for him I'd still be trapped on the Queen's island and you…YOU would be dead! Besides, do you really think you can force them to leave? None of us can change the path we find ourselves on." Aillil stepped towards her brother as she continued, "including you."

Trapped with the knowledge that he was not old enough, wise enough, nor strong enough to fight these demons, Miko lowered his head. Caught in that miasma of regret and defeat, all he could do now was nod in agreement. Suddenly his head came up and he stared at DeSpon. "I will agree as long as you keep your promise that none of you will ever try to enter the fortress." He waited for DeSpon's answer.

DeSpon simply said, "Agreed."

V-Tor helped Cephas drink the warm tea that Eirian had made to help with his recovery. He gave Cephas a pleading look as he leaned in. "You better hurry up and get your strength back. Eirian is all hell bent on going to Solveig and then back to the Walled City to save Broan, and she will not listen to me."

Cephas coughed and sputtered tea everywhere. "EIRIAN!" he screamed. "You are not going anywhere near the city."

Eirian walked over and glared at both of them. "I will be going. Once we get Deeton and Leif back to Solveig, I'm leaving. There is some unfinished business needing my attention." Her eyes narrowed as her mind played over the scene that she knew would happen.

"Forget it!" Cephas threw his head back and yelled in total frustration.

Eirian stood with her hands on her hips and looked down at Cephas. "Too late, I've already asked Braz to send word to the Duronykians to join me. I'm calling them to arms against Tybalt."

Cephas shook his head. "That will do nothing. Storming the city will not save Broan or anyone. As soon as they see us coming, they will put everyone to death. No, an army will not help."

Eirian raised an eyebrow as if to challenge him. "We won't be storming the walls. We will be going in by the tunnel. Once dressed in Iarnan's guard uniforms, we will make our way to the dungeons and free the others."

"You can't just walk into a dungeon and expect to be welcomed, in uniforms or not!" Cephas yelled.

"Yes you can, especially if you just caught one of Broan's top men and we need to imprison him." She smiled sweetly at V-Tor. "Right? And in the meantime Hywel and the others can storm the guard houses and get the gates open to BroMac and anyone else that wants to fight."

Cephas stared at Eirian, his strength now fueled by anger. "Good idea, not bad …but you are not going to the Walled City. V-Tor are you going to help me with this?" he asked over his shoulder, keeping his eyes firmly locked on Eirian's.

"Help you! I woke you up to HELP me. As far as I can see, we'd be wasting too much time going to Solveig first. I think we should just send Deeton, and Leif back alone."

Cephas' eyes nearly bugged out of his head. "You call that helping? I think you both are mad."

V-Tor shrugged his shoulders. "Well it's better than sitting around and waiting for something bad to happen. Come on, Braz can make sure they get to Solveig in one piece, and we can head out tomorrow. Eirian's men can join us on the way."

Cephas rolled his eyes. He knew he wasn't going to win this one. "Why wait for tomorrow? If you can get me on a horse, we can ride out now."

"NOW, that's crazier than any of my ideas," Eirian said.

"Just get me up."

Achurst took refuge in a simple log-sided structure nicely tucked among the pine trees not far from his destination. He sat anxiously wondering how he was going to get inside the Walled City. The one person he was supposed to see and relay a message to was on the other side of those overwhelming walls. He cursed Ryu for sending him on a fool's mission.

Suddenly, Achurst froze. There was a shuffling sound just outside the building. He inched back into the shadows and waited. He couldn't afford to get caught right now. He listened intently trying to determine who or what was out there.

"Damn that whore of a horse!"

"Well this makes my job easier." Relief flooded Achurst as he stepped forward. "Only you, Mohr, would swear like a woman."

"Is that you Achurst? I thought you had gone with Ryu." Mohr said as he stood at the entrance of the building.

"I did and almost got myself killed." He walked over as he eyed the large box and full saddlebags Mohr carried. "I wouldn't have even come back if Ryu hadn't sent me." He took the bags from Mohr's arm. "Everything was going well until the Giants got involved and tossed Ryu over the edge of a canyon. Lucky for him I made my way down to the river and fished him out." Achurst grunted as he started to walk to the back corner. "What is all this stuff?"

"Things...my things," He shifted the heavy box in his arms and followed Achurst. "I'm cutting my losses and heading east."

"East? No, no," Achurst looked back at Mohr, "Ryu sent me here to collect you."

"ME?" Mohr's eyes narrowed.

"Yeah," Achurst smiled as he shook his head. "There is a small village halfway between Remdor's border and Harbor City, called Lanberg. He said he'd stay there until our return."

"So he is safe there while all hell breaks loose here." Mohr mentally counted everything he had with him and then he looked up at Achurst. "Where is your horse?"

"Tied up just inside the tree line," Achurst turned to put the saddlebags down. "Why?"

Mohr drove his knife into Achurst's back twice, making sure his attack was lethal. "Because I need one and right now there is a shortage." Mohr took out the compass that Sobus had given him. All six arms pointed to where DeSpon and the Shadow Dwellers were which was northeast. He glanced over to Achurst's dead body. "Sorry, but Ryu will just have to wait."

The Walled City was in chaos. The soldiers that followed Tybalt looked for resistance everywhere within the city. Their purge of an opposition was unstoppable. Many of the citizens rushed to the gates of the city with bundles of belongings. Rickety handcarts groaned under the weight of possessions, children and the elderly. They wanted nothing more than to leave. But high up on the walls that surrounded the city, Tybalt's new ruling army was enjoying their newfound power. They shot arrows into the air and watched as the arrows found their marks among the unarmed people. It didn't take long for the crowd to disperse in a panic, followed by soldiers that stormed down the cobbled streets on horseback. Those who fell to the ground were simply crushed under the hooves. If you did not support the new regime, you suffered the consequences.

Eirian's head was the first to poke through the underground chute on the far end of the cave. She slowly inched up a little more and glanced around. The little old man from the Ancients was there again. He had shown up three times since she had left the lodge. She backed down a bit wanting to hide from his dark piercing eyes. Now that Stamas was gone she wasn't sure who to talk to about this ghost that kept following her around.

Concerned, V-Tor lifted himself up to check out what had spooked Eirian. He spotted Ke-Hern and Laeg and his spirits brightened. "Come on," he called to those behind him and quickly climbed out of the tunnel and into the cavern.

Laeg and Ke-Hern turned towards the new arrivals and frowned when they saw Eirian. "What on earth are you doing here?" Laeg asked as he stood with his hands on his hips. "Broan's going to have a fit when he finds out. Do you know how dangerous it was to come here?" Then he looked at Cephas. "By the gods Cephas, what were you thinking?"

Cephas shrugged his shoulders. "You know Eirian. When she gets something into her mind, there is no way of stopping her."

"Nice to see you too, Laeg," she said as she passed him on her way to Ke-Hern. "Cephas will tell you what we have planned."

Eirian stood in front of Ke-Hern, observing his bound chest. "Are you okay?" she asked.

"Yes of course."

She eyed him with stern eyes. "Well you don't look it."

Ke-Hern tossed his head over to a flat slab of stone. "Compared to the others, I'm looking great."

Shocked and relief filled Eirian at the same time. She walked over to Bronagh and picked up her hand and leaned in close. "They are alive, Bronagh. Leif and Deeton are at Solveig waiting for you. Don't disappoint them by giving up now." Bronagh smiled weakly.

Queen DaNann rose up on her elbows and watched as Eirian talked to Bronagh. Her heart caught in her throat as she watched Eirian turn and walk towards her. Like her mother, Eirian was akin to a force of nature and DaNann wondered if this encounter would develop into a confrontation. Eirian had disliked her for such a long time.

"Are you going to be alright?" Eirian asked.

DaNann gave her a sideways glance. "That's a strange thing to ask someone you've hated all your life."

Eirian smiled down at her. "But it's the right thing to ask your grandmother."

DaNann closed her eyes and took in a deep breath of relief. "I never thought I'd hear those words. Ke-Hern never told me about you." She opened her eyes and looked at Eirian. "I wish he had." She paused for second then continued, "I have to ask. Why did you choose to kill Sobus and not me?"

"He left me no choice. He killed Broan's mother and sister. He didn't give them a chance. You at least gave us Duronykians a way out of the curse." Eirian smiled down at the Queen.

"It wasn't my curse. I just altered it. Of course Sobus wasn't happy but I didn't care." She studied Eirian for a moment. "Do you still have the ring on your toe?" Eirian nodded cautiously. "Even though the Ancients gave you something to aid ridding this land of Sobus, do not bind yourself to them. They've been known to stack the odds hopelessly against our kind."

"Ancients? I'm barely willing to bind myself to Broan."

Miko caught a movement in his periphery vision. He cursed under his breath. He hadn't counted on Aillil being such a problem. Quietly he got up and followed.

The canyon was a magical place to DeSpon. His friends were here and his hope for their salvation was still alive. He took a deep drink of herb tea and then smiled when he noticed Aillil. "It appears we have a guest this morning," he called out to the others as he pointed towards Aillil.

Aillil stopped when she heard DeSpon's voice and smiled in his direction. "I hope I'm not interrupting," she said.

"Not at all," Bacot answered. He rose from his seat and walked towards Aillil. "Come take my arm, and I'll walk you to the fire. Join us for some morning tea."

"The only tea she will drink is with ME," yelled Miko as he entered the clearing just behind his sister.

Bacot shrugged his shoulder and continued to guide Aillil to a place by the fire. "Then join us as well. We will not harm you."

"But you would harm children." Miko glared at him. "You think your ill ways are behind you, yet you all plot to snatch children to gain your freedom. How is that harmless?"

"Children?" Everyone repeated as if they all were unsure they heard right. "What's this about children?"

"Nothing," Aillil said as she let go of Bacot's arm. "Miko doesn't know what he is talking about!"

"Yes I do. I heard you talking to the Ancients about it. I heard your plan. All of it!"

"Really Miko," Aillil said as she nervously smiled. "He tends to overplay everything."

"Aillil?" DeSpon questioned, unsure if he really wanted to hear this. "Tell me what you have planned?"

"It is nothing bad. The children are just a little incentive. That is all. No harm will come to the twins. I promise."

"Whose twins?" DeSpon asked as he now gave Aillil his full attention.

Quickly Miko he blurted out, "Eirian and Broan's twins. Aillil has already set the plan in motion. Once they are born, they will be abducted and brought here."

"Shut up Miko!" Aillil cried. "You don't understand and are only making things worse."

"Who takes the children, Aillil?" DeSpon asked as he stepped towards her. "Who will kidnap the twins?"

Aillil reached out trying to find DeSpon. "Laeg, one of Broan's seconds. It was one way to make sure no harm came to them. Don't you see? Laeg will be unable to stop himself, yet he will do everything he can to protect them."

"This is crazy," Marcoff growled. "I thought the plan was simple."

"I agree," Larden said as he stood up from his seat and glared at DeSpon. "Once again you have led us towards the darkest of circumstances. I don't know if getting my freedom is worth condemning my soul."

Aillil began to cry. "Please. Please listen to me. Nothing bad is going to happen. The Ancients have far too much to lose in this. They will make sure all goes well."

Marcoff angrily looked at Aillil and then at DeSpon. He emptied his cup of tea on the hot fire, causing it to spit and sizzled. "If you are in such good company and know the secrets of the Ancients, why don't you just get them to release us?"

"I can't," Aillil dropped her head. "That's why I did this...and now we have no choice but to follow through."

Marcoff bared his teeth. "How can you, a woman, come up with such an evil plan, a plan that is headed towards a bad ending?" Confused and ashamed, Aillil took off running.

DeSpon shook his head. This was partly his fault and he knew it. His single minded purpose to free his friends from the curse had set in motion a plan that had no right to be. Suddenly he was hit with a bone-jarring fist to the jaw that momentarily laid him out. He turned onto his back and looked up at Falzon.

"I've waited a long time to do that."

DeSpon started to get up but Falzon forced him back down with his apelike knuckles. "Stay there. I have words to say and I'm going to say them. It is rare to find something that is unequivocally, indisputably this bad, yet you have." He looked down at DeSpon. "It's not hard to tell the girl likes you and thought to help you in your mission to free us. Love has a way of sometimes robbing us of sense and wisdom. But if I find that you tricked her…"

Miko stood rooted to the ground. He hadn't thought that they, of all beings, had no knowledge of Aillil's plan. "I'm worried about Aillil," he slowly said. "The Ancients don't agree with her plan either."

"Shit." Falzon looked at the others. "You are sure?"

Miko simply nodded.

Bacot went up to Miko and gently pushed him in the direction his sister went. "Go to her Miko. What is done is done. Now we just have to make sure it is done right for everyone's concern."

Broan never dreamed that Eirian would return to the Walled City, let alone enter the dungeons. He was so sure that she was safely tucked away with Stamas. The most he had hoped for was her returning to Solveig and waiting for him there. Yet she was a vision on the stairs. He stared at her with sheer wonder as she approached him.

When Eirian saw Broan, beaten and chained to the wall, everything else around her seemed to stop and stand still. All she could hear was Broan's ragged breath as she gazed at him. Suddenly a rough hand grabbed her by the arm. Eirian swiftly spun as she brought up her knife. She drove her knife viciously into the enemy's chest and quickly whirled around the other way, slashing the guard's the neck, sending blood spraying across the landing. No one was going to keep her from Broan.

Broan let out a fierce growl as he helplessly watched her fight. It was as if time slowed down. Each turn she took, each side step she made was like a dance with time itself. He pulled at his bindings, trying to get free, desperately wanting to help her. Enraged, he let out battle roar.

V-Tor and Cephas quickly worked their way to Eirian and took up the fight, effectively protecting her back. Eirian focused her talent on the cell doors, iron bars, and locks. A large and sudden explosion rocked the very ground the dungeon was dug into. The doors of the cells were blown open and the prisoners sprang free joining the fight.

Eirian ran over to Broan. Cradling his face in her hands, Eirian drew it to hers. She pressed her mouth fervently on his, kissing him as if both their lives depended on that very thing. Slowly and tenderly she removed her lips from his and smiled. Then she ran her hands over his bare chest. She looked deep into his eyes. "This is going to hurt, but I must do it, or your broken ribs will rob you of even more than just air."

Broan just kept his eyes fixed on her. She had come to him unbidden. She could do anything to him right now and he wouldn't care. He was transfixed by the knowledge that she was really there in front of him.

"Ready?" she asked as she placed her hands on his chest and then lowered them to his sides. She concentrated and with one swift movement, she pushed, widening the compressed ribs back into place.

Broan threw his head back and screamed as the intense pain shot through him, then blinked his eyes, quickly realizing that he could breathe again. The strangle hold on his chest was gone and air filled his lungs again. He raised his head and smiled at her.

"Come," she said as she unlocked his chains from the wall. "Let's get you out of here."

Even though the dungeon was at the edge of the training fields, Eirian and the others could clearly hear the sounds of liberty as BroMac and Deeton lead their warriors through the gates. The two armies faced the enemy together and with each step the horses advanced, good overcame evil. Civilians rushed to help the warriors of Solveig and Duronyk.

Eirian led the way with knife in hand, willing to use it on anyone or anything that got in their way. Cephas and V-Tor helped Broan across the field, down the side alleys, to the main residence and then into the cave. Immediately Ke-Hern took over Broan's care giving Eirian a chance to turn and go back the way she had just come. Within a breath she was gone, back to the city in its turmoil, back to finish this once and for all.

Broan pushed everyone's hands away from him. He didn't want their attention. He wanted to see Eirian again. He sat up and looked around the cave. "Where is Eirian?" he yelled.

"I think I know," Laeg growled as he handed Broan a sword. "Are you coming?"

Within an hour of the invading army entering the city, ninety percent of the city had been retaken. The loss was staggering to Tybalt. He had no place to go, no place to run. He sat on Iarnan's high council chair and waited. He had no idea what had happened to Mohr. He didn't know if Mohr had been captured, killed or if he was just damn smart to get away before the wrath of Broan came down on them.

Eirian found Tybalt in the council chamber, all alone, looking small. At first she hesitated, then anger rushed through her body as she thought of all the people that had suffered because of this arrogant man. His greed for power and wealth had taken the land down the sad slope of civil war. "Ryu told me you were looking for this?" she said as she twisted Cian's ring off her thumb and tossed it at him. The ring landed a few feet from him. Tybalt didn't move. He glanced around the room nervously.

She stood in the middle of the council room and glared at him. "Was it worth it?" she asked. Tybalt had no answer for her. He lowered his eyes and turned his face away from her. "I thought not," she said as she turned and walked away. She would not waste anymore time or energy on the man.

Tybalt felt the heat of his own disgrace. He grabbed the knife from his belt and started after her when Broan suddenly stepped through the side door. "Going someplace?" he said.

Surprised, Tybalt stumbled to a stop. "You? But…" Tybalt raised his knife and charged. Swiftly Broan raised his sword and swung permanently stopping Tybalt.

Eirian walked out of the main residence and turned towards the east gate of the Walled City. She would have made it if Laeg hadn't caught up with her. "Haven't you forgotten something?" he said to her as he took one of her hands and placed Cian's ring in it. "You shouldn't leave things laying around for just anyone to pick up."

Eirian blinked the moisture from her eyes. She looked at the ring and then back up at him. "I want to go home! I want to go to Solveig and get away from here!"

"Then let's go," Broan said as he strolled up next to Laeg, gingerly holding on to his ribs. "Go get our horses," he told Laeg, "You can catch up to us on the road."

As they started out again, Broan pulled Eirian nearer. "Are you sure about Solveig being home?"

Stopping, Eirian looked up at him. "Yes" she said smiling.

Overwhelmed by an avalanche of relief, Broan pulled her to him. "So we're done with running away and with the Ancients, magic and wars to free Faeries?"

An intense, exciting sense of trust and belonging filled Eirian. "Yes" she said. "It seems that despite all your faults… I love you."

CPSIA information can be obtained at www.ICGtesting.com
Printed in the USA
LVOW100818270513

335467LV00002B/2/P